ALSO BY PHILIP SINGTON

Zola's Gold

PHILIP SINGTON

The Einstein Girl

VINTAGE BOOKS
London

Published by Vintage 2010

6 8 10 9 7 5

First published in Great Britain in 2009 by
Harvill Secker

Vintage
Random House, 20 Vauxhall Bridge Road,
London SW1V 2SA

www.vintage-books.co.uk

Addresses for companies within The Random House Group Limited can be found at: www.randomhouse.co.uk/offices.htm

The Random House Group Limited Reg. No. 954009

A CIP catalogue record for this book
is available from the British Library

ISBN 9780099535799

Mixed Sources
Product group from well-managed
forests and other controlled sources
www.fsc.org Cert no. TT-COC-2139
© 1996 Forest Stewardship Council

FSC

The Random House Group Limited supports The Forest Stewardship Council (FSC), the leading international forest certification organisation. All our titles that are printed on Greenpeace approved FSC certified paper carry the FSC logo. Our paper procurement policy can be found at:
www.rbooks.co.uk/environment

Printed and bound in Great Britain by
CPI Bookmarque, Croydon CR0 4TD

For Uta

&

Leo

'He who is unable to live in society, or who has no need because he is sufficient for himself, must be either a beast or a god.'

Aristotle, *Politics*

'We are all agreed that your theory is insane. The question that divides us is whether it is insane enough to have a chance of being correct.'

Niels Bohr, *Reply to a presentation by Wolfgang Pauli*

Zürich, 18 October

Dearest Elisabeth,
Here, tied up in this parcel, is the manuscript of a book, which I finally completed the day after you came to say goodbye.

I call it a book even though it is as yet nothing more than a pile of papers, lacking even a title. Nor will this change while I am alive. I don't dare to seek out a publisher, for reasons which will become clear to you before you reach the end. Yet my book I still call it, not out of vanity but because the moment when a book becomes a book is hard to pin down, like the moment when a succession of musical notes becomes a melody. It takes a mind to realise its character, just as it takes a mind to discern a melody.

I ask that you take it with you when you leave. I know from experience what a long journey you have ahead of you, and I hope the story will serve, at least for a time, to distract you from the clattering of the wheels, the stale air and the tiresome intrusiveness of officialdom. In other words, I hope to shrink both time and distance so that we remain closer to each other in both.

I hope also that my book helps prepare you for your mission in Berlin. There is so much I should have told you already. But I have found that in fiction one is freer to speak the truth, if only because in fiction the truth is not expected or required. You may easily disguise it, so that it is only recognised much later, when the story and the characters have faded into darkness.

I have one further hope, even more selfish than the others: that once you have finished reading, you will give me your opinion as to a title. If I leave the matter unresolved, then a title will only be chosen for

I

me after I am dead. And I should hate that, even if, being dead, I am not in a position to hate anything.

But all that is for the end of your journey. For the moment this book shall remain nameless, which you may discover in these times of fear and upheaval, is the safest way to be.

nameless

One

Two weeks after her fiancé disappeared, Alma Siegel travelled across the teeming city to the edge of the eastern districts to look at photographs of the unnamed dead. They were displayed in a corridor at police headquarters, lined up inside glass cabinets, beneath each one a slip of paper bearing information on the place and date of discovery: waste ground off Danziger Strasse, 24 January; Anhalter station public lavatories, 7 February; Landwehr Canal at Kottbusser Bridge, 15 April. The corridor was busy. People came to police headquarters for many different reasons: to present themselves at the Alien Registration Office, to obtain a visa, to look for lost property or report a theft. They jostled her as they hurried by, all purpose and expedient haste, never pausing to look at the rows of frozen faces staring at them through the glass.

Her old friend Robert insisted on coming with her. It was he who had introduced her to Martin Kirsch in the first place. The two men were colleagues at the Charité Psychiatric Clinic; and no doubt Robert felt it was his duty to rally round. In any case, he assured her, the trip to police headquarters was just a formality. Her fiancé wasn't likely to be found among the faces in the cabinets. They belonged to labourers, immigrants, maids and 'working women' – by which he must have meant prostitutes. A man of Martin's standing, a doctor of psychiatry, didn't keep that kind of company. And so it had proved. The stiff white collars of the professional classes were rarely to be found around the necks of the unnamed dead. Their shirts were open-necked and dark coloured so as to hide the dirt. And there was a coarseness about them, a raggedness that went beyond the condition of their clothes.

They were photographed at the scene, rolled onto their backs where necessary, lit up in the brilliance of a magnesium flash, skin starkly white against bottomless black shadows. Gravity tugged at their cheeks and their hair, which gave many the appearance of facing into a gale, eyes squinting or half-closed, mouths open as if gasping for a final breath. Since the beginning of the year more than a hundred of them had been gathered from all over Berlin.

Identification was the sole purpose of the display. The slips of paper made no distinction between unsolved murders, suicides and deaths from exposure – although sometimes the distinction was all too evident: a trickle of blood running down a man's face, a leather tourniquet twisted tight around a woman's outstretched neck. The drowned were the worst: caked in slime, flesh bloated and split open, as if they had eaten themselves to death. The bodies were kept at the morgue for a few weeks, then disposed of. Most of the nameless dead had, in fact, already ceased to exist in any physical sense. All that remained of them, the only evidence that they had ever lived, were the police photographers' snapshots pinned up in the corridor. Even this courtesy was temporary. After a few months the prints were taken down and filed away in the basement, never to be seen again.

Alma brought along a photograph: Martin looking uncharacteristically suave in a three-piece suit, hair a little longer than usual so that it flopped gamely over his forehead, smiling as he squinted into the light. The police officers examined the picture and declared that they had never seen him before.

'He wears spectacles,' she said. 'For reading.' But still they shook their heads.

She came back every few days, alone. The officers got used to seeing her and would give her a smile as she walked in. She wasn't like the women they usually had to deal with, with her strawberry-blonde curls and pretty retroussé nose, her tailored jackets and polka-dot scarves. Everything about her gave off an aura of expense: her skin, her slender legs and delicate ankles, her upright bearing, the melodious clack of her heels. They escorted her

assiduously to the cabinets. Sometimes they let her see pictures that had not yet gone up, that still awaited their correct bureaucratic designation. They even showed her the pictures that were usually considered unsuitable for public display: bodies cut in two on railway lines, burned black in house fires, or lying in shallow graves, grinning through decomposed flesh.

'Now these aren't pretty,' they would say, as they opened the files. And then they would watch her closely as the dark, coagulated masses took form before her eyes, became flesh and bone, became gradually human. For all their show of reluctance, she had a sense that they enjoyed introducing her to these horrors, as seducers took pleasure in the corruption of innocence. There was camaraderie in braving the extremes of corporeal ruin and not turning away. Or perhaps what pleased them was to see her wobble on her society pedestal. That she was complicit in her degradation, came back again and again as if satisfying some depraved appetite, made them all the more eager to oblige.

One of the older sergeants had a patch of shiny smooth scar tissue down the side of his face and an eyelid that was never fully open. 'What makes you think he's dead,' he asked her one day, as they stood before the cabinets, 'your Dr Kirsch?'

There had been some rearrangement of the pictures since Alma's last visit. It took her a moment to get her bearings. One of the drowned women had migrated to the bottom row, as if dragged down by her own weight, and in the top row there was now a gap.

'We were going to be married,' she said.

'Yes, Fräulein, but did he say anything? Anything that gave cause for alarm? Did he have enemies, for instance?'

Alma shook her head. She had thoughts on the matter, instincts, but nothing she could explain. They concerned one of Martin's patients, a young Slavic woman. The case had been in the newspapers for weeks, the subject of much lurid speculation. As her doctor, Kirsch had been photographed and written about, a development Alma had welcomed at the time. But that was when Martin had begun to change. The case seemed to act on him like a drug.

He had been seduced, poisoned. Robert had complained about his remoteness and his secrecy. He had hinted at a fixation. This was not the Martin Alma knew, or anyone knew.

His superiors were reluctant to discuss the case. They could not say if it had anything to do with Martin's disappearance. They were politely unhelpful, as if concealing some professional embarrassment. But their lack of alarm betrayed a belief that Martin had disappeared of his own volition. Or if he had fallen victim to a criminal act – a street robbery gone wrong, a kidnap, an assassination – it was a crime they had no intention of investigating.

Martin had rented rooms off the Schönhauser Allee, a mile and a half from the hospital. Alma had not been there often – only once, briefly, inside – but she knew it was not a reputable neighbourhood. To the north lay the tenements of Pankow, to the south, the seedy nightspots that were clustered like a rash around Alexanderplatz station. The area was inexpensive, he had explained, and convenient for work. But when she found him more suitable accommodation out west in Charlottenburg, he had dragged his heels.

'I've become used to this old place. Besides, if we're moving out of town next year, what's the point?'

She had put his reluctance down to inertia and a bachelor's disregard for appearances. Space for his books and peace to work in were all he needed. But in the days after his disappearance, she had been forced to question that assumption. She wondered if what people said was true: that there were fascinations in this part of the city to which she had been oblivious.

Her parents did not understand why she kept going in. As far as they were concerned, the sooner she forgot about Kirsch the better. They had taken a house on the Baltic for the summer and had insisted she join them there. Alma got herself a part-time job as a receptionist, just so they would stop bothering her about it.

After work she rode the S-Bahn as it hurtled roof-high over the streets, plunging into hollowed-out buildings, squeezing past apartment blocks so close she could see her own reflection dance

across the window-panes. She made the journeys her fiancé used to make, determined to see the city through his eyes. From the S-Bahn you could see things invisible at street level: a solitary cherry tree flowering in a courtyard, children washing in a tin bath, a young girl hanging up a turquoise dress from a tenement balcony. The railway was part scalpel, part movie camera, slicing the city open, parading its inner workings at fifty frames per second. It was on the S-Bahn that she felt least abandoned, as if the act of travelling turned back the clock, and brought her nearer to the future she had lost.

Sometimes she rode the tram beyond Alexanderplatz, heading into places that had only ever been names to her before, émigré quarters officially void of interest for any recreational visitor. The capital had grown bigger and messier since the war. It had spread, metastasising over fields and forests, its proletarian masses swollen by hordes from the East: Russians and Poles, gypsies and Jews. It was not truly a German city, measured against any other German city; that was what her father said.

Alma stared out at the strange, foreign streets, with their watchful crowds, their covered markets and temples, haunted by the thought that these were places her fiancé knew, where perhaps he was still known. Once she saw him standing in front of a shop window, hunched over to light a cigarette. She was off the tram and over the street before she realised she had made a mistake.

'Do excuse me. I thought . . .'

The stranger had smiled and tipped his hat, saying something in a language she could not understand.

Alma went to the Prussian State Library to read through the old newspaper reports. A group of eager young students in blazers were helping reorganise the book stacks, wheeling trolleys up and down the corridors, talking and joking in loud voices. Berlin boasted dozens of newspapers. Alma sat in the Periodicals Room, skimming the pages, breathing in the oily stink of newsprint, fingers and palms turning slowly black. Somewhere amidst the topical

clamour were surely some grains of truth, some portents of her private catastrophe.

Martin's patient had been found in woodland near Potsdam, thirteen miles south-west of the city. Two young boys out cycling had made the discovery. They were pictured in the *Berliner Morgenpost*: Hans and Ernst Waise, standing stiffly with their bicycles as they stared into the lens. They had gone out early that morning, a Saturday in late October, intent on reaching the lakeside town of Caputh, where they had heard the great Albert Einstein lived and sailed boats. But it had been foggy and they had lost their way. In the end, it was the younger boy who had spotted something lying by the water's edge.

THEY CAME LOOKING FOR A GENIUS AND UNCOVERED A SEX CRIME, the piece began. The girl was found half-naked and soaked to the skin. Her legs were cut and scratched. Other unspecified marks of violence had been found all over her body, which was so pale the boys thought she was dead. When they detected a faint pulse at her throat, they covered her with their jackets while Hans, the older boy, peddled off to get help. It was over an hour before he returned with the police.

An imaginative feuilleton in the *Berliner Illustrierte Presse* reflected on Ernst Waise's ordeal, a child of eight, left alone in the mist-shrouded forest with a beautiful, dying woman, his head filling up with tales of ghosts and evil spirits, hardly daring to breathe in case they noticed him. The boy himself later claimed that the girl had spoken before lapsing into unconsciousness again, though he could not repeat her words. He said he had even kissed her, thinking that might somehow keep her alive.

Details of the girl's immediate fate took longer to come out. Alma found the most detail in the topical weeklies, brash two-tone publications full of blotchy black-and-white photographs, the kind her father's driver, Hans-Peter, read as he waited at the wheel.

The police that attended the scene had been unsure what to do. They had taken the unconscious woman to a first-aid station in Caputh, which was equipped only with blankets, bandages and

disinfectant, and then to a sanatorium in Potsdam. The staff there were also inexperienced, most of their clients being consumptives and sufferers from bronchial disease. Fearing hypothermia, they submersed the girl in a bath of hot water to raise her body temperature, a ploy the doctors at the Charité later suggested might have made matters worse. The sudden warmth would have caused the blood vessels in her arms and legs to dilate from their narrowed state, they said. Cold blood trapped in her extremities would have flooded back into the core of her body and her brain, further lowering their temperature. The same blood would have carried elevated levels of toxins and acids. It was acidosis that had probably sent her into a coma.

The girl had a brief convulsive episode. The staff prevented her from swallowing her tongue. Then her pupils dilated and she lapsed into deep unconsciousness. With her pulse growing fainter, the chaplain was summoned from the dining room on the off-chance the girl was Roman Catholic. She was read the last rites. Finally, at around two o'clock, as a rainstorm broke over the city, an ambulance arrived and raced her up the Avus speedway to Berlin. When she finally awoke, her memory was a blank. She did not even know her name.

A police search was hastily organised the next day. In the woods around the capital, tent colonies frequently sprang up, full of unemployed men and their families – a tiny fraction of the workless millions who drifted like human flotsam from one conurbation to the next. The papers speculated that it was in such an 'enclave of despair' that the truth would be found. With the press looking on, sixteen officers trudged through the woods outside Caputh, searching for evidence. The Tuesday edition of the *Berliner Morgenpost* carried a photograph of the men hunched beneath their oilskins or crouching down to examine depressions in the leaf-strewn earth. But they found no tent colony, nor evidence that there had ever been any. From a forensic point of view, the operation yielded little: a few scraps of fabric, a hairclip, a boot caked in mud that appeared to be almost new. They also recovered the soggy remains of a hand-bill issued to advertise a public lecture at the Philharmonic Hall. The lecture

was entitled *The Present State of Quantum Theory*. The principal speaker was Professor Albert Einstein.

The library closed its doors at six. Alma stepped out onto Unter den Linden, sheltering her eyes against the evening sunshine. It had rained while she was inside. The cobblestones were dark and slick. Music blared from a loudspeaker nearby, male voices and marching bands echoing back and forth between the sooty imperial façades.

Robert was waiting for her in a new Daimler. As soon as he saw her, he climbed out, giving her a hopeful smile as he held open the passenger door.

The students had taken their work outside the library, wheeling trolley-loads of books towards a waiting truck. One of them winked at Alma as she came down the steps. His smile was white, like the triangle of handkerchief protruding from the top pocket of his blazer. Alma frowned as he began to throw his load onto the truck with all the care of a labourer shifting coal.

'What are they doing?' she asked.

'Having fun, by the look of it,' Robert said.

He put a hand on her shoulder. His concern for her was surprising. He had always been a cheerful soul, but she had never believed him capable of real tenderness. The fact that they were equally bewildered by recent events, were both struggling to come to terms with Martin Kirsch's disappearance, had brought them closer.

As they drove past the little square in front of the opera house, Alma saw the books again. They were in piles six feet high. It was then she understood: they were about to be burned.

Two

Martin Kirsch was in the washroom when he heard it: a rasping, metallic scream. It seemed to come up through the plug hole – a terrible scream of pain and horror. He stood frozen before the sink, hands dripping, staring down into the rusty O of darkness.

Kirsch had come in early to catch up on some paperwork in peace and quiet. All week, truck-loads of election campaigners and para-militaries had been driving up and down the Schönhauser Allee, sounding horns, singing and jeering. Fights erupted when the police weren't watching. Smashed teeth and splintered bones. His land-lady, Frau Schirmann, kept the front door bolted and deadlocked. He'd been forced to wake her just to get out.

It was still barely light outside. The patients were always asleep at that hour. The dormitories were on the other side of the building anyway. Still he remained transfixed, listening, in case the scream came again. But all he heard was the water as it dripped from his fingers onto the cracked white porcelain.

Pipes, it was just the pipes. A boiler playing up. An air lock. Stupid of him. He straightened up, reached for a towel. These old buildings, they creaked and groaned worse than old men.

A voice again, only different now: faster and softer. Panting – or was it sobbing? He held his breath, leaned closer.

'No no no no no no no no.'

Water going down a drain somewhere. The air lock clearing. Not a human voice at all.

He replaced his spectacles and peered under the row of sinks. The plumbing was fifty years old: heavy galvanised iron, blisters of rust bubbling through a skin of grey paint. After the water trap, the outlet

took a dog-leg towards the stalls before disappearing through the floor. Underneath the washroom were the ground-floor offices, and underneath them lay the basement, partially cleared out for the deputy director's experiments. There were sinks down there, he recalled, in the old laundry. The plumbing was all connected, like a giant telephone exchange.

He looked at his watch: seven o'clock. He leaned down again and gingerly put his ear to the outlet.

Just whispers now, a distant gurgling. A tap, tap, tap. Then voices again, funnelling through metal – women's voices.

'Disgusting pig.'

He jumped. The voice was perfectly clear.

A rattle of taps. Water hissing through the system.

The door swung open behind him. The deputy director walked in, heel-caps clacking on the tiled floor: Dr Heinrich Mehring, wing-collared and meticulously bald, under his arm his usual copy of *Kreuz-Zeitung*.

'Good morning, Dr Kirsch.' Kirsch straightened up. 'Forgot your coat again?'

All medical staff were supposed to wear their white coats on duty. The director insisted upon it. It was important, he believed, to maintain a clear professional distance between patient and practitioner.

'No, Herr Doctor. I don't plan to see any patients today.'

Mehring opened one of the cubicle doors and raised himself on tiptoe. He liked to get a view of the pan from a safe distance before committing himself. 'But *they* might see *you*. I think that's the point, isn't it? There's a spare one in my office if you need it.'

Apparently the pan passed muster. Mehring closed the cubicle door and locked it. Kirsch heard him open the newspaper.

He hadn't been down to the basement since Mehring had requisitioned it. He recalled a warren of storage rooms, a repository of redundant medical texts, an ancient boiler maintained by a watchful janitor of few words and fewer teeth. Mehring preferred the basement to the available rooms above ground. He wanted to conduct

14

his experiments in conditions of scientific isolation, as if contact with the rest of the clinic might invalidate his findings.

The focus of his work was a new form of treatment, pioneered at the Lichterfelde Sanatorium a few miles away. A psychiatrist there, called Manfred Sakel, had injected recovering opium addicts with insulin, a hormone used to reduce sugar levels in the bloodstream. The agony of their withdrawal – the tremors, the vomiting, the anxiety – seemed to lessen. But Sakel got the best results when the dose was so high it put them into hypoglycaemic shock. With brains starved of sugar, his patients went into comas from which they could only be revived with heavy doses of glucose. Sakel was unclear whether it was the shock aspects of the treatment that were effective or the resulting comas, but he reported finding his patients' behaviour much improved. They were less argumentative, hostile, uncooperative. He had continued his work at the University of Vienna, applying the same techniques to patients diagnosed with *dementia praecox* – or schizophrenia, as it had become known. Although a formal paper was still awaited, it was rumoured that his results were equally impressive. Patients sent into comas five or six times a week were no longer plagued with psychotic thoughts. Their delusions evaporated, or seemed not to affect them. And while they were prone to disorientation and memory loss, they also became less wrapped up in themselves, and far less prone to inappropriate displays of emotion. As Sakel had put it, they became less 'complicated'.

Dr Mehring had followed Sakel's work with interest. As soon as a nursing vacancy had become available, he had filled it with a member of Sakel's old team at Lichterfelde. He had theories of his own on how to take the shock approach further. He believed it was changes to the brain's electrical activity that lay behind the effects Sakel reported, opening up the prospect of exciting new treatments.

Kirsch had read reports of the procedure. The subject was woken at six every morning and taken at once to a windowless room. There the staff laid him on a bed and propped up his head with pillows. Then they fed a greased rubber tube through his left nostril and

down through his oesophagus into his empty stomach. At the other end of the tube was a glass reservoir of sugar water suspended behind the bed. The sugar was there to bring him out of the coma at the designated time. Equipment for faster intervention was laid out on a tray: sealed bottles of thirty-eight per cent glucose solution and syringes.

At seven o'clock they injected insulin into a vein in the subject's left forearm, the dose mounting day by day from twenty units to forty to eighty until the comas began. Some patients showed unusual insulin resistance. They fought to stay awake, arms and legs twitching and trembling, as if to lose consciousness meant descent into some place of terror. As their bodies went into shock, goose pimples came up on their arms, they began to sweat, their mouths filled with saliva, so that they had to be rolled onto their sides to keep from drowning.

Kirsch had asked that his schizophrenia patients be exempted from Mehring's experiments. He was sure that putting them through such trials would disrupt his treatment, which depended on winning their trust. He had raised the matter with the director, Dr Bonhoeffer, and, when that did not produce results, with the patients' families. As far as he could tell, Mehring had taken no notice.

The service lift came to a stop. Kirsch left the door open and headed down the central passageway. Electric light bulbs had been suspended from the ceiling. They pulsed brighter then dimmer with the fluctuating voltage of the hospital generators. The air was thick with a sour smell of paint.

The books had all gone. The repository and the old laundry had been turned into treatment rooms. Heavy self-closing doors had been freshly installed. He pushed the nearest door open an inch. Two of Mehring's nurses were standing over an iron bed. One of them had a sponge in her hand, the other a clipboard. A patient lay between them, bare gnarled feet sticking out from under a woollen blanket.

The feet were bent towards each other, the toes clenched tight

like fists. Clasp-knife rigidity, they called it, usually a symptom of spasticity or lesions in the brain.

The feet twitched.

'Clean him up later. He'll just do it again.'

Nurse Regina Honig had been recruited from the Lichterfelde Sanatorium. She didn't take orders from anyone but Dr Mehring. She was tall and heavy-set, with pale skin that looked permanently sunburned. The other nurse was called Ritter. She was a thin, nervous woman with deep-set insomniac eyes. Kirsch had never heard her speak, at least not in conversation. He had the impression she was painfully shy.

Nurse Honig looked at her pocket watch and made a note on the clipboard. The patient began to convulse. The blanket was kicked to the floor. Kirsch recognised one of his patients: Andreas Stoehr. A strangled, gargling noise sounded in his throat.

Nurse Ritter bent over him. 'Do you think we should turn him over?'

Kirsch couldn't stand and watch. He stepped into the room. 'What's happening?'

Nurse Honig looked up, frowned, then came marching towards him, a hand held up in front of her.

'Dr Kirsch, we're in the middle of a procedure. If you'd be so kind . . .'

She'd been warned about his interfering.

He pushed past her. They had Stoehr strapped down on the bed. From wrist to elbows his arms were bruised from the insulin shots, circles of black and purple like the progress of a disease. His face had the drawn look of the imminently dead. His thick, spiky hair was unevenly dappled with tufts of white and grey. From his freshly soiled pyjamas rose a stink of urine.

Stoehr's head was rocking from side to side, mouth contorting as he tried to vomit up the rubber tube plumbed through his oesophagus.

'He does this,' Nurse Honig explained. 'He fights the coma. It's just a transitional phase.'

17

'He's choking,' Kirsch said.

Nurse Honig placed herself in front of him.

'He can't choke, Dr Kirsch. He has nothing to choke *on*.'

Stoehr's jaws began working furiously. He was trying to bite on the tube, to force it out of his mouth. A streak of saliva ran down his cheek.

Nurse Ritter looked on nervously, turning a ring round and round on her finger. 'Shall we put him on his side, Sister?' she said again.

Stoehr made a rasping noise. His eyes blinked open.

'B-b-black dogs!'

He bellowed, tugging at his straps.

'He's having a fit,' Kirsch said. 'Take him out of it.'

The foam was bubbling from Stoehr's mouth like a pan boiling over. The gargling sound was horrible.

'Sister?' Nurse Ritter looked worried.

'We have everything under control.' Nurse Honig put her hands on Kirsch's shoulders, trying to turn him away. 'The deputy director will be back presently. I don't think he'd –'

A violent, strangling sound sent her scurrying back to the bed. 'Get his head over.' She dropped her clipboard and thrust a pan under Stoehr's chin while Nurse Ritter rolled his head onto his left, using the flat of her hands. His arms jerked in their restraints.

Kirsch scanned the instrument trolley, looking for hypodermics. They were supposed to keep shots of glucose ready for emergencies. Intravenous injection acted quicker on the brain than ingestion through the stomach.

There were two syringes lying side by side, primed and ready.

Stoehr's whole body lurched. The legs of the iron bed screeched against the floor. Nurse Ritter staggered backwards.

'Hold him!' Nurse Honig shot Kirsch a hostile look, as if this were all his fault. 'I don't know why he's playing up like this.'

Kirsch picked up the hypodermic, squeezing out the air. 'Stand back. Please.'

'Doctor, you can't. We're in the middle –'

'I'll take full responsibility.'

'But Dr Mehring's *programme* . . .'

He took Stoehr's hand, straightening the arm. The surface veins had been cut into so many times, there wasn't a good spot left.

Stoehr's hand suddenly tightened around his. The grip was surprisingly strong for such a skinny man. 'They found me.' He was staring at Kirsch, eyes bulging. 'You told them. *You.*'

'Just try to relax.'

Stoehr's body convulsed. He slumped back, moaning. Kirsch fought to undo the strap around his wrist. He would have to give the shot in the upper arm, like a vaccination.

'Doctor, that isn't advisable.' Nurse Honig's face was flushed. 'Without the straps he could –'

'Get away? Can you blame him?'

'Dr Mehring gave specific instructions that glucose was not be administered until –'

She had grabbed Kirsch by the arm. He shook himself free.

'Dr Mehring is not here.'

'Nonetheless –'

Nurse Ritter screamed. With his free arm Stoehr had swung out and grabbed her by the hair. Now he was pulling her towards him.

'*Black dogs!*'

Her cap tumbled off as he dragged her head down, long brown hair spilling over them both.

Stoehr's mouth gaped open. Kirsch saw canines and incisors, cracked and yellowed, a sickly white tongue. Stoehr's eyes were open but unfocused, a bestial blank.

'*B-b-black.*'

Before anyone could reach him, Stoehr sank his teeth into the flesh beneath Nurse Ritter's ear. There came a squelching, crunching sound. A squirt of blood shot up his cheek.

Nurse Ritter was on the floor, clutching her bloody wound and screaming when Dr Mehring hurried into the room.

Three

Kirsch had taken a special interest in Andreas Stoehr. The case was difficult — certainly none of his colleagues had been in any hurry to work on it — but Kirsch knew the moment he read the file that it was one he had to take.

Stoehr was thirty-four years old, a one-time sergeant in the 140th Infantry Regiment. He had been arrested outside the opera house carrying two stick grenades and a can of paraffin, with which he said he intended to destroy the building. Upon interrogation, he had insisted that the opera house concealed the mouth of a secret tunnel connecting the surface of the Earth to the ninth circle of Hell, where traitors were incarcerated and those who had plotted to destroy the rightful God. These vengeful souls, he said, had been recruited by Satan and were returning via the opera house to colonise the Earth. Stoehr had been sent for psychiatric evaluation to the Charité Psychiatric Clinic, where he had been diagnosed as suffering from *dementia praecox* of the paranoid subtype.

Stoehr had dreams of drowning. The dread of suffocation haunted him day and night. He would not take the U-Bahn in wet weather for fear of being trapped in the tunnels. Walking over a bridge he would tremble with fear at the thought of the dark waters sliding by beneath his feet. In the middle of the night he would wake up screaming for air.

Kirsch had encountered phobias of this kind before, among veterans of the Great War. They afflicted men who had suffered poison gas attacks, or who had witnessed the effects of them close up, the way chlorine gas stripped away the inner lining of the lungs, causing the victims to drown in their own fluids.

Stoehr had volunteered for military service at the age of fifteen.

He had lied about his age to the recruiting officer and been sent west in time to take part in the Battle of Verdun. Kirsch reassembled the facts as best he could, though Stoehr's recollections were often confused. In France he had gone down with dysentery from drinking water out of a shell hole full of corpses. At some point he had been decorated for bravery and promoted to sergeant. He had been shot through the hip during an assault on Fort Souville, and had laid untreated and delirious for half a day or more, listening to the pleading and the screams of other wounded men.

After the war he had returned to his home town of Bremen, where he had worked for a year as a railway porter before following his sister to Berlin. There he had drifted in and out of casual work before finally securing a position as a nightwatchman at the Sklarek brothers' garment warehouse. This job seemed to suit him. For once there were no complaints about absenteeism or insubordination. But then, after a few years, the Sklareks had gone out of business in the wake of a financial scandal, liquidating their stock and closing the warehouse. It was around this time, according to his sister, that Stoehr's behaviour had become erratic and increasingly alarming. In particular, she suspected that he had killed a neighbour's dog. After a disagreement with his brother-in-law, Stoehr had moved out to lodgings in Pankow. The next the family heard of him, he had been arrested outside the opera house.

There was a pattern to Stoehr's madness, if you looked for it. In his mind the epicentre of all dread, all horror, lay beneath his feet, in the churning earth and the fetid waters. The shell holes had corpses in them, he said, but there was nothing fanciful about that. At Verdun, ten months of artillery warfare had sown several thousand tons of human flesh into the soil. Sergeant Stoehr had breathed in the stench of the dead, he had crawled and fought over their remains, he had filled his stomach with their putrefied blood. Their flesh had become his flesh.

Kirsch's colleagues were baffled by his interest in the sergeant's ravings. Different types of neurological disease caused different types of symptom, they believed. The character of a patient's

madness was a means of identifying which disease he had, according to a system of classification. But how that madness found expression, the particular delusions and fantasies that took hold of a patient's mind, were irrelevant. The job of the psychiatrist was to find a cure, through trial and error if necessary, so the patient could return to his place in society. How could psychiatry call itself medicine, if it were not in the business of finding cures?

But what would a cure mean, in Andreas Stoehr's case? What aspect of his mind, of his thinking or his behaviour, would be changed for the better? Where did his particular illness lie, if indeed he was ill? At the root of his troubles were his experiences of war. That, at least, seemed likely. But the past could not be mended, only forgotten. And as far as Kirsch knew, inducing amnesia was not a recognised form of treatment in any school of psychiatry.

They wheeled Nurse Ritter to the main hospital in a trolley. She was shaking too much to walk. As soon as Stoehr's blood sugar levels had returned to normal, he was tied into a security harness and locked up in the south wing, in one of the cells they kept for dangerous patients. Kirsch checked on him every hour, but Stoehr no longer seemed to recognise him. He sat on his mattress with his knees drawn up under his chin, staring at the wall.

Kirsch spent the rest of the morning in his office, waiting for Dr Mehring to reappear. In the commotion that followed Nurse Ritter's injury, there had been no chance to explain his actions, why he had removed the restraints from Stoehr's arm, why he had felt compelled to terminate the treatment. He didn't expect Mehring to accept his explanation, but he did expect him to demand one.

But then, his own was not the only conduct deserving scrutiny. Mehring, after all, had been absent during a dangerous procedure. The nurses he had left behind might be competent, but they could not be expected to take critical decisions. Mehring had been increasing the doses of insulin given to his patients day by day, inducing comas of increasing length and depth. Close supervision was required at every stage. Would he have dared disappear to the lavatory (with a

newspaper, no less) at any other day of the week but Sunday, when there were fewer medical staff around to observe his negligence?

The hours ticked by and Mehring did not appear. It grew dark outside. Flecks of rain tapped against the narrow, filthy window. Kirsch switched on the lights, but it was hard to concentrate on his work. He decided to seek Mehring out. Perhaps his difference in rank demanded no less, but when Kirsch went to the deputy director's office, he found it locked. He had no more success on the wards and the recreation areas. When he asked around for Nurse Honig, he was told she had gone home.

Mehring was in no hurry to discuss the incident, after all – at least not with him.

Kirsch hurried back to his office. What he needed was someone to back up his version of events, to acknowledge that Stoehr's seizure had been a genuine cause for concern. And he had to talk to them before Mehring did.

In his office he picked up the telephone. The operator put him through to the Emergency Department.

'I wanted to enquire about Nurse Ritter.'

'She's sleeping now. We gave her Luminal. She was in a lot of pain.' At the other end of the line Dr Oswald Brenner sounded faintly exasperated. 'She just has the five stitches, but they're deep, and there's extensive bruising. As far as infection goes, it's too early to say if we have a problem.'

Kirsch remembered the crunch of cartilage and the spray of blood – blood surprisingly bright coming from such an anaemic-looking woman.

'Is there anything she needs? Anything I could –'

'Rest. That's what she needs. We'll take another look in the morning.'

Kirsch remembered Nurse Ritter's face when Stoehr started foaming at the mouth: she'd been scared. It was the one glimmer of hope that she might see things his way. 'I don't suppose she's said anything about the incident?'

'We asked her about the circumstances. It's standard procedure.'

'And?'

'She was bitten, I understand. By some maniac.'

'A patient, yes. Although he wasn't . . . I don't think he knew what he was doing.'

Dr Brenner grunted. 'We'll get to the details later. I've advised her to stay in overnight.'

'Is that really necessary?'

'Just a precaution. Bite wounds are often dirty, and therefore susceptible to infection. Especially in this case.' There were voices in the background, the sound of hurried footsteps. 'Now if you'll excuse me –'

'Just one more thing: has Dr Mehring been in? I've been trying to find him.'

'He was here a while ago. I told him what I'm telling you: if you want to talk to Nurse Ritter, you'll have to wait until visiting hours tomorrow.'

Four

It was after five o'clock when his train pulled into Alexanderplatz. An hour of rain had driven the crowds from the streets. Most of the campaigners had given up for the day, leaving the soggy remnants of their literature plastered on walls and lamp-posts. By the exit, a solitary gang of girls were handing out leaflets and shouting 'Germany Awake!' in ragged unison. They looked out of place with their plaited blonde hair and sunburned faces. Most of the leaflets were tossed into the gutter.

The number 69 tramway snaked its way north towards the Schönhauser Allee, but he passed the stop and kept walking. He didn't go the shortest way home, but instead took a detour along Grenadierstrasse, by day a busy thoroughfare of small shops and market stalls, by night a haunt of streetwalkers and scavenging cats.

Kirsch felt at ease on Grenadierstrasse. In the winter months the air smelled of roasting chestnuts and burned sugar. The shops sold things no department store would stock: animal skeletons, prescription medicines, nuggets of amber and red gold. Bearded men gathered beneath the awnings – to gossip probably, though it did not look like gossiping, the way they shook their heads and frowned as if at the untimely passing of a friend. On the shop signs and nameplates the Hebrew lettering was jagged and monumental, as if bearing the import of divine edicts, or the codes of a secret society. No one knew him there, and the chances of running into a colleague, or anyone in his circle of acquaintance, were slim. The district was too shabby for that, and too foreign.

At the far end of the street, opposite a cheap hotel, was a corner where rainwater always collected, making a huge puddle beside the

pavement. It was there, on a Monday one week earlier, that he had first seen Elisabeth.

He had been walking back from the S-Bahn at about five o'clock. He had just bought some Salvarsan from his usual supplier and had stopped in front of a shop selling gramophone records. He was peering through the plate-glass window at the discs fanned out across a crush of red velvet, when he caught her reflection as she walked by. He had only a fleeting impression of her face – full, parted lips, dark eyes – but the realisation that she had been looking at him (or was it at the records?) gave his heart a gentle jolt. He turned. She was walking towards the edge of the pavement, the unbridgeable puddle barring her way. She wore a plain brown cloche hat, and a coat that was too bulky to be fashionable. She looked like a poor country girl just off the train, come to work as a housemaid in the great city. Tucked securely under her arm was a thick white envelope, with an address written on the front.

Anyone else would have walked around the puddle. But instead, she extended one foot over the water – Kirsch could still picture the heavy black lace-up shoes – and leaped across, landing with the grace of a ballerina. And when her trailing foot caught the very edge of the puddle, making a gentle splash, instead of fretting or cursing, she laughed.

She carried on across the road, hurrying a little as a taxi cab trundled by on Hirtenstrasse. Kirsch watched her intently, hoping the balletic leap had been for his benefit and that she might look back, if only to witness its effect. But in a few moments she had vanished among the crowds and the traffic, leaving nothing behind but a feathery swirl of mud in the water.

He stood now on the same spot, looking down at his reflection, dark against the street light glare.

The shop owner had eventually noticed him and opened up specially. Kirsch had found it hard to concentrate on what to buy. In the end, he took a recording of piano music by Artur Schnabel because the owner recommended it, and then set off home. Perhaps it was the gathering darkness, perhaps he simply wasn't concentrating, but after a while he found himself on a street he didn't recognise.

There was nobody around to ask for directions so he pressed on, passing a pumping station and a synagogue before turning down an alley that he thought might bring him out onto a main thorough-fare. He had reached the corner, could just make out the walls of a cemetery ahead, when a window opened above him. Then he was looking at her again.

She had a small iron balcony, just big enough for a clothes horse or a couple of pot plants. She leaned out and picked up a bottle of milk, thumbing open the stopper and bringing it to her nose. She wasn't wearing her hat, but even in the half-dark, he knew it was her. She had the look of a southern European, a homely broadness in the face, eyebrows that any Berliner would have plucked into unnatural arches. It came to him that she had just run out to post the letter she had been carrying and gone home again while he'd been in the shop.

She pulled the window shut.

'Excuse me! The Schönhauser Allee? Is it this way?'

He was surprised at his own boldness. His heart was pounding. All the nerves of a schoolboy asking for a first date.

Hesitantly, the window opened again.

'Fräulein?'

She stuck her head over the balcony railings. On the floor above a light came on.

He pulled off his hat. 'I seem to have lost my way. To the Schönhauser Allee? I'm sorry to trouble you.'

She studied him for a moment then pointed up the alley. 'One hundred metres. Go right and then left.' She spoke with a foreign accent.

'Thank you. Thank you very much.'

He saw her smile as she looked down at him. For a few seconds – it couldn't have been longer, though it seemed like it – they were both very still. Then she closed the window.

Standing on the corner of Grenadierstrasse, he wondered at his behaviour that night. He *had* been lost. It had been sensible to ask for directions. But that wasn't why he had done it. Some-thing had changed outside the music shop. The intensity of his feelings had been a revelation: exhilarating and disturbing, equally.

He feared – no, he *knew* – it was an intensity he had never felt with his fiancée, for all her innumerable virtues. He had long ago ceased to believe it *could* be felt, at least by him.

He followed the same route now. A glance at a street map had revealed his original mistake, the turning he had missed. He went by the pumping station and the synagogue, before heading towards the cemetery and into the alley at the corner of Wörtherstrasse. It was a route he took most days – healthier than being packed onto a tram full of people coughing and sneezing. And, like every day, he stopped outside the rooming house to look up at the girl's window.

For three days now, he had seen no light.

The Café Tanguero was doing good business for a Sunday, but the girls sitting round the dance floor were seeing little benefit. The tables were taken up with couples taking shelter from the rain. The smell of wet wool and leather mingled with the fug of cigarette smoke and spilled beer.

Kirsch took a seat at the bar. At the far end of the room, beneath a flaking pastoral fresco, an old man in a chalk-stripe shirt was squeezing the bandoneon. The tune was slow and sad, but then one of the girls leaned over and shook him by the knee, and he switched into a polka. She called herself Carmen these days, though Kirsch had it on good authority that her real name was Ludmila and she came from Warsaw. She had recently re-styled her appearance, ditching the unfashionable bob for a Latin look, hair pulled back tight and fastened behind. It was a style that complemented her black dress and long lace-up boots.

She caught his eye and walked over to the bar. 'Back again? You must like it here.' She elbowed her way in beside him and put a hand on his wrist. 'Let's have a dance.'

It was a familiar sequence: for dances the customer paid with a round of drinks, usually expensive ones, cocktails or cognac – or a kümmel if money was tight. That part was for the house. Then, after the drinking and the dancing, there was the option of a less euphemistic transaction, involving a trip to a room or a cheap hotel somewhere in the vicinity.

He shook his head. 'I don't dance.'

'Of course you do. Everybody dances.'

Two of the other girls had taken to the floor and were slinging each other around, trying to attract attention. The raincoats and umbrellas had dripped onto the boards. The girls slipped and slithered, shrieking with forced laughter.

'Not me.'

The barman placed the glass of beer in front of him. Carmen pouted. Her hand was still on his forearm. She slid it up to the elbow and down again. 'You shouldn't tell lies. It isn't nice.'

There was a smell of liquor on her breath. She was already tipsy.

'Lies?'

'I've *seen* you dance.'

'Here?'

'Don't pretend you've forgotten. You took long enough to get up the nerve.'

It was true. The previous week, a busy Thursday, he'd wandered into the Tanguero for a nightcap. The girl from Grenadierstrasse had been sitting there in the corner, wearing the same baggy coat and rustic shoes, earthiness and innocence bundled up together like the ends of her laces. The moment he saw her, he felt his pulse quicken. She sat watching the dancing, a drink in front of her, nobody else at her table. Eventually, he had asked her to dance. Without saying a word, she had stood up and offered him her hand.

He still couldn't recall very much about what happened then. He didn't remember the music or the crowd or the other dancers. He remembered the girl's shoulder, dark pleated fabric below the yoke of her dress; the vanilla sweetness of her hair; the way her body felt light – light enough that he could have swept her up with one arm, or thought he could. A couple of times she stumbled against him. The steps, it seemed, were unfamiliar and required her to concentrate.

'Shall we sit down?' he asked her after the second time.

She shook her head, refusing to be defeated.

'Are you here alone?' he asked her, as the number drew to a close.

She nodded.

'Me too.'

They held their position, each looking past the other's shoulder.

'Aren't you from here?' she said.

'Yes, I am.'

'Then why? Why are you here alone?'

He was at a loss to answer. Around them, couples were breaking apart or coming together, leaving the floor or walking onto it. Before he could say 'I don't know', the music started up again. He remembered that she looked at him then, just before the room was plunged into darkness.

It was another power cut. A groan went up, mingled with ironic cheers. The staff, who had become accustomed to such interruptions, began lighting lanterns above the bar. The band started up again, more raggedly than before. Kirsch felt the girl's forehead brush against his cheek.

In the darkness he kissed her.

It only lasted a second, perhaps two. He felt her break away, startled or disgusted. He felt stupid and ashamed of himself. But then, before he could stammer an apology, they were kissing again, longer and harder. In his arms her body was a dark, gentle heat.

The lights flickered and came back on. The crowd at the bar was even bigger than before. And there, elbowing his way through, was Robert Eisner with one of the nurses from the Charité. Of all people.

Eisner saw him and waved. Kirsch waved back.

'Please excuse me,' he said to the girl. 'I have to . . . I'll be just a minute.'

The girl seemed to understand. She nodded and turned away. Kirsch just had enough time to ask for her name. She hesitated before answering, as if the matter required some thought, and then said 'Elisabeth'. He suspected at once that this was not her real name, but a fiction she had made up on the spot.

It proved difficult getting away from Eisner, who seemed in no hurry to be alone with his date. Out of the corner of his eye, he watched Elisabeth dance with another man, and then another. Both were drunk and importunate, pulling her closer than she wanted to

be. Finally Eisner took to the dance floor, but by this time, Elisabeth was nowhere to be seen.

Kirsch went back to the Tanguero the next night and the next, and every night after that. But he had never seen her again. Perhaps she had gone back to wherever she came from. More likely she had met someone, someone who had whisked her away to a better life in a better part of town.

It was all for the best probably, he told himself. His interest had been a manifestation of pre-marital panic, an episode best forgotten.

He looked into his glass. Carmen was playing with one of her big silver earrings. 'So, you were here that night,' he said.

'I'm always here.'

'Do you remember the girl I danced with?'

Carmen looked over his shoulder at a man who had just walked through the door. 'Not really.'

'Try.'

'Are you going to dance with me?'

'Try to remember. She called herself Elisabeth.'

Carmen studied his face for a moment. 'Oh *her*. The dark one.'

'That's right.'

Carmen giggled. 'She looked like she cut her own hair.'

'Tell me her name, her full name.'

'Why? You want to look her up?'

'Maybe.'

'Well, I can't help you. She isn't . . .' Carmen lowered her voice. 'She doesn't work around here.'

'I know. I just thought perhaps you'd talked to her. Since you're always here.'

A sly look crossed Carmen's face. She reached up and took off his spectacles. 'I tell you what: you have a dance with me, and I'll tell you everything I know.'

But it was obvious from the way she said it that she didn't know anything at all.

Five

Robert Eisner was outside the common room with two of the junior psychiatric nurses. As soon as he saw Kirsch at the end of the corridor, he hurried over. It was clear from the anxious pinch of his eyebrows that the news about Nurse Ritter was out.

'There you are. I was afraid you weren't going to show up.'

Kirsch had intended to come in early, but an uncomfortable night had put paid to that plan. 'Why wouldn't I? I'm not sick.'

He realised he had been holding his left arm. The Salvarsan injection had produced a steady ache that even alcohol wouldn't mask. He carried on towards his office.

'I'm talking about yesterday,' Eisner said. He was five years younger than Kirsch, but with his smooth skin and clear blue eyes, he could have passed for twenty. 'What in God's name got into you?'

Kirsch wasn't sure whether to resent his curiosity or welcome it. 'Nothing got into me. I was passing the treatment room –'

'In the basement?'

'The patient was having a seizure, and Mehring wasn't there.'

Eisner fell silent as they climbed the stairs, the unfamiliar furrows deepening on his brow. 'Look, I know you're not happy with these insulin procedures, but –'

'Ten per cent of patients go into an irreversible coma. For the rest, the effect is about the same as a sharp blow to the head.'

'Yes, yes. But what I don't understand is: why you and Nurse Honig . . .' Eisner shrugged helplessly. 'Why you had to assault her.'

Kirsch stopped. 'Is that what she's saying? I *assaulted* her?'

'That's what I heard.'

Kirsch pictured the confrontation, Nurse Honig's puffy red face

up close to his, eyes red-rimmed and bulging. At worst, he had nudged her aside.

'Mehring. He put her up to this.'

'Mehring?' Eisner thrust his hands deep into his coat pockets. 'So you didn't . . . ?'

'She's making it up.'

Eisner fell behind a little as they reached the corridor. 'Well, of course, she and Mehring, they're thick as thieves.'

'Exactly. She owes him her job.'

Eisner nodded firmly. 'Then Nurse Ritter, she wasn't –'

'I suppose it was me who bit her. Is that the story?'

'No. Sergeant Stoehr did that, after you . . .' Eisner came over and put a hand on his shoulder. 'The important thing is: can anyone back up your side of the story?'

He hurried across the road towards the main hospital, Eisner in tow. There were no visiting hours until the afternoon; so they decided to evade the formalities by going through Triage.

'That Dr Brenner's a stickler for procedure,' Eisner said, as they crossed the road. 'And he thinks psychiatrists are quacks. He'll send us away for sure.'

An ambulance was parked outside the entrance. A wounded man was being carried inside. His shirt had been torn off and across one shoulder the purple-black flesh was badly swollen. They followed, the wounded man staring at them with a frozen look of shock on his face.

In the Emergency Department every bed was taken. Teams of doctors and nurses were working on both sides of the room, all talking at once, trying to stabilise their patients: establishing airways, plumbing in drips, administering morphine. Blood was smeared across the grey linoleum. Overnight, the street fighting had flared again, in Friedrichshain and Neukölln. Shots had been fired at a beer hall in Pankow. Eisner said some of the ambulance crews had refused to pick up the wounded until first light.

At the far end of the room, someone started yelling. A nurse ran

out from behind a screen, bumping into Kirsch. A sterile bowl and instruments went crashing to the floor.

'Uh! You . . . *sch–schwein*!' The voice crackled with demonic rage.

The nurse bent down to pick up her things. A lock of hair had slipped out from under her cap. It hung limply across her forehead. Through a gap in the screen, Kirsch glimpsed a pair of legs in baggy brown trousers kicking wildly.

Two orderlies were trying to hold the patient down. He was young, twenty-five at most, got up head-to-foot in the pseudo-military regalia of a storm trooper. He was staring in stunned outrage at the torn remains of his shirt and undershirt and the blood-soaked dressing taped across his stomach.

Kirsch watched the doctors and nurses work. Perhaps it was just the gravity of the wound, the rate of blood loss, but they seemed edgy, flustered. Two weeks earlier a storm trooper had been rushed to a hospital in Lichterfelde with head injuries. He had been struck with an iron bar, and died a few hours later. The next day a posse of his comrades had appeared at the hospital, accusing the resident surgeon of letting their man die deliberately. They had clubbed him to the ground and thrown him from a second-storey window. He would have died if there hadn't been a motor car parked underneath with a canvas roof. At least a dozen people had witnessed the assault, but no arrests had been made.

Everyone at the Charité knew the story, though it wasn't often discussed. Politics, even political violence, was considered an unsuitable subject for conversation, as if discussion could only lead to disagreement and division, and in the process, make matters worse. If it was acceptable to give voice to any political view, it was only to the consensus of the professional classes generally: that the republic was falling apart, that political violence was a symptom of its failure and that sooner or later, something would have to be done.

The storm trooper went pale. He blinked slowly, then his head lolled back onto the pillow. Around him, the pace of activity grew frantic as they prepared him for surgery.

Kirsch felt Eisner's hand on his arm.

'Not our problem, eh?'

Outside Triage they took a wrong turn and found themselves in a storage area. Three of the trolleys had bodies on them. A grimy forehead and a head of ragged hair peeped over the top of a sheet.

It was quieter on the next floor. The ceilings were high, the walls white, everywhere a background echo of measured footsteps and hushed voices. Kirsch began to have doubts about the chances of getting Nurse Ritter on his side. He *had* disobeyed instructions and she *had* been wounded because of it. Perhaps the best thing was to go directly to the director and explain himself, but Eisner was having none of it.

'Attack is the best form of defence. Catch the old bugger in a lie and you're in the clear.'

A porter was pushing a laundry basket down the corridor. They asked him for the women's wards. He pointed absently back the way he had come.

'There was a nurse brought in here yesterday,' Kirsch said. 'Her name was Ritter. She had a wound?' He indicated the place, an inch beneath the ear. 'A young woman, dark hair.'

The porter reeked of tobacco. He had pitted skin and dyed hair. 'I know who you want,' he said.

They were bending over her, like pathologists over an interesting corpse. Dr Brenner shone a penlight into her eyes while the ward sister made notes on a clipboard. Something had gone wrong. Nurse Ritter lay motionless, apparently unconscious. A drip had been plumbed into her wrist.

Brenner was fifty, unkempt and short-sighted, his fleshy face folded in on itself by the action of perpetual squinting. He was well enough known at the psychiatric clinic. Over the years, he had shared a number of patients with Dr Bonhoeffer, mostly neurological cases brought about by head injuries. But this was not a neurological case, nor a psychiatric one. It was a case of routine injury, a flesh wound.

The blood drained from Kirsch's face. When last they spoke, Dr Brenner had been concerned about infection. Bite wounds were

dirty wounds. But an infection would have taken days to set in. Even a bite from a rabid dog wouldn't have rendered her comatose that quickly.

Brenner sighed and leaned closer. Nurse Ritter's pale arms lay at her sides, palms upward.

'Pupillary reflex present,' he said. 'We've essential brain stem function at least.'

The brain stem. The nut-sized morsel of grey matter that kept the vital organs functioning: heart beating, lungs pumping. It performed a host of essential tasks, none of them requiring either consciousness or thought.

'We'll move on to the deep tendon reflexes.' Brenner straightened up, realised that he and the sister were no longer alone. 'Can I help you, gentlemen?'

Kirsch stepped closer to the bed. In his mind all he could see was the bite wound. He saw it opening like the petals of a flower, straining at the web of stitches, purple, swollen and suppurating: a bite from Cerberus, a taste of Sergeant Stoehr's internal world.

'That's all right, Dr Brenner,' Eisner said. 'Our mistake.'

Kirsch didn't move. He could see her face now for the first time. But it wasn't Nurse Ritter's face.

Eisner leaned towards him. 'Wrong patient, Martin. Let's go, shall we?'

Brenner frowned and went back to work, pulling a small wooden hammer from his coat pocket. The ward sister folded down the covers. They were going to test the reflexes, checking for nerve damage.

'Martin? What's the matter?'

Her skin was like wax, her bloodless lips cracked and swollen, her eyelids puffy. But it was her – Kirsch was in no doubt: the girl from Grenadierstrasse. They had dressed her in a hospital smock, the kind that was laced up the back like a straitjacket. Smeary black bruises discoloured her neck.

It was the last place he had ever expected to find her. He felt a surge of panic, a sudden shortness of breath. A better part of town. She was supposed to have gone to a better part of town.

Brenner turned the girl's hands over. 'You're Dr Bonhoeffer's people, aren't you? Did he send you?'

Eisner shot Kirsch a quizzical glance. 'We were looking for Fräulein Ritter. We were told –'

'Nurse Ritter was discharged this morning,' the sister said. 'She went home.'

Kirsch was standing at the foot of the bed. The girl's stillness was horrible. It was a stillness like death. 'What happened to her?'

Brenner gently smacked the hammer against her wrist. There was no response. 'Unclear. She was found unconscious. The temporal lesion doesn't look serious; so I suspect it was hypothermia that put her in the coma.'

'A coma? How long has she been –'

'We're not sure. Forty-eight hours or so. Possibly longer.' Brenner brought the hammer down again. The forearm twitched. 'Brachioradialis reflex present, but weak.'

The sister made a note. Brenner leaned across the bed and repeated the test on the left arm.

'But she'll come out of it. She *will* come out of it?'

'Hard to say. It depends on the extent of the brain damage. In my experience, the longer the coma, the worse the prognosis.' Brenner continued to work, tapping and probing the girl's arms from elbow to fingers, checking for impairment of the central nervous system with the precision of a violinist tuning up. 'The likelihood is, she won't survive.'

Kirsch steadied himself against the end of the bed, surprised at the strength of his own reaction. It was disproportionate, unnatural. Physical. This was a woman he hardly knew.

Brenner flexed one of the girl's legs and placed it over the other, cradling her foot as he struck the Achilles tendon. The toes were bruised. It looked as if she had fractured a toe. There was dried blood beneath her nails.

'Do you know her name?'

Brenner pulled the gown up to the girl's knees. She had fallen, judging from the grazes and the bruising.

'Not yet,' Brenner said. 'The police are hoping someone will come forward.'

'Wait a second.' Eisner was at his side. 'This was in the papers. I read about this. Two little boys found her in the woods, near Caputh.' The sister frowned at him over her clipboard. 'All they found was a programme, for a physics lecture.'

'A physics lecture?' Kirsch said. 'Are you sure?'

'Didn't you read about it? It was a lecture by Albert Einstein.' Eisner folded his arms as he looked her up and down, like a man surveying a new make of car in his neighbour's driveway. 'That's why they call her the Einstein girl.'

quanta

Six

Dr Oswald Brenner lurched awake. He was still behind his desk, the departmental budget estimates for the coming year spread out before him, numbers that a whole evening of trimming and paring had not brought down to the requisite size. He fumbled for his spectacles, aware now of hurried footsteps clacking down the corridor outside. Hastily he hooked the spectacles over the back of his ears and squinted up at the clock. It was almost eleven o'clock. He had been asleep for –

A door banged. He heard voices, what sounded like an argument. The footsteps got louder, then stopped outside his office.

'What in God's name . . . ?'

There was an urgent knock, then one of the junior nurses stuck her head round the door. 'Dr Brenner sir? I think you'd better come.'

Nurse Friedrich: *very* junior, highly strung and inadequately educated.

'Nurse Friedrich, please do not run in this hospital. It will do our patients no good at all to have you blundering into them.'

'I'm sorry, Doctor. It's the coma patient. The Einstein –' Nurse Friedrich checked herself. 'The patient they found in the . . .'

She was so out of breath she could hardly get the words out.

'I know who you mean. What about her?'

Someone else ran down the corridor. Footsteps pounded up the stairs towards the women's wards.

'She's . . .' Nurse Friedrich's legs flexed at the knees, as if she was struggling to contain a full bladder. 'I think you'd better come.'

Someone had tipped off the newspapers. Reporters began arriving at the hospital even before the police, though Dr Brenner barred them from the premises. Hours later they were still hanging around

outside, buttonholing anyone who looked like they might have information. Standing at the common-room window, Kirsch watched them pacing up and down beside the police inspector's car: thin, hungry-looking men with shifty demeanours, like dogs expecting to be kicked.

He had been told the story by Robert Eisner, who had heard it from the nurses. The Einstein girl had woken suddenly from her coma, screaming. A duty nurse had hurried over, but the girl seemed hysterical. She had smashed a glass against the bedstead and tried to push it in the nurse's face. The nurse ran for help, but by the time she returned, the patient had vanished. After a hue and cry they had finally found her out on the fire escape. It wasn't clear, Eisner said, if she was hiding or intent on throwing herself off. It took two male orderlies and a shot of phenobarbital to get her back inside. She had remained sedated ever since.

Eisner was in the common room now, slouched in a worn leather armchair, his nose in the *Neue Berliner Zeitung*. Stories about the election results covered the front page. As far as the Reichstag was concerned, it was another stalemate. Except for the Communists, most political parties had lost seats. But then, since President Hindenburg had taken to appointing his governments without reference to the people's elected representatives, it was hard to see how this would make any difference.

'Looks like von Papen won't last much longer,' Eisner said. 'The army are sick of him.'

One of the reporters sauntered round the back of a parked truck and began to urinate against the wheel.

'You'd prefer Hitler?'

'For Chancellor?' Eisner turned over a page. 'Hindenburg would rather cut his own throat. Hitler's far too plebeian.'

'Then who?'

'Generals are like stinging nettles. Cut one down, another pops up. The army'll get who it wants. There's always someone.'

Kirsch's future father-in-law had been a guarded supporter of Franz von Papen, the present Reich Chancellor, and what the Berlin press deridingly referred to as his 'cabinet of barons', a fact that

had given rise to some tense moments around the Siegels' dining table. Under the pretext of restoring order and national unity, the one-time cavalry officer and amateur racetrack rider, whose long face strikingly resembled that of a horse, had used the army to remove the state government of Prussia. It was clearly the first step in dismantling the despised republic in its entirety. But the economy had continued to deteriorate and the violence was still getting worse.

Kirsch's breath flared against the cold glass. Once again, men in uniform were making all the decisions, just as they had during the war. No one seemed to think it odd, despite the outcome of that particular conflict. And why should they? Square bashing and boot polish were the principal prerequisites for good government. Everyone knew that.

There was movement outside the hospital, a burst of harsh light and shadow. The reporters hurried forward, casting aside their cigarettes.

The police inspector was gaunt and lanky. Most of his energy seemed to have been absorbed by his moustache, which was thick and lustrous. He scowled as another flashbulb went off in his face, refusing questions with irritable shakes of the head. Kirsch stood on tiptoe as he reached the kerb.

'What's up?' Eisner said, peering around his newspaper.

By the car, the police inspector turned and faced the reporters. It looked like he was going to take questions, after all.

Kirsch dug his hands into his pockets. 'Think I need a breath of fresh air,' he said.

It was starting to rain. Fat drops, large but infrequent, smacked against hat brims and overcoats. The police driver turned on his headlamps as Kirsch hurried across the road.

'I am assured by Dr Brenner that the patient is in no immediate danger. Physically she appears quite healthy.' The inspector coughed and cast a resentful glance at the sky. 'For the time being, however, she remains disorientated.'

'What does that mean?' a reporter shouted. 'Has she gone mad?'

'It *means* she is disorientated.'

Another reporter smirked as he wrote. He seemed to enjoy some advantage of professional rank; the other reporters kept quiet and listened when he spoke.

'Inspector Hagen, have you made *any* headway in finding her attacker?'

The inspector frowned. '*Mister* Lehnert, we have no firm evidence that she *was* attacked. Her injuries are minor, and consistent with a fall.'

'In the woods? What did she fall from, Inspector? A tree?'

The other reporters laughed.

'She is yet to make a complaint,' Hagen said, 'of any kind.'

The reporters couldn't believe their ears. It was a cue for them all to shout at once.

'Isn't it obvious she was kidnapped?' Lehnert demanded. 'Otherwise, where are her clothes?'

'We haven't found them. But that doesn't mean —'

'Is it the police's hypothesis that the victim was out for a swim?' The other reporters laughed again, louder. 'Or is it your contention that she was sunbathing up this hypothetical tree?'

The reporters could hardly contain themselves. Inspector Hagen shook his head in disgust, clearly regretting his decision to say anything.

In recent years the detective powers of the civilian police had become an object of derision in the German press. Their poor record in hunting down serial murderers was largely responsible. First there was Karl Denke, a minor church functionary and purveyor of smoked pork from Münsterberg, whose meticulous records catalogued thirty murders, and whose cellar had been found to contain barrels of smoked human flesh, bones, cured skin and pots of human lard. In Berlin itself, there was Carl Grossmann, a one-time butcher and door-to-door salesman, who had confessed to the murder of twenty-four young women, all newly arrived migrants to the city, whom he had hired as a succession of housekeepers before killing, dismembering and selling them for meat in discreet paper parcels. Then there was Georg Haarmann, a police informer from Hanover, who had befriended

young migrant workers at the railway station. He would take them home, sexually molest them and then kill them by tearing out their throats with his teeth, an atrocity he committed on at least twenty-five occasions, by which time human skulls were washing up on the banks of the Leine River. Haarmann too had seen no reason to let the bodies go to waste, and so had skilfully dismembered them, boiling up the flesh and selling it on the black market as potted veal and pork. Like the others, it was said, his eventual arrest had been accompanied by much discreet vomiting around the town.

What interested Kirsch was the killers' lack of remorse. Whether or not they were insane was a matter of debate. Beyond serious doubt was their inability to empathise with their victims or their families. Examination revealed that they were able to experience only a limited range of emotions altogether. Theirs was a condition of emotional poverty and isolation from the mainstream of human life. An American psychiatrist called Partridge had proposed calling such individuals *sociopaths*, on the grounds that the causes of their condition were social, a conclusion he had reached after studies of juvenile delinquency.

Kirsch was interested to know if the condition was reversible, but the press had fixed on more immediate issues. In their reports and editorials the incompetence of the civilian police was the constant theme. Intentionally or not, the effect was to provide implicit justification for the existence of paramilitary groups who frequently took the law into their own hands.

Lehnert and the other reporters were still laughing. Red-faced, the inspector turned away, then immediately turned back again, levelling an angry finger. 'You may indulge in whatever fantasies you like, gentlemen. I shall deal in facts. The young woman has undergone an ordeal of some kind, but it is *not* clear that any other parties were involved.'

He climbed into the back of the car, refusing to answer further questions. The passenger window on the far side was partly open. Kirsch rapped on the glass.

'What's her name, Inspector? Have you found out her name?'

The inspector looked at Kirsch, took in the white coat, realised that

he was not another reporter. His expression softened. 'I'm afraid not, Doctor. She says she doesn't remember.' The driver cursed as the interior of the car was lit up with a blinding flash. 'If you ask me, she's –'

But Kirsch never heard what she was in the inspector's opinion, because the car had already pulled away.

Later that day, a fight broke out in the refectory. It was not the first. Since the start of the election campaign, the patients at the clinic had exhibited signs of increasing agitation. The bitterness of the contest and the vehemence of its rhetoric had somehow inflamed them, despite their having only sporadic contact with the world outside.

National Socialist propaganda in particular cast a spell. Several of the patients proclaimed themselves to be leading members of the party (though they were plainly not), and demanded that the other patients submit to their authority. Others denounced what they claimed were traitors in their midst, calling for purges and retribution. Almost every day Franz Scheck, a dentist and manic depressive, stood at the top of the stairs and proclaimed himself *Führer*, vowing to take revenge upon the devils and Jews of high finance who were orchestrating Germany's ruin, on one occasion concluding his remarks by casually urinating upon the upturned faces of his audience. Some patients were roughed up, appearing at mealtimes with split lips and swollen faces, but it was impossible to identify the guilty parties. Kirsch suspected that some of the orderlies were involved. Several times he had been forced to rebuke them for shouting or excessive force. He had tried to remove a notorious bully called Jochmann, but his notes to the director requesting action went unanswered. The isolation cells filled up, sedative doses were doubled and still the nights were punctuated with outbursts of demonic ranting, accompanied by whistles and cat-calls that echoed round the building. With the director struck down with flu and his deputy fixated on his insulin experiments, the sense of disintegration was palpable.

More than a week had gone by, and still Kirsch had heard nothing

further about Nurse Ritter's injury and the alleged assault upon Nurse Honig. He began to hope that the issue had blown over; that he might not be dismissed after all. So far, he had told no one about his precarious position, neither his family nor Alma. He knew they would worry. And what was the point of that, when it might turn out that there was nothing to worry about?

He spent all day on his cases, noting their progress or the lack of it, planning his responses. The threatening atmosphere had affected everyone. Even his more amenable patients treated him distrustfully, as if wary of speaking their minds. Again and again, he found himself thinking about the Einstein girl, lying in her hospital bed. He could have speeded up police inquiries by revealing what he knew, which included her likely address off Wörtherstrasse. At least that way they could have established her identity. But how would he explain being in possession of such knowledge? What would the newspapers make of it, not to mention his fiancée and her family? It was not the kind of knowledge a man in his position was supposed to have.

He wished the girl would recover her memory, and soon. He wished – though he was not yet ready to admit it – that she would recover her memory of him. But if she did remember him, then what? What could possibly happen next? Nothing, of course. Nothing good. He was a professional man, about to be married. His future with Alma was all mapped out. This was his chance for a new beginning, for family life and children – wholesome, bright prospects that would purge his system of the past. What good was the Einstein girl next to that, this stranger whose misadventures had somehow found their way into the newspapers?

She was nothing to him, with or without her memories: a fantasy lover, devoid of all substance – except that when he closed his eyes and thought of her, the pull he felt, the hunger, seemed substantial, urgent and real like nothing else.

Seven

They had moved her away from the women's wards and into a room at the top of the building with bars on the window and a door that could be locked. It was a place reserved for highly infectious patients, or ones who were considered a threat to the smooth running of the hospital for any other reason.

'Dr Brenner thought it best,' the nurse explained as she showed Kirsch in, 'after everything that's happened. She'll be gone soon anyway.'

'Gone where?'

The nurse shrugged. 'Dr Brenner says there's nothing more we can do.'

Peeling grey paint and faded anatomical drawings covered the walls. Above the bed hung a small wooden crucifix, with an old garland of flowers around it, shrivelled up and faded to the colour of straw. A solitary electric bulb was screwed into the ceiling. The nurse's footsteps retreated down the corridor.

The girl was asleep on the bed, her head turned away from the door. They had cut her hair. It gave her a youthful, tomboyish look, a different, androgynous kind of beauty. The split lip had mostly healed and the bruising on her face had gone down, leaving shadows around her cheekbones and beneath her eyes. She seemed more fragile than ever.

Her injuries are minor, and consistent with a fall. That was what Inspector Hagen had said.

Kirsch took a step closer. The girl let out a sudden, terrified gasp. Her whole body bucked and twisted, as if she were shackled and desperate to wrench herself free. A sob rose from her throat, then, just as suddenly, she was still again.

Night terrors, he knew all about those. Recently, more or less coincidentally with the Stoehr case, they had returned: horrible visions he could only recall with difficulty by day, but which he felt lying in wait for him at night. He had taken to staying up later and later – reading, drinking, walking the streets from bar to bar – so as to postpone the moment when they might return. The best sleep, the most oblivious sleep, was the sleep of utter exhaustion.

He sat down beside the bed and reached for the girl's hand: it was smooth and soft, not the hand of a housemaid or factory worker. Nor were there any scratches, just a graze and some swelling on her wrist. He felt for a pulse, surprised at how cool her flesh felt. The room was too cold. With his coat on, he hadn't noticed. He eased her blanket up higher, folding it under her chin. Then he took her hand again, looked at his watch and began to count, wondering as he registered the tremulous beat, how Dr Brenner could have allowed his patient to be injected with barbiturates, whatever the circumstances. They could easily have put her back into a coma. She might never have woken up again, might have died without anyone even knowing who she was.

There were bruises on her arms. The catheters had irritated her veins: they stood out darkly, like the tendrils of an invading tumour.

Seventy-two beats per minute: a little fast, but no cause for concern. The unsteadiness of the pulse was more worrying. He looked into her face, realised that the lids were no longer fully closed. Behind the dark lashes, there was movement among the tiny points of reflected light.

Her eyelids flickered, then opened.

'Good evening,' he said.

She sat up sharply, brought her hands to her mouth, hurriedly felt her lips, the outside and the inside, pushing her fingers between her teeth. She was terrified.

'Just a bad dream,' Kirsch said. 'You're safe now.'

She took her hands away, looked at them, then at him. He searched for some hint of recognition in her eyes, but saw none.

'Do you know where you are?'

She shrank from him, pulling the sheets up to her chin.

'If you want the book you're too late.'

'Too late?'

'I don't have it any more. I sent it back.'

'What book are you talking about?'

She opened her mouth to speak, but no words came out. Slowly she shook her head. 'It was just a dream.'

'Are you sure?'

She didn't answer. Her gaze drifted towards the window, a blankness in her face now, a descending stillness Kirsch had often seen in dementia patients and others in the grip of psychosis. The gravitational pull of the interior world; in certain states it became irresistible, distorting the geometry of conscious thought, its straight lines and perpendicular angles. Memories ran in circles, unable to reach a destination. Without the discipline of chronology, they crossed over and doubled back, undoing the indispensable logic of cause and effect. From a presence to a half-presence to no presence at all, that was his perception of it – of insanity generally: a kind of leaving. It was how loved ones experienced it too. The patient remained physically present, but his or her mind travelled a different road, one that no other human being, even the closest, could follow.

He had to reconnect her to the outside world, to bring her back into the living present.

'Let me introduce myself,' he said. 'My name is Dr Kirsch. Martin Kirsch. I work at the Charité Psychiatric Clinic.' He nodded towards the window. 'Across the road.'

'Kirsch.' She kept her gaze on the sky, which was turning blue in the twilight. An ambulance set off from the hospital, alarm bells clanging. 'You're not what I expected.'

'You were expecting me?'

'You're in the book. I thought you'd be older.'

She was clearly confused.

'We met once, briefly,' he said. 'Don't you recognise me?'

She frowned, swallowed. 'Have I lost my mind?'

Kirsch picked up the accent again: Slavic, was it? Or from somewhere further south: Greece perhaps, or Italy?

'Of course not. Under the circumstances it's natural that you should experience some . . .' He groped for a palliative term. '. . . disorientation. Do you have any idea how you got here?'

'In an ambulance. I remember the bells.'

'And before that?'

'They t-told me I was found. In the woods.'

'But you don't remember that?'

She shook her head. 'Amnesia. Isn't that the name for it?'

'Loss of memory, that's right.'

She nodded. 'I have amnesia.' As she said the words, her chin lifted, as if the condition were some source of comfort. 'Can you make me better?'

She looked at him, a hard clarity in her eyes.

'The thing is . . .' The frankness of her stare was disconcerting. 'I'm not your doctor. You're not my patient. Dr Brenner is in charge of your case. I was just . . .'

The girl frowned. 'Just what?'

'Curious.'

Kirsch thought of the reporters outside and wished he had said something else. The girl looked down at her blankets. Her fingers absently traced the line of her throat.

'You must be thirsty,' he said. 'Would you like some water?'

Without waiting for an answer, he went to fetch a glass from downstairs. But by the time he returned her eyes were closed. One of her feet was uncovered, sticking out from under the blanket into the chill air. The ankle was still swollen and there was dried blood around the toenails. He remembered the first time he had seen her, her foot extended over a wide black puddle on Grenadierstrasse, laughing as she kicked up the water. She had been on her way to post a letter. But who was the intended recipient? A lover perhaps? In which case, where was that lover now? For that matter, where was her family? Why had they not come to claim her? How was it that she was alone?

Carefully, he pulled the blanket down and tucked it under the mattress. 'Sleep now,' he said, but she was asleep already.

He found Dr Brenner in the Anatomy Department.

'Her amnesia is retrograde. She remembers everything that's happened to her since she came out of her coma, including what the medical staff told her this morning. What she can't access reliably are memories pre-dating the coma. When I asked her about her past, she seemed unable to answer.'

'Or unwilling,' Dr Brenner said under his breath, 'if we're keeping an open mind.' He hesitated, then led the way into the storage room.

'Unwilling?'

Brenner shook his head. 'It doesn't matter. I should thank you for taking an interest, I suppose. I had thought of asking Dr Bonhoeffer for a psychological assessment. Certainly I see no evidence of head trauma, or any other form of impairment, besides the amnesia. I had her do some mental faculty tests, and the results, if anything, were rather better than average.'

'Is there any evidence of alcoholism?'

'No. We took a blood test when she arrived, but of course quite some time had gone by. It can't be ruled out.'

'I noticed a slight stammer, although she could have had that before.'

'Indeed. In any case, after a coma that's to be expected. The faculty of speech is the first thing to disintegrate.'

Kirsch was brought up short by the sight of a complete human brain, pickled in formaldehyde, sitting on a bench in a large glass jar. All around the dimly lit room were shelves full of similar jars, each one containing a specimen of some kind: brains, fetuses, lungs or other internal organs. It was brains Dr Brenner was interested in. He had written several papers on head trauma and the pattern of its effects.

'She's also been having vivid dreams,' he said. 'Nightmares. Possibly involving injuries to the mouth area, which may be significant.'

'Really? How so?'

'I've found them to be associated with issues of enforced silence, an inability to speak out. Or sometimes with strong feelings of guilt.'

'Well.' Brenner frowned. 'Her dreams aren't my concern.' He switched on a light above the table. 'But I concur with your tangible observations. As you know, I believe the damage was done when she went into her coma. In such cases neurological symptoms can take almost any form.' He paused to admire the larger of the two brains in front of him, squinting through the heavy glass. The last traces of colour had been bleached from the tissue, leaving it a creamy, fibrous white. 'In any case, the patient doesn't appear to be in any immediate danger. In fact, she's almost recovered, physically.'

'I understand you plan to discharge her.'

'Unless there's some deterioration in her condition. We'll watch her for a few more days. But there's no point in her being here if we can't effect an improvement.'

'But she has nowhere to go.'

'Someone will come forward eventually. Missing persons and so forth. I'm sure the papers will be only too happy to run a photograph. In the meantime, there are residences, aren't there, for destitute women?'

There were, a few, some run by church organisations, others by the municipal authorities. Most were run along prison or military lines, with residents put to work for their keep. Suicides were regular occurrences. Most of the women Kirsch had spoken to preferred life on the streets.

There was only one thing he could do.

'I'd like to investigate the possibility that the cause of the amnesia is psychiatric,' he said, 'rather than simply neurological.'

Brenner looked mildly affronted. 'I've never heard of a psychiatric disorder that puts its sufferers into a coma. Perhaps I've missed something in the literature.'

He turned to a second, noticeably smaller brain specimen. He picked up the jar, peering at what appeared to be an area of tumorous tissue above the right temporal lobe.

'We could be seeing the effects of shock.'

Brenner turned the jar around in his hands. The brain bobbed. 'She wasn't raped, you do know that? In fact, I saw no evidence of recent sexual activity.'

Kirsch could not help picturing the examination, the patient dragged unconscious onto the table, Brenner squinting between her upraised legs as his stubby fingers delved and probed.

'That said,' Brenner added, 'she's certainly no blushing virgin. She almost certainly gave birth at some time. And there's no wedding ring on her finger.'

'An attacker might have removed it.'

'It would have left a mark. I found none.'

Brenner's indifference was suddenly easier to understand: the Einstein girl was not, in his eyes, respectable. She belonged to a class of women who were prone to misadventures, usually at the hands of men, but which they had invariably brought upon themselves.

'In any case,' Kirsch said, 'she's clearly undergone a traumatic experience.'

'I'm not sure anything's exactly *clear*, Dr Kirsch. The police have found no evidence of foul play.'

'Then how do they explain –'

'They have a theory, for what it's worth, that the woman is simply deranged, and was all along. They say they've seen similar cases. A deranged woman might well decide to take a swim in a lake in late October. She might think to herself it was the middle of July.' Brenner smirked. 'Of course, this theory is very convenient, since it means they've nothing to investigate.'

Brenner took a pen from his pocket and began to write in the log-out book. Nothing could be removed from the department without a record being kept. Finally he looked up. 'Was there anything else?'

'If you've no objection, I'd like to request that the patient be transferred to the clinic for observation.'

Brenner's pen was still for a second. 'I can understand your interest, Dr Kirsch. Patients this unencumbered are hard to come by. One has a free hand, more or less.'

'I can assure you, it's not my intention –'

'Of course, she has no means that we're aware of. No way of paying.'

'Her fee would be waived.'

'With the director's approval, I assume.'

'It's potentially a very interesting case. I'm sure he'd agree.'

Brenner looked at Kirsch over his spectacles, then went back to work. 'Very well, I shall request a referral. Just as soon as I see his signature on the paperwork.'

After his visit to the main hospital, Kirsch returned to his desk at the clinic to find a sealed envelope resting on the blotter. It contained a letter from Dr Bonhoeffer informing him of the director's return the following Monday and summoning him to a meeting first thing in the morning.

Eight

Dearest Martin,

I just heard about the transport strike in Berlin, and I hope it doesn't mean you won't be able to receive my letters, or that they'll sit in a depot for weeks and weeks, uncollected. Father says I should be careful what I write to you, because sooner or later the strikers will open the envelope looking for money, especially if the whole thing drags on. Do you think the strikers will interfere with the mail? I can't bear the idea that my words, which are only for you, could end up being passed around for entertainment among such awful people. It's silly of me, but I can't get the idea out of my head. It's not that I imagine the words I have for you are so very special. I dare say they have all been used a million times before. But they are special to me, because they come straight from my heart, and are words that I have never used before to anyone else, and hope never to use again to anyone but you — there! You see, I am already minding what I say. There is no need to _hope_. I _know_ I could never replace you in my heart, however that were to come about . . . And now I am sinking into all kinds of sad speculations when there is no reason — when I should be happy. All because of a silly strike!

So please, dearest, let me know as soon as you can that you have received this letter, and set my mind at rest. I haven't heard from you for over a week as it is, and there is so much I need to talk to you about, so many things to be decided before June. I know it seems like a long time yet, but if we don't make up our minds, the whole event will be decided for us. I am already having quite a struggle keeping Mother from taking charge. She has such fixed ideas about how a wedding

56

should be (a 'society wedding' she keeps calling it, although I think the concept is faintly loathsome, don't you?), but I am afraid to give way to her all the time without consulting you first. She is already drawing up a list of the magazines she deems suitable to cover the reception, and will no doubt enlist Father's support to make sure she is not disappointed. Do you really want a whole <u>hour</u> of opera before the dinner? Mother is so anxious to show off her acquaintance with Ruth Jost-Arden, who I know sings marvellously, but an <u>hour</u>? And do you want your poor little bride struggling down the aisle with a train, like a big queen ant? But then I suppose that is not something you should worry yourself about, being a man, but it worries me. I think Mother has been watching too many newsreels.

I expect you are wondering about going down to Reinsdorf on the 13th, and of course I will be there on the Sunday as you suggest. I haven't seen your mother and father for so long. Tell them I am looking forward to seeing them. I think the war memorial idea is splendid. What better way could there be to remember your dear brother Max, and all those other brave young men? I am sure the necessary funds will be forthcoming.

I have to finish now or else I will miss the post. Hans-Peter is going to drive down for me. Do write, my dearest, when you can, or whenever your poor lunatics allow it. I hate it when I don't get a letter. Mother says it puts me in a foul mood all day.

Your loving (there I go censoring myself again — that should be <u>adoring!</u>)

Alma

Nine

He used to see Max when the autumn came, when the fogs crept in at dawn, making haloes round the gas lamps, crackling on the tramway power lines, softening the lofty outline of the apartment buildings on the Schönhauser Allee. He remembered his little brother when the ends of the avenue vanished into cloud; so that it was possible to think of it as small and incomplete, a splinter floating in a grey void – full of detail, stained and decayed with the passage of time, yet isolated, like the fragment of a frieze, or a picture torn from an illustrated book.

What he remembered most were the holidays they had in Mecklenburg, when they were boys. He and Max would go down to the lakeside and watch the mist rising off the water, twisting in silver threads towards the sky. They would stand with their backs to the woods as it rolled landward, until the white light enfolded them and they could see nothing else. It was their secret game. They would get up early, before anyone else was awake, and take out a rowing boat (something they were under strict instructions not to do unsupervised). Max always manned the oars, pulling out across the water until they had reached the deepest part of the lake. Out of sight of everyone, they would drift in the silence, feeling like explorers on the edge of the world.

They discovered that if you lay back in the boat, it felt as if you were rising, floating free of everything, drifting up into the sky. You were cut off from the world, but at the same time closer to the heart of Creation, souls on the threshold of Heaven. And when the mist began to clear and the shore reached out to them again, it was like drifting back down to Earth.

Max loved astronomy. On his twelfth birthday their Uncle Stefan

gave him an old brass telescope. On clear nights he would stare through it for hours, even taking it with him on their trips to the country because, he said, the air was cleaner out there and the stars brighter. Their parents encouraged him. Their mother taught French at the local high school and their father ran the family firm making mathematical instruments: compasses, dividers, protractors. They held learning – science, particularly – in high esteem. Religion hardly merited a mention. It was a subject that produced impatient sighs or dismissive paternal mutterings from behind the newspaper. The churches had simply been wrong about the universe too many times. The Earth was not flat, despite appearances, and the sun did not travel around it once a day. For all their claims of intimacy with the Supreme Being, the men of God had merely tried to set in stone everyday human perceptions. It had taken imagination, scepticism and the rigorous methodologies of science to reveal that these perceptions were false.

Years later, during the war, they went up to Mecklenburg one last time. They were days of forced good humour and unspoken foreboding. Max had received his commission in the infantry and was a few days from heading out to France. Their elder sister Frieda had just got engaged to Julius, a lieutenant in the navy. Martin was on leave from the Rumanian campaign, where he had been serving as a medical officer with the 9th Army. Back then, his hands were still steady enough for surgical work. Everyone was there – for the last time, as it turned out.

It was their father's idea: a holiday among the lakes near Schwerin, like they used to take. Better than skulking around at home, he said. Kirsch was sure he had other reasons: the farewells would be less solemn at the end of a holiday, less final. It was a way of making the fear more manageable, for their mother mainly; a way of marshalling optimism. The woods and the lakes did not change. They would always be there. In Mecklenburg they could believe in the possibility of living by their own measure of time.

All the same, there was a fragility about the celebrations. Even the delicacies were artificial: lemonade laced with spirits instead of

champagne, the cigars Frieda's fiancé had given them as a present, which turned out to be made of dried cabbage leaves soaked in nicotine. Everyone tried not to talk about the war, but news of the revolution in Russia intruded. Kirsch remembered his little sister Emilie running into breakfast with a newspaper. Violence had erupted in St Petersburg and Moscow. The Tsar had been forced to abdicate. Surely this meant the war would soon be over, and the boys could stay at home. Everyone crowded round to read the report, but Kirsch caught the look in his father's eyes. The country was in no mood for peace, even if peace was on offer. The mood was for victory at any cost, if only so that the dead would not have died for nothing. There had been cheering in the streets when the U-boats were told to sink neutral ships in Allied waters, though that was almost certain to bring America into the war.

In the Kirsch family there had been the same absence of celebration at the start of the conflict. With the parades and marching bands and the singing in the streets, it was as if a huge party was going on to which they had not been invited. When Martin declared his eagerness for the fight, his mother had slapped his face and run out of the house. In the event, his eyesight had proved too weak for front-line duty. But that did not lift the sense of foreboding at home. They still had Max to worry about, Max with the blond hair and the eyes like jade, the boy who never stopped asking questions, though he seemed to know everything. The boy who made everyone laugh. He had no Achilles heel to keep him safe.

All through his officer training he had been reading Albert Einstein. He turned up in Mecklenburg with the professor's latest book. He was eager to talk about it – because no one at the barracks was interested, Kirsch assumed; or perhaps because it kept them from talking about other, more important, things.

Of all the great men of science, Einstein had always enjoyed a special place in Max's affections. Growing up, he pounced on any book or paper that set out to explain Einstein's work, even when the mathematics was beyond him. Visitors to the house were quizzed on their knowledge of differential calculus and asked to help decipher

it if they could (which was not often). Back then, what seemed to please Max most was Einstein's demolition of received ideas – the more inviolable the better. For Max, Einstein was an iconoclast, smashing the false idols of accepted wisdom, however jealously guarded.

One of Einstein's first targets was the aether, a sacred concept for theologians and scientists alike since the days of Aristotle. The aether was supposed to be everywhere in the universe, invisible and undetectable, just as God was everywhere. As far as science was concerned, it was the medium through which light waves passed, just as sound waves passed through air and sea waves passed through water. It had to exist because simple experiments had proved beyond doubt that light was not a material thing, but an undulation, a disturbance that travelled through something else. When pairs of light beams fanned out from two narrow points, they interfered with each other, producing alternate bands of greater brightness where peaks and troughs coincided and darkness where peaks met troughs and troughs met peaks. It was an effect only waves could produce. But about the mysterious aether Einstein was suspicious. Was it scientific to accept the existence of something that eluded all attempts to observe it?

'Two thousand years of religion and two hundred years of science.' Kirsch could still picture the delight on Max's face. 'Demolished in a single equation.'

Max loved nothing better than to see the great and the good proved wrong. For him it meant freedom, a weight being lifted. He was free to imagine anything.

Einstein's equation said light was not a wave, but a stream of energy particles he called *quanta*. Like a volley of tiny bullets, a light beam was quite capable of travelling through the voids of space without the need for aether to carry it. And, unlike a wave, these *quanta* had mass, just like the objects that emitted them, which meant they would have to be affected by gravity in the same way. A beam of light passing by a massive object like the sun would change direction, giving to an observer a false impression of where it had come from.

At the time, all this had struck Martin Kirsch as fantastical. How could light – the purest form of energy – have weight? Mass and energy were two different entities, one material and permanent; the other intangible, a quality not a thing. An object might be hot, but heat itself had no substance. It needed mass to exist, the way a thought needed a mind. But Einstein said mass was simply energy in a different form. He denied both its solidity and its permanence, even its clear distinction from the space that surrounded it. Mass was simply energy vastly concentrated. As Max explained it, the material universe could be thought of as nothing less than frozen light. At the heart of all material was the immaterial.

What Max did not know was how Einstein's ambiguous *quanta* would change the world. Or how Einstein would come to detest his creation, and devote himself to its destruction. All that was still to come.

In any case, Martin did not share Max's enthusiasm for the science of light. He felt stupid when they talked about it, which is not how an older brother wants to feel in the presence of a younger one. He listened and pondered only so that Max would not have to repeat himself and make him feel stupider still. He even wondered, from time to time, if that wasn't Max's real intention, the spur behind his relentless curiosity: a secret need to outshine the first-born son.

Kirsch learned later that he was wrong. The truth came to him the last time he saw Max alive: Einstein's vision was not just a source of fascination for his brother. It was something much more important.

That last morning they took a boat out on the lake, just the two of them. It was Max's idea.

'We'll sneak off at dawn, like the old days. I've already found a boat.'

No explanation. It was something Martin was just supposed to understand, even though it was early April and cold. As if they were boys still, and nothing – not time, not war – separated the past from the present.

Kirsch assumed Max wanted to ask him about what to expect at the front. He had to be afraid. New recruits were always afraid, though they did their best to hide it. But it turned out all Max wanted to talk about was his Einstein book. All weekend he had been carrying it around like a preacher with a Bible. He was close to understanding it, he said. He was close to seeing clearly how everything in the universe – matter, energy, space and time – was really one thing, like a giant snake, twisting and turning as it swallowed its own tail.

'Is that what's on your mind? Giant snakes?'

Max smiled as he looked out across the water. The sun was up. Yellow sunlight lanced through the clouds. 'Well, what's the point of having a mind if there's nothing on it?'

'And yours is on Einstein, even now.'

'Yes.' Max frowned as he pulled on the oars. Reflected light danced over his face, gilding his pale skin. 'In fact, I hope he'll be on my mind for a while yet.'

Kirsch wished he'd insisted on rowing. It might have kept him warm. He wished he understood what they were doing out there.

'It isn't that there's a lot to learn,' Max said. 'It's more a case of *un*learning – forgetting, if you like. That's much harder. You have to let go of your intuition. You have to accept what seems impossible.'

Kirsch remembered blowing on his hands.

'Such as?'

Max stopped rowing and reached into a knapsack. 'See for yourself.'

It was the book: *On the Special and General Theory of Relativity, Generally Comprehensible.*

Kirsch laughed. 'You expect me to read that now?'

'Not now. After we've left here. It's a present.'

Max held out the book. Kirsch looked at it. His smile slowly vanished.

'Keep it,' he said. 'It's wasted on me.'

'How can you say that when you haven't read it?'

'We can talk about all this when you get back. There'll be plenty of time then.'

For a split second there was silence, an interval just long enough for Kirsch to understand that his brother did not expect to come back; that this book, which he so treasured, was a final parting gift.

'Of course, of course,' Max said. 'Still.' He tossed the book into his brother's lap and picked up the oars again. 'It'll amuse me to think of you racking your brains over it. I'll need something to laugh at when I'm up to my neck in mud.'

It was the first time he'd mentioned what lay before him, the first acknowledgement that there was anything troubling about it at all.

'And when we're back again – just like you say – we can argue about the non-existence of time.'

Kirsch didn't read the book until several years later. By that time, Einstein's theories had been brilliantly confirmed by observations of starlight as it passed by the mass of the sun, observations that were only possible during a total eclipse. They had made the German scientist the most famous man in the world.

But any chance of arguing with Max had gone. Two months after their visit to the lake, on 7 June, the British army detonated a million pounds of high explosives beneath German positions on the Messines Ridge. Second Lieutenant Max Kirsch was among the ten thousand men who died in the explosion, the sound of which was heard over three hundred miles away, as far as the borders of Mecklenburg. No trace of him was ever recovered.

Ten

Max's room was at the top of the house in Reinsdorf. Everything
was just as he had left it, except that some of his possessions had
found their way back there from other parts of the building: a
tortoiseshell comb with his name engraved along the side, a pearly
white nautilus shell, a china figurine of a spectacle-wearing terrier,
which he had been given as a gift and had never liked. On top of
the chest of drawers, at an angle to the mirror, so that its reflection
was visible from the door, was a framed photograph of Max taken
a month before he had left for the front, posing in his cadet's uniform
– stiffly, but with a discernible hint of self-parody. The photograph
had faded over time so that his skin was now a uniform white, his
features etched in faint sepia lines. The mirror, too, had clouded
with age, so that in the reflection Max was already lost behind a veil
of mist.

No one had planned to create a shrine. It had happened by degrees.
Because Max's body had not been found, nor a single item of his
personal effects, he had been designated as Missing in Action. The
hope had remained that he might one day come home, that he had
been taken prisoner by the enemy, or, like the girl in the Charité,
lay in a hospital somewhere, stricken with amnesia and unable to
remember his name. Now and again, the missing did come home.
The newspapers carried stories about it, reports of soldiers
wandering out of the East, having fought with the Cossacks, or
fallen captive to the Reds. For the family there was never any particular moment when hope was finally extinguished, no crisis from which
it was possible to recover and rebuild. A state of suspension, somewhere between mourning and normal life, went on for years.

All the while, Max's room remained Max's room. The sheets were

changed from time to time, though no one ever slept in them, and the gaslights replaced with electric ones, as they were throughout the house. But that was all. In the end, it became unthinkable that anything else should be disturbed. Emilie still had the tiny box room she had always slept in as a child, though it was far too small for a grown woman. Once Kirsch had tentatively suggested she move upstairs, but she had shaken her head vehemently: she was quite happy where she was. Besides, their mother still spent time in Max's room, she said, in the afternoons, especially when it was raining.

Emilie, blonde and willowy, verging on awkward, had never left Reinsdorf. She worked as a schoolteacher in Wittenberg, as her mother had once done, cycling there and back every day rather than waste money on the train. Instead of French, she taught geography and elementary mathematics.

For a few years before the war Kirsch had been very close to Emilie, closer than to Frieda, who was the eldest, or even to Max, whose head had always been in a book. As a child she had been high-spirited and intensely curious about the world. When grown-ups came to dine, she would sit in the corner of the sitting room, her hands tucked under her legs, listening attentively to the conversation. Yet somehow all that curiosity had played itself out. In its place were now sobriety and reserve, and an almost wilful plainness in dress and appearance, as if any display of vanity would invite scorn. With her dull, pale skin and pinned-up hair, it was hard to believe she had once been thought a beauty.

Her closeness to her brother Martin had diminished along with her looks. At some point, perhaps during those long years after the war, when he was mostly away, she must have decided he was not a suitable confidant any longer. He wondered if she had come to resent him: if, deep down, she felt he had abandoned her, leaving her to grow up in a house full of grief.

In all, fourteen young men from the village of Reinsdorf and the surrounding hamlets had fallen in the Great War. The Keil family had lost both sons – Erich in 1917, Fritz in 1918 – both, coincidentally, at

the age of twenty-one years and three months. An iron plaque in the church bore their names. But ten years on, plans began to be drawn up for a free-standing memorial at the heart of the village. It was a complicated project. Money had to be raised, a site purchased, a design approved. His mother sat on the steering committee, busying herself organising fund-raising events and liaising with artists. These days it absorbed most of her energies. When Kirsch went home, the latest developments were always discussed at length. This weekend was an important one for the memorial cause: a chamber concert was to be held on Sunday afternoon in the old school house, with an ensemble travelling in specially from the conservatory at Leipzig.

'Bach, Beethoven and a transcription from Wagner,' his father said, as they walked to church that morning. '*Siegfried*, I think.'

'Worthy choices,' Kirsch said. He had decided to tell the family about events at the Charité, and the all-too-likely prospect of his dismissal. But an opportunity to raise the subject had yet to present itself.

'Oh yes, very worthy,' his father said. 'They suggested Rossini as an opener – the ensemble, I mean. Some overture. But the committee . . .' He shook his head despondently.

'Too light?'

'Too Italian. Fought on the wrong side. Even Mozart was frowned upon, apparently, not being *entirely* German.'

Once he would have mocked such unsophisticated thinking, but no longer. In the lingering aftermath of war, expressions of patriotism were irreproachable, no matter how idiotic. Only those who had made the supreme sacrifice were entitled to criticise. Strangely, they never did.

'I'm not sure van Beethoven was *entirely* German,' Kirsch ventured. 'Wasn't his family from Flanders?'

'Possibly.'

His father stopped and looked anxiously back down the path. The women were following on behind, sharing an umbrella. Kirsch's mother walked stiffly, as if the weight of her winter clothes was too much for her.

His father continued along the track, subject closed. 'It's a pity Frieda can't be here. We don't see enough of her. Nor Julius either, of course.'

Kirsch agreed that it was a pity, although the fact was hardly anybody saw Julius these days. The same year Max died, his ship had taken a direct hit from a British cruiser, and although he had survived, that was where his luck had run out. The blast had taken his left arm and disfigured him so brutally that he refused to show himself in public. In France, so Kirsch had heard, the state had established special homes for old soldiers with *gueule-cassées* – broken faces – so that no one should be forced to look at them. But as far as he was aware, no equivalents existed in Germany. The disfigured took their chances on the streets or, like Julius, dwelt spectre-like in the shadows, preferring to be thought of only in the past tense, in the memory, rather than be seen for what they were.

The approved design for the memorial was on display at the front of the church, rendered in watercolour and propped up on an easel. Obelisks and blocks of carved limestone had been eschewed in favour of a massive slab of granite. A Maltese cross – the simplified military version – was gouged out of the dark rock over the words FOR GOD AND THE FATHERLAND.

The new pastor was short and overweight, with a florid complexion. With the memorial in mind, the theme of his address that morning was sacrifice: the sacrifice of Christ, Abraham's sacrifice of his son, the sacrifice of those who had fallen in battle. Sacrifice was as old as Creation and brought about renewal, he said, just as the fallen leaves of autumn enriched the earth and made possible the arrival of spring – an analogy that greatly pleased him, judging from the way he smiled as he made it, bouncing up and down on the balls of his feet. Kirsch stared at the design, hearing only the water dripping from the roof and the squeaking of the pastor's shoes. He pictured Max's name, chiselled into the granite, his allegiance and purpose in death unequivocally set down for all eternity, lest

there should be any doubt. Max and the others, the monument boasted, had died for the very ground beneath Germany's feet. They had poured their blood into its foundations, like so many tons of human cement, and the earth in turn had rendered up the proof.

For God and the Fatherland. Kirsch wondered at his mother going along with the assertion. Max's hero, after all, had been Albert Einstein, an inveterate pacifist who despised and ridiculed all things military. In any case, it was hard to see how God was the beneficiary of the sacrifice, or how a general European war could have advanced his interests one way or the other. Some memorials sensibly left God out of it. The fallen there had died simply *for the Fatherland*, a more tenable claim, though it left the choice of preposition still open to question. Given that most men at the front had been conscripted, wouldn't it have been more accurate to say they had fallen *in the service of* the Fatherland? Or even *by order of* the Fatherland, since it was the Fatherland that had placed them deliberately in harm's way, without giving them any say in the matter?

Kirsch looked across the aisle at the rows of care-worn faces, at Frau Keil and the farmer, Herr Kehlitz, whose boy had died at Mons during the first month of the war, and it came to him that remembering was not, in fact, the point. The memorial wouldn't help them remember. What they most wanted was to be proud, and for that they needed their sons to be cast as heroes who had offered up their lives in a conscious and necessary act of self-sacrifice. They could not be proud of mere victims, however blameless they might be. A victim's death was without meaning or purpose. And that, for some reason, made it impossible to bear.

One evening, when the design had first arrived and still awaited approval, Kirsch had shared these reservations with Emilie. He couldn't speak for the other dead men, he said, but the memorial was completely wrong for Max. He would never have wanted anything so brutal and bombastic in the heart of the village. Emilie had told him urgently to keep his voice down, for their mother's sake: 'It's what she wants. Don't interfere.'

Emboldened by two glasses of brandy, Kirsch had pressed home

his point. 'I can tell you, I wouldn't want my name on that damned lump of rock.'

Emilie had come over and yanked the glass from his hand, spilling half the contents over her dress. 'It's a pity it *isn't* your name on it,' she said, 'instead of Max's. Then no one would care either way.'

After a dreadful silence, Emilie had apologised, assuring him that she hadn't meant it, that she had let her temper get the better of her. He had accepted her apology, waving away her concern with a smile.

He had never mentioned the memorial again.

After the service they all hurried home and prepared for lunch. Kirsch grabbed an umbrella and hurried out to meet Alma's taxi, surprised to discover that it had stopped raining and that the sun was breaking through the clouds. He had to shelter his eyes as she climbed out of the car.

She was wearing a smart tweed outfit beneath her raincoat, and a cocked hat with a feather in it, like a huntswoman in a pastoral operetta. Her blonde hair was freshly curled. She placed a hand on his shoulder and offered her cheek. Her skin smelled of roses.

'Why didn't you tell me about the paper?' she said, giving his arm a squeeze.

'What are you talking about?'

'You haven't seen the picture?' She reached into her bag and pulled out a copy of *Die Berliner Woche*. 'It came out yesterday. Hans-Peter spotted it.'

It was the kind of publication Alma didn't buy for herself, an illustrated weekly full of crime stories and scandal. She turned over a couple of pages and handed it over. The headline read: EINSTEIN GIRL — *MYSTERY DEEPENS* — POLICE BAFFLED. Underneath there was a photograph. The girl was sitting up in bed, caught in the flash-bulb glare, one hand clutching the blanket to her chest. The picture was at least a few days old, because her hair had not yet been cut short. The scratches and grazes on her face looked dark and ugly, but nothing could disguise the pretty pout of her mouth or the dark lustre of her eyes.

'Not there, *there*.'

Alma's gloved finger pointed to a pair of photographs at the bottom of the page. They had both been taken outside the hospital: Inspector Hagen, holding his impromptu press conference, mouth gaping open, hands held up as if in abject surrender; then Hagen in the back of his police car, talking through the passenger window to a man in a white coat. The man's face was partially obscured by the flash bulb reflecting off his spectacles. The caption ran: *Inspector Hagen in consultation with Dr Martin Kirsch, the eminent psychiatrist assigned to the case.*

'Isn't it wonderful?' Alma said. 'My fiancé is *eminent*. And the whole world knows it.'

Kirsch shook his head in disbelief. 'How did they get my name?'

The way he was leaning in through the open window made him look like an autograph hunter.

'You shouldn't be so modest,' Alma said. He sensed her watching him closely as he read the piece. 'She's rather beautiful, isn't she?'

'Who?'

'Who do you think?'

He shrugged. 'If you like your women black and blue.' He folded up the paper. 'Do you mind if I borrow this?'

'Keep it.' She took his arm as they walked towards the house. 'I must say, I thought you'd be more pleased.'

He thought of his upcoming interview with Bonhoeffer and shook his head. 'I'm sorry.'

'What's the matter?'

'It just isn't helpful, this kind of nonsense.'

'For the patient, do you mean, or . . . ? Because if it's true what they say, that the poor girl has lost her memory and doesn't know who she is, surely it can only help.'

Before he could explain, his mother had appeared in the kitchen doorway, holding out her arms in welcome.

The dining table was covered with their best lace cloth. Silver they hadn't used in years sparkled in the pale winter sunlight. The meal

was a friendly interrogation. Kirsch's mother wanted to know everything about the wedding preparations and barely gave Alma time
to eat.

'Have you thought about a place to live?' she asked.

'Martin hasn't told you?'

'Martin doesn't tell me anything. I'm his mother.'

'Well, I found this pretty little place in Zehlendorf, not far from
the Wannsee.' Alma smiled as she cut into a potato. 'It isn't for sale
just yet, but I've spoken to the owners. In the meantime, I suppose
we shall have to get an apartment in town.'

'Martin's always worked in Berlin,' his mother said. 'I can't see
the attraction. From what I read, it seems so dirty and dangerous.
What does your father think?'

Alma gave Kirsch an apologetic look. 'I'm afraid he agrees with
you, Frau Kirsch. He's always saying the city needs a thorough
cleaning out.'

'A doctor has to go where he's needed, Klara,' his father said.
'Not where he happens to enjoy the scenery.'

His mother shrugged. 'Are there really no mad people in
Wittenberg? Or Leipzig? Or is it just their kind of insanity is too
dull and provincial?'

Kirsch reached for his wineglass while everyone laughed. His
father had unearthed a bottle of Riesling from the cellar, one of a
case bought for some putative celebration long ago, and now past
its best.

'There are no posts,' Kirsch said.

'What about the university? Couldn't you teach there?'

Alma put her hand on his forearm. 'I've always thought Martin
was a born teacher.'

His mother nodded. 'He was a wonderful surgeon when he was
in the army. I still have a letter from his commanding officer, Colonel
Schad. He said Martin was the best man in his unit.' She turned
towards her son. 'I've never understood why you left the profession, Martin. Good surgeons are always in demand.'

Kirsch had never explained to the family the real reasons why

he had abandoned conventional medicine. As far as they were concerned, he had simply followed a new interest, the way the Kirsch men always did, with no regard for the financial consequences.

'He's his own harshest critic,' Alma said.

He shook his head. 'Not at all.'

'But I'm sure he won't have to stay at the clinic much longer, unless he wants to, of course.' Alma made it sound like a prison sentence. 'He's becoming quite well known. That paper he wrote, for example –'

'That's nothing,' Kirsch said, because it *was* nothing, or at least not much. His one and only contribution to psychiatric literature, it had been published in the *Annals of Psychiatric Medicine*, a new publication with a derisory circulation, printed in Munich.

'Well, my father said –'

'Your father read my paper?'

Alma squeezed his arm. 'Of *course* he did. He was very impressed. In fact, he said he was going to show it to some people.'

A gratified look passed between his mother and father.

'What kind of people?' Kirsch asked.

Alma smiled and shrugged. 'Medical people, I suppose. His company does make medicines you know, darling.' She looked down at her plate and began delicately dabbing at her meat. 'And he supports all kinds of institutions in the medical field.'

Kirsch was about to tell them that he had no intention of leaving the Charité, that Dr Karl Bonhoeffer was arguably the most distinguished psychiatrist in Germany and that there could be few more experienced mentors. But then he thought about the summons he had received for the next morning and the idea lost its appeal.

'It's as well Martin has you to look out for him, Alma,' his mother said. 'He cares a great deal about his books. But getting on in the world . . .'

His father made to refill Alma's glass, but smilingly she covered it with her hand. 'The funny thing is, when they were boys, it was Max who was the thinker,' he said. 'Martin was the practical one. We thought he'd be an engineer or a businessman. He was always

taking things apart to see how they worked.' He chuckled as he poured himself another glass of wine. 'There are still clocks in this house that tell the time most eccentrically, thanks to Martin's boyhood *interventions*. Isn't that so, Klara?'

But his mother didn't seem to be listening any more. She was staring down at the lace tablecloth, absently smoothing it out with her fingers. His father grimaced momentarily, as if suddenly aware of having said the wrong thing. For a moment nobody spoke. Then his mother took a sharp breath and glanced up at the ceiling in the direction of Max's room.

The committee had done its best to make the old school house hospitable. Paraffin lamps burned in the corners. Winter bouquets of willow and jasmine had been placed either side of the door and in the corners of the room. Footlights had been strung along the bottom of the platform so that the musicians' shadows would play over the wall behind them, where an old imperial flag was on display. But with the ensemble tuning up, most of the seats were still empty.

Kirsch's mother was distraught. 'The weather may have held people up,' she said. 'Tell them not to start yet.'

She stood by the door, holding the programmes, refusing to come inside. The reward for her persistence was a solitary latecomer who arrived on a bicycle and then left again without paying. When she was finally persuaded to come and sit down, she did not stay, but got up at the end of each piece and went outside again just to see if there were any more people waiting.

The music itself seemed curiously out of place. Most of the performers were slight, bespectacled young men, the kind that usually failed to pass muster for military service on grounds of general delicacy, if not bad eyesight, and their playing had a wistfulness and refinement that evoked nothing of the parade ground, let alone the battlefield. The audience, a mixture of veterans, villagers and local dignitaries, sat motionless on their folding chairs, staring blankly at the proceedings, respectfully aware that such examples of high culture were the ultimate proof of the superiority of German

civilisation, but at the same time wishing there could be more in the way of a tune. All things considered, Kirsch thought, a brass band would have suited the occasion better, except perhaps that Max had always hated brass bands and would invariably cover his ears if one marched by.

After the ensemble had taken their bows, everyone stood up and sang the national anthem. Then finally the audience trailed out, visibly relieved to be out of their seats. A collection box had been placed by the door for any further donations to the memorial fund, but having already paid for their tickets, most people seemed to think they had made sacrifices enough.

The pastor, who had breezed in without even attempting to buy a ticket, was the only person who seemed oblivious to the mood of disappointment. 'A beautiful occasion, Frau Kirsch,' he said, bounding up afterwards. 'It should become an annual event.'

'We had rather hoped one event would be enough,' his father said. 'We shall have to think again.'

'But it *was* beautiful,' Alma said. 'I shall never forget it.'

Kirsch's mother looked at her in surprise, then smiled gratefully. 'Then it was all worth it. No matter what else.'

They filed out of the school house and wandered through the village in the gathering dusk. They passed the spot where the memorial was supposed to go, a triangle of grass which, as children, Kirsch and his brother had used as the finishing line for their bicycle races.

Alma took his arm again. 'How much more money do they need?' she asked softly.

'For the memorial? A few hundred Reichsmarks. The problem is, the longer it takes them to raise it, the more they have to raise.'

Alma pulled him a little closer. 'Tell your mother not to worry. It's such a good cause. She'll have the money, I'm quite sure.'

Eleven

Back in his rented room that night, Kirsch pulled the curtains closed. He stripped off his jacket, sweater and shirt, and turned towards the mirror. On his upper arm what had begun as a small bruise had deepened and blackened, the surface skin around the puncture wound turning dry and shiny. The muscle ached, as if a splinter of cold stone were fixed inside it. What he had feared was true: the subcutaneous tissue was dying. It was a danger with Salvarsan, as with any compound of arsenic. Besides the hours of nausea, the cramps and the vomiting, the injection had to be completely within the walls of the vein. Any fluid leaking into the surrounding tissue would cause necrosis. Then there was the vein itself: Salvarsan could induce blood clots at the site of injection, causing the vessel to swell and become irritated, and creating a risk of infection. Maybe that was the problem. Squinting in the dim electric light, he traced the basilic vein with his fingers, searching for sensitivity, but it was hard to feel anything through the dead weight of pain.

By now most doctors had switched to administering the drug via intravenous drip. Injections were too hazardous. But for Kirsch, going through the normal medical channels presented difficulties. Another doctor might not agree to prescribe the drug, and certainly not on demand. Confidentiality could not be taken for granted either. A medical man undergoing treatment for a serious communicable disease, even if in a latent phase, was fodder for gossip. Word of such things had a habit of leaking out, if not through the physicians themselves, then through their attendant nurses and secretaries. Besides, some in the profession considered it their duty to report infectious cases to the authorities, especially where they thought the risk of spread was significant. Others believed that infected patients

should be prohibited from marrying, on pain of exposure, until their serological tests had been negative for several years. All in all, it was simpler and safer to handle things himself, even if that meant buying the powder from unlicensed traders and preparing the injections, likewise the mercury and bismuth ointments that he kept hidden beneath the washbasin, in case any sores or lesions reappeared.

The electric lights were too weak. He lit the paraffin lamp and pulled off the rest of his clothes. In his case, the first sign of infection had appeared during the war, in the form of small circular swellings on the insides of his fingers. They were brownish and hard, somewhere between a nettle rash and a blister, but barely sensitive, and certainly not painful. They had lasted a few weeks and then healed before there was time to worry about them. Several months went by before further symptoms began to appear: fevers, aching joints and an angry red rash under his arms and across his chest. Even then, it did not occur to him that he was under attack from a lethal disease, that the tiny worm-like spirals of *Treponema pallidum* were coursing through his body, multiplying, clustering and clumping in his glands and his blood vessels, tunnelling into his nervous system and laying siege to his brain.

Hundreds of the men he treated at the field hospital suffered from the same infection, even the Austrian officers who were brought in on special orders from the High Command because they did not trust their own surgeons. Venereal disease accounted for more loss of manpower at the front than any other kind, except, in the winter months, for pneumonia. But the primary and secondary symptoms of syphilis varied from person to person, and were easily confused with other, less serious conditions. In any case, with so many men dying from their wounds, treating diseases that might take twenty years to prove fatal was not a military priority. Even casualties with the distinctive open sores of the secondary stage, moist ulcers that teemed with bacilli, were not usually isolated or handled with special caution. There was not enough time. Kirsch had no way of knowing when exactly the disease had entered his bloodstream, or which

patients might have been responsible. Scalpel cuts were common in the operating rooms, and hygiene frequently sacrificed to speed of intervention. But that did not stop him thinking about it. In dreams he even saw the face of the carrier: he was one of those who had survived his turn on the table, only to die later at the front. This Kirsch knew from the uniform he wore and the blood that covered his face.

It was possible he had caught the disease somewhere else, in more conventional circumstances, but the chancres – the medical term, he later realised, for the small brown swellings – were supposed to appear close to the site of infection. That was why most began in the groin or on the genitals. But in his case they had erupted on the soft flesh of his hands.

The secondary stage of the disease brought headaches and fevers. These plagued him in bouts of several days' duration, then disappeared so that he was able to function normally again. With the fevers came the bad dreams, visions so starkly clear that even afterwards they seemed more real than any memory of waking life. In those dreams, patients whose faces he thought he had forgotten stood waiting for him wherever he went, blood drained, wounds gaping or partially stitched. They watched him work at the operating table; they stared at him from the ends of corridors. By night and at dawn they stood sentinel in the hospital grounds. He had only to wipe the condensation from a window-pane or a shaving mirror to see the face of a dead man. Even when he was awake, he lived in fear of them. He shunned darkened rooms or empty stairwells. He stayed always close to the light, and where possible in company, although his participation in conversation became noticeably sporadic and forced.

Sometimes in his dreams he saw Max. He would stand on the far side of the drainage ditch that ran along the edge of the grounds. In those days he still had a face, though it was always deathly pale. Once, they brought a man in on a stretcher whose legs had been blown clean off, a man Kirsch knew at once could not be saved. And for a moment that was Max too.

His hands started shaking: first at mealtimes, then as he was shaving, razor in hand, then in the operating theatre. The shaking came and went, unpredictably. He couldn't tell if it was another effect of the disease or simply his nerves, the cause neurological or psychological; but the loss of control scared him even more than the visions, because it was a symptom he couldn't hide. It was then that he turned to medication, helping himself to the necessary supplies from the hospital stores, and preparing them late at night in the privacy of his room: compounds of potassium, iodine, bismuth, mercury, arsenic.

The worst of the second-stage symptoms faded away a few months after the Armistice. It was possible he had cured himself outright. More likely, he had entered what the manuals called 'the period of latency', which could last anywhere from a few weeks to thirty years. One in four patients then experienced the tertiary stage, characterised by disfiguring tumours and lesions, the eating away of internal organs, progressive paralysis, insanity, blindness and death. Treatment during the third stage was the most drastic, and the least likely to succeed.

He had no way of knowing if he was safe or not. At different times, he had tested both positive and negative for the disease. But recently he had begun to grow especially uneasy. A familiar stiffness had returned to his joints. Short bursts of fever came and went, so that at night he would sometimes wake up from his nightmares drenched in sweat. And all around his waist and stomach, faint red-brown smudges had appeared on his skin, each one the size of a large thumbprint.

Standing now in the greenish glow of the paraffin lamp, he traced the pattern of discoloration, twisting this way and that. The smudges were more numerous than the last time, especially on his flanks. They overlapped, darkening and reddening. Some were slightly raised. Only his back and shoulders remained unaffected, though the definition of muscle and bone seemed exaggerated, suggestive of an anatomical model. He was losing weight, subcutaneous fat daily melting away.

Alma had noticed it that evening. She had put her arms around him at the station in Berlin when the time had come to say goodbye.

'You mustn't work too hard,' she had said, a hand running up and down the back of his coat. 'You mustn't wear yourself out. Promise me?'

He had promised.

'You wait until we're married. I'm going to fatten you up like a prize pig. I'll make you eat steak and dumplings twice a day.'

And she had kissed him with unusual urgency, holding on to him until the last train for Oranienburg was almost pulling out of the station, as if not sure whether to take it or to miss it and, in so doing, strand herself in the city for the duration of the night.

Twelve

Dr Bonhoeffer stood by the window, looking out through the fog at the ivy-clad exterior of the main hospital. This part of the building, the side where his counterparts in conventional medicine had their offices, was south-west facing, and the ivy, which grew thickly, had turned to a coppery gold. Being taller than the clinic, the hospital caught the evening sun, the display stopping passers-by in their tracks. Attempts had been made to soften the martial exterior of the clinic by planting various species of creeper, but the aspect was unfavourable, and the spindly limbs that did get a purchase on the brickwork never managed more than a desultory patina of foliage. Worse, the persistent northerly damp had warped the window frames, so that even with the double-glazing there was always a draft.

'I wanted to give you advanced warning,' he said. 'So that you'd have time to look for another position.' He frowned at his reflection in the window. He was sixty-four, his tall forehead deeply lined, his always tidy hair a ghostly white. 'I'm sorry it can't be longer. But I've very little discretion in the matter.'

They were not even giving him a chance to explain himself.

'Shall we agree on Christmas? That should give you time to make arrangements with respect to your existing patients. Of course, you'd best refrain from treating any new ones.'

Kirsch saw now that he had been naïve. The director had no appetite for formal disciplinary procedures. Such things were embarrassing for all concerned. Furthermore, they would give him an opportunity to fight his corner and to question the judgement of his superiors. Lawyers might even be dragged in. How much easier it was to elicit a resignation, in return for decent references and an unblemished record.

'I know you've heard some unfavourable reports, Herr Director,' he said. 'But I would appreciate an opportunity to answer the accusations levelled against me.'

'Accusations?'

'I believe that is my right.'

Bonhoeffer sighed. 'The issue is not one of accusations, Dr Kirsch. The issue is one of suitability, and the wider need to effect reductions in our budget.'

'But the incident with Nurse Ritter . . . Dr Mehring's experiment –'

'All of that could be – *can* be overlooked.'

'If I resign.'

'If you seek a position elsewhere, giving your notice at the appropriate time. If you do that, there will be no need to examine the matter further.' Bonhoeffer sat down at his desk, spreading his hands across the unruly mass of paperwork. 'Frankly, I wonder at you wanting to waste your talents on a profession you no longer believe in. I read your paper. It's practically a letter of resignation in itself. I should have realised sooner, but I'd no idea you would seek to put your ideas into practice.'

Some last-minute cuts by the editor of the *Annals of Psychiatric Medicine* had left the language of his paper starker and more uncompromising than Kirsch had intended, but the central proposition was unchanged: that the classification of psychiatric illnesses was unscientific. The nineteenth-century pioneers of the discipline had set out to create a mirror of general medicine. They had adopted its assumptions and its methods. They held it as axiomatic that there was a clear dividing line between the psychologically ill and the psychologically healthy; that there was a finite number of distinct mental illnesses, and that these would be identifiable through a rigorous delineation of symptoms. They also assumed that the causes of these illnesses would turn out to be biological, and therefore treatable only through medication or surgery.

It was for this reason that the early decades of modern psychiatry had been spent painstakingly breaking down, categorising and

labelling the behaviour of mental patients. The modern panoply of psychoses sprang from these efforts: schizophrenia, schizotaxia, paranoia, hypomania, personality disorder, mood disorder, neurotic depression, psychotic depression, involutional depression – with every year more types and sub-types being added until they could be counted by the dozen. When a patient's behaviour did not fit neatly into an existing category, the usual response was simply to propose a new one: a paranoid sub-type of depression, perhaps, or a depressive sub-type of paranoia.

It all seemed as rational as clockwork, but it didn't fit the facts. In Kirsch's experience, definitions of the most frequently identified psychoses varied from place to place and from time to time. To the great Emil Kraepelin schizophrenia or *dementia praecox* was a disease afflicting the intellect, the ability to reason; to the leading Swiss psychiatrist Eugen Bleuler, its sphere was cognitive and emotional; whereas to Kurt Schneider, a contemporary whose work was widely admired, it was a disorder inducing hallucinations and delusions – an imagination running wild. Kirsch had noticed these differences even as a student. As a practitioner, he often came across equally striking inconsistencies in his patients' psychiatric histories.

This was what his paper was about. Kirsch had identified fifty patients in Berlin institutions who had been diagnosed more than once by different psychiatrists. He had successfully tracked down their records in all but seven cases. Just as he had come to expect, the diagnoses were often at odds with each other, even where the most reputable practitioners were involved. As far as he was concerned, the inescapable conclusion was that the edifice of modern psychiatry was built on sand. How could different diseases be identified if practitioners could not agree on the symptoms? And if individual diseases could not be identified, what hope was there of developing individual remedies? Perhaps the mechanism of the mind was not, after all, like the mechanism of the body, something that could be broken down, function by function, organ by organ. Perhaps aberrant behaviour – itself a concept that resisted precise definition – should not be seen as a symptom of something else, part of a code

that only the expert practitioner could decipher. Given the complexities, it seemed to Kirsch that the most reliable guide to the mental landscape of a patient was the patient himself. He was better placed to explain his behaviour and his experiences than anyone else. Yet wherever Kirsch went, the patient was the very last person anyone thought to consult. Because, of course, the patient was insane.

These more constructive suggestions had been cut from the published article. For some reason, the editor had only found room for Kirsch's critique of existing psychiatric methodology. At the time he had not objected, since it was only his critique that was supported by evidence. But now, he was aware of how exposed it had left him.

'It is one thing to take issue with a colleague's approach,' Bonhoeffer said. 'It is quite another to systematically disrupt his work.'

'There was nothing systematic about my intervention, Herr Director. I had reason to believe Sergeant Stoehr's life was in danger.'

'Dr Mehring says you were mistaken in that assumption. And I'm inclined to believe him, given that he is familiar with the procedure and you are not.'

'I've read what there is on insulin coma therapy. I have data from the Lichterfelde Sanatorium showing unequivocally how dangerous it is.'

Bonhoeffer pushed back from his desk. 'Why would you bother to study a procedure that you consider a waste of time?'

'Because it was being used on one of my patients, to his detriment.'

'Or his benefit. Surely it's too early to say, isn't it? Or have you entirely dismissed the possibility that you might be wrong?'

Bonhoeffer's sarcasm was like something uttered under the shadow of pain. Kirsch tried not to look flustered.

'I don't doubt that the treatment will make Sergeant Stoehr more pliable. It's done that already. But I see no evidence that this amounts to an improvement in his mental health, or that it's to his benefit in any other way.'

'You seem to forget why Patient Stoehr was brought here. He was plainly a threat to those around him. If Dr Mehring's treatment reduces this threat, surely that's a worthwhile improvement.'

'For society perhaps, but not for the patient.'

'I see. So society's interests are of no importance to you.'

'They may be important, but they aren't my responsibility. My responsibility is to my patient.'

Bonhoeffer shook his head. Kirsch could sense his disappointment at a promising career turned bad.

'You were a military surgeon before you turned to psychiatry, weren't you? During the war.'

The dead flesh in Kirsch's arm began to throb. Instinctively he covered the wound with his hand.

'Yes.'

'You patched up the young men who were brought to you, didn't you?'

'The lucky ones.'

'And you sent them back to the front, where no doubt many of them were subsequently killed. Correct?' Kirsch didn't answer. 'Now, was *that* in their best interests? Or was it in the interests of the war effort, of the Fatherland, of society?'

'I didn't send them.'

The pain was worse now, pulsing and hot. Kirsch felt it in his veins.

'Perhaps it would have been better for them if you had let their wounds fester a little, or carried out some precautionary amputations. They would still be alive.'

'I didn't send them.'

Bonhoeffer regarded him steadily. 'No. You just let them *be* sent. As your duty required.'

Kirsch got to his feet. In his dreams the man who had infected him was always one of those who had gone back. It was revenge, of course. One death for another. Quid pro quo.

It was a struggle to keep his balance. 'If you'll excuse me, Herr Director.'

'That's how it is now, Dr Kirsch. Nothing's changed. The medical profession's first priority – civilian or military – is to safeguard the health of society. The interests of the healthy cannot always be subordinated to those of the sick. You must see that.'

Even now, Kirsch wondered if a complete retraction of his position might save the day. Bonhoeffer's declarations had a forced quality that suggested even he was not convinced by them.

'I cannot judge those things, Herr Director: the interests of society, the interests of the healthy. I can only deal with what I see, one patient at a time. All the rest is . . .' He thought for a moment, wanting to find the precise words, though his pulsing temples made it hard to think at all. '. . . an abstraction.'

Alone in his office Kirsch began to draft his letter of resignation. The nib of his pen moved unsteadily across the paper. It scratched and scored, then dried up completely. He shook the pen violently, but the reservoir was empty.

In one of the recreation rooms a gramophone was playing. The sound of strings drifted up through the courtyard, as if from the bottom of the sea. He listened, trying to catch the tune.

He closed his eyes, but Bonhoeffer was still there, staring at him over the top of his spectacles. *You just let them be sent.*

What was he going to tell Alma? How was he going to explain? It wasn't going to be easy finding another position. He brought his hands to his face. Perhaps he should refuse to resign: go down fighting and take Heinrich Mehring with him. That way, he might at least do some good.

He looked out across the courtyard, through the widow's veil of tangled branches towards the windows on the other side. Out of the corner of his eye, he saw something move. He peered out further. Outside the kitchens, partially obscured by the fire escape, stood a man in a brown felt hat. He was not a member of staff, but something about him – his baggy, ill-fitting suit, the way his hands were thrust deep into his jacket pockets – was familiar. Then Kirsch remembered: he had been among the reporters camped outside the Charité, a thick-set man with sandy hair and a blush of broken veins across his cheeks. He was talking to someone across the threshold. The stranger nodded, then turned and walked away. It was then that Kirsch saw Robert Eisner close the door behind him.

The Einstein girl was still newsworthy, apparently: good for a few more column inches, perhaps even a photograph. In his head Kirsch heard the *whump* of a flash bulb, saw in stark contrast the dark pupils, the pale cheeks, the beautiful bruised mouth. He closed his eyes, reliving the touch of her lips and the sweet scent of her skin.

He had planned to make her his patient, but that was hardly possible now. Bonhoeffer probably wouldn't have given his consent even before the Nurse Ritter incident. As far as he was concerned, amnesia was a neurological condition, not a psychological one.

What would Max have said about it? What would Max have *done*? Kirsch brought his head to rest against the window-pane. Max would have been fascinated by the Einstein connection, however insubstantial or imaginary. And the girl was his type: small, dark, demure, yet with a directness in her words and actions that cut through the tiresome pretences of life. Max would have liked that, very much.

The music from the gramophone grew louder, then abruptly stopped. Kirsch felt sure he was no longer alone. He could detect a pressure on the floorboards beneath his feet, hear a steady drawing of breath that was not his own.

'What can I do?' he asked out loud.

But Max had already told him.

He found a pot of ink in the bottom drawer of his desk and refilled his fountain pen. He reached for the form he had prepared, approving the girl's admission to the clinic and releasing her present custodians from all financial obligation. Then, at the bottom, he wrote Bonhoeffer's name, carefully forging the signature with the help of a staff memorandum pinned up on the wall outside.

Thirteen

The next day, two weeks after she had first been found, Dr Brenner discharged his still unnamed patient to the care of the Charité Psychiatric Clinic. On Kirsch's instructions, she was allocated a single room on the second floor of the women's wing, a narrow space with a wash basin, two iron beds, a small wardrobe and a barred window looking out across the yard. The previous occupant, Frau Wassermann, since moved to a private asylum outside the city, had been gripped by an irrational terror of germs. During her time at the clinic she had stolen cleaning materials from the stores, and had been found several times scrubbing the floor or dousing the walls of her room with carbolic and disinfectant. In spite of thorough airing, the smell remained strong. The clinic had other single rooms, but none were available. Kirsch had the floors mopped. He bought lavender pouches and hung them up behind the door and above the iron beds, in an attempt to make the air more breathable. Then, as an afterthought, he stopped at a stall on Grenadierstrasse and bought a pot-pourri of rose petals which he balanced on the shelf of the wash basin, between the taps.

The registration of the patient was complicated by her lack of identity. Kirsch entered her in the record as 'Patient E', the E standing for Elisabeth, the name she had given him at the Tanguero. Unfortunately, because he couldn't explain his reasoning, the rest of the staff assumed that the E stood for Einstein, 'the Einstein girl' being how several newspapers still referred to her. It was a choice that seemed to underscore the importance of her fame, which was the last thing Kirsch had intended, but until a better name came along there was nothing he could do.

'What would you like us to call you?' he asked her that first afternoon.

There were armchairs available around the sides of the treatment room, but she had chosen to sit in an upright chair, one of a pair on either side of a small table. Kirsch had taken the other.

'Any name that feels right,' he said. 'We have to call you something.'

She looked at her hands. The nurses had put her in a grey woollen dress that was at least a size too big. Her slender frame was lost inside the heavy folds. She was paler than before: her lips the colour of coral, her bloodless cheeks shiny like bridal satin. One of her eyes was still puffy and on the side of her neck were the purplish traces of a graze.

He waited, but she said nothing. 'You know, usually we don't get the chance to chose our names. Other people chose them for us. Isn't there any name you like?'

She looked him in the face for the first time that day. 'Maria,' she said. Her pupils were dark as jet. 'Will that do?'

Maria. The Holy Mother. The blessed Virgin.

'Of course.'

In his mind Kirsch saw Dr Brenner, squinting between her open thighs. His busy fingers. *I saw no evidence of recent sexual activity*.

He cleared his throat, aware now of the disinfectant taste in his mouth. He took out his notebook and wrote *Maria* at the top of a clean page. At that moment his feelings were not important. The important thing was to establish exactly what the patient did and did not remember. The pattern of memory loss, according to the literature, would be a strong indicator of its cause: concussion, alcohol poisoning, tumour, dementia, psychological trauma or (contentiously) hypnosis.

'I know the police have already questioned you, but it's important we cover the same ground.'

'Am I yours now?' The girl was looking down, one leg swinging. He saw her slender white ankles beneath the table, half-concealed by a pair of black woollen socks. 'My case, I mean.'

'Yes.'

'You changed your mind.'

'I see you remember our conversation. That's good.'

'Why?'

'Anterograde amnesia is indicative of brain damage. It's not usually treatable.'

'No, I meant *why*?'

'Why isn't it treatable?'

'Why did you change your mind?'

Kirsch put down his pencil. 'Would you rather have someone else? I could try to arrange it.'

The girl frowned. 'Someone t-took my photograph. When I was in the other hospital, in bed. I looked up and he was s-standing there. The flash blinded me. That's rude, isn't it? You're s-supposed to ask permission, aren't you, if you want to take someone's photograph.'

'You should. The newspapers don't usually bother, I'm afraid.'

'The newspapers?'

'They're intrigued by your story. They think you might be a princess or a spy. It would be best to ignore them.'

'What do you think I am?'

Kirsch smiled and opened his briefcase. 'I'm keeping an open mind,' he said, and immediately wondered if that was actually true. 'Now, I've some things for you to look at.'

He took out a small stack of postcards, and placed them on the table between them. Hohenzollern palaces, soot-blackened and monumental, were captured in sepia tones, all except the summer palace at Sans Souci, which had been coloured in with washes of yellow, green and an implausibly brilliant blue. Finding them had entailed a lengthy trawl through the street markets and a special visit to Schropp's geographical bookshop.

'All these places are close to where you were found,' he said.

The first postcard was of a church, its odd cylindrical steeple rising high into the air, like an ornate factory chimney. The second was of a sturdy baroque mansion with stone steps at the front, flanked with thickly growing ivy. The third showed a lakeside boathouse, with a rowing boat going by on the water.

'The nearest village is called Caputh. People go boating out there. Maybe that's why you went.'

He slid the pictures across the table. On the third postcard the name of the town was visible on a sign above the jetty, where the passenger steamers docked in the summer.

Maria picked it up, frowning. 'Caputh. That's a funny name. Like *kaput*.' But she wasn't smiling.

'Do you remember it? The church perhaps?'

He picked up the first picture. The steeple was unusual; she would know if she had seen it before, but she only seemed interested in the lakeside boathouse.

'I had a ticket.'

'A boat ticket?'

'I don't know, I . . . I was holding a ticket.'

The boathouse was not distinctive in any way. It could have been anywhere. Kirsch questioned Maria further, but she remembered nothing else. It was the same when he asked her about Berlin, about her childhood and where she was born, her education and schooling, her family, her sweethearts. Sometimes she would open her mouth to speak, as if on the cusp of remembering, as if poised on the very brink of a breakthrough. But then a shadow would fall across her face and whatever thought had been so close to forming would dissipate, leaving nothing.

Her stammering was less pronounced. That was the only clear improvement. On the other hand, she seemed even less connected than before to the here and now, even more prone to drift into silent introspection. The change made Kirsch uneasy.

'That's enough for today,' he said finally. 'We'll talk again tomorrow. In the meantime, there's something I want you to do.' He reached into his briefcase again and took out a sketch-book and some pencils. 'I want you to draw: anything you like, it doesn't matter what. The more drawings the better. When you run out of paper, I'll get you more. Will you do that for me?'

She nodded, watching him silently as he got up. He gathered the postcards from Potsdam, then changed his mind and placed them

back on the table. At the same moment she reached for the sketch-book. For an instant his fingers brushed against the back of her hand before she hastily withdrew it.

Walking away down the corridor, he could still feel the touch of her skin on his, like static.

He worked into the evening, travelling to and from the reference library with as many volumes as he could carry. Among the case histories there was one in particular that caught his eye. The patient, known as Hans J, had been found wandering aimlessly around the market square in Nürnberg. He was taken at first for a vagrant, but on questioning was found to have no knowledge of his identity, nor any memory of how he came to be there. He was taken to a local hospital and examined for signs of injury. He was also questioned extensively by police officers and medical staff, whereupon he claimed his name was Peter Kleist and that he himself was a police detective. He had travelled from Berlin, he said, in pursuit of a criminal, whom he called Schwarz. Although there were palpable inconsistencies in his story – and no record of a Detective Kleist in the Berlin police force – he insisted it was true more and more forcefully, day by day. He even engaged the nurses and patients at the hospital with elaborate stories of the cases he had cracked.

A week later his real identity was discovered. Hans J turned out to be an unmarried bank clerk from a small town in Swabia, around a hundred and fifty miles away. He had apparently left the bank for lunch as usual one afternoon and then vanished. For a time it was feared that he had drowned himself in a nearby river – he had appar-ently been seen on the bridge – and the local police went as far as to organise a search downstream. Although Hans J was able to return to his former life, he continued to experience periodic bouts of amnesia and was eventually discharged from the bank. His memory of the Nürnberg episode also disappeared with unusual speed, and when examined by a psychiatrist a year after the event, he had apparently no recollection of it whatsoever.

According to one paper, similar cases had been documented

elsewhere: two in France, another in Switzerland, several in England. The author referred to the condition as *psychogenic fugue*, a rare type of amnesia characterised by sudden, unexpected journeys, often taking days. In addition, sufferers frequently lost all notion of their identities, and sometimes assumed new, fictitious ones. In each case, investigation of the circumstances had revealed an episode of psychological trauma immediately prior to onset. Hans J, for instance, had that very morning received a letter from a longstanding female acquaintance rejecting a proposal of marriage. He was also later accused, although not convicted, of embezzling money from his employers in the months leading up to his disappearance. Although the cases were few, there was evidence to suggest that flight was not merely a means of escaping painful or embarrassing circumstances, but a defensive response, intended to protect the individual from suicidal or homicidal impulses. In several cases, suicide, actual or attempted, had followed a return to the normal pattern of life. In one, admittedly controversial case (controversial in that the authorities did not believe his claims of amnesia to be genuine), a man whose wife had betrayed him had gone on to attempt murder.

There was a lengthy addendum to the case history of Hans J, which Kirsch was still reading when the telephone rang. It was Inspector Hagen. He was anxious to know if there was any improvement in the patient's condition.

'Fundamentally, no, there isn't.'

'Fundamentally?'

'She still remembers nothing, or next to nothing. She recalls having a ticket, for a boat or a train.'

'This is near Potsdam?'

'I think so.'

'Then it'll be the train. The steamers don't run this time of year. Where did she buy this ticket?'

'She doesn't remember.'

There was a pause on the line, a sound of muffled voices. It came to Kirsch that there were other people at the other end of the telephone.

'In your opinion, Doctor, is she insane?'

'That may be a legal term, Inspector. It's not a medical one.'

Hagen sighed. 'You know what I mean. Is she *normal*? Might an unbalanced mind be responsible for this whole incident?'

Kirsch recalled what Dr Brenner had said about the police and their theory of choice: that his patient had been of unsound mind all along. No one had abducted or assaulted her; so there was nothing more for them to do, and nothing for the visiting public to fear. Kirsch was happy for them to think that if it meant they would leave him alone.

'Some form of psychological trauma may well be involved. I think it's very likely.'

'Trauma?' Hagen was disappointed. What he wanted to hear was that the girl was mentally ill, plain and simple. But that was a dangerous path, at the end of which lay incarceration in an asylum. 'And who might be responsible for this trauma? If anyone.'

'When I have some answers, I'll be sure to let you know.'

Hagen wasn't finished. 'What about suicide? Have you considered that possibility? Maybe she threw herself off a bridge.'

'And why would she do that?'

'She has a child and no ring on her finger. For plenty of people, that's reason enough.'

'She gave birth at least a year ago, Inspector. Probably several years.'

'Guilt has a way of creeping up on you.'

'We don't know if the child is even alive.'

Kirsch felt a sharp stab of pain in his arm. The whole of the left side of his body had become cold and heavy, as if turning slowly to stone.

'I suppose it's commendable that you should be so protective of your patient, Doctor,' Hagen said. 'All I'm suggesting is you avoid jumping to conclusions. If this girl's really the victim of a crime, it's the oddest one I've ever come across.'

Fourteen

Frau Schirmann was throwing the bolts on the street door when he arrived home that evening. The door to her own apartment stood open behind her, a smell like cats and fish glue drifting out into the hall.

'I was afraid for you, Dr Kirsch. I was going to telephone the police.'

She peered out at the dark street, one hand braced against the jamb, revealing a heavy silver bracelet around her scrawny wrist. Kirsch wasn't sure of her age – about seventy-five, he supposed. There had been a Herr Schirmann once, but he had died years ago.

'You know I often work late. You shouldn't worry.'

He helped her push the door shut.

'Herr Bronstein's been taken to hospital. Some men broke into his shop.'

Kirsch didn't know any Herr Bronstein, but that was no surprise. Frau Schirmann often regaled him with news of people he had never heard of, people, he assumed, who lived locally and with whom she had contact. The news was almost always bad, death and disease being the mainstays. Once a son of Frau Hammerstein had won a useful sum of money with a lottery ticket, but this was bad news too, since it revealed a tragic predilection for gambling.

'I'm sorry to hear it,' he said, beginning to climb the stairs to his rooms on the second floor. 'Let's hope he makes a swift recovery.'

'They say he may *never* recover,' Frau Schirmann said. 'And his wife can't manage the shop. She knows nothing at all about music.'

Kirsch stopped. 'Music?'

'Eight ribs broken and his face blown up like a balloon. They punctured a lung.'

'He sold music?'

Frau Schirmann looked up at him with her milky pupils. 'The little place at the top of Grenadierstrasse. With the red velvet in the window.'

He knew the place. It was there he had bought a gramophone record the evening he first saw Maria. He tried to picture the man that had served him, but all he could recollect were his rectangular spectacles.

'Of course. Send Herr Bronstein my best wishes.'

Kirsch carried on up the stairs, but Frau Schirmann didn't move. 'Oh, Dr Kirsch? You had a visitor earlier. Did you see him?'

'A visitor?'

'A man called Bucher. He said he would wait for you in his motor car.'

Kirsch hadn't noticed any car outside. The name Bucher meant nothing to him either. 'What did he want?'

'He had something to deliver, he said, but he wouldn't leave it. A big man. I didn't want to let him in. Should I have done?'

It came to him that there had once been a patient called Bucher at the clinic, a paranoid schizophrenic with a history of violence. Or was it Buch*ner*?

'No, Frau Schirmann,' he said. 'You were right to be careful.'

Kirsch had a narrow bureau desk with a fold-down top, which he had bought second-hand from a dealer on the Kurfürstendamm. It was the only thing he could lock except for the wardrobe, and he was sure Frau Schirmann had a key to that. It was in the desk that he kept Alma's letters, an old scrapbook, mementoes and photographs from the past that he wanted neither to look at nor to discard. It was also where he kept the Salvarsan and the needles and the book Max had given him that last morning in Mecklenburg: *On the Special and General Theory of Relativity, Generally Comprehensible*.

He picked up the book – Max's Bible – and carefully turned over the pages. He had begun to read it after Max left for the front, but had soon put it aside. Generally comprehensible it might have been,

but it required more concentration than he had been willing to give it. Besides, he wasn't ready to give his attention to the work of a pacifist, a man whose loyalty to the Fatherland was at best invisible, and who regarded the sacrifices of his countrymen with indifference.

One incident in particular had set Kirsch against him. Two months into the war, ninety-three of Germany's most eminent scholars and scientists had put their names to an open letter entitled *An Appeal to the Cultured World*. It was published in all the leading dailies and translated into ten foreign languages. Its aim was to champion Germany's cause abroad, and to justify the violation of Belgian neutrality. The war, it explained, was a war of self-defence, which had been forced on Germany by her enemies. Most of Einstein's colleagues had signed it, including his mentor, Max Planck.

Planck's work on energy *quanta* had been essential to Einstein's. It was Planck who had lured Einstein back to Germany from a life of obscurity in Switzerland, Planck who had championed the Special Theory of Relativity, helping to get it accepted across the scientific world. But still Einstein would not sign. His name, when it appeared at all, was found on leftist appeals for the creation of a united Europe, and tracts that placed the blame for the war on aberrant male psychology. To Einstein, it seemed, there was no justice in war, no right and wrong. There was only madness, a congenital, collective insanity eclipsing both free will and self-interest. As the war dragged on, year after year, even these surfacings ceased, as if Einstein himself no longer saw any point to them. Germany – the whole of Europe, indeed – was a madhouse. And madness was not a condition that even science had the means to cure.

But Einstein didn't leave. He didn't return to Switzerland, or take up a post in neutral Holland, where life would have been easier. Apparently the madhouse had its attractions. This was the time when he completed the General Theory of Relativity, his most important work to date. Being at odds with the people around him, cut off from non-scientific discourse, didn't cloud his vision or dull his intelligence: if anything, it made them sharper.

The war shuddered to an end. Kirsch felt bewildered, lost.

No one could explain the sudden paralysis on the western front any more than they could explain the war. Certainly the generals would not explain it. The word *defeat* never crossed their lips. The talk was all of betrayal: of the army, of the working class; above all, of the two million dead. The war could not be over, because they hadn't yet won. And they were always going to win.

People wanted answers. Kirsch wanted answers. He wanted to know what it had all been for. Every effect had a cause – so reason told him – but what had caused this war? He had always taken for granted that European civilisation led the world in industry, art and science. But what had it led the world *to*? That was when Albert Einstein strolled onto the stage; a man who had been right where the rest of the human race had been wrong. A prophet, vindicated.

For Kirsch it began with the *Berliner Illustrierte Zeitung* on 14 December 1919. The front page was still there in his scrapbook. It was given over completely to a photograph of Einstein, eyes cast down, one hand curled thoughtfully beneath his jaw. Beneath it was written: *A New Giant in World History: Albert Einstein, whose researches mean a complete overthrow of our views of Nature, and which rank as equal with the discoveries of Copernicus, Keppler, and Newton.*

Einstein's theories of light had at last been confirmed by observation. British astronomers had recorded the deflection of starlight by the gravitational pull of the sun, exactly by the degree that Einstein had predicted. Every paper in Berlin carried the news. Einstein's face was everywhere. It turned out the German press were not even in the forefront of the coverage. The papers in America and Britain had been running the story for days. It didn't matter that the physicist was German, or that his discoveries had no obvious practical consequences. It didn't matter that the theory was mathematical and hard to follow – the American press reported that only twelve people in the whole world understood it. What mattered was that it overturned everything that had gone before. The old certainties of the mechanical universe, the crowning achievement of European thought, had been revealed as a fiction. In their place was a universe whose nature could be accepted by the human mind,

the way a mathematical proof was accepted, but which, like infinity or the Divine purpose, could never be truly perceived, let alone felt – except perhaps by Einstein himself and the twelve unnamed Illuminati described in the *New York Times*.

Kirsch was among the crowds that clambered for a glimpse of him. He was among those who crowded into his lectures at the University of Berlin. Thousands did the same. Talk of Einstein was everywhere. In bars and shop queues, people who had never given a passing thought to the nature of light or gravity argued over the meaning of his work. Sitting in the smoky darkness of the picture house, Kirsch watched the newsreels: everywhere Einstein went, the crowds turned out for him. Statesmen, monarchs and movie stars lined up to be seen at his side. Kirsch watched his triumphal visits to London, Paris and New York, then Scandinavia, South America and Japan: Einstein on podiums, Einstein descending from ocean liners or open-topped limousines, Einstein drawing diagrams on blackboards, talking or smiling or shaking hands, always a sea of faces turned towards him, like bathers basking in the glow of a bright new sun. Einstein's enemies, the nationalists and anti-Semites, started calling him 'the Jewish saint'. By the end of the year, his was the most famous face in the world.

Kirsch did not rejoice at Einstein's fame. To him it was an intrusion. Max had been there ahead of the millions. He had felt the truth of Einstein's vision instinctively, had absorbed and understood it, long before it reached the newspapers. He had seen what was to come. The last days and weeks of his life he had been living in Albert Einstein's universe.

This was when Kirsch finally returned to the book. It was obvious that Max was never coming back. Kirsch would have no guide through Einstein's strange new universe, except Einstein himself. If he wanted to learn its secrets, if he wanted to see what Max had seen, he would have to travel alone.

When he was a child, Einstein said, space and time made up a universal system of reference, an invisible box inside which the galaxies turned and the planets spun. A mile was always a mile,

no matter where it was measured; and time ticked by at a constant rate throughout the universe. Every object, position and trajectory could be measured against this absolute scale. The motion of objects, or of observers, no matter how fast, changed nothing. It was a vision founded on the everyday experiences of men whose lives were governed by the clockwork regularity of day and night, tides and seasons, and the fixed geography of planet Earth. It was a universe ruled by Newton's laws of motion and gravitation; a celestial mechanism, balanced, precise and predictable. It was a universe in which nothing happened without a reason, in which every effect had a cause. It was a universe in which all it took to know the future was to know the past.

But by the time Einstein was a student, cracks had begun to appear in the sacred notion of the absolute scale. Observations in the field of electro-magnetism, the science of light waves and electricity, were proving hard to explain. First in Berlin and then in America, physicists had carried out experiments to measure the effect of the Earth's motion on the speed of light. The Earth, they knew, travelled around the sun at thirty kilometres every second, while at the same time spinning on its axis. Using a form of triangulation, they compared the speed of light leaving the Earth in the direction of its orbit, with light beams leaving in the opposite direction. They expected the planet's speed would add to the speed of the light beams in one direction and subtract from their speed in the other. In the mechanical universe, where time and space were fixed, velocities had to add up. The speed of a man walking forward along a moving train was, with respect to the world outside, simply the sum of his walking speed and the speed of the rolling stock. But the experiments yielded a different result: no matter at what speed the source of light was travelling, or in which direction, light itself always reached the observer at exactly the same speed. Light – in fact the whole spectrum of electromagnetic radiation from radio waves to X-rays – didn't obey Newton's laws of motion. Its speed could not be added to or subtracted from.

Albert Einstein, working alone in Switzerland, dared to ask if the

problem lay with the absolute system of reference itself. After all, in the end it was, like the aether, an abstract construction of the human mind, lacking tangible existence. No invisible box surrounded the universe; no clock ticked away at its heart. These concepts belonged in the realm of metaphysics. But light, *that* was measurable, observable. And its velocity in a vacuum was always the same. How would a model of the universe look if its laws were based on that?

The distance an object travelled was revealed by multiplying its speed by time. A train travelling at forty miles per hour for half an hour would cover twenty miles. But light took no notice of distance or time. Its speed remained the same even when the body emitting it was hurtling through space at immense speed. What then did this additional motion, the motion of the emitting body, affect? If it was not the speed of light, then the only remaining elements in the equation were space on one side and time on the other. It was these that had to change, these that were local, flexible, *relative*. Einstein realised that motion did not take place independent of space and time, as common sense dictated. It changed them.

Einstein's mathematics shook the very principles of scientific observation, as understood since Galileo. That was what Max loved about it. For hundreds of years, astronomers had struggled to improve the accuracy of their measuring equipment, their telescopes, astrolabes and sextants, only to discover that the distance between two points could not be measured in any objective way. Distance was not simply a relation between two points. It also involved the observer, whose relation to those points directly affected the outcome of the measurement. As for intervals of time, they had no absolute value either, since the flow of time directly depended on the relation between object and observer. What Man had taken to be the universe, was in fact only a subjective perception of the universe, seen from one specific frame of reference.

Max had talked about this revelation, in breathless monologues at the supper table that only their father pretended to understand. To the rest of the family it was the product of an over-active

imagination, too many late nights or an incipient attack of fever. For in this strange new universe, clocks in motion ran more slowly than clocks at rest. Time at the Equator ran more slowly than time at the poles. Different observers could perceive two events as occurring in different sequence, while others might see them as simultaneous. Their perceptions might be different, but none of them would be wrong. If the dimensions of space and time were relative, there could be as many right answers as there were observers.

The Special Theory of Relativity had been published when Kirsch was still a boy. But there had been no newspaper headlines then, no crowds of onlookers eager for a glimpse of the visionary behind it. The scepticism of his family was universal. Even many physicists assumed that Einstein was only concerned with theoretical problems of astronomical observation, rather than the nature of reality itself. Only when he extended relativity to the laws of gravity, the dominant force in the universe, did it dawn on them that he was building a completely new model of creation, with the speed of light as its founding principle. For while motion affected time and space, it was an observable fact that gravity affected motion. You only had to let go of an apple to see that.

For eleven years he worked to derive the equations, juggling Newton's laws of motion with the new geometry of flexible space. He completed the General Theory of Relativity in 1916, the year of the great offensives on the western front. While armies clashed at Verdun and the Somme, in a desperate attempt to redraw the notional frontiers on their notional European maps, Einstein remained at work, quietly stripping space and time of all objective reality. In this new model of Creation, matter and space were part of one single continuum, a fabric of existence running unbroken throughout the universe, coalescing in different forms but never breaking apart. Geometry was dictated by gravity, and gravity by mass. All fixed points of reference were banished: they had to be, because time and space were nothing more than artefacts of the gravitational field. If the Earth travelled in circles around the sun, it was not thanks to a mysterious and invisible force of attraction.

It was because space and time were pulled out of shape by the presence of the star. The Earth was travelling through curved space and curved time, like a tram riding curved rails round a bend on the Schönhauser Allee.

This was the work Einstein completed in Berlin, after years of working at the frontiers of scientific knowledge. He had been making a new world just as the old one was marching off to war, killing off redundant metaphysical certainties just as the youth of Europe was being sacrificed to defend them. Did Max understand the irony? Was that why he had given his brother Einstein's book? Or was there more to it than that? Were the discoveries set out on its pages, the scale and wonder of them, supposed to render human losses minuscule and insignificant, and therefore easier to bear?

Kirsch was still looking through the book when he heard knocking downstairs. It was after half past ten. He waited for the sound of Frau Schirmann's door opening, the old woman bustling out into the hall, but there was nothing. The knocking came again, louder this time. He could hear the bolts rattling, but still Frau Schirmann did not stir.

He went to the window. His view of the front of the building was obscured by the small stone balcony and the branches of a tree. A motor car was parked by the kerb, its polished black panels beaded with rain. He put down the book and went out onto the landing.

'Frau Schirmann? Are you going to answer that?'

The knocking came a third time. Kirsch hurried down the stairs, wondering what his landlady was playing at. Was she too afraid after what had happened to Herr Bronstein? Or was it that she had taken her make-up off and couldn't bear to be seen in her natural state?

His hand was on the bolt when something made him hesitate. It *was* late, too late for social calls.

'Who is it?'

He heard the crunch of grit against stone.

'Dr Kirsch?' A man's voice.

'What do you want?'

'Excuse me for disturbing you. My name is Bucher. I called before.'

Bucher. Kirsch was still not sure if this was his paranoid schizophrenic or not. He turned on the light. 'Do I know you?'

The door moved gently against the locks and bolts.

'I have an invitation from Dr Fischer. He wanted me to wait for a reply.'

'Dr Fischer? I don't know any Dr Fischer.'

'Dr Eugen Fischer, Director of the Kaiser Wilhelm Institute of Anthropology.'

Kirsch had heard Fischer's name, knew he was considered eminent, but could recall little of his work, only that some of it had concerned the effects of racial intermarriage in southern Africa.

'He certainly knows of you, Dr Kirsch.'

The stranger sounded hurt, but it was hurt of the playacting kind.

Kirsch hesitated, then threw open the door. The stranger stepped back, pulling off his hat. He was younger than the Bucher Kirsch remembered, and a great deal smarter.

'Dr Fischer leaves for Munich tomorrow afternoon, and wishes to know if you can meet him beforehand.' The stranger smiled, revealing a marked overlap in his upper incisors. 'He apologises for the short notice.'

He handed over an envelope and stood back while Kirsch read the contents. It was an invitation to lunch at the Adlon Hotel. *I was much impressed by your paper, and am most anxious to discuss it with you before my departure.* Kirsch was surprised. He had always assumed his study was too brief and insubstantial to impress anyone. But then he recalled what Alma had said about her father showing it to *some people*, and all the learned institutions he supported with his money.

'Will you be available tomorrow, Dr Kirsch?'

Kirsch folded up the letter. The Adlon was reputed to have the best restaurant in Berlin.

'Tell Dr Fischer I shall be honoured,' he said.

Fifteen

The kitchen doors swung open, releasing an aroma of seared meat. An affable clamour rose above the crescendos of sizzling and the clattering of pots and pans. Kirsch wished he had put on a better show. His collar was a day old and there had been no time to get his suit pressed. His waistcoat was patterned with parallel creases, like an overextended concertina. Worse, he had spent another bad night; not sleepless, but filled with tortuous dreams in which he was always on the move, running for assignations that he couldn't miss, riding on express trains as they hurtled through tunnels and crowded stations, everything accompanied by the scream of steel on steel.

The head waiter led him into the dining room. Inside, more waiters in tailcoats moved between the tables or stood to attention beside the great log fire. Kirsch's stomach rumbled. From nothing, the smell of the grill had summoned up an appetite. It was never like that at the Charité canteen. The smell there was always of stale grease and boiled cabbage, a permanent, ineradicable stink that seemed over the years to have seeped into the walls.

He was taken to a table by the window with a view across Pariser Platz. Outside, traffic moved steadily along the avenue, passing beneath the arches of the Brandenburg Gate. He declined the offer of an aperitif and glanced around the room. The Adlon was renowned for its celebrity clientele. Before the war it had played host to the Kaiser and the Tsar of Russia; in more recent times, Henry Ford and the Rockefellers, Marlene Dietrich and Albert Einstein. Such was its fame abroad that Hollywood had made a film about it, starring Greta Garbo. It was also where Alma's father stayed on his rare trips to the capital, a fact that left Kirsch wondering if

he wasn't being drawn deliberately into a more comfortable and elevated social sphere, as befitted Otto Siegel's future son-in-law.

Kirsch recognised none of the other diners. Instead his gaze came to rest on a tall bearded man twenty years his senior, striding across the room with one hand tucked into the pocket of his waistcoat, addressing affable remarks to the head waiter.

'The eminent Dr Kirsch. Delighted to meet you.'

Kirsch got to his feet. 'Dr Fischer.'

In spite of his lanky frame and huge hands, his host had an impish appearance, with a high forehead, protruding ears, and a narrow chin accentuated by a beard. He took Kirsch's hand and shook it warmly, bringing his other hand to his elbow, prolonging the gesture as if to underscore that it was more than a matter of mere politeness. 'I do hope this place suits you. Not too far from the clinic?'

'Barely a ten-minute walk.'

They sat down, Fischer unfurling his napkin and accepting a menu. 'You walked. Excellent. Even a thinking man must take exercise. Too many neglect it. The same goes for food. Scholars have a regrettable habit of starving themselves.'

Kirsch opened the menu, read in disbelief the prices. 'I fear some have no choice.'

Fischer laughed. 'Allow me to address that lamentable state of affairs. I hope you've brought a good appetite.' And he began interrogating the head waiter, whom he addressed as Konrad, on the dishes of the day.

For ten minutes the talk was of food and Dr Fischer's personal routines. Kirsch felt like a favourite nephew on the receiving end of avuncular wisdom and a good meal. Fischer's familiarity was such that he wondered if he was not, in fact, related to the Siegels in some way, and would therefore be shortly related to him. Only when they were tucking into a venison terrine did he bring up the subject of his paper.

'What you wrote was courageous,' he said. 'It takes courage to be radical, especially in a profession as conservative as medicine.'

'I was simply drawing attention to a few diagnostic inconsistencies.'

'Inconsistencies that call into question the basis of modern psychiatry, as practised by your superiors.' Fischer broke apart a loaf of fresh bread and handed Kirsch the larger piece. 'A self-interested man would have been more accommodating in his choice of study. He would have ignored those inconsistencies, just as everyone else does.'

The terrine was delicious. Kirsch struggled not to talk with his mouth full. 'It did surprise me that no one had really studied the question before.'

Fischer made an appreciative noise. Everything he did – eating, talking, gesturing – was done with an intensity verging on impatience. 'Status. It's the Achilles heel of the whole profession.' He made little circles with his butter knife. 'Psychiatry's been so caught up in this headlong rush to establish itself, to achieve the same status as conventional medicine. But conventional medicine is grounded in centuries of anatomical study. Do we have any such grounding where the workings of the mind are concerned? No. And it will be a very long time before we do.' Another waiter appeared, pouring wine. 'But to suggest that psychiatrists might be getting ahead of themselves, to even suggest that the founding assumptions of the whole business are not, in fact, rock solid – that, Dr Kirsch, is heresy.'

Fischer was right. What had Bonhoeffer called his paper? *Practically a letter of resignation in itself.*

Fischer brought his wineglass to his nose, rolled it around for a moment and smiled. It was as if he had been in Bonhoeffer's office the day before, and overheard the argument. Kirsch toyed with the base of his glass, wondering how much Fischer *did* know.

'Was there anything in particular that prompted your . . . ? I had the impression there was some urgency . . .'

For a moment Fischer stopped chewing. He smiled again, then eased himself back from the table, brushing the crumbs from his lap. 'You are quite correct in divining an ulterior motive.' His tongue smacked against his hard palate. 'I have a proposal, one I hope will appeal to you.'

Kirsch's findings to date had relied on too small a sample, he said. The inconsistencies in diagnosis could be dismissed as anomalous and unrepresentative. But that would not be the case if a new study took in a broader swathe of the German-speaking world and covered a longer period.

'A body of evidence on such a scale couldn't be ignored. It would force the profession to re-examine its approach to mental abnormality. It might bring about real change.'

Kirsch thought about Sergeant Stoehr and the other patients subjected to Heinrich Mehring's experimental treatments – treatments for diseases classified and schematised the way medieval theologians had once categorised different types of demon, and with just as much regard for observable fact. He thought about the 'improvements' they were said to effect, and the half-baked theorising that was sure to follow about the nature of the diseases themselves.

'It'd be a huge undertaking,' he said. 'It'd need almost everyone to cooperate; many different institutions.' Fischer was looking at him expectantly. He reached across the table and topped up his wineglass. 'You aren't suggesting *I* should do it? I'm afraid that's impossible.'

'You'd be paid, of course. The Kaiser Wilhelm would commission the study. And publish it.'

'The anthropology institute?'

'Or the medical. We've commissioned a great deal of research: family genealogy, craniometry, blood groups. We work increasingly across disciplines nowadays, not to mention frontiers. Very much an international effort. It's time men of science stopped living in their intellectual ghettoes and pulled together for the common good. Don't you agree?'

'Yes, but –'

'I think I could promise you the equivalent of a year's salary. In advance.'

With particular care, Fischer began buttering another piece of bread, leaving Kirsch to wonder if all this really had been arranged behind the scenes by Otto Siegel.

'Forgive me, but I thought your particular field was anthropology.'

'It is. But I study the origins of mankind for a reason. Like you, I believe that to protect the race one must first understand it.'

'The race?'

Fischer cut into his slab of terrine. 'The Nordic race. The one we all belong to. As far as psychiatry is concerned, I believe many forms of mental illness have a hereditary component. It's to be expected. Intelligence runs in families, after all, to say nothing of physical disabilities. Your own study contained a number of instances of mental illness passing between the generations, the schizophrenic type in particular.'

Kirsch frowned. 'Incidentally perhaps. But not enough to –'

'Oh, I agree: incidentally. Quite so. But then a much larger survey might clear up the matter once and for all. We can't have too much information, can we?'

'I suppose not.'

Kirsch sipped his wine, considering briefly how useful a year's pay in advance would be. He had to do something once he left the Charité. A commission might provide a cloak for his departure. It would be perfectly understandable that he should give up practising psychiatry in order to concentrate on academic studies. Alma would understand it, her family would understand it, and so would potential future employers.

'May I ask,' he said, 'if you're acquainted with Otto Siegel?'

Fischer looked blank.

'My future father-in-law.'

Fischer shook his head. 'I didn't know you were engaged. My dear fellow, congratulations.'

'Thank you. I just thought perhaps . . .'

But before Kirsch could explain, the waiters reappeared, pushing a trolley on which sat a roast leg of lamb, browned and glistening.

Fischer took his time with the meat, eating it largely unaccompanied and remarking on the importance of protecting the digestion as the years went on: 'The digestion is like a conscience,' he said.

'Treat it badly in youth and it'll return to give you sleepless nights when you're old.'

Kirsch had to admit that he usually ate in a hurry, especially when at work.

'I can understand that,' Fischer said. 'Some food is better not dwelt on, especially the kind served up in hospitals. Unappetising establishments at the best of times. And a man like you is always anxious to get back to his patients.'

'I can't give them half the time they need. At times it's overwhelming.'

Fischer clasped his hands together in front of him, the fingers flexing and twitching. 'Still, it must be tempting to concentrate on the more interesting cases, the unusual ones. I expect one learns so much more.'

'Every case is unusual. The closer I look, the more unusual I find they are. Like people.'

'Take this case in the papers, this girl they found in the woods. Now *that's* an interesting case.'

'Potentially.'

'The complete loss of identity, the nakedness. And yet no evidence of sexual assault. As if it was her very identity that was the target. Like something from a detective novel.'

Kirsch mopped gravy from his plate. 'That's just the newspapers. It's really just a straightforward case of amnesia.'

'Come, come. Straightforward? How do you account for it then?'

'I can't. Not yet.'

'You must have a theory. Everyone I speak to has a theory, even my driver.'

Perhaps Fischer didn't realise it, what with all the speculation in the newspapers, but individual case histories were confidential. Kirsch thought about how he could say so without appearing ungracious, but Fischer seemed to read his mind.

'Of course. She's still your patient, isn't she? You mustn't say another word. My curiosity is idle and reprehensible.'

'It's quite natural.' Kirsch glanced around the room. Some of the

diners had left and those that remained were comfortably pushed back from their tables, sipping coffee or brandy, or puffing on cigars. 'Perhaps if I could have your assurance –'

'Of course, my dear fellow, of course. I shan't breathe a word. Call it a professional consultation. No harm in that, surely.'

'I suppose not.'

'I hate to rely on the gentlemen of the press. One can't believe a word they say.'

'In that case . . .' Kirsch finished with his plate and put it aside. 'I believe the amnesia was caused by some form of trauma. But I'm not convinced the trauma took place immediately before she was found. I think she may have travelled some distance. There have been cases like it in the past, a coincidence of amnesia and sudden flight. Psychogenic fugue is the preferred term. We do know the patient is not a native German speaker.'

'Really?' Fischer edged closer. 'Then where's she from?'

'Hard to say. Somewhere in the East, I think, judging from her accent. Russia perhaps, or the Balkans.'

Fischer nodded slowly. 'So you agree with the police. The inspector – what was it?'

'Hagen?'

'Yes. He thinks the girl escaped from an asylum. There was no crime, no maniac in the woods.'

Kirsch shrugged. 'I've no information either way.'

Fischer leaned back, gathering his knife and fork on his plate, and tucking his fingers into his waistcoat. 'I have a theory of my own, one you shall no doubt disprove with ease.'

'And that is?'

Fischer reached for a toothpick and screwed it between two of his upper incisors. 'She'll turn out to be an impostor.'

Kirsch laughed, though he didn't feel like laughing. 'How can she be an impostor if she has no identity?'

'That will follow in time. Have you forgotten Anna Anderson? That woman they pulled from the Landwehr canal? It was eighteen months before she declared she was the Grand Duchess Anastasia.'

Kirsch knew the story. After her failed suicide attempt the woman had been taken to the Dalldorf asylum, where she had refused to give a name. Only later did she declare that she was the child of Tsar Nicholas II, and had survived the massacre of the Russian royal family by the Bolsheviks several years earlier. Though she apparently spoke neither Russian nor French – the language of the Russian aristocracy – several exiled Russian aristocrats and courtiers had confirmed her identity and pledged their allegiance. The bandwagon had rolled on, with donations being elicited and financial claims made, even after the Berlin newspapers had positively identified Anderson as a Polish factory worker called Franziska Schanzkowska, a woman with a long history of mental illness. It was said that she and her advisers had grown rich on the proceeds of her celebrity.

'You can see the parallels,' Fischer observed. 'These days one only needs to attract the attention of the press to make money. And your patient has already done that.'

Kirsch didn't know what to say. It wasn't unheard of for people to fake psychiatric illness as a means of gaining attention, but it had never occurred to him that Maria's might be such a case.

Fischer watched him for a moment, then waved a dismissive hand in front of his face. 'It's just an idle thought. Don't let it trouble you.' He reached inside his jacket and produced a gold cigarette case. 'Do you smoke, Dr Kirsch?'

Sixteen

For a long time, Eugen Fischer's theory played on Kirsch's mind. He was sure Maria couldn't have faked a coma, one so deep that Dr Brenner had thought her unlikely to survive. But that aside, the similarities with the Anderson case were undeniable: the amnesia, the suggestion of a near-drowning, the fact that no one had come forward to make an identification. There was even a passing resemblance between Anderson and his patient, as well as a similarity in age. And the press interest – reporters and photographers still lurked outside the clinic, waylaying staff as they went in and out – that too gave the affair the flavour of a performance, an entertainment for popular consumption. Fischer had sensed a degree of manipulation in the pattern of events and now Kirsch found he did too. Had his coming across Maria at the hospital really been an accident? The question nagged at him on his daily rounds, in the common room and at work in his office. Had he been chosen for his role in a plot of some kind? The more he thought about it, the more he felt in the presence of unseen forces, like a small planet drawn into the orbit of a massive but invisible star.

He watched Maria whenever he got the chance, between the long hours of therapy and the endless writing of reports, to see if anyone made contact. The clinic was notionally secure, patients wandering off being a constant danger, but it was not a prison. Staff and tradesmen came and went all day, as well as visitors. He watched her in the refectory, where she generally ate alone. He watched her in the library, where she went after lunch, turning the pages of the books, never settling on a page for more than a few seconds at a time. He watched her walking in the little triangle of grass and trees that passed for a garden, or sitting on the bench with the dappled

winter sunlight playing over her skin. Once, from a window on the second floor, he saw a man walk over to her. He had a cigarette in his mouth and a brown felt hat pulled down low over his eyes. Kirsch climbed up on tiptoe to get a better look. He felt sure it was the reporter he had seen before, talking to Robert Eisner outside the kitchens. Or rather, he wasn't sure, because the man's face was hidden. In any case, if anything passed between him and Maria, it was over in a few seconds, the man tipping his hat and walking briskly away.

Kirsch asked the nurses to report such incidents and to keep back any correspondence for his attention. From then on, almost every morning, something turned up on his desk addressed to Maria, using one or other of her newspaper sobriquets: 'the Potsdam Patient', 'the Lady of the Lake' or 'the Einstein Girl'. Some were love letters, apparently inspired by her picture in the press.

When I saw your face, I thought it was my beloved Susanne come back to me. You are so like her it is a miracle. I swear you could be her sister, though she never had a sister that I know of. She died of the influenza thirteen years ago and I have been alone since then.

One, written in an erratic hand, asked if her name was not Elsa Mühlhausen, a child snatched from her cradle at the age of six months back in 1895, and never seen again. Maria was too young to fit that bill. Another letter claimed to have met her during a seance. Kirsch thought of investigating the claim, until he realised that it was on the other side of the Great Divide that this encounter had supposedly taken place. Several letters, all anonymous, were obscene. One offered to pay Maria for performing a variety of sexual acts and enquired after the price of each one (in what appeared to be ascending order). Another contained a drawing of a young female, presumably Maria, copulating with a frock-coated man whose forehead was decorated with a Star of David. Others asked for a photograph and enclosed money. As far as Kirsch could tell, none of them were from an accomplice, or from anyone who knew Maria's real

identity, unless the accomplice was using some form of code. Not knowing what else to do with them, he put the letters in a box file and stowed them under his desk.

He visited Maria every day. Whenever he could, he brought post-cards, which he propped up on the top of the wainscoting in her room; so that she was soon surrounded as she slept by the land-marks of Berlin. He arranged them according to location, with the bed as the notional centre of the city: the Tiergarten propped up against the window at one end of the room; the colonnaded façade of the National Gallery below the light switch at the other; in between, the Brandenburg Gate, the opera house, cathedrals and churches. He had an idea that if he could rekindle her sense of local geography, a sense of chronology and purpose might follow. He searched for postcards of Grenadierstrasse and the Tanguero as well, but none were to be found.

At first Maria received these additions to the decor with puzzlement or indifference; then later with flickers of amusement. Encouraged, Kirsch branched out from Berlin landmarks into other subjects: roses, ocean liners and steam engines, dogs, cats and horses. But the days went by and there was no improvement, at least as far as the amnesia was concerned. Maria tried to remember, to answer the questions he casually put to her (Had she ever been to sea? Had she ever owned a dog? What was her favourite breed?); but the harder she tried, the more confused and distressed she became. She would start to stammer, her hands twisting together in her lap. He would see the tears welling, the panic rising as she struggled for an answer, a fragment of concrete truth that would tell her she was real and alive. He would glimpse the swirling darkness beneath her feet and feel compelled to stop, to change the subject and bring her back to the present. He couldn't banish the irrational conviction that she was slowly dying, just as surely as if from a fatal infection. Without a past, she struggled to believe in her own existence, that she was more than a flight of imagination, a ghost or a memory to be banished on waking.

The nurses reported that she still had nightmares. She talked in her sleep, they said, sometimes in a foreign tongue, sometimes

in German. They couldn't make sense of her words. Once Kirsch returned to the clinic at dead of night and sat listening outside Maria's door. He heard her murmur in her sleep, get up and pace the room for several minutes before returning to bed. He never heard her screaming, although the nurses assured him that she did scream, especially in the hours before dawn. They wanted to sedate her, but he wouldn't allow it. At least in her nightmares, he thought, it was possible she knew who she was.

Then one day she began to draw. She would sit barefoot at a window in the women's recreation room, with her sketch-book propped up against her knees. The window looked out across the canal towards the arched roof of the Lehrter station. When the wind was in the west, the trains could be heard rattling over the points, their whistles echoing across the city, like the calls to prayer of some shrill, mechanised religion. She had acquired a heavy woollen shawl, which she held tight around her, her mouth and chin hidden in the folds. Perhaps because of that, or because she seemed so absorbed in her work, it was rare for other patients to disturb her.

She sketched most mornings. When she was done, she would close the sketch-book, put her shoes back on, tying the laces with neat bows, and return to her room. There, before anything else, she would put the sketch-book and the pencils in their place: on the top shelf of the battered closet in the corner.

What she drew were faces. They covered every page, faces drifting up into the light through clouds of shading. They were executed with some skill. Fine lines traced the contours of the flesh: faces gazing upward or captured in profile; old, careworn faces and youthful, expectant ones, yet all marked with the same hesitant, ephemeral quality, as if aware of their incompleteness, or unsure how they came to be trapped in their strange two-dimensional world.

Some faces occurred again and again: a child – female, he thought – with her head wrapped in a scarf, and two men. The first looked young enough to be a sweetheart or a brother. He had narrow eyes, a broad forehead and a beautiful, delicate mouth, the lips pushed

together in an attitude of contemplation. She had drawn him several times, from different angles, the expression shifting, but always troubled. Kirsch wondered if this could be the stranger he had seen in the grounds.

'What shall we call him?' he asked her one day. 'What name suits him?'

But she could not give him a name. 'He's a writer,' was all she could say.

The other man was old. He had dark eyes, the same full lips and wild white hair, like an Old Testament prophet or a Renaissance image of God. She could not name him either.

As Kirsch looked through the sketch-book, it came to him that Maria drew nothing from life. He saw no patients, no staff. These were visions seen with the inner eye, a cast of remembered souls. The people who surrounded Maria at the clinic might as well not have been there. It was not what he had hoped for.

'What about a self-portrait?' he suggested.

'Why?'

'I'd like to have one.'

A self-portrait might help re-establish her sense of identity. It might reveal how she saw herself.

Maria shook her head. 'There are no mirrors.'

It was true: mirrors were not allowed, for safety reasons. Over the years several had been smashed by patients disturbed by the sight of their own reflections, the shards of broken glass causing injury, or even being used as weapons. In the women's shower room there were two mirrors left, but they were small and securely bolted to the wall.

'What if I brought you one?' Kirsch drew a square in the air, framing her face. 'So big. I think I know where I can get one.'

'If it's what you want,' Maria said, tugging absently at a lock of her hair.

'It is,' he said.

To prove it, he slipped out at lunchtime and bought a mirror in a gilded frame from a furniture dealer on the Kurfürstendamm.

* * *

There was no word from Dr Fischer in the week following their lunch. There was no confirmation of the proposed commission, which had seemed so pressing at the time, nor any further information about how Kirsch should go about it. He wondered if the anthropologist had meant what he said, and if he really had the necessary means at his disposal. He came to suspect that Fischer was just a lonely, if well-heeled, eccentric, a man who filled up his days with superficial enthusiasms, only to drop them when something more intriguing came along. Kirsch's paper had resonated with some intellectual bugbear of his, and so he had sought out the author with all the impatience of someone with time on their hands and nothing useful to do with it. Already Kirsch regretted having talked so freely about his work and about Maria.

He had finally sat down to write his letter of resignation when Robert Eisner strolled in carrying the morning post. Kirsch still hadn't told him about Bonhoeffer's decision, hoping the director would in time relent, but a fortnight had gone by and there was still no sign of that happening.

'A letter from the Kaiser Wilhelm Institute of Anthropology, Eugenics and Human Heredity,' Eisner announced, reading the back of a stiff white envelope and slinging it into his in-tray.

The envelope had been sealed with wax. Kirsch put down his pen and picked up a knife.

'You writing another paper, then?' Eisner continued to hover beside his desk. 'I wouldn't have thought human heredity was your field.'

'It's not,' Kirsch said, peering at the contents without taking them out. He looked at his watch. 'I have to be going.'

He tucked the envelope away in his inside pocket and left the room.

Fischer didn't stop at sending money. He enclosed a short list from the Kaiser Wilhelm Institute for Psychiatry of psychiatric hospitals and practitioners across Germany, Switzerland and Austria that he considered likely to be cooperative in the quest for diagnostic records.

My institute is not concerned with individual cases, he wrote in his letter, *so there is no reason they should worry unduly about breaches of confidentiality.*

At the Adlon, Kirsch had been careful not to commit himself. Fischer, though, seemed to assume that he had done just that. He wanted Kirsch to begin approaching the institutions at once, setting out his goals and methods. *I consider this work to be of the highest importance, and I feel sure it will result in a significant publication. I trust you will be able to set aside the necessary time from your regular duties.*

For two days Kirsch did nothing. Dr Bonhoeffer had made clear his feelings about his first paper. For Kirsch to announce that he was about to undertake a larger study along the same lines would be tantamount to a slap in the face. All hope of rehabilitation would be lost. It was as if Kirsch was being asked to choose sides – or choose masters. But then, thanks to Heinrich Mehring and Nurse Honig, that decision had already been made for him.

On the third day, he banked the cheque.

Seventeen

Later that day Kirsch was struck down with a sudden bout of fever. It came upon him as he was riding the crowded tram from Alexanderplatz. He was hanging on to one of the overhead straps, feeling hot and tired inside his heavy overcoat, but otherwise normal, when the driver slammed on the brakes. Gasps went up. A small jam jar slipped from a woman's shopping bag and rolled down the aisle. Then everyone steadied themselves and the tram moved off again. Kirsch bent down to pick up the jam jar which was still rolling towards him. It jumped neatly into his hand, showing him its label, which had a pair of cherries on it, red and shining, which struck him as strangely comic, given his name. He had a sensation of being watched from somewhere high above, toyed with and laughed at, as if by the ancient gods. The next thing he knew he was in darkness.

There was shouting and a deafening rumble of guns. It came into his head that he had to find his surgical instruments. There would be injured men coming in, wounds full of filth and soil. No time to take shelter. He shouted for light, saw lanterns dancing in the gloom, coming closer. Pale faces hurried by. Then his vision cleared and he found himself lying face up on the tram's ribbed floor, a crowd of passengers staring down at him.

No one helped him up. They must have thought he was drunk. He elbowed his way to the doors and got off at the next stop, forgetting his briefcase. A young man tossed it to him from the tram as it pulled away. The briefcase hit the kerb and burst open, scattering papers, journals and postcards across the cobblestones.

He was shivering by the time he got home. Frau Schirmann saw him on the stairs and offered to send for a doctor, but he told her

not to bother. It was just a touch of influenza, something he had picked up at the clinic, he said. He would be better in no time.

Frau Schirmann was frightened of influenza on account of her weak lungs. She needed no more encouragement to stay away. Kirsch locked himself in his room and collapsed on the bed. The fever raged all night. At dawn he prepared another dose of Salvarsan, but his hands were shaking too much to use the needle safely. Arsenic poisoning could result from a botched injection.

He didn't need the Salvarsan anyway, he told himself. He probably *had* gone down with influenza, his system weakened by long hours at the clinic and the stresses of his professional situation. The main hospital at the Charité was full of sick people, and it was only yards from the clinic. Ancillary staff and delivery men visited both buildings, carrying germs from one to the other. His fever had nothing to do with syphilis or the shadowy brown marks that were spreading across his ribs.

Around noon, Frau Schirmann brought him bread and vegetable broth, leaving them outside the door. By the middle of the afternoon the fever had subsided. It had been like the memory of an old illness, a reminder of suffering gone by. It wasn't the portent of suffering to come.

Still, Kirsch wished he could be sure. He wished there was someone he could trust, someone who would discern the truth of his condition and then keep the results to themselves. But though he thought long and hard, no one came to mind.

He returned to the clinic on the Wednesday. In his brief absence, Maria's sketching had changed. Kirsch sat with her in the usual treatment room, looking through her sketch-book. For the first time, fellow patients and Charité staff loomed up through the fibrous mesh of shading: Nurse Honig, complexion typically florid, but with a weight of sorrow in the arch of her brow that he had never seen before; Nurse Auerbach, pretty but expectant, her lips pressed together in an impatient line; Dr Mehring, the dome of his head as smooth as an egg, his bearing stiff and remote, as if aware of how easily he might crack. In her quest for new subjects, Maria was at

last sketching from life. Her pages were crowded not with ghosts, but with living people.

Kirsch smiled to himself. This had to be progress of some sort. Maria's past might be no clearer, but at least she was reconnecting with the present; resisting the pull of the internal world and engaging with the real one. His greatest fear had been that she would lose her grip on reality, sinking into psychosis as the weight of her predicament bore down.

'This picture of Dr Eisner, the likeness is striking.' He held up the sketch-book. Robert Eisner had been captured with a hesitant, loitering look on his face, like someone listening in on a conversation but undecided about whether to join in. His eyes were ghostly pale except for the hard black points of his pupils.

'Is he a doctor?'

'Didn't he say?'

Maria shook her head. 'Sometimes he wears a white coat, like you. Other times not.'

Kirsch wondered how many times there had been.

'I didn't know he'd spoken to you.'

Maria put her head on one side. A shaft of light from the window fell across her cheek. Her hair, just long enough now to tie back in a knot, had a coppery sheen, a hint of fire in the darkness. 'Oh yes,' she said. 'He pretends he's just passing. It's not a very good act. He's very curious.'

Kirsch smiled. 'I expect he is.'

'Like you were.'

'Me?'

'That's what you said. When you came to the hospital. You were curious.'

'Of course.' Kirsch coloured. He wished he could reassure her that she was more than an interesting specimen, more than a potential key to professional advancement, as cases in the public eye often were. But he could think of no way to do it.

He turned over another page of the sketch-book. 'So no self-portrait, then?'

'I've tried, but it's hard. I look at myself but the picture never sticks.' She shrugged. 'I've no sense of it. I draw the first line and then it's gone.'

He turned over another page, the last. Here there was only one face, and it was his. She had drawn him looking down and to the side. The shading had a roughness and energy that was different from the other pictures. It had been done in haste, as if Maria had been concerned to capture the likeness before it was lost – as if she feared he would soon be gone. It was like looking in a mirror, but without the blank mimicry of a pure reflection. Kirsch sat staring, surprised at the intensity of the image: the lined brow, the troubled gaze.

'My God.' He forced a laugh. 'Do I really look this unhappy?'

Maria nodded. Then she reached up and touched his face.

Something scuffed against the outside of the door. It closed against the jamb with a faint bump. Footsteps tapped lightly down the corridor.

The lunch bell sounded. Maria took her hand away. 'I must go,' she said.

She got up and hurried out of the room. It was a moment before Kirsch realised that she had left her sketch-book behind.

That evening it began to snow. Kirsch left the clinic earlier than usual, catching the tail end of the evening rush. The S-Bahn carriage was full from end to end. He stood pressed up against the door, being buffeted by the other passengers, breathing in the fug of tobacco and wet leather, his mind churning, his breath short. The crowds streamed through Alexanderplatz, mute and huddled, faces flaring into living detail as they passed beneath the street lamps, then plunging once again into shadow.

Up until that day, it was if he had been playing a game, even if the game was masked by all the seriousness of scientific and medical enquiry. But it was a game no longer.

East of the Schönhauser Allee it was quieter. The snow was starting to settle as he hurried up Grenadierstrasse, pausing only to

take in the boarded-up front of Herr Bronstein's gramophone shop and the splinters of glass glistening like frost on the cobblestones. A few minutes later he was outside the Jewish cemetery, staring up at the rooming house, just as he had two months before.

It took him a while to find the street door. It was located up some steps at the side of the building, partially obscured beneath the rusting spiral of a fire escape. He pulled on the doorbell, to no obvious effect, then pounded on the door with his fist.

'Hello?'

His voice reverberated between the walls of the alley, compressing into a single note. In the tenement opposite a light went out, plunging him into darkness.

'What do you want?'

A man was looking down at him from a first-floor window. He had a shaven head and wore spectacles.

'I've come about a room. I'm looking to rent.'

'I only rent to ladies.'

'It's not for me.'

'Come back tomorrow.'

The man pulled the window shut.

'I'll pay in advance,' Kirsch shouted. 'If I can see something now. Tomorrow will be too late.'

The landlord was called Sebastian Mettler and he spoke with a rasping Swiss inflexion. He couldn't have been much more than forty, but he carried himself like an old man, stooping, one arm clamped to his side as he hauled himself up the bare wooden staircase. Frau Mettler, his mother, an obese woman with a pince-nez clamped on her nose, watched from the open door of their apartment, as if afraid the effort might prove too much for him.

'I've just the one vacancy, at the back. Not much of a view.'

They were up on the second floor of the rooming house, where Kirsch had seen Maria. An electric table lamp threw shadows across an expanse of faded floral wallpaper. A redundant glass chandelier hung from the ceiling.

Herr Mettler opened up a door with a brass '2' nailed to it. 'So who's it for?' He switched on a light and stood back to let Kirsch pass. 'I told you, I only take –'

'It's for a student of mine.'

'A student?' Herr Mettler pushed his spectacles up his nose. 'Well, as long as you can vouch for her.'

The room was simply furnished, but tidy. The wrought-iron fireplace and plaster cornices lent it a Spartan gentility. Kirsch took in the table with the lace tablecloth draped across it, the sturdy wardrobe, the crucifix over the bedstead. The window looked out onto an enclosed space, washing lines and snow flakes criss-crossing the darkness.

'A view of the street. That's what I'm looking for.'

Herr Mettler shook his head. 'I've just the one room.'

He pointed across the hall at the door marked '3'. It was a dark shade of red, though the paint had been thinly applied so that the grain of the wood was visible. 'What about that one?'

'Taken. For the time being anyway.'

'For the time being?'

'It's been paid for till the end of the month.'

'Today's the twenty-ninth.'

'Then it's paid till Thursday.'

'Is anyone home?'

Herr Mettler squinted across the landing. 'Couldn't say. I don't keep tabs.'

'Can I take a look?'

'What for? I told you: it's not free.'

'Not yet.' Kirsch opened his wallet. 'I'd be only too happy to pay for your trouble. Seeing as it's so late.'

Herr Mettler slowly straightened up, his back clicking ominously. The tip of his tongue made a circle around his lips. 'I'll have to fetch the key.'

Kirsch took out a five-Reichsmark note. 'I'll come down with you. That way you needn't trouble yourself about coming back up.'

* * *

Two minutes later he stood alone outside Maria's door. The iron key was cold and heavy in his hand. He tried to picture the room. Was it as bare as the room across the landing? Was it tidy or disordered? Was there evidence of a crime, of the fraud Dr Fischer had suspected? Or of a descent into madness? He had seen rooms like that, rooms the like of which he never wanted to enter again.

It came to him that this was why he hadn't come sooner. It would have been hard to explain, his knowing where Maria lived. It might have led to all manner of awkward questions. That was still the case. But it was not the reason: he had been afraid of what he might find.

With the exertion he felt giddy. The dark red door drifted before his eyes, squeezing and stretching as if it were alive. He gripped the key, held the cold metal to his face for a moment, then pushed it fumblingly into the lock.

madness

Eighteen

How do I come to be here after all this time? It is natural that you should want an explanation, and though I have had long enough to prepare one, still I don't know how best to convey it. The simplest thing would be to tell you in person, but that idea fills me with trepidation. I am not gifted when it comes to conversation, and often think of what I should say only after the occasion to say it has passed. So I am writing it all down, so that at least I may consider my words before I commit to them.

Let me first reassure you that the circumstances of my upbringing put me at no material disadvantage. In the village of Orlovat the family I grew up with was one of considerable note. The father of the household, Zoltán Draganović, had one of the largest and grandest houses, which, unlike most, was set back from the road, with a courtyard in front to shield us from the summer dust and the gaze of passers-by. At the back there was a whitewashed veranda and enclosures for chickens and geese, an orchard of apple and cherry trees, and several outbuildings where we kept the horses and an old carriage — at least, a carriage was what my father called it, although in truth it was little better than a tinker's wagon. We also had land which others rented from us.

The house itself was wide and yellow, with windows painted green and plaster escutcheons above each one. The heraldic motifs, most of which had fallen off, were Austrian. This was because the Draganović clan had Austrian blood in it through the maternal line, as my father frequently explained. I understood from an early age that this was important to him, and therefore to me, but I soon discovered it was not always a wise thing to talk about. I was only seven years old when the schoolmistress accused me of giving myself airs, and the boys took to calling me names and throwing pebbles when no one was looking. For a while I was so frightened of going to school that I would faint or pretend

to be sick, dousing my face with water and muttering as if in a fever. I became quite skilled at dissembling, and sometimes put my mother in such a fright that I was sorry and feigned a swift recovery. I did not tell my father about the trouble he had caused me, or about the boys who threw pebbles, because I was afraid he would march down to the school and wring their necks, as he threatened to do with anyone who insulted our family's honour. I did not especially mind the idea of the boys being strangled, but I did not want my father to be punished for the crime. For I still cared for him in those days.

At this time I envied my sister. Senka was a year younger than me, and although she had started school, she was soon excused and no longer had to attend. Instead she took her lessons at home, from our mother. But her lessons were not like school lessons, with hour upon hour of copying out and learning by heart. Hers were outdoors, except in bad weather, and involved learning the care of the animals and the names of the plants and insects. If it was raining she would have lessons in sewing and needlework by the kitchen fire, which I would gladly have swapped for my cold school bench and the endless exercises in spelling and arithmetic. The only schooling I received at home was in German, which my father insisted I learn for reasons once more connected with the maternal line.

At that time he held a position in the imperial customs service and was away a great deal in Novi Sad. I was very anxious to please him and so studied hard during his absences, so that he would be impressed with my progress. My proudest moments were when he would pick me up in his arms and call me his schlaue kleine Dame. It was the first praise I ever earned from him, because it was no secret in our family that what a man most needed from his wife was a son, and that until he had one, children of the other sex were a luxury, and an expensive one at that. However, since my proficiency at German had succeeded in earning my father's praise, I decided to work hard in all subjects, so that he would see I was some use after all, and might yet bring some credit to the family name. This did not make me any more popular with the other children but it did at least keep me away from the playground, and out of the range of their pebbles.

As for Senka, I imagined that, as the youngest, she was being groomed for the running of the house, and this was why she did not have to study. I only discovered the real reason from one of the boys at school who, as a change from throwing stones, decided one day to throw insults instead. My sister was an idiot, he shouted, and he pulled a strange ugly face that did not look like Senka at all, but which I knew was, in some cruel way, true. By the time I got home that day, I had understood everything, and my jealousy had disappeared, to be replaced by shame.

I grew closer to Senka after that. Her name means 'shadow' in Serb, and that is how close we were, always together when I was not studying. I even took over some of her lessons, which pleased my mother (though not my father, who said I was wasting my time). I taught her some reading and arithmetic — not too much, as her attention would wander after a while, and there was nothing I could do to regain it. But she did learn, and I tried to learn from her, especially her way with the animals. The geese would follow her around, pecking gently at her sleeves and the hem of her skirts with their orange beaks. They would let her stroke their long downy necks too, which was a privilege granted to no one else. Whenever I approached they hissed and puffed up their feathers and sometimes chased me out of the yard altogether, if they were not in a sociable mood.

I said that Senka was my only sister, but I learned a few years later that there had once been another. One summer day there were guests in the house, and the talk around the table turned to scarlet fever, which had returned to some villages not far away. I could tell the way my mother fell silent, and from the way my father looked at her, that the subject was painful to her. I knew that scarlet fever was much feared, and had taken many children in years past. So later I asked my grandmother if anyone in our family had died of it.

At first she was shocked, and said it was not the sort of question a young lady should be asking, which, of course, made me quite certain that someone had died. I told her that I was good at keeping secrets and would keep this one if she would share it, and this seemed to satisfy her. She told me that the fever had taken my mother's first-born when she was still a baby, but that I should never speak of it to anyone, or

the fever would surely return to our house. This seemed quite reasonable to me at the time. One did not speak of the Devil for fear that to do so would summon him, and I assumed this was a precaution built on a similar principle. It was only after some years that I began to wonder why my family had chosen to add the burden of secrecy to what was already a burden of sadness.

After she had shared the secret, my grandmother was worried that it might trouble me. By way of comfort, she told me that what God took away with one hand, he gave back with the other. This idea appealed to me considerably, as it suggested that there was a fairness to the universe and a pleasing degree of symmetry — much like the algebra I had begun at school, where a problem could only be solved when both sides of it were of equal value. In this instance, what God gave to balance the equation with respect to my mother was me. And the proof of it was that the dead child and I shared the same name. My sister Senka, I noted sadly, was not included in the equation, but I knew why that was: because she did not go to school as I did, and consequently had no knowledge of either algebra or God.

I had by this time been identified as a scholar of some promise. My studies had been greatly improved by the arrival of a new teacher from Zagreb whose name was Bošković. He had been to the university, and arrived with many new theories about the curriculum. One rainy day, when I was not yet eleven years old, he turned up outside our house wearing his best frock-coat and asked to speak with my father. I didn't know what to think, and was much afraid that I had done something bad, such that I might be punished or barred from the school. I tried to listen at the door of my father's study, but was shooed away by my mother, who told me sternly to go to my room and stay there until I was sent for. So I sat in my room, on the verge of tears, while Senka sat in the corner singing to herself and drawing, at which she was quite proficient. Seeing that I was upset, she offered to make a portrait of me, which helped take my mind off my worries, especially since she made me look pretty and grown up, which pleased me a good deal.

From the window I at last saw Mr Bošković leaving, and ran downstairs, though I had not yet been sent for. My parents had gone back into

the study and were in earnest discussion, as I plainly heard: my mother excited and entreating, my father truculent, which was very much the norm for their discussions, regardless of the subject. I heard several references to money and whether enough could be procured, which again did not surprise me, since that was in my experience the only subject that ever engaged the two of them together for more than a minute at a time – unless it was the manifest failings of my mother's family, which was a theme my father never tired of raking over.

It turned out that I was not in trouble after all. As my mother informed me, the teacher had recommended that I be sent to continue my education at the gymnasium in Bečkerek, where the principal happened to be an acquaintance. Considerable expense would be involved, for there were fees, not to mention the cost of travelling daily on the train, Bečkerek being some fourteen miles away. For this reason, my father added, it was most unlikely that the recommendation would be followed, which disappointed me sorely. I had grown tired of the school in the village, of the taunts of the boys and the lessons, which were far too easy, especially in mathematics. And while Bečkerek was very far from a great metropolis, or for that matter a city of any kind, still it seemed to me at that age infinitely grand and impressive. In tears, I ran back to my room and hid my head in my arms, and would not lift my face to the light even for Senka, who drew me in that posture with shading all around me as dark as my mood.

I need not have been so disappointed. I do not know exactly how the money was found for the gymnasium, but found it was. I do know my mother wrote to our Aunt Helene in Belgrade, and after a month or so received a welcome answer. Such was the timing of this, coinciding as it did with my father's sudden change of heart, that I perceived a connection without being told what it was. I went as far as to ask if Aunt Helene had sent money for my education, but was smartly told to stop talking nonsense. So I left the matter there, and thought no more about it.

From that time onward my life was scarcely my own. The classes at the gymnasium were more demanding than any I had known before, especially since I was by some months the youngest in my class. The daily

train journeys ate up most of the waking hours that remained and left me with neither time nor strength for play. Then there was my father, who now took greater interest in my studies, critically perusing my home-work (even though much of it, especially in mathematics, was soon entirely beyond him), and demanding of my teachers constant reports of my progress. Worst of all, he took to boasting of my achievements, and telling people that I was a child prodigy, and that a girl like me had never been seen in the region before, which was not true, as you of all people know very well.

In short, the attention which once I had sought soon became a burden; but I could have borne it gladly had his neglect of my sister not grown worse at the same time. It was as if my father had only a very limited stock of paternal love, if such it was, and had decided to spend it all on me. He spoke to her harshly and made sly jokes about her slow wits and complained that she ate too much for a child that did nothing all day — which was unfair, because she laboured hard to keep the animals in good health, and both the chickens and the geese laid for her in great profusion, such that it was remarked upon around the village. In the past my mother would have upbraided him for such slights, but her health was not of the best at this time, and she was often in her bed by the time I got home.

I knew what angered him, well enough. Senka was a Draganović, and the fact that she was backward in her learning and unlikely to make a good match for herself, if any at all, shed a bad light on the family name. It was another sign that the line was fallen into decay and corrup-tion, like the escutcheons above the windows and the land we no longer had (though we had enough, and more than most). Every time he looked at her, that was what he was reminded of — that and the fact that he had no son to restore the family fortunes, nor no longer any chance of getting one while our mother lived. That burden had fallen to me, if only as a last resort, but I was under no illusions that should I fail in that regard, my treatment would be no better than my sister's.

It was during the war that I finally began to see my father for what he was. Until then, we had kept the geese for laying, but he announced a few days before Christmas that we should have to kill one for the table.

He told Senka that she should choose the plumpest of the birds and see to it that its neck was wrung so that it could be gutted and dressed by our mother. Poor Senka fell silent, for she was very afraid of him. I knew how his words must have horrified her, for the geese were all her friends, and she had a name for each and every one. But I did not guess what she would do, which was to steal out that night and lead them all away across the fields — so far away, in fact, that she herself did not return until dawn. I suppose she was afraid that they would come home again otherwise, for they had certainly never shown the slightest inclination to escape, and were only fenced in for their own protection.

I went off to school first thing in the morning, and did not discover what had happened until I returned in the late afternoon. I found the geese gone and Senka nowhere to be found. My father was not in the house and my mother had once again taken to her bed. Eventually I found Senka in the disused part of the stables — disused because by that time we had just the one horse. She was shivering in the corner, half-covered in straw for warmth. She dared not go back inside the house, and when I tried to help her up, I began to see why. Her lip was split, and there were welts and purple bruises on her shoulders, arms and legs, and I dared not even look at her back. Until then, our father had never been much of a one to hand out beatings. As far as he was concerned it was our mother's job to keep us in hand. Now it was as if he had made up for lost time all at once.

Over the days that followed some of the geese came back to the village and were rounded up and returned to us, though Father claimed that many had been stolen. We had goose for Christmas, as planned, though Senka did not eat it. In fact, she did not eat with the rest of us from that day onward, except when our father was away, because, he said, the very sight of her took away his appetite.

I continued to study, harder now than ever, though the war often interrupted the railways, such that I could not get to school. By now I was not studying to please my father, but mainly to make good my escape when the time came. I did not know to where, only that it would be far away, and that I should take Senka with me. And my only doubt was how we would manage to make our getaway with her geese in tow, for,

just as it says in the Roman legend, geese are noisy birds and prone to raise the alarm whether they mean to or not.

In spite of what had happened, I did not hate my father exactly, though some might say he deserved to be hated. Rather, the notion sank in deeper than ever that we were different in every way – so different that if we were indeed family and shared the same blood, then those connections meant little, and certainly much less than was generally supposed. For, from that day onward, I perceived no great difficulty, no revolt against nature, in the idea of being parted from the Draganović clan for ever – from all its lines, but most especially the maternal line, of which I saw no reason on Earth to boast, and never would again.

Nineteen

The first thing he saw when he opened the door were sprigs of lavender in a cut-glass vase, and a pile of neatly folded petticoats on the wicker chair. On top of the chest of drawers there was a small stack of post-cards – unused, as it turned out: Berlin scenes just like the ones he had bought for Maria. Beside that was a matching hand mirror and hairbrush, a few strands of dark hair still clinging to the bristles. On the bed sat an antique doll with a porcelain face and oriental eyes, dressed in a Chinese costume of reds and greens. A pair of black lace-up shoes, the shoes he had seen Maria wearing outside Herr Bronstein's music shop, stood neatly lined up behind the door, the toes pointing outwards.

Everything in its place. Everything normal. Nothing torn to shreds. Nothing scrawled on the walls. No blood. The pile of petticoats still gave off a clean, laundered smell.

Her possessions had been positioned so as to make best use of the available space, and to display the few objects of worth to advantage – the doll, the lace tablecloth, the hand mirror with its mother-of-pearl in-lay. The place had not been left in a hurry. Its tidiness anticipated a return. It set out to create an impression. But for whom?

Apart from the antique doll, Kirsch saw no evidence of a child, not even a photograph, or a brooch with a lock of hair. He went to the window and looked down into the street, picturing himself there, hat in hand, a stranger looking for directions. Snow clung to the lamp-posts and the top of the cemetery wall. It was settling on the pavements. A pair of huddled figures hurried past the gates, their footsteps making no sound at all.

He closed the door and went to the chest of drawers, opening them one after another. They contained mostly clothes, all clean and folded but few in number; and a sewing kit, with spools of thread in various

colours. Some items of clothing had been patched. She had several pairs of cotton stockings, all black and of the coarser, heavier variety eschewed by the girls at the Tanguero. He checked for laundry marks, but found no trace of identification.

Three dresses were hanging in the wardrobe, simple prints on dark fabrics, one skirt pleated. None of them had labels. On one side there was the brown velvet cloche hat he had seen her wearing in the street. The label read *Herrmann Gerson, Werderscher Markt, BERLIN*, but the hat was not a recent line. Either she had shopped in the city years before or she had acquired it second-hand, perhaps at one of the stalls on Grenadierstrasse. The coat was there, too; and the dress she had worn at the Tanguero.

He closed the wardrobe door, caught his frowning reflection in the smoky glass. What then had she worn on her trip to Potsdam? A different hat, a different coat, a different dress, different shoes — wasn't Alma always telling him that such things made all the difference to a woman? He looked around the room, saw now with a squeeze of panic the blankness of it. There was no obvious history, no discernible past. A few objects, sensibly arranged, just as they might be by someone waiting for a new life to begin. An empty stage awaiting the arrival of the cast.

He sat down on the bed. Were his impressions to be trusted? Other interpretations of the scene were possible. Perhaps Maria had come with few personal possessions because she *had* few personal possessions. Or because she had never planned to stay long. The pillow case and sheets were pristine. He turned the pillow over, found a few faint creases in the cotton. He laid his head down, picking up a faint, musky scent.

His heel knocked against something hard. It was under the bed: an old travelling trunk, varnished yellow canvas stretched over wood, the initials Z M D stencilled in red across the front. He moved it out into the light. A faded label on the lid read: *Hotel Sacher, Vienna*. From downstairs came the thud of a door closing. He listened for a moment, then eased open the catches.

The lid came up with a sharp crack and a musty smell he knew

138

only too well. Kneeling on the floor, he pulled out the books, two at a time, turning their spines towards the light. They were textbooks: mathematics, physics, chemistry – all German editions, none recent. A translation of John F. Herschel's *Outlines of Astronomy* had been heavily annotated in pencil. A copy of the original 1913 edition of *The Principal of Relativity* by Lorentz, Einstein, Minkowski and Sommerfeld had a broken spine, so that the folios came loose as he opened them. What was Maria doing with books like these?

Among them was a notebook with a hard cover. It was full of mathematical calculations – line after line, page after page, of equations and symbols, many amended or crossed out. Kirsch recognised the notation of differential calculus, the same mathematical puzzles with which Max had once bamboozled visitors to Reinsdorf. At once he was reminded of something he had read in the newspaper: how the police had found a programme or a flier in the Potsdam woods, close to where Maria was found. It had been printed on the occasion of a public lecture by Professor Albert Einstein at the Philharmonic Hall, entitled *The Present State of Quantum Theory.*

'What did I tell you?' Max said, as clearly as if he were standing at Kirsch's shoulder.

'You didn't tell me anything,' Kirsch replied.

There was a cough from the hallway below, other voices: the landlord and his mother in hushed disagreement. Kirsch tucked the notebook inside his coat and went back to the trunk. At the very bottom, under the textbooks, there was something bulky wrapped up in a white cloth.

Herr Mettler called up the stairs: 'Dr Kirsch?' It seemed five Reichmarks bought limited privileges. 'Are you finished?'

Hastily Kirsch unwrapped the cloth. Inside it was an old photograph album with an embossed leather cover. There had been one just like it in his grandfather's house, a big sturdy tome kept, like the family Bible, in a special place where neither sunlight nor prying hands could damage it.

He found a brass clamp at the side. It bore evidence of damage. He had to force it open with both hands.

Down below Herr Mettler sighed audibly and began to climb the stairs, letting out an exasperated grunt every few steps. Kirsch opened the album.

The pictures had been secured with corners made of silvered paper. They were on every page, framing rectangular spaces large and small. But the photographs themselves were missing. All that remained of them were faint shadows and what seemed to be knife marks in the surface of the card.

Halfway through the album, someone in the family had acquired their own camera. Small prints, a few inches square, had been evenly spaced across the pages, held in place with the same corner mounts, though here several were missing.

Near the bottom of the last page Kirsch found one picture still in place. Two girls with scarves round their heads, aged ten or eleven, were feeding a flock of geese. One of them stood back a little, holding a scrap of bread between her hands. The other was squatting down, caressing a bird with one hand and feeding it with the other. Both were looking up at the camera, smiling. Either of the girls could have been Maria, or neither of them.

Herr Mettler was crossing the landing, coughing to announce his presence. 'So is this what you're looking for?'

He stood surveying the scene through his thick lenses, clearly unsure whether or not to object to the invasion of privacy.

Kirsch closed the album. 'Forgive me, Herr Mettler,' he said, 'but something tells me you don't read the newspapers.'

Herr Mettler adjusted his spectacles. 'The newspapers?'

'Because I think you've quite a famous tenant.'

Her name was Mariya, just as she had said – only it was spelled the Slavic way: Mariya Draganović. At least, that was the name she had given on arrival. Herr Mettler admitted that he had never asked to see her passport. She had arrived at the beginning of October from Zürich, where she said she had been a student. Someone there had recommended his premises for their cleanliness and convenient location. She hadn't revealed her reasons for travelling to Berlin. She had paid her

rent six weeks in advance, lived quietly and entertained few guests, if any. That was all he knew.

Mariya: she had remembered it correctly. That had to be a good sign, a hopeful sign – unless it was a mistake, a slip-up in an otherwise faultless performance.

If we're keeping an open mind, Dr Kirsch.

Walking back to the tram stop along snowy, luminescent streets, Kirsch went over the facts. His patient was a student of mathematics from Zürich, although presumably not a native of that city, given her accent. Mariya Draganović. The family name added substance. It placed her in the world again, the world outside the Charité – a good thing, he reminded himself, the goal of psychiatric treatment being a return to society. On the other hand, according to the literature, it was typical in cases of psychogenic fugue for the subject to assume a new identity. Hans J, the bank clerk from Nürnberg, had sworn his name was Otto Kleist, a detective from Berlin. Until Kirsch saw the name Mariya Draganović on some official document, he couldn't be sure it was genuine.

Mariya Draganović. Why hadn't she given him her real name at the Tanguero? Why had she lied? To hide her Slavic origins, perhaps, the way the working girls did? Or had she thought that concealing her identity might keep her safe?

She hadn't trusted him, of course. It was as simple as that.

He thought of going back to the clinic at once and sharing with her everything he had learned. But how would all that information affect her? Where psychogenic fugue was concerned, the case histories were not encouraging. Hans J, his identity recovered, had returned to his home in Nürnberg and his job at the bank. But after that, his life and his mind had slowly fallen apart. It was the same with one of the English cases, a twenty-eight-year-old woman called Ethel. Ethel, too, had recovered her lost memories and returned to her home in Manchester. But in subsequent interviews, members of her family claimed that she was not the same woman, that she had become secretive and was apt to disappear for hours at a time without explanation. An aunt even claimed

that the new Ethel was an impostor and had reported the matter to the police.

The root of these afflictions lay not in the fact that information had been lost. It was to be found in the mind's decision to forget, to blank out memories with which it was dangerous or impossible to co-exist. In Mariya's case, it might make the same decision again. And this time, Kirsch would be forgotten too.

Back at his apartment, he shrugged off his heavy overcoat. The notebook landed on the floor with a thud, several loose scraps of paper spilling out. He knelt down to gather them up again. One was an old letter. The paper was yellowed with age, the address written in a neat, feminine hand. It read: *Fr. Mileva Einstein-Marić, Tillierstrasse 18, Berne, Switzerland.*

Belgrade, 21 April 1903

Dear Mileva,
I am taking this opportunity to write to you quickly while the children are asleep, Milivoj is out, and there is some peace in the house. I should like to have replied to your letter earlier, with all its warm wishes, but the baby has taken up so much of my attention that it has been hard to stay on top of my other duties – while continuing to give little Julka the attention she deserves too.
I read with some surprise your enquiry about finding work here in Belgrade. Is this really something you have discussed with your husband? It is regrettable, of course, if his present employment is not to his liking, but the kind of academic posts he has searched for in the past are not to be found here, even at the university, which, as you know, is not of the first rank when it comes to science. As for your teaching German here, I cannot but think that would be a waste of your talents in mathematics and suchlike, which led you to study in Switzerland in the first place.
I know that Lieserl is on your mind when you ask such things. But I urge you to be cautious in this matter and observe, as much as it is in your power, the agreements that have been entered into. We were

fortunate in being able to find people who were prepared to help us, and it would be most unfortunate, for the child as much as for everyone else, if matters were to unravel now. I hope I can at least set your mind at rest for the time being with news from Orlovat, which I have from my friend Irena who was there a week ago. She said the child appears quite healthy, has a good appetite and is well looked after. It further appears that she will soon have a little brother or sister, for Frau D is expecting again, and is due in six weeks or so. She has been poorly of late, however, and they have some fears for the health of this child, as for the last.

Now that you are married, and Albert has found employment to support you both, I hope with all my heart that you will be blessed with a family of your own, and will be able to put these concerns behind you. Milivoj and I are of course delighted to hear of your plan to visit later this year, but I do hope you are not thinking of using your time here to undo what has been settled according to your wishes and for the good of all.

I will write to you at greater length in a few days' time. In the meantime, I send my very fondest regards to you both.

Your dear friend,

Helene Savić

Kirsch sat down on his bed. The names in the letter meant nothing to him. They were thirty years old in any case; the preoccupations of strangers, long since overtaken by the march of history – memories now at best, lacking all substance.

What was Mariya doing with this old letter? Had someone given it to her? Or was it like one of those scraps of private correspondence he sometimes found hidden between the leaves of a second-hand book: a thing of no more significance than a bookmark?

He lay down. He felt exhausted but anxious without knowing exactly why. He should have been reassured by what he had found in Mariya's room – the cleanliness, the order – but he was not reassured. It came to him that the room was ghostly, sepulchral, like a tomb awaiting its occupant.

He looked at the letter again. Spring, 1903. A world before the war, a world he could hardly remember. A world that was certainly dead.

Twenty

The next day Kirsch received a letter from his old commanding officer. He hadn't heard from Gustav Schad in more than twelve years, but the colonel had seen his name in the newspaper and felt encouraged to write.

> *I heard a rumour that you had moved into psychiatric medicine. I'm delighted, though not at all surprised, to see you have made a success of it.*

After years of working at a hospital in Essen, Schad had recently returned to the capital and set up a private practice.

> *I got tired of breathing smoke and decided it was time to sample the famous air that you Berliners are always singing about. I have as yet few acquaintances and would welcome a chance to mull over the bad old days with a comrade.*

Kirsch made a note of the address: it was in Charlottenburg, in the west of the city, a relatively genteel district, populated with rheumatic old ladies and querulous dogs. Though he had always respected Schad, he doubted if he would find time to make the trip. Similar reunions, for all their back-slapping and bonhomie, invariably awoke memories he preferred to leave alone, as far as he could. The knowledge that others felt the same way didn't make them any more enjoyable. Some old comrades he would gladly have seen again, but as far as he knew, they were all dead.

He spent the morning trying to catch up on paperwork. The backlog of unwritten reports and case notes had begun to grow,

and new patients were being admitted every day. Nor had he made a start on Dr Fischer's project, despite the anthropologist's impatience for results. He began work at once, hammering away on his old Adler, typing relentlessly and fast, not pausing to correct mistakes, trying to maintain the noise and motion.

He finished one report, filed it, began another: *Preliminary Assessment of Patient Joseph Grossman*. Grossman was a musician, a violinist in one of the city's symphony orchestras: forty-seven, small and balding. His playing had become increasingly erratic; so much so that he had begun to disrupt rehearsals. It was only then that other peculiarities were noticed: the detached and unstructured nature of his conversation (and, it turned out, his correspondence), his habit of talking to strangers in the street and on the train, the nonsensical music that he had written in his apartment, not only on piles of manuscript paper, but on the walls, the door, the lampshades and the furniture. When his landlady had tried to scrub it off, he had threatened to cut her ears off.

Grossman's behavioural abnormalities were textbook indicators of schizophrenia, and clearly recognisable as such; but what was puzzling to Kirsch was how long it had taken anyone to notice them. In spite of the sociable nature of his work, Grossman seemed virtually friendless, a situation that had only begun to be remedied after he entered the clinic. There his playing had made him quite popular with the other patients, especially Mariya. Even when he played outside, she would come and listen, her gaze fixed on the action of the bow and his nail-bitten fingers as they shuffled crab-like from string to string, slowly turning blue in the cold.

For a moment, Kirsch thought he could hear Grossman playing now, a distant cadence echoing in the yard, but it was only the wind, catching on the side of the building.

He went on typing, got as far as recording the patient's name, then stopped. His fingers were paralysed. His mind would no longer form the appropriate words. It was just a report, a routine statement of preliminary findings, a provisional conclusion. But he couldn't write it. He flipped through his notes, hoping to find some purpose

there, some sense. But it was hopeless. Everything he read, every phrase, every professionally crafted observation, felt like a fraud.

He turned to the notebook he had taken from Mariya's trunk. He stared at the lines of exotic symbols and numbers. There was something poetical about them. All mathematics of this kind was an attempt to bring the world into balance, to reveal the precise equivalence between apparently disparate things – acceleration and gravity, energy and mass; to balance reality on a single fulcrum, represented by the two parallel dashes than made up an equals sign. In theoretical physics the task was delicate and monumental, heroic even: a journey into a world where nothing, no matter how fundamental, was set in stone; where human perceptions and human language were as likely to prove enemies as friends.

But what was the object of Mariya's search? What problem was she trying to solve?

Perhaps there was no problem. For all he knew, he might be looking at gibberish, like the music Joseph Grossman had scrawled all over his lodgings.

Max would have known. For him it would have been perfectly clear, like so much else that his older brother found opaque. But Max was only alive in his dreams.

They had labour gangs out on Unter den Linden, stooped, haggard men recruited from the doss-houses and the soup kitchens, shovelling grit onto the icy pavements for a few Pfennigs an hour. Unlike the labour, the grit was in short supply. The men queued to fill their shovels from small piles deposited at intervals along the road. They stood, backs bent, waiting for well-heeled pedestrians, scattering a little of their loads ahead of them as they scurried alongside, as if they were casting palm fronds before a conquering hero, in hope their deference might earn them a tip.

Kirsch's pockets were empty by the time the sooty columns of the opera house loomed up ahead of him. Slithering on slush, he hurried across the road towards the Academy of Sciences, dodging a procession of taxis. A raw easterly wind tugged at his clothes,

threatening to strip the hat from his head. It would have been easier to stay balanced with his arms outstretched, but his arms were occupied with the notebook he held tight under his coat.

He was at the corner of Franz-Joseph Platz when he heard the urgent rasp of a car horn. He looked up in time to see a green Mercedes lurching around the inside of a truck, bearing down on him at racetrack speed. He leaped for the kerb, lost his footing, went down hard on one knee. The notebook spilled out onto the ground, landing face down. He scrambled to recover it, but the damage was done. Ink had smeared across the pages, the numbers and symbols blurred and streaked. The paper was of low quality. It soaked up water like a rag, clumping together into a pulpy mass. The Mercedes blasted past, showering him with slush. He cursed out loud, spun round in time to see the driver's head framed in the open window of his car. It was a man, at least fifty, with a drooping moustache and sad, bloodhound eyes. His face wore a sheepish expression, as if he knew an apology was called for, but was in too much of a hurry to give it. The Mercedes braked, took a hard right into the square and disappeared, leaving a trail of smoke.

The porter at the Academy of Sciences looked Kirsch up and down, taking in the muddy trousers and the water that still dripped from his raincoat. 'What did you say your name was?'

'Dr Martin Kirsch of the Charité Psychiatric Clinic.'

The porter sighed and disappeared into his office, leaving Kirsch alone in the lobby. A grand marble staircase led up to the first floor, where another porter – a burly man with a shiny bald head – stood looking down at him. From the corridor came the sound of a lecture in progress. The lecturer said something humorous. Polite laughter briefly filled the space.

What if the lecturer were Albert Einstein? It had to be a possibility. It was at the academy that many of his most important papers had been presented. The thought that he might be there in the building, might any moment come walking down the stairs, set Kirsch's heart beating faster.

'Dr Kirsch?'

A man wearing pince-nez and a wing collar stood before him. His name turned out to be Klepper and he held an administrative position at the academy.

Kirsch produced the notebook. He explained that it appeared to contain calculations attempted by one of his patients. 'No one at the clinic is qualified to judge whether they're sound. The mathematics is too complex. But one of your distinguished members would know at once.'

Klepper glanced at the notebook, at the wrinkled pages and blurred ink. 'I'm not sure I follow. This is a mental patient you're talking about?'

'Yes.'

'And this patient is a mathematician?'

'A student of mathematics. Or perhaps of physics.'

'So you want . . .' Klepper frowned. He could not have been more than thirty, but everything in his dress and manner said he yearned for the *gravitas* of middle age. 'You want *tuition* for him?'

'I want to know if these calculations show evidence of a disturbed mind. I want to know if they make mathematical sense.'

'If your patient is a student, surely you should consult his teachers.'

'I'm afraid that's impossible.'

Herr Klepper shrugged. 'Be that as it may, Dr . . .'

Kirsch felt a cold draft at his back. Someone was coming in through the front door. 'My name is Kirsch.'

'Our members are not in the habit of providing free consultations to . . .' Klepper's gaze came to rest on his muddy shoes '. . . anyone.'

'It would only take a few minutes. To a physicist –'

'Out of the question, I'm afraid. These are extremely busy men. As I'm sure you can appreciate, their time is valuable.' Klepper gestured vaguely towards the street. 'You might try the university.'

Kirsch turned and found himself looking at a middle-aged man with a high forehead and a white moustache.

'Good morning, Professor,' Herr Klepper said. 'Can I be of assistance?'

The professor gave Kirsch a regretful look, and it was then that

he remembered the speeding Mercedes that had nearly run him over, and the driver's face framed in the window.

The professor pulled off a pair of heavy leather gloves and offered his hand. 'Max von Laue. You were looking for a physicist, you said?'

Von Laue. He had won the Nobel Prize just before the war for his work on X-rays. He had written a book on general relativity.

Kirsch introduced himself and explained the purpose of his visit. The professor nodded gravely and accepted the notebook, turning over a couple of damp pages. But the light was poor in the lobby and the way he squinted, it was obvious he could make out very little.

'Perhaps you could leave this with me,' he said. 'I promise to take good care of it.'

Upstairs, the lecture had drawn to a close. Applause briefly interrupted the atmosphere of reverential calm. This was Max's world, a world of ideas, of pure thought; the world he was born for, but had never lived to share.

Kirsch handed over his card and left, casting a final glance up the marble staircase.

In the staff common room the talk was all of General Schleicher and his elevation from Minister of War to Reich Chancellor. Most were of the opinion that it was only a matter of time before martial law was declared, as there was little chance of his being able to assemble a workable majority in the Reichstag. Others thought a coalition with the more pragmatic wing of the Nazi party would be cobbled together, leaving Adolf Hitler out in the cold. Economic conditions were showing signs of improvement, and popular support for the nationalists was already waning. The Nazis might never get their hands on power again.

Kirsch went back to his office and continued with the backlog of paperwork, but after a few hours his eyes were aching and he couldn't write anything more. His arm felt cold and heavy, as if the flesh were slowly petrifying. He hadn't examined it in days. He went out to the landing and lit a cigarette. Across the grounds, the snow and

slush were blue in the twilight. On the far side of the canal what looked like a pile of refuse was burning, the fitful yellow light colouring the misty air.

There were prints in the snow outside, animal as well as human. Stray dogs came sniffing around at night, especially when it was cold, drawn by the smell from the kitchens. More than once they had knocked over the dustbins, strewing peelings and offal across the yard. Kirsch traced their looping paths until the light was gone.

He left the clinic at around eight. Outside, the air was damp and raw. The slush on the pavements was turning to ice. It crunched underfoot, like broken glass. He hunched his shoulders, burying his chin beneath the lapels of his coat.

A car was turning around outside the main hospital. Kirsch saw his shadow drift across the brick walls. He squinted into the headlights as the car edged along the kerb beside him.

'Dr Kirsch?'

The rear passenger door swung open. Billowing exhaust fumes masked the interior. Then he saw the bearded face, the weathered sea-dog complexion, the angular frame canted forward.

'Dr Fischer?'

'What luck! Get in, get in. Bucher and I are entirely at your disposal.' Fischer's driver got out and held open the door. 'Be quick now. It's getting cold.'

Kirsch climbed in. 'I'm afraid I wasn't expecting you, Dr Fischer. Did we arrange . . . ?'

'I just got in from Munich. Thought I'd stop by on the off-chance. I called from the station, but no one seemed to know where you were.'

They turned right onto the main road, heading east. Either side of them the apartment buildings stood tall and black against the lowering city sky. For the conditions, Bucher drove fast.

'Did you receive the cheque?' Fischer asked.

'Yes I did, thank you.'

'The sum is adequate, I hope, to make a start on the matter we discussed.'

'More than adequate. I've started drawing up a list of institutions and practitioners to approach.'

It was all he could think of to say, having, in fact, done nothing.

'But I thought I sent you that.'

'Your list was useful as a starting point. But I thought I should enquire as widely as possible.'

Fischer reached into his pocket and took out his cigarette case. 'I've a pretty good idea who's likely to cooperate with your research and who isn't.' He offered Kirsch a cigarette. 'Stick to my list. You'll find it saves you a lot of time.'

Kirsch declined the cigarette, wondering how it was that Fischer was so well acquainted with the rank and file of Germany's psychiatrists, and by what criteria his list had been drawn up.

Fischer lit up, one hand cupped around the flame. 'Not that I'm trying to rush you. Far from it. You must take all the time you need.'

They caught up with a tram on the north side of Luisenplatz, bars of yellow light rolling past, the dark outline of heads and faces staring through the misty glass. To Kirsch it felt as if he *was* being rushed. But perhaps that was simply Fischer's way of doing things.

Fischer pushed back in the seat, plucking a strand of tobacco from his tongue. 'So how's your special patient? Have you made any progress?'

'A little,' Kirsch said.

Fischer turned towards him, exhaling forcefully. 'And?'

Bucher was watching him too, in the driver's mirror. By the light of oncoming headlamps Kirsch could see his eyes.

He shrugged. 'She's a student, visiting from Zürich.'

'She told you this?'

'No. Her landlord came forward. He saw her picture in the papers. Her name's Draganović. Mariya Draganović. I decided it was best not to make any announcements.'

'Very wise.' The leather squeaked as Fischer gently braced himself against the seat of the cab. 'But she still remembers nothing? Her amnesia is not improved?'

'No.'

Fischer turned back to the window, hardly seeming to notice the ambulance that came screaming past them on its way to the hospital. He dragged on his cigarette and smiled. 'So is my theory entirely exploded in your view?'

'I see no reason to believe this is a scam, if that's what you mean. I can't see how anyone stands to gain.'

Fischer laughed. 'Someone *always* stands to gain, Herr Doctor. Perhaps you might stand to gain, if the whole matter were dealt with in the right way. If the press don't turn it into a circus.'

They were on a wider, busier thoroughfare now, one that followed the course of a defunct city boundary. Bucher accelerated again, pulling clear of the tram, riding over a set of points with a jolt.

'It is an interesting case,' Kirsch said, not sure if that was what Fischer meant.

'Most interesting. It could be the making of you.'

He saw Mariya sitting in the window, frowning as she worked at her sketch-book. If he closed his eyes, he could recall the scent of her pillow.

'Of course,' he said, 'that depends on whether she remains my patient. I'm afraid as things stand that looks unlikely.'

'Unlikely? Why?'

Kirsch decided to tell the truth. He couldn't hide it much longer in any case. 'Because Dr Bonhoeffer is expecting my letter of resignation.'

He told Fischer about his dispute with Dr Mehring, about the insulin coma therapy and the injury to Nurse Ritter. He said little about Sergeant Stoehr, how his suffering had affected him, reawakening memories of the war. He was afraid Fischer would think him sentimental.

Fischer listened in silence. He was too old to have served in the war. He would have been safely ensconced at some university, able to regret the suffering at the front, perhaps even to imagine it; but free from the numbing shock and the visions that never faded.

'So you see,' Kirsch concluded, as they waited at a junction, 'my days at the Charité are numbered. And if I leave the Charité, I must give up the case.'

On the corner a group of policemen were descending from the back of a truck. Two of them were carrying rifles. Fischer's fingers caressed the line of his jaw.

'Dr Mehring's a Jew, isn't he?' he said.

'I don't know.'

'Heinrich Mehring? I think you'll find he is. Your profession is full of Jews. Ever since Dr Freud.'

'Dr Mehring is no Freudian, that I can say.'

'Not that I have any objection, you understand. Many Israelites have excellent analytical brains, though there's an unhealthy preference for the abstract.' As they moved off again one of the policemen slipped on the ice. The others laughed. 'On the other hand, there are many that have a less internationalist outlook. And I fear it may be unwise to provoke them.'

'I'm not sure I follow,' Kirsch said.

Fischer pulled down his window and flipped out his cigarette butt. 'It doesn't matter.' He leaned across and patted Kirsch on the forearm. 'A man with your gifts cannot be discarded in such a manner. I will use my influence, which is not inconsiderable.'

'I'm supposed to be gone by Christmas. It was all agreed.'

Fischer tut-tutted. 'Don't be too hasty. Let me see what I can do. It may all blow over yet.'

They passed beneath the massive stone spire of the Zionskirche. Lights burned behind the stained glass, but the great doors were shut. A few minutes later they were turning into the Schönhauser Allee.

Kirsch climbed out of the car without waiting for Bucher to open the door for him. Fischer looked up at Frau Schirmann's doubtfully, tapping another cigarette against the case. Kirsch thanked him for the lift.

'My pleasure,' Fischer said. 'I'm looking forward to seeing your work. Very much. Trust me, it's more important than you think.'

He lit the cigarette and extinguished the match with three emphatic flicks of the wrist.

Twenty-one

On a Sunday, a few years earlier, when he had been leaving the house at Reinsdorf, Kirsch had taken his overcoat down from its peg in the hall, only to find, when it was too late, that it was not his coat at all. Max had owned an almost identical one – dark grey and double-breasted with black felt around the collar – except, as Kirsch discovered as he wrestled with it on the railway station platform, his brother's was several sizes smaller. Since then it had been hanging in his apartment in Berlin, untouched and unworn. Kirsch had no use for it himself, but neither had he ever taken it back to Reinsdorf. He had made a mental note to do so many times, but in the event he had always forgotten, or the occasion had not felt right. In truth, it was not how he wanted any visit to begin, with a reminder of Max. Nor did he relish the idea of explaining how he came to be in possession of the coat, or why he had not brought it back sooner. For that would raise, at least implicitly, another question: why so many of Max's things were still in the house, things that no one would ever use again. That was a subject nobody wanted to acknowledge, let alone discuss, as if the fact of Max's death was not simply an impersonal mischance of war, but some dark and shameful secret, a crime in which they were all implicated.

The coat gave off a musty camphor smell, tinged with an aroma that reminded Kirsch of the travelling sweets their father used to given them when they were children. As far as he could tell, it had not been cleaned since the last time Max wore it. But even that was not something Kirsch felt able to remedy. What if the coat were damaged at the laundry? What if the black dye on the collar ran, or a button went missing? He did not want to be responsible for that. And in all that detergent and water, wouldn't something of Max be washed away too?

So the coat had hung on a hanger behind the door, doing no one any good, keeping out no wind or rain; serving only to remind Kirsch of his thoughtlessness in having taken it from its rightful place and his absolute inability to make amends.

Now at last, on a Friday at the beginning of December, Kirsch took down Max's overcoat, brushed it off carefully and draped it over his arm for the journey to work.

He found Mariya in her room. 'Here,' he said, holding the coat by the shoulders. 'It's cold outside.'

Mariya was sketching one of the other patients. They sat for her willingly now, although not always for long before wandering off. That morning it was Frau Becker's turn. A widow in her fifties, she had been a beauty in her heyday, though the scarlet lipstick she preferred was no longer flattering. She sat on a stool, her hands between her knees, patiently watching the artist at work, betraying no sign of the disordered mind that had caused her to walk naked into the street one morning, claiming that she was late for church.

Mariya looked up from her sketch-book. 'Where are we going?'

'Out.' Kirsch continued to hold open the coat. A smell of old mothballs mingled with the prevailing disinfectant fug.

'I have to stay here,' she said, 'until I'm finished.'

'I just want you to try on the coat. We can go later.'

'I have to stay *here*.' She jabbed her pencil towards the floor. 'If I move, it changes. And I have to start again.'

It was the drawing she was talking about. Or was she displeased with him for some reason?

'It'll only take a second.'

She stared at her subject and went on drawing. Perhaps she was afraid of losing her perspective, the fall of the light, the angle, or her sense of them. Perhaps her amnesia made such transient things more precious, the need to hang on to them greater.

He watched her for a moment then rested the coat down on her bed, pausing to smooth out the creases. 'I'll come for you at three,' he said.

* * *

When he returned, he found her sitting on her bed, wearing the coat. She got up when she saw him, standing in the middle of the room, her hands by her sides. Kirsch shuddered. It was as if Max were looking at him through the girl's eyes, a faint trace of him suddenly catching the light, like an image locked inside a prism. But the fit was not as good as he had imagined. Even as a youth, Max had been taller and broader at the shoulders than Mariya. The coat looked borrowed, like her heavy ankle-length boots and her shapeless woollen dress.

Outside, they hailed a taxi and headed across the river towards the centre of the city. Sunlight pierced the clouds, reflecting off wet roofs and cobbles, so that Kirsch had to shelter his eyes. They crossed Unter den Linden and nudged their way down Wilhelmstrasse, passing beneath the stately masses of banks and government buildings. Mariya sat in silence, staring at the pedestrians. Sometimes, when she spotted someone of particular interest, she would kneel on the seat so that she could continue to watch them out of the back window. Then, as soon as they had disappeared, she would spin round again and fix on someone new, as if every face were a painting in a gallery, unique and interesting. As they stopped to let a tram go by on Leipziger Strasse, a beggar rapped on the window, rattling his tin cup. His face was covered with burn scars, and where his left eye had been there was nothing but a sunken red slit. She looked at him without flinching, her hands pressed against the glass.

They got out at the Anhalt station. It was there that travellers from Zürich arrived in Berlin. It was the middle of the afternoon, but already the pavements were busy with office workers and civil servants making their way home. While Kirsch paid the driver, Mariya looked up at the building, its lofty portico and vast brick arches. Kirsch saw her swallow. He should have made greater efforts to dress her. For one thing she needed a scarf. The way her bare throat emerged from the heavy fabric of the overcoat looked simply wrong.

'Is this where you're going to leave me?' she said.

'Now why would you think that?'

She dug her hands into her pockets. 'You aren't sending me away?'

He turned up her lapels, covering the V of pale flesh beneath her throat. 'How can I send you anywhere when I don't know where you're from?'

Her hair had grown just enough that he had to lift it free of the collar. As it brushed against the back of his hand he caught a familiar trace of her scent, masked but not obliterated by the chemical cocktail of camphor and bleach, like a flower blossoming in a field of rubble.

Two women were watching from the steps above. One of them held a dachshund under her arm. The dachshund yapped at him, baring yellow fangs. No doubt they suspected some impropriety. Mariya was certainly not dressed as a lady, and if she was not a lady what was she?

Kirsch turned back to the taxi. 'I've changed my mind. Take us to Karstadt's.'

The Karstadt department store was the biggest building in Berlin, a vast fortress of cement and stone, with squat square towers at the southern corners rising twenty-five floors into the air. With its rigid adherence to perpendicular forms (there was not a curve or a diagonal anywhere), it reminded Kirsch of a power station, but Alma swore that for everyday clothes and household items generally, it could not be bettered. 'One wouldn't go there for evening wear,' she said, 'but one can waste so much time in little shops just looking for a pair of gloves.' Twice the previous summer she had dragged him up to the roof garden, where a string orchestra serenaded the clientele as they stuffed themselves with coffee and cake. On the first occasion she had bought him a tie which, at her suggestion, he wore to visit her family in Oranienburg. On the second occasion she had bought him a set of nail scissors in a leather case.

Mariya seemed unfamiliar with escalators. On the first ride her legs wobbled and she held on to the handrail with both hands, stealing glances at the glimmering spaces overhead. Kirsch found it hard not to laugh at the alarm on her face as the steps above her vanished one

by one beneath the steel teeth of the comb-plate. Finally she let go of the handrail altogether, extended her arms like a tightrope walker and leaped across the threshold, clearing it by a good four feet.

'We can take the stairs if you like,' Kirsch said.

'No.' She squared her shoulders. 'I want to try again. How do you go down?'

But there was no need to go down, because the ladieswear department was still a floor above them. On the second escalator, Mariya managed to hold on with only one hand, though now and again, as the staircase shuddered, she would reach for Kirsch's arm to steady herself. Thus occupied, she did not notice the looks people gave her, the backward glances and frowns. Kirsch was not sure what so disconcerted them – the absence of headgear or coiffure, her labourer's boots, the lack of make-up on her face, or simply the fact that she was more beautiful than she had a right to be. As they rose floor by floor through the great emporium, Kirsch found he enjoyed their discomfiture.

He picked out a suit in brown worsted. Alma wore a lot of suits these days, even, on one occasion, a suit with trousers, like Marlene Dietrich. But Mariya was not impressed. She picked out a blue patterned house dress with puffed sleeves and a pin-tucked skirt. She held it up against herself, turning this way and that as she looked at her reflection in the mirror.

'Try it on,' Kirsch said.

It was like the dresses in her wardrobe at Herr Mettler's, only brighter, newer.

'Why? I can't buy without money.'

'Try it anyway. Doctor's orders.'

He took her to the changing area and waited outside, listening to the rustle of fabric and the gentle pop of fasteners that came from behind the curtains. He heard voices, a scandalised chuckle: two women were in the next cubicle together. More women walked past him, various items of clothing draped over their arms. It came to him that he was probably the only man on the floor.

She came out from behind the curtain barefoot. After her usual

inmate-garb, the dress looked pretty and feminine. She spun round for him so that the skirt flared outward, revealing faint blue bruises on the backs of her calves. She had lost weight since they danced, he could see that now. Her waist was as slender as a girl of thirteen's.

'You need stockings,' he said, and he called over one of the assistants.

Two pairs of silk stockings, a suspender belt, the dress, a pair of black Oxford pumps, they spent almost an hour acquiring the outfit. Then they went up a floor and tried on some hats: a cream-coloured fedora with a brown ribbon, a black cone hat folded over at the top in what the assistants called 'the Swiss style', a moulded felt hat that reminded Kirsch of the helmet worn by Mercury the winged messenger, thanks to the shiny black feathers fixed to the sides. One after the other he placed them on Mariya's head as she stood before the mirror, wrinkling her nose. Choosing was difficult. Each hat seemed to cast her in a different light: the fedora as worldly and rakish, the cone as playful, the moulded hat as poised and delicate, like a dancer. Her innocence lent intensity to every look, lustre to every nuance.

'You choose,' he said.

'Is this a test? Is this part of my treatment?'

He still had not told her where they were going and she had apparently decided against asking.

'It's not a test. But you have to wear something. You don't want to look like a convict.'

She pulled off the fedora and handed it to him. 'I can't chose. They all look so pretty.'

'They're the latest lines.'

She turned back to the mirror and without any show of embarrassment, hitched up her skirt, straightening the hem of her stocking. Kirsch caught the reflection of two shop assistants whispering to each other behind the counter.

'These stockings are special too,' she said.

'They're silk.'

'I've never worn silk before.'

'Perhaps you couldn't afford it.'

She let her skirt down again, brushing off some lint that had caught in the fabric. 'My father wasn't poor. He had a government job and wore a uniform on feast days.'

Were these clear memories, Kirsch wondered, or another dream?

'And where is he now, your father?'

'Dead.' She walked over to another stand, where more hats were on display, fingering the rims in a perfunctory way. 'All my family are dead.' She picked out a black felt Derby. 'How about this one? Does this suit me?'

'For a day at the races perhaps. What makes you think all your family are dead?'

She pulled the Derby down low on her forehead, so that her eyes were lost in shadow.

'I was outside yesterday, in the grounds. There's a bench I like to sit on.'

'I know. I've seen you there.'

'Oh, you have.' She brought a hand to her cheek.

'And?'

'I remembered finding my father's grave. The snow and the fresh earth. That wet earth smell. I think he was buried in that uniform.'

'That's all you remember?'

'I remember how I felt.'

'And how was that? Sad, I suppose.'

'No. I remember the feeling very clearly.' She took off the Derby and replaced it with a blue straw cloche, the brim turned up at the forehead in a style Alma had said was *passé*. 'I felt free.'

After Karstadt's they travelled on crowded trams to Alexanderplatz, then set out on foot along Kirsch's usual route: past the stalls on Grenadierstrasse, though they were fewer in number than usual; past Herr Bronstein's boarded-up music shop, past the pumping station and the synagogue on Rykestrasse, where a lone policeman steadily eyed the procession of worshippers making their way inside.

If Mariya recognised the surroundings, she did not say so. She did not say anything. She walked ahead steadily, neither looking around nor stopping to take her bearings. Now and again, as they reached a street corner, Kirsch would hold back, watching to see if she became confused or disorientated; but each time she carried on, giving him not so much as a backward glance.

Outside the cemetery she stopped. The gates stood open. In the half-darkness Kirsch could see a handful of figures moving around; caretakers perhaps, clearing away dead flowers or digging new graves. The light of their cigarettes floated in the gloom.

'I came this way before,' she said, her breath making a plume in the cold air.

Herr Mettler took a long time to answer the door. Even then he seemed reluctant to open it more than a few inches.

'What do you want? I thought . . .' He caught sight of Mariya waiting on the pavement. His voice fell to a whisper. 'What's *she* doing here?'

'I want you to show me that room again. Number three.'

A wireless was on inside: rasping voices and crackles of applause. Herr Mettler stepped back from the door. Kirsch took Mariya by the arm and led her into the hallway. She was slightly out of breath.

'If you give us the key, we'll find our own way,' Kirsch said.

Herr Mettler grunted and went back into his apartment. There came the sound of a brief consultation, then he reappeared, beckoning Kirsch over.

'I've a party interested in taking that room,' he said, breathing on his spectacles and polishing the lenses against his sleeve. 'So if she wants her things, you'll have to take them now.'

They were standing in a narrow parlour. Keys hung from hooks. Old shoes were lined up along the wall. A smell of boiled potatoes drifted in from the kitchen.

Kirsch reached into his jacket. 'Suppose I pay her rent for another week?'

Herr Mettler shook his head. His prospective tenant was a good

one, he said, the kind that settled in for the long term – an aristo-crat, in fact: the kind of tenant you did not want to lose. The more he explained, the more certain Kirsch became that he was lying.

'Suppose I pay two weeks then, just to be going on with? I think it might be good for Mariya to move back here, away from the clinic.'

'Here? You mean, permanently?'

'For a few months at least.'

'No, no, that's impossible.'

'Why? She wasn't any trouble. You said so.'

'That was before.' Mettler glanced back towards the kitchen. 'No one wants her kind in the place.'

'I don't know what you mean.'

'People don't feel safe.' Herr Mettler screwed a finger against his temple. 'Never know what they might do, do you? What are asylums for?'

Kirsch opened his wallet. 'Thirty days, cash in advance. I can leave a deposit now.'

Herr Mettler looked past him into the hallway. 'Where's she wandered off to?'

Kirsch turned. Mariya was gone. So was the key to Room 3. 'She must have . . .' He went to the foot of the stairs. 'Mariya?'

In the street outside, a bottle burst against the cobblestones. A dog started barking. Herr Mettler hurried to the front door and threw the bolts. Kirsch set off up the stairs.

Rapid footsteps echoed in the alley.

'Mariya?'

Nobody answered. He hadn't wanted her to go up alone. He'd wanted to takes things one step at a time. A sudden rush of recol-lection might have unforeseen consequences. It might be dangerous.

What about suicide? Have you considered that possibility? Maybe she threw herself off a bridge.

A light went on in one of the first-floor rooms. Kirsch hurried up to the second floor. Just as he arrived outside Room 3, the door clicked shut.

She wanted to be alone. It was her room, after all, or had been. Her things were still in there: clothes, books, the photograph album. He knocked gently.

There was a cold draft at his ankles. He knocked again.

'Mariya?' He listened: nothing. He tried the door handle. It was not locked.

Inside the lights were still off. A bar of yellow from a nearby street light was stretched across the ceiling. It was surprisingly cold.

He flicked on the light switch. The bulb had gone. He squinted into the darkness, took a few steps forward. Mariya was not there.

Noiselessly the window swung open. The curtains billowed. The faraway roar of the city grew louder.

He ran to the window, flung it open, looked out over the little iron balcony. The gas lamps down below were unusually bright. Kirsch had to shield his eyes. But there was no body lying shattered on the pavement, no crowd of onlookers gathered round. A man was lighting a cigarette. He looked up at Kirsch as he tossed away the match.

'What's the matter?'

Mariya was standing beside him.

'What are you doing out here?'

She hunched her shoulders. 'I saw you down there. Is that possible? I thought I remembered seeing you.'

He put his arms around her and held her close. She seemed impossibly light. He picked her up, carried her inside and set her down on the floor.

'I thought I'd lost you.'

Her arms were still around his neck, her face hidden in the folds of his coat. He felt himself moving closer again, a brief weightlessness like the moment before a fall.

She kept her eyes firmly shut while he kissed her, as if making a wish. Then she framed his face in her hands and kissed him back, her eyes flickering shut again as their bodies slowly relaxed. They stayed that way for a long time, standing in the cold darkness, the bare boards beneath their feet creaking. Kirsch did not

think to ask her what else she remembered. For once, it did not seem important.

It came to him that this love was not, after all, a dream or an indulgence or a flight of madness. It was a gift, a rescue.

He shivered. The room had a small fireplace, the fuel already laid, but it would take a long time to heat up the room.

'I'm starving,' Mariya said. 'Can we eat something? I didn't have any lunch.'

'No lunch? Why not?'

'I was nervous. Couldn't you tell?'

'As a matter of fact, no.'

What kind of a psychiatrist am I? Kirsch thought. And the answer came back: *one who has affairs with his patients.*

'I know a place,' he said.

Twenty-two

He winced when Alma threw her arms around him. The cold weather had inflamed the wound in his arm. Beneath his coat, the flesh was bloated and angry.

'What is it? What's the matter?'

'Nothing. I fell. Ice.'

It was Sunday morning. Shafts of blinding sunlight pierced the railway station canopy, dappling the cavernous interior.

'You're lying.'

Kirsch rubbed the spot. 'What makes you say that?'

'I know what happened,' Alma said. 'One of them attacked you, didn't they? Daddy was telling me about it: how people who work in asylums are always being attacked.'

'That's nonsense. Anyway, it's a clinic, not an asylum.'

The train driver blew his whistle. Kirsch opened the carriage door, lending Alma his good arm.

'Even worse,' she said. 'At least asylums have guards. If something happened to you, I don't know what I'd do.'

Her scolding was good-humoured, but the underlying purpose was serious, just as it was familiar: Alma wanted her future husband to leave the clinic and find work in a more wholesome branch of medicine, one less steeped in misery and degradation. Psychiatry was fine at the theoretical level. But the mentally ill themselves were tainted, and that taint rubbed off on anyone who lived among them.

It came to Kirsch that this would have been the perfect moment to tell her about his likely departure from the Charité and his new research for Dr Fischer. But there was no point any more. He had resolved to tell her that the engagement was off. Now that he was

no longer deceiving himself, he could not go on deceiving her. He had only to work out what to say, and when to say it.

He had suggested they spend the day at Potsdam, by the lake. He told her he wanted to get out of the city for a while. She had agreed gladly, although it was not until they were on the train that Kirsch found out why: they would be able to stop off at Zehlendorf and visit the villa she planned to make their home.

'It'd be good to get the feel of the neighbourhood,' she said. 'They say it'll soon be the most desirable in Berlin. A lot of famous people live there. We'll hold parties, and there'll be photographs in the press.'

'Only if we invite the press,' Kirsch said. 'Which we won't.'

Alma extracted a pin from her hat. Her blonde hair had a freshly curled bounce to it and smelled faintly of alcohol.

'You sound like Daddy.'

'I do?'

'You know how he feels about the newspapers.' She shrugged. 'He's very . . .'

'Reactionary?'

'Old-fashioned.'

'That's letting him off lightly.'

She sighed and squeezed his arm as the train dived beneath the S-Bahn. Grey steam funnelled past the windows. 'He just wants things to be how they used to be. You can understand that, can't you? For his generation change always means losing something they care about.'

Kirsch thought of his mother, still crying alone in Max's room; of his sister, Emilie, listening from her little box room down below.

'It's too late,' he said. They were crossing a freight yard. The spires and chimneys of the city were shrinking into the distance, stark against a fold of cloud. 'Things can never be how they used to be. Time may not be linear, but it isn't circular either.'

Alma wrinkled her nose and nestled against him, her head heavy against his shoulder. 'Well, it doesn't matter. We'll go and live in Zehlendorf and do as we please.'

She straightened up as the conductor appeared. A few minutes later they were rolling through a tangled landscape of fences and muddy plots still harbouring ice and snow in their furrows. Alma talked about the wedding preparations. The important issues had already been decided, but there were endless smaller details to mull over: the bridal bouquets, the bridesmaids' dresses, the order of service, the musical entertainment, as well as the seating plan for dinner, which was reorganised almost daily, even though the invitations would not be going out for months.

'Do you think your sister Emilie could be persuaded to be a flower girl?' Alma's hands were cupped around his. 'I know she'd be a lot older than the others, but it would be so nice to include her in the ceremony, don't you think?'

'A flower girl?' The idea seemed faintly preposterous.

'Of course, we'd make the dress for her,' Alma added.

Kirsch wondered if this was really the point, to make sure Emilie did not let the side down with one of her dowdy school-room outfits. 'The thing is, she's rather shy. I'm not sure she'd want the attention.'

'But she's a teacher. And she plays the piano, doesn't she? She played the very first time I was there – rather passionately, I thought.'

Kirsch remembered the occasion, the trance-like state that his sister seemed to enter, the way her body swayed, much like patients he had known at the clinic in various stages of disconnection from the world.

'That's different. When she plays, I don't think she's really . . . there.'

'What do you mean?'

'In her mind.' He looked at Alma. Two tiny vertical creases had appeared between her eyebrows. 'I suppose I could ask her if you like.'

The train rocked them so that their bodies gently collided. Alma was sitting close to him, her thigh in contact with his, an unusual occurrence in a public place.

'It doesn't matter,' she said, 'if she's shy as you say. As a matter

of fact, I sometimes got the impression when she was quiet like that, it was because she didn't like me.'

There was so much noise at the lakeside restaurant that it was impossible to talk without shouting. Most establishments around Potsdam had closed for the winter, but the good weather had tempted a late influx of day-trippers from the city, and every table was taken. Some chubby-faced boys were playing outside while their parents finished their meal. Unsupervised, they were soon punching and kicking each other, the smallest of them screaming unheeded.

Again and again Kirsch's gaze drifted towards the lake. In the distance a sailing boat was tacking into an easterly wind.

'It's so bright out here. I should get some sunglasses.'

'Your head's been buried in books too long,' Alma said. 'Your eyes aren't used to the sky.'

Kirsch watched as the boat came about, the white sails filling, the stern carving a foamy arc through the water. A few years earlier, Albert Einstein had told a newspaper about his new love of sailing. It had been different in his youth, he said. Then he had preferred trekking in the mountains. He had done some of his best thinking in the high passes of the Alps, on long walks with friends. But recently he had grown tired of the uplands. Mountains impeded his view. Instead, he had grown to love the Earth's desolate places, the sea and the prairie, anywhere vast and unending to the gaze. At first, Kirsch had been puzzled by these reports. The majesty of nature, it seemed to him, was nowhere more visible than in the mountains, among the glaciers and the soaring peaks. Countless artists and poets had found their inspiration there. But the more he read of Einstein's work, the better he understood: to escape a thousand years of received ideas required boldness and independence of mind. It was not majesty the physicist needed, nor inspiration, but emptiness, *distance* – a place to think what, for the mass of humankind, was unthinkable. On the water Einstein came closest to the perfect objectivity he craved. Was it possible Mariya had travelled out here in search of the same searing clarity? Perhaps that

was why she had come to Berlin: to break old ties and devote herself instead to knowledge and truth. Kirsch found himself wishing that were not the case. For if Mariya saw everything clearly, then she would see him clearly too.

'I was only concerned that you might want a rest.'

Alma was talking about their honeymoon.

'A rest?'

'Instead of traipsing round basilicas all day. Still, we needn't do that. We can lie around on the Lido and stuff ourselves.' She pushed a hand across the table so that their fingers intertwined. 'You do look on edge these days. You're working too hard, everyone says so.'

'Who's everyone?'

Alma looked at her plate, pushed at some vegetables with her fork. 'I talked to Robert the other day.'

'Ah, Dr Eisner.'

'Don't be like that.'

'Like what?'

'I don't know why you're so mean about Robert. He's done nothing to you.'

'What did I say?'

Alma shook her head. This was apparently something that had been on her mind for some time. 'I know he plays the fool sometimes, but he's really a very good sort. I've known him for years. And have you forgotten he's the reason we met?'

Kirsch did not reply. He was thinking back to Friday evening: he had returned Mariya to her room at the clinic and found Eisner hanging around in the corridor. It was unusual for him to stay later than he had to. 'Looks like you're making progress,' he had said with the trace of a smirk on his face. Kirsch had not stopped to talk. He had gone straight to the washrooms and checked in the mirror for smudges of lipstick, before remembering that Mariya did not wear any.

'What did he say exactly?'

Alma sighed. 'He said you've been taking on too many difficult cases. Beating your brains out. He's concerned about you.' Alma

took a sip of iced water. 'That girl, for instance, the one in the papers. You've been spending an awful lot of time on her.'

Kirsch picked up his fork and dabbed at his food. 'Of course. I can't have the press saying the *eminent* Dr Kirsch isn't up to scratch.'

'Suddenly you care what the press say? I know you better than that, darling.'

Alma put down her glass. The ice clinked against the lip.

'It's a difficult case,' Kirsch said. 'But I think I'm making progress.'

At a table across the room laughter erupted. *Tell her now*, he thought.

'Alma –'

'The Einstein girl. Why do they call her that? Is it a joke?'

'A joke?'

'Because she's very stupid or something.'

'She's not stupid. It's because they found her –'

'What do *you* call her, by the way?'

Kirsch reached for his glass. 'Does it matter?'

'Is it a secret?'

'We made up a name, to be going on with.'

'What name?'

He didn't want to say it. As if Alma was taking something that he didn't want to give her. But then, she only had to ask Robert Eisner.

'Mariya. She chose it. We don't know what her real name is.'

Alma was silent for a moment. Then she gave her fiancé a conciliatory smile and reached across the table. 'I think it's wonderful, the way you treat your patients, putting your heart and soul into it.' She put her head on one side, a finger tracing the tendons of his right hand. 'Only you must be careful not to go *too* far. There are limits to what they can expect from you. You mustn't sacrifice yourself. It wouldn't be fair.'

Kirsch glanced at the sailing boat again. It had turned south towards Caputh, a brilliant white splinter in the distance. He pictured Mariya on board, the sunlight on her face, sailing towards some horizon that would forever be beyond him.

'Don't worry,' he said. 'I'm not the self-sacrificing type.'

* * *

After lunch the weather closed in. They were caught in a shower running back to the station. The train to Berlin was crowded, the day-trippers evacuating all at once, their dripping waterproofs and umbrellas making puddles on the floor. Kirsch gave his seat to an elderly woman and stood out in the corridor, watching the glimmering waters of the Havel vanish among the trees. It was not until they were clear of the terminus that he and Alma spoke again.

'Have you time for a coffee?' he said.

It was still too early for the dance halls to open, at least the more respectable ones that Alma was used to. But she was insistent: she wanted music and something to warm her up.

'Take me to your favourite *dive*,' she said.

'I don't have a favourite. Some are just more convenient than others.'

'Then take me to your most convenient one.'

'All right,' he said.

By day the Café Tanguero looked especially tatty: the way the pictures on the walls had faded to brown, the dust that clouded the glass, the paintwork peeling and nicotine stained. Business was slow: a couple smoking in the corner and an old man on his own, reading a newspaper. There was no music and no one was dancing. At this hour only the prostitutes were interested.

They sat down at a table, Kirsch with his back to the dance floor. Alma ordered lemonade and a shot of kümmel. Kirsch stuck with beer.

'You wanted a dive,' he said.

Alma looked flushed, tiny beads of sweat glistening beneath her hairline and in the hollow of her neck. 'It isn't quite what I expected, I must say.'

'What did you expect?'

She shrugged. 'I don't know: something more . . . I just don't see you fitting in here, Martin. It's so dirty.' She looked up at the cracked and yellowed ceiling. 'It all looks like it needs a jolly good scrub.'

Kirsch shrugged. He had always felt more comfortable in this

dirty, ruined place than in the tidy world she inhabited. But how could he expect her to understand that?

'We should have gone to a café,' he said, 'a proper one.'

'Never mind.' Alma took a mouthful of kümmel. It was the first time Kirsch had seen her drink spirits. She grimaced as it went down. 'At least now I know where you go when I'm not around.'

Customers were trickling in. Electric lights came on above the narrow stage at the back of the dance floor. The pianist struck up with an awkward rendition of 'The Prettiest Legs in Berlin'. A couple of working girls came through the door. Carmen was one of them. She had one of her regular clients in tow, the visit post-coital to judge from the blank, sated expression on his face.

Alma ordered another kümmel and downed it. 'Let's dance,' she said.

'Here?'

'Why not?'

'You don't want to dance here.'

'Why not? It's a dance hall, isn't it?'

'It's a dive with a dance *floor*. Not the same thing. No one really dances.'

'Then what do you call that?'

Carmen had dragged her customer onto the floor. Already they were glued together, the man a little the worse for drink, Carmen with her lacquered head buried in the nape of his neck.

'Well, if you don't want to dance, I shall ask someone else.'

'That wouldn't be a good idea.'

Alma tossed back the rest of her kümmel and got to her feet. She pointed towards a mean-looking stranger at the bar. 'He'll do.'

Kirsch caught her by the wrist. 'All right, you win. Let's dance.'

Reluctantly he led her onto the floor. Everyone in the place was looking her up and down. It was obvious she did not belong. She was too smart, too young, too clean. The old man lowered his newspaper and stared, running his tongue around the front of his teeth.

They were playing a slow waltz. Alma's dancing stood out as much as she did. The Tanguero's regular clientele slouched or

stumbled their way around the floor, intent only on the feel of body against body. But Alma danced with the upright posture of a ballroom regular. When she stumbled on a broken board, a raucous laugh went up from the shadows.

Kirsch saw her blush. 'Maybe we should —'

'It doesn't matter.'

She held him tighter. They went on through several numbers until the sharp, scented sweat trickled down their faces. He had danced with her before, in the grand hotels around Unter den Linden and Friedrichstrasse, but never this close, with the curve of her breasts brushing against him. The music slowed and she was clinging to him, her body taut and hard like a weapon. He looked up, saw Carmen staring at them from her corner of the bar, a wide yellow grin on her face. In the Tanguero, dancing was almost always a preliminary — just as it was in the other places where he went to drink and watch.

'We should go,' he said at last. 'Or you'll miss your train.'

'Fancy,' she said, her head nestling against his lapel. He could smell the alcohol on her breath. 'Where *would* I go then?'

Kirsch tried to extract himself from her embrace. Alma was tipsy and strangely reckless.

'Not to my place,' he said. 'Frau Schirmann is very strict about women callers. Besides, people might talk.'

'They're talking already,' Alma said, waving a finger at him. 'About you. Maybe it's time I got in on the act.'

'I'm not sure your father would agree.'

Kirsch took her hand and led her off the dance floor. Thankfully the band were taking a break.

'You worry too much about Daddy,' Alma said. 'Daddy does exactly what I tell him. Always.'

Twenty-three

The introduction of callisthenics into the weekly regime had been Dr Mehring's idea, but from the start he had left the business of conducting the classes to other members of staff. The patients were led out into the grounds behind the building, arranged into three or four ranks and taken through the motions by two of the nurses. Provided it was not too windy, a large wind-up gramophone was deployed, playing a variety of uplifting numbers. The reedy strains echoed around the adjacent courtyard, so that from inside the clinic it sounded as if the orchestra were playing under water.

On Monday morning it was the turn of the female patients. From a window in the refectory, Kirsch watched them file out of the back door. As he had hoped, Mariya was among them, wearing her old boots and Max's grey overcoat. Kirsch pushed open the window, making as much noise as possible. Mariya heard him and looked up. So did several of the other women. Hesitantly, Kirsch waved. Mariya smiled, then looked away.

The women took their places, standing an arm's length apart. The gramophone was wound. A gust of wind blew Mariya's hair across her cheek. Kirsch watched her push it back and curl it behind her ear. How long would he have to wait before she looked his way again? How long before he could smile at her, or wave or nod; anything to show her he was still thinking of her, that she was no longer alone? She was less than fifty feet away, but in that short distance he already felt a deprivation, a grievance – just as he had all that weekend: time wasted, love lost. He braced himself against the frame of the window. His impatience to hold her again, to crush her against him, made him giddy.

Someone was standing next to him.

'Good weekend?'

It was Robert Eisner with a newspaper tucked under his arm.

Kirsch straightened up. 'Yes, thank you.'

'How's Alma doing?'

I don't know why you're so mean about Robert. He's done nothing to you.

'Extremely well, under the circumstances.'

Eisner nodded sympathetically. 'Of course. Well. Biggest day of a girl's life, isn't it?'

Before Kirsch could close the window Eisner placed his hand on the sill and surveyed the scene outside. 'Can't be easy either: you up here and her down there.'

'What do you mean?'

'Down there. In Oranienburg. With all the wedding preparations to sort out.' He turned. 'Why? What did you think I meant?'

'Nothing.' Kirsch hoped he was not blushing. 'Anyway, the Siegels have everything under control.'

Down in the grounds, the gramophone was playing a nautical number. The nurses were standing to attention, moving up and down on the balls of their feet in time to the music. The female patients joined in, some on the beat, some off it, some tottering around to a rhythm all their own.

'What about Patient E? Any progress?'

'Hard to say.'

'I heard something about an identification.'

Kirsch pushed his hands into his coat pockets. He hadn't expected the news to travel so fast. 'That's right.'

'When did this happen?'

'Friday. I don't want to make a song and dance about it. The press, you know.'

Eisner stepped closer. Kirsch caught a whiff of cologne. 'So who is she?'

Kirsch gave him the name. Mariya's landlord had recognised her photograph and telephoned the clinic, he said. She was a recent arrival from Switzerland and had been staying at a ladies' rooming house off Wörtherstrasse. To date, these were the only details.

'Have you told the police?'

'I suppose I shall have to. Not that it'll help them much. She still doesn't remember what happened to her.'

The nurses raised their arms above their heads and began waving them from side to side. The patients followed. Even in her bulky overcoat and boots, Mariya managed to be graceful. Kirsch watched her outstretched fingers reaching gamely for the sky, no hint of self-consciousness.

'So why is she in Berlin? This landlord of hers must have some idea.'

'For work probably.'

'Work? Well, there's not a lot of that right now. Anyway, have you seen her hands? They're not the hands of a housemaid.'

Kirsch closed the window. 'I expect she was looking for something clerical.'

He turned to go, but Eisner tapped him on the arm with the newspaper. 'I've an idea how we could find out. Take a look.'

He passed Kirsch the newspaper. On page four a small headline read: AMERICANS DISCOVER TRUTH SERUM. The piece underneath was only two paragraphs long. Chemists at a pharmaceutical company in Chicago had been conducting experiments on a new class of sedatives, synthesised from barbituric acid. They had stumbled on some unexpected properties: patients rendered semi-conscious by injections of these new compounds were apparently unable to tell lies under questioning. More extensive research was planned.

Kirsch handed the paper back. 'You aren't serious.'

'Why not?'

'It's just a newspaper story.'

Eisner shook his head. 'I've done some checking. They used a short-acting barbiturate, a kind they've been using for years as an anaesthetic.'

'Mariya isn't lying. She has amnesia.'

'How can you be sure? Besides, this drug might work on that too. Think of it: a direct route to the subconscious. No higher brain

functions muddying the water. We could be looking at a major break-through.'

'You're worse than Mehring.'

'We'll take it slowly, of course. Start with small doses.'

Kirsch walked away.

'I know where we can get some,' Eisner called after him. 'Sodium pentobarbital. I have a contact. We could make history.'

Kirsch stopped by the door. 'Why don't you ask Dr Bonhoeffer what he thinks? Maybe he'll agree to your experiment. Then the only obstacle you'll have to negotiate is my dead body.'

Later that day Kirsch found a letter from Dr Bonhoeffer waiting in his pigeon-hole. The stark tone did not surprise him; the substance did. Dr Mehring, the letter said, had re-examined the events surrounding Nurse Ritter's injury and retracted his complaint in full. Nurse Honig's allegations of assault had likewise been withdrawn. As for Nurse Ritter herself, she had resigned in favour of a new position at the public hospital in Friedrichshain and had expressed no desire to take matters further. There was therefore no justification in continuing to ask for Kirsch's resignation. He was at liberty to consider the matter closed.

Kirsch went to see Bonhoeffer at once, to ask for clarification. The director did not provide any. Dr Mehring, it seemed, had simply changed his mind. 'Perhaps he has finally come around to the view that you were acting in the patient's best interests, as you saw them,' was the only explanation he was prepared to offer.

Twenty-four

Colonel Schad's surgery was just off the Bismarck Strasse, with its busy tramlines and avenues of trees, but the immediate area was not as genteel as Kirsch had expected. Schad practised on the first floor of a sooty apartment building whose yellow stucco had come away in places, revealing naked brickwork underneath. A corner of the building was under scaffolding. He employed the services of a receptionist, but otherwise worked alone.

'I'd planned on having a partner,' he said, as he showed Kirsch around. 'A fellow I trained with years ago. But it didn't work out.'

Schad had aged a good deal since their last meeting. Unlike most men in their fifties, he had lost weight rather than gaining it, his plump, martial face becoming drawn and almost gaunt. His moustache had gone, and his hair was shorter and whiter than it had ever been in the army.

'You've enough clients, I hope,' Kirsch enquired.

'Mainly old ladies so far, and children with respiratory problems. I'm afraid the Berlin air isn't all it's cracked up to be.'

Schad showed Kirsch into his consulting room, which was large but sparsely furnished. Books took up most of one wall, anatomical charts another. To make patients feel at home, a quartet of watercolours were arranged symmetrically opposite the window: rustic scenes involving meadows, farmyard animals and barns in good repair.

Over cups of bitter coffee they discussed professional matters: Schad's years at the hospital in Essen, Kirsch's work in psychiatry, and various aspects of living in the capital. The one thing they did not talk about was the war. Kirsch tried to broach the subject – it felt unnatural to say nothing – but when the moment came, he could not think of what to say. He sensed that for his old commanding

officer it was the same. Perhaps a certain bleak commonality could be found in that silence.

Eventually Schad looked at his pocket watch. 'There's a tolerable restaurant opposite the Schiller Theatre,' he said. 'I'd be honoured if you'd accept an invitation to lunch. I've a patient in about fifteen minutes, but I shouldn't be very long with her. Frau von Hassell. A chronic malingerer, like most of them.'

'My own visit isn't entirely social, Colonel. I wanted –'

'Please, no military formalities. I'm not a colonel any more.'

'I wanted to consult you as a patient.'

Schad regarded Kirsch steadily. Then he nodded. He had guessed the nature of the problem at once, Kirsch realised. The circumstances made it all too clear.

'You can count on my discretion,' Schad said.

He pulled down a thick paper blind while Kirsch undressed. The examination took only a few minutes. The wound on his arm had begun to heal, the dead flesh hardening into a glutinous pellet beneath his skin. But the marks on his chest and flanks were darker than before. Here and there the flesh was raised, tiny dark red spots showing through the flesh as if he were bleeding beneath his skin.

'You're concerned these indicate the onset of the tertiary stage?' Schad said, stepping behind him.

Kirsch kept his gaze on the wall. 'Should I be?'

'Not in my experience. Granulomas return in many forms and in many places on the body, but not like this. Curious how your back is unaffected.' He ran his fingers over Kirsch's ribs. 'These marks, are they sore?'

'Sometimes, a little. In the morning mostly. They feel like bruises.'

'Perhaps they *are* bruises.'

'How could that be?'

Schad rubbed his chin. 'Just a thought. You can get dressed now.'

He went and sat down behind his desk while Kirsch pulled on his clothes. Kirsch knew he should feel relieved, but something was not right: not least the suggestion that the marks on his body were

self-inflicted. He sensed the colonel watching him closely as he fumbled with his cuffs.

'So.' Schad rested his chin on the points of his fingers. 'What else have you noticed?'

'What else?'

'Symptoms. Possible symptoms.'

Kirsch had taken his tie off too quickly, pulling the knot into a tight ball. He struggled now to loosen it. His fingernails were too short to catch on the fabric.

'Nothing much. Lack of sleep. Bad dreams sometimes. Nothing remarkable.'

'No stabbing pains?'

Kirsch shook his head.

'Loss of sensation? In the limbs, for example?'

'Not really.'

'That's good.' Schad picked up a pencil from his desk. 'So no loss of reflexes? Involuntary movements, that sort of thing?'

Kirsch remembered a glass he had broken the evening before. But what did that prove? Everyone was clumsy now and again.

'No.'

'What about hallucinations?'

The tie slipped through Kirsch's fingers. 'None. None that I'm aware of. Although I suppose one can never be completely sure.'

Schad smiled tightly. 'No. I suppose not. Now, I want you to look at my hand. Step a little closer, would you?'

Kirsch did as he was asked. At the same moment, Schad quickly pulled up the blinds. Even though the sky was overcast, the light was too bright. Kirsch had to look away.

'I'm sorry. I had to check.' Schad let the blinds drop again.

'Check what?'

'Your eyes. They're not adjusting to the light, are they? As quickly as they should.'

It was true. Kirsch was forever sheltering his eyes these days. It was December and yet he had often thought of buying sunglasses.

'What does it mean?'

'Please, Martin, sit down.'

Kirsch lowered himself onto a chair.

'It's a strong indicator for neurosyphilis. It suggests that the micro-organism has reached your brain, probably via the nervous system. In my experience, it happens to about three patients in ten. It doesn't mean the disease has reached the tertiary stage, or that it ever will. But there's a high chance you will start to experience certain impairments.'

During the war, when the secondary symptoms had appeared, Kirsch had investigated the pathogenesis of neurosyphilis. The symptoms read like a catalogue of divine punishment: from the headaches, vertigo and numbness of the early stages to strokes, paralysis, dementia and death. In between, there were disturbing changes in personality, memory loss, hallucinations and the decay of mental faculties.

'How long before . . . ?' He hesitated, not knowing how to frame the question. 'How long will I be able to go on working?'

'That's impossible to say. Anything from a few months to a few years, perhaps even longer. I'm sure you appreciate there are a great many variables.'

The colonel got busy taking a sample of blood with a hypodermic syringe. Serological tests were not wholly reliable, he said, but it might be helpful to get an idea of how numerous the bacteria had become. He would send the blood to a local hospital without using Kirsch's name. He expected the results some time after Christmas.

'In the meantime, it would be wise to assume that you're contagious. You did say you were unmarried?'

Kirsch put on his shoes. His hands had stopped shaking, but still it took an effort of will to manipulate the laces, to make the loops and secure them tightly.

'That's right. I'm not married.'

'Perhaps that's just as well, under the circumstances.' Schad was carefully transferring the blood into a small, sealable phial. 'Trying to explain these things to loved ones, it's hard. They always assume the worst. At least you have the luxury of being able to keep quiet about it.'

Schad was right. Under the circumstances, matrimony was out of the question, the engagement to Alma an act of insanity, or of wild optimism, at the very least. And yet none of this had been clear to him until Mariya crossed his path. Only then had he seen.

Schad closed the phial and pulled off his rubber gloves. From behind the door came the sound of Frau von Hassell arriving.

Kirsch reached for his coat. 'Is there any hope of recovery?'

Schad nodded slowly. His cheeks had coloured slightly. Apart from that his face expressed nothing. 'There's always hope,' he said.

That night Kirsch telephoned Alma in Oranienburg. He had to arrange to see her again, and soon. If he was going to break off the engagement, it would be best to do it face to face.

'It's sweet of you to call,' she said before he'd had a chance to explain. 'I expect you've heard.'

'Heard what?'

'About Daddy. He's going to be all right, I know he is. He's as strong as an ox. Everyone says so.'

Otto Siegel had been taken to hospital after suffering what the doctors called a cardiac episode. It was not clear how long they intended to keep him there. Pretty much the entire family had scurried to the old man's bedside nevertheless.

'Mother's desperately worried,' Alma said. 'But I keep telling her he's going to be fine. I saw him this morning and he was sitting up reading the newspaper and swearing at the nurses for keeping him there. He can't *wait* to be up and about.'

Between Frau Siegel and her daughter, Kirsch felt sure, it was Alma who was the more petrified. That her father might actually die, that something loved and irreplaceable might be snatched away from her, was a possibility that was sure to shake the foundations of her world.

'I suppose you won't be visiting for a while then,' Kirsch said.

'You know I'd love to, but Mother really needs me here. You do understand?'

'Of course,' Kirsch said. 'Of course. You must be where you're needed.'

Twenty-five

The next morning, a handwritten note arrived via the pneumatic post from the Prussian Academy of Sciences:

Dear Dr Kirsch,
I have looked over the notebooks you were good enough to leave with me last week. I should be happy to discuss them with you at your soonest convenience. It might be best if we were to meet in person. I shall be lecturing at the university every afternoon this week. Please feel free to call on me at any time.
Yours sincerely,
Max von Laue

There were several new admissions to the clinic that day and it wasn't until four in the afternoon that Kirsch was able to make his way to the university. After trawling around the Department of Physics for a quarter of an hour, he was told that the professor was lecturing and sent to another part of the building. He arrived just as the corridors were filling with students on their way out. He went from room to room, saw tiered seating and blackboards covered in diagrams and mathematical notation, lecturers gathering their papers or talking with colleagues. At last he found von Laue alone, smoking a cigarette beside one of the big sash windows, apparently deep in thought.

'Herr Professor.' Kirsch offered his hand. 'I hope this is not a bad time.'

'Far from it,' von Laue said. 'Good of you to come. I'd have come to you at the Charité, but I wasn't sure . . .'

'That's quite all right.'

'The notebook's in my office. Shall we?'

There was an old-fashioned grace about von Laue. Kirsch had noticed it even at their first, brief meeting. There was no condescension, no sense that his time was more valuable than the next man's.

'You said you'd looked it over.'

'Yes.' The professor picked up his overcoat and briefcase and ushered Kirsch back into the corridor. 'Did I understand you correctly? The calculations were made by a psychiatric patient?'

'I assume so. The notebook was found among her possessions.'

Von Laue stopped. '*Her* possessions? Your patient is a woman?'

'Is that so unlikely?'

'Let's say it's unexpected.'

'But they *are* calculations? They make mathematical sense?'

'Well . . .' Von Laue shrugged, as if the issue were a delicate one. 'There *are* those who'd say they're fanciful. The idea of a fifth dimension as anything more than a mathematical construct, that's certainly not gained *wide* acceptance. But as to the execution, I'd say it's quite rigorous.'

They were crossing the entrance hall, heading out into the cobbled yard. It was getting dark. Everywhere students were putting on their bicycle clips and wheeling their bicycles towards the road.

'So my patient, she'd have to be a student of physics.'

'I'd say so,' von Laue said. 'And a curiously well-informed one. These aren't the kind of problems you'd normally give to a student. They're too experimental, too . . . contemporary. That's why I'm curious to know whose student this is.'

'I wish I could tell you. But it's an unusual case. Amnesia is involved.'

'Amnesia, you say?'

Kirsch saw a glimmer of recognition in von Laue's eyes. The professor frowned, drawing on the last of his cigarette before tossing the butt into the gutter. In spite of the raw December wind, he didn't seem bothered by the cold.

'It's the timing, you see,' he said after a few moments. 'It's troubling.'

'The timing? I'm afraid I don't –'

'Let me explain. The calculations you showed me, they're part of an attempt to reduce a number of equations – equations describing physical laws – down to one equation: a law from which the others are derived. The first set of equations applies to the motion of objects in a gravitational field: stars, planets, asteroids and so forth. The other applies to objects in an electromagnetic field: atoms, electrons. The two sets of laws appear contradictory, that's the difficulty. We have one set of laws for the motion of big things and another for the motion of small ones, which isn't very satisfactory, or even plausible to most minds. It's an important problem, perhaps the most important in physics.'

Von Laue didn't know it, but Kirsch had read about this before, as he knew Max would have done, and with the same hunger. When Albert Einstein had proved that light, like all forms of pure energy, was a stream of particles, and that the particles had mass, he had opened the door on a world of uncertainty. Observations and experiments had proved him right. Light *was* made up of *quanta*, pellets of energy like tiny grains of sand, travelling at immense speed. There was only one problem: the old experiments, the ones that had revealed light to be a travelling undulation, like a ripple moving across water, remained as valid as they had always been. The interference patterns continued to prove, as Einstein acknowledged, that light *was* a wave. The mathematics were irrefutable.

No matter how they examined the problem, no matter what experiments they attempted, physicists were forced to acknowledge what reason and experience said was impossible: a beam of light could be either of two completely different things depending on how it was observed. The two possibilities co-existed in a perpetual state of ambiguity until interaction with an observer resolved the question one way or the other. The implications were disturbing, to say the least. If the nature of a thing was determined by the act and method of observation, how could the scientist hope to arrive at any definitive conclusions? It was as if the principles of relativity had moved on from space and time to unpick the very fabric of knowledge.

And that was not the end of it. The old planetary model of the atom, in which electrons orbited a nucleus, the way planets orbited the sun and obeying the same physical laws, was soon dead and buried. Einstein's young disciples – Niels Bohr, Werner Heisenberg, Erwin Schrödinger – soon showed that the laws of motion did not apply in the sub-atomic sphere at all. Neither did conventional geometry. Electrons and *quanta* of light had no fixed positions, like objects in the larger world – if they could be said to be objects at all. Their position depended on how they were observed. It seemed they had a range of possible positions, all existing simultaneously. Their behaviour could not be predicted individually, only statistically en masse.

Classical physics said everything, even the smallest motion of the smallest particle, happened for a reason. If one electron behaved differently from another, it was because the forces acting upon it were different. With enough information, everything could be predicted, at least theoretically. The classical universe was a mechanism, set in motion at the beginning of time, its every motion predetermined. The young apostles of quantum mechanics ridiculed this idea. In the very substance of energy and matter, they argued, the link between cause and effect was absent. A universe founded upon the physics of light was a universe in which individual events occurred for no reason at all. For the first time, the behaviour of matter became not just unknown, but unknowable. Reality was built not on the rock of action and reaction, but on the shifting sands of chance. Einstein had shown the world that the heart of all material was the immaterial; now his precious *quanta* were showing him that at the heart of all reason was unreason.

But to the great physicist, this was a step too far. To the dismay of Bohr and the others, he determined to bring quantum mechanics to heel. His weapon would be a new mathematical model, one that would subordinate the upstart physics of the *quanta* to the strict causality of the cosmic realm. A Unified Field Theory would reveal the hidden laws that dictated to the quantum world, as they dictated to all others. Einstein would prove that everything was knowable after all, the randomness of quantum reality just an illusion.

Four years before Mariya's notebook led Kirsch to the Prussian Academy, the Berlin press had been camped outside, waiting for news of Einstein's final victory. Kirsch's scrapbook still bulged with their fantastical articles about what might follow: a future with unlimited energy, the instantaneous transportation of matter, even time travel. He himself had queued outside the offices of the *Berliner Morgenpost*, because it was rumoured they were going to carry an authorised report in their first edition (a rumour that turned out to be false). But so far the breakthrough hadn't come.

Kirsch had wondered often as he read the newspapers and journals, which side Max would have been on in this great battle of realities. Would he have wanted Einstein, his hero, to emerge triumphant? Or would the strangeness of the quantum world have proved too seductive to resist? In Kirsch's dreams he was always evasive on the subject, as if he knew what he thought, but was not yet ready to share.

Von Laue led the way through a courtyard full of students. It was cold.

'You said the timing of these notes was troubling,' Kirsch said. 'What did you mean?'

'Forgive me,' Von Laue said, 'I expect I haven't been very clear. What I meant to say was, the last time I saw *that* field of mathematics – a five-dimensional geometry – applied to *this* particular problem, I was listening to Professor Einstein deliver a paper to the members of the Prussian Academy. That was in April. The paper wasn't actually published until a couple of months ago.' They had reached another, smaller entrance. Von Laue held open the door. 'So you see, those notes you left me must be the work either of a leading physicist or of someone *close* to a leading physicist. At least, that was my assumption.'

Von Laue showed Kirsch into his office and turned on the lights. It was smaller than Kirsch had expected, though comfortably furnished, with bookshelves lining the walls, a mahogany desk, a faded Persian rug, and an old ivory and brass model of the solar system on top of a filing cabinet. With a key from his waistcoat

pocket, von Laue unlocked the drawer of his desk and produced Mariya's notebook. Gingerly, Kirsch opened it. The lines of letters and symbols stared up at him, blurred and unintelligible, evidence of the dousing it had received on the way to the Academy.

'These calculations then, are they complete? Do they prove something?'

Von Laue smiled as he moved behind his desk. 'In theoretical physics things are rarely proven, Dr Kirsch, at least in the sense that they're shown to be true. We can't yet observe an individual atom, any more than we can travel among the stars.' He pulled open a pair of wooden shutters and looked out across the avenue towards Franz-Joseph Platz. 'As I often tell my students, the human perspective places almost as many limitations on our ability to observe as it does on our ability to understand. It's no easy matter to go beyond it. True objectivity demands dedication and considerable sacrifice.'

Kirsch turned over a page. It was stiff and warped, but the writing was clearer. A single sheet of blotting paper had been carefully inserted among the leaves. A few pages on, he found another.

'If nothing is proven,' he said, 'how do you know when you're right?'

Von Laue was gazing at the street lights. They flickered against a cobalt sky. 'It's a question of finding what's beautiful. We look for elegance, simplicity, economy. Those are the solutions Nature prefers. Of course, it's a very rare form of intuition that knows where to look for them. Most of us can't see beyond the fog of our own suppositions.' He turned. 'Unfortunately, in your patient's case, the work is incomplete. The last pages are missing.'

Kirsch hadn't noticed it before: but the final folio of the notebook had been pulled out – twenty pages or more. He plucked out the loose threads of the binding.

'I don't suppose you know where those pages are, by any chance?' von Laue said.

'I'm afraid not.' Silence fell. After a moment, Kirsch stepped forward and offered his hand. 'You've been most helpful, Professor. I won't presume to take up any more of your time.'

A look of resignation crossed von Laue's face. 'When your patient recovers I should be most interested in meeting her. Be under no illusions: she has a remarkable intelligence – assuming, of course, that those really are her calculations.'

'I've no reason to doubt it. The handwriting appears to be hers.'

Von Laue showed him out. 'I don't wish to sound disparaging about the fairer sex, you understand. It's just that in all my years as a physicist, I've only ever known two women who could absorb Albert Einstein's work so readily. One of them was Marie Curie, and she has a Nobel Prize.'

'And the other?'

Von Laue hesitated. 'The other was his wife.'

'Elsa Einstein?'

Von Laue laughed. 'No. Elsa has trouble with the household accounts. I meant his *first* wife.'

'I didn't know he was married before.'

'Not many people do. It was in Switzerland, some years ago. She and Albert were students at the Polytechnic.' Von Laue opened the door. 'I think she still teaches there, as a matter of fact.'

'In Switzerland?'

'In Zürich. Private pupils only, mostly young women. A witches' coven, Albert calls it.' Von Laue smiled for a moment. 'There's a great shortage of female teachers, in physics especially. Many universities still won't admit women to study science, regrettably.'

'Can you tell me her name? If it's not . . .'

Von Laue shrugged. 'Mileva. Mileva Marić.'

It took Kirsch a few seconds to place the name.

'It's Serbian,' von Laue said. 'That's where Mileva comes from, you see. Some small town miles from anywhere.'

Kirsch hurried back to the clinic. Supper was under way and most of the building was quiet. He went to his office and closed the door, fishing in his pocket for the key to the filing cabinet. He pushed the Adler aside, took out Mariya's file and emptied the contents onto the desk. The letter was there, between a sample of Mariya's sketches

and the photograph in *Die Berliner Woche* that Alma had given him: *Fr. Mileva Einstein-Marić, Tillierstrasse 18, Berne, Switzerland*.

The first time he'd seen the name, he'd wondered if it wasn't a joke. 'Dr Einstein-Kirsch' was just how Robert Eisner might have addressed him in one of his more sarcastic moods. But there was no doubt now: the letter was addressed to Albert Einstein's first wife.

He read it again. April 1903. The Einsteins were thinking about moving to Serbia. Mileva was concerned about a young child there, called Lieserl. Her friend Helene reassured her that the child was well, and warned against undoing arrangements previously entered into *for the good of all*.

The child had been Mileva's. It was the only plausible explanation. Lieserl had been put up for adoption – privately and secretly, to judge from the tone. There was no clue as to why, or to how Mariya came to be in possession of the letter twenty-nine years on – still less, why she had brought it with her to Berlin.

An ugly thought occurred to him. If the letter was evidence of impropriety, it could have been used for blackmail. Perhaps that had been the intention: to threaten the Einsteins with a scandal.

Eugen Fischer had suspected a scam, and he was not alone. Even the police were reluctant to treat Mariya as a victim. Seen from the outside, there was something strange and calculated about the way she had come to the public's notice, as if she were doing her utmost to gain attention and, in the process, leverage.

Kirsch looked at the sketches lying on his desk. The young man and the old man, they were there again, looming up through the delicate shading. Had the young man been her accomplice? If so, what had become of him? Kirsch looked at the broad forehead and the beautiful, delicate mouth. Perhaps he hadn't been as lucky as Mariya: perhaps he had not been found. Kirsch pictured them out on the lake, in a rowing boat; an argument, a struggle. Maybe she'd killed him and dumped his body over the side. Maybe it lay still undiscovered, the pockets weighed down with stones.

Kirsch thought of her exercising in the grounds, her pale white

arms, the way she had looked down as she tucked her hair behind her ear. She was no murderess. She wasn't capable of blackmail or deceit.

But, of course, she *had* deceived him. At the Tanguero. When he had asked for her name, she had told him it was Elisabeth.

He picked up the letter again. *I know that Lieserl is on your mind when you ask such things.*

Lieserl. Not a proper name, not a name for a birth certificate or a passport. It was an old-fashioned German diminutive, an affectionate moniker given to a small child.

He got to his feet, tipping over an empty coffee cup. It rolled off the desk and smashed on the floor. He stared at the shards, thinking only of Mariya, their fleeting exchange at the Tanguero, the way she had hesitated before answering him, the hint of a smile on her lips.

A baby called Lieserl grew up to be woman called Lisa or Elsbeth – or *Elisabeth*.

He'd thought she was playing with him, making up a name on the spot to put him off the scent. But he'd been wrong. She hadn't been out to deceive him at all. She had been trusting him with a secret. She was the child in the letter. She was Lieserl.

The young man and the old man. He closed the file and locked it away in the cabinet. He'd always wondered who the old man was. Now he knew.

First thing the next morning he telephoned the university, but it took several attempts before anyone would take a message. At noon, von Laue finally returned his call.

'I need to get in contact with Professor Einstein,' Kirsch said. 'It concerns this case of mine, the student.'

'Albert Einstein? Are you serious?'

'I know it's a lot to ask.'

Kirsch heard footsteps, the thud of a door closing. After a bad night – a kaleidoscope of memories, dreams and speculations – he felt tired and edgy. 'Professor von Laue?'

'You want to show him the notebook. Is that what you had in mind?'

Von Laue's tone was wary. The mention of Einstein, of seeing him, meeting him, had changed everything.

'No. The issue isn't strictly scientific.'

'Then what makes you think it would be of interest? Professor Einstein is a scientist. He has no expertise in psychiatry.'

'This particular case, the case of Mariya Draganović: I believe it *would* be of interest to the professor, if he were fully acquainted with the facts. But I wanted to consult you before presuming to approach him directly.'

It was tempting to tell von Laue about the Savić letter, about what it meant — tempting, but dangerous. What if the letter had been stolen? It had clearly been private correspondence. Besides, regarded objectively, it was hardly proof of anything.

'Draganović, you said?'

'It's a Serbian name. I believe she comes from Serbia. Like the professor's first wife.'

There was a pause. For a moment he thought von Laue was going to hang up.

'Go on.'

Kirsch sat down. 'I believe there's a strong possibility this patient was once known to Professor Einstein. There may be a connection between them, one that accounts for her presence in Berlin.'

'I'm sorry, but I fail to see —'

'The professor may be the one person who can help her.'

Von Laue sighed, as if he had heard all this before. 'Dr Kirsch, we're talking about the most famous man alive. Have you forgotten that?'

'I realise —'

'Albert Einstein is recognised in every corner of the civilised world. The newsreels follow him night and day, and there can't be a newspaper in existence that hasn't carried his photograph. As a psychiatrist, you must know that to many people, sane and insane, such exposure *constitutes* a connection, even a relationship. I assure

you, hardly a week goes by without some deluded soul making one kind of claim or another.'

'Nevertheless, in this instance, I believe the professor would want to learn what I've learned. The matter would remain strictly confidential, of course.'

Von Laue took a long time to reply. 'I would like to help you, Dr Kirsch, but I'm afraid it's impossible. Professor Einstein and his wife are leaving for Bremerhaven this afternoon.'

'Bremerhaven? Will they be gone for long?'

'I hope you understand that their travel plans shouldn't be broadcast, even now, for reasons of safety. Albert is not only the world's most famous scientist. He is also the world's most famous Jew. Not to mention a vociferous opponent of National Socialism.'

'I understand.'

'Very well. They sail for America in a few days. They aren't due back until March; although, the situation being what it is, I shouldn't count on them returning at all.'

It occurred to Kirsch that this might be a lie, a way of denying his request without giving offence. But then, von Laue had proved he wasn't the type for lies.

'I'm sorry I can't do more for you, Dr Kirsch, or for your patient. But I wouldn't have Professor Einstein delay his departure on any account. His enemies here grow bolder and more dangerous every day. Whatever this *connection*, it cannot be allowed to divert him from his work, let alone compromise his safety.'

'The thing is –'

'I'm sorry, but I'm afraid I shall have to leave matters there.'

'I think this may be his daughter. Einstein's daughter, Elisabeth. Wouldn't that change everything?'

There was another pause on the line.

'Goodbye, Dr Kirsch.'

Twenty-six

Mariya had not seen Dr Kirsch for several days. When he came walking towards her across the grounds, she could tell that something was wrong. His hands were dug deep into the pockets of his coat so the knuckles pushed through the fabric; and there was a stiffness in the way he carried himself that she had not seen before.

'Don't tell me you're drawing the clinic?' he said.

Mariya was seated on her usual bench. She faced the building with the pad on her lap, though she had yet to make a start. Afternoon sunlight was breaking through the clouds. 'Why shouldn't I?'

Kirsch squinted up at the barred windows and stark brickwork, obscured only by the skeletal remains of dead creepers. 'There must be prettier views.'

She moved along the seat of the bench so as to make room for him, but he sat down on the arm. Mariya looked down at her paper, drew a curved line, waiting for Kirsch to speak. The line became a cheekbone. Beneath the cheekbone she drew a jaw.

'Is it bad news?' she asked.

'No,' he said. 'No, it's progress. Definite progress. With luck, you'll be out of here very soon. You'll be able to go on with your life.'

She drew the arch of an eyebrow. A man's or a woman's? She didn't know. Her stomach squirmed.

'Where are you going to send me?'

'Only to where you belong.' He was looking at her for the first time, but she kept her eyes on the page. 'This place, it's just a temporary refuge. Soon you won't need it any more.'

She drew the eyes dark and piercing. 'What about you?'

Up on the top floor of the clinic, a figure in white drifted past

194

one of the windows. How many others were watching? Mariya wondered. Awkward for Dr Kirsch, having an audience. Or was that what he had wanted: to have others enforce a distance between them?

'Mariya, what happened at Herr Mettler's . . .' Her pencil came to rest. 'It was wrong of me. Entirely wrong.'

'Was it? Why?'

'I'm a doctor. My role . . . my *place* is to restore you to health. Anything else can only complicate your recovery.'

She felt tears in her eyes. She clenched her teeth. She was afraid if she opened her mouth to speak, they would run down her cheeks. How stupid, she thought. How *abnormal*. She forced herself to concentrate on her drawing, filled in the pupils and the eyelids with hard jabs of her pencil.

'You must understand,' Kirsch said. 'You're bound to feel isolated at the moment. Any feelings you may have, that's the cause of them. But once you're better, all that will change. Your horizons will broaden. You'll be able to forget this place.'

'And everyone in it. Is that what you mean?'

'Yes.'

'Forgetting is something I'm good at.'

She heard him sigh. Her cheeks burned, knowing now how much of a burden she had become.

'Apart from anything else . . .' He placed a hand against his chest. 'I'm engaged to be married. So you see . . .'

She shivered. She wanted to run away, but where would she go? Beyond the grounds of the clinic, the world was a fog of half-remembered pictures, daunting and lonely.

She got to her feet. 'I understand, Doctor. Thank you.'

She took a few steps towards the clinic, but Kirsch put a hand on her arm. She did not dare to turn and look at him.

'I've received some information.' His voice was softer, though there was nobody around to overhear them. 'If it's true, it changes everything. You see, all this time I've been fixed on the idea of rebuilding your past. I thought that was the only way to address

your amnesia. But I think in your case it's your future that's really important. It's your future we should be trying to reclaim. Perhaps a brilliant future.'

She reached for his hand and gently removed it. 'How?'

'Just give me a little time.' His voice was normal again now, a doctor's voice: level, reassuring, distant. 'I shall have to go away for a while. I've taken a leave of absence, with the director's approval. There's more I need to learn, you see, and I won't learn it in Berlin. In the meantime . . .' He was holding something out to her, a book. 'I want you to read this.'

She glanced at the title on the spine: *On the Special and General Theory of Relativity, Generally Comprehensible*. What a strange gift, she thought: a gift to pass between strangers. Anything but a gift of love.

'Think of it as a new beginning,' Kirsch said.

She took the book, not wishing to seem churlish. 'Of course, Doctor. Whatever you think best.'

the writer

Twenty-seven

So it was that I began to study not for the praise or good opinion of others, but for the independence I thought it could give me. My studies were soon my life. They gave me refuge as well as occupation, for when I was sunk in my books I felt myself not alone, but in company: a company of enlightened souls whose passion was the enlightenment of others. I felt privileged to eavesdrop on the discourse of these great minds, and sometimes resented the intrusions of daily life. I can admit this to you because I know you will understand the temptations of a scholarly existence. Sometimes I think if I had not taken that road, a tumult of emotions might have overwhelmed me. Anger, sorrow and loneliness lay in wait on every side. I had only to stray a step or two from the path and I would be lost to them, and to despair. For what use are the tears of a few gentle souls against the cruelty of so many?

Yet I was not happy. I took pride in my accomplishments, all the more so as they were rare for a young person of my sex, but I did not see the worth of prizes. I wanted my learning to make me happier, and others whom I cared for, and I wanted that happiness to endure. Until then, my successes had served only to isolate me. The girls at school thought me boyish and strange, with my pursuit of mathematics and science; the boys regarded me as an upstart. I believe I was therefore receptive to the notion that learning might at least bring me closer to God.

Not that I received this suggestion in church. I had the impression that, if anything, ministers of religion regarded too much learning with suspicion, especially those kinds that touched upon the natural world. God and his Great Plan were mysteries beyond the reach of human reason, they said. There was a presumption in mortal men propounding on the subject of natural law. Faith was the quality that mattered — blind or otherwise, it made no difference. All the learning in the world,

they reminded me repeatedly, did not bring a soul one step closer to the Kingdom of Heaven, unless it was a learning of the scriptures.

Fortunately, there were teachers at the gymnasium who had a different opinion of science. My last teacher of physics, Dr Stanić, suggested that God and the laws of nature were one and the same, since the character of the universe was an expression of natural law, and all things subject to it. So in understanding better natural laws, how could we fail to understand God better? In this way he placed a new prize before me. I saw that the pathway of learning and investigation led not only to understanding, but to the source of all goodness and love.

These words were a great comfort to me, and a spur. My father never had cause to rebuke me for wasting the money he spent on my education, although this did not deter him from reminding me of the sacrifices he was making. This he did so often I feared he would remove me from the school, even though I had by this time obtained a scholarship, so that the greater part of my fees was waived. Had I known then how he boasted of his prowess around the district, claiming that he had tutored me himself, and that there had been many such prodigies in his family in generations past, I would have worried less.

I suppose he had little else to brag of at this time, for the end of the war had brought an end to his position in the customs service. The border had disappeared by order of the great powers, and the customs posts with it. More welcome to me was the news that the new Kingdom of Yugoslavia would open all its universities, including the schools of medicine and science, to female students. Dr Stanić said neither the university at Zagreb nor its sister in Belgrade were of the first rank when it came to science, and that if it were at all possible I should study abroad. But I knew my father would never pay for that, for since he had lost his position there were more arguments than ever between him and my mother on the subject of money.

Usually I absented myself from the table when these began, as I felt sure my presence would not incline any outcome in my favour. I was still afraid that my father would change his mind about my education (which, as far as I could see, had yet to bring in so much as a penny) and decide that I should come home to work. He had taken to spending his days

either fishing by the river or drinking in the company of other idle men. Instead of looking for work – the little there was available being beneath him – he talked more and more about how we could make a profit with this-or-that grand scheme. One of these was to cultivate silk worms in the attic and the outbuildings. He came home from Novi Sad one day with several baskets full of shiny brown cocoons, none of which ever hatched. Another plan was to turn over our land to growing vines, to which end he ploughed up a good meadow and turned it into a bad one full of weeds. But if he did not persist with these schemes (which thankfully he did not), there was always a need for more help around the house, especially with my mother's health being poor. So usually I got busy clearing the plates when the subject of money came up, and disappeared into the scullery, especially when Father started in with his complaining – that our mother was extravagant, which was not true, and that her family had not given him the dowry they had promised, and numerous other slights and grievances.

One night, however, I strayed within earshot. I had returned that day with a report from the gymnasium, which I knew was to be one of my last. For once I had obtained my diploma I should have to leave, my education being complete. The question of whether I should have further studies could not be postponed much longer. My mother and father were talking in hushed voices, which was not usual, but which only served to make me more curious. So, I confess, I listened at the door, hardly daring to breathe in case the floorboards in the hallway should creak beneath me.

They were talking about money, just as I'd expected, and whether they should ask for more – from whom, I could not make out. My mother was all against it, because of a promise they had made, but my father was insistent. 'We never agreed to shoulder this sort of burden,' I distinctly heard him say. 'They can't expect it. Besides, they have money to burn now. And we have next to nothing.'

My heart sank, for I knew only too well what the burden was. Still, I was curious to know who it was that had been giving us money. Then I heard my father say that Helene should be prevailed upon to intercede on our behalf again, since she had some responsibility too, which once

again my mother opposed, although not as vehemently. I wondered if this could be my Aunt Helene, whom I had not seen for a year or more.

Aunt Helene was what my mother called her, but this was out of affection, and not because she was any blood relative. Her husband Milivoj was an old school friend of my father's and had a job at a ministry, although that did not prevent Father calling him a buffoon and a damned fool dreamer behind his back, which he frequently did, mainly on account of his radical politics. They lived in Belgrade and visited occasionally, Helene sometimes coming on her own, because she had relatives outside Novi Sad. My mother, in particular, treated her with great respect. Aunt Helene was a highly educated woman, small and refined in her dress, though with a deformity in one leg that caused her to limp. In particular, I was much impressed with the fact that she had been to university in Switzerland before her marriage. She told me about the great mountains and glaciers of that country, the likes of which I had never seen except in books — for, as you know, the land where I grew up is as flat as a duck's foot. Once she added in a whisper, as if it were a secret for the two of us, that if I continued to excel in my studies, I too might study in such a place. For it was not unknown for clever Serbian girls to find a welcome in Zürich. Indeed, she said, some had gone for a degree and come back with a husband into the bargain.

I blushed at this, being still too young to think of the opposite sex, except either as teachers or as scuff-kneed tormentors best avoided. And I wondered if the second glass of apple brandy had gone to her head.

On at least two occasions, when I was still very young, Aunt Helene arrived with a female companion: a dark, quiet lady, very soberly dressed, but handsome. At first I took her for a companion or a maid, for she sat silently in the corner most of the time, watching us children play and smiling warmly at us whenever our gaze met hers. I think I would have forgotten about her altogether, had it not been for the way her melancholy presence seemed to cast a spell over my mother and father. Aunt Helene's visits were normally accompanied by a torrent of conversation — about mutual friends, the news from Belgrade, even politics. But when Aunt Helene's companion was present the conversation kept lapsing into silence, as if everyone in the room were preoccupied with something else.

Then when she left, they became light-headed, as if some catastrophe had been narrowly averted. Whenever I saw this lady, I wondered what great sadness it was that she kept locked in her heart, and why no one would speak of it.

Always, after she had gone, I would dream of her. I dreamed I saw her walk into my room and stroke my hair as I slept, and that she was standing in the doorway watching me, silhouetted against the light. I became convinced that she must once have had a daughter and that she had lost her, perhaps to the scarlet fever that had taken so many children of my age. And on that account her heart was broken.

I remembered that the companion's name was Mileva. She and Aunt Helene had met when they were both students in Zürich. She still lived in Switzerland, but had family in the villages of Kać and Titel, which were all within a day's ride of our house. I did not find out until some years later — in fact from my teacher, Herr Bošković — that she had once been famous in Serbia as the most brilliant female physicist our country has ever produced, and none other than the wife of the great Professor Einstein.

Twenty-eight

Mileva Einstein-Marić lived on the slopes of the Zürichberg in an affluent residential district, just above the Polytechnic where she and Albert Einstein had first met thirty years before. Kirsch went on foot, trailing up the long flights of steps that intersected the zigzagging roads, pausing only to catch his breath. Low cloud rolled over the grey waters of the Zürichsee, parting now and then to reveal densely wooded hills on the far shore. Snow was falling. Down below, the trams rolled by on freshly cushioned rails.

Einstein's first wife was the one person who was in possession of the facts. No one else – not even Einstein himself – was a completely reliable source where Lieserl was concerned. After all, the child had been born before she and Einstein were married, in circumstances that were far from clear. Only Mileva could say for sure who the father was. For the same reason, she was the best authority on what had become of the child and where she was now. More than anyone's, these were Mileva's secrets to keep or to share.

Number 62 Huttenstrasse was a heavy four-storey apartment building, rendered in cement, with massive stone footings. It had been finished in a sombre version of the art-nouveau style, with stained glass above the doors and in the windows, and delicate ironwork on the balcony railings. Kirsch did not have an appointment. He had decided to give no warning of his coming. Letters were easy to ignore, and the telephone unsuitable for discussions of a delicate nature. He climbed the stairs to the third floor and rang the bell.

A maid answered the door, took his card and, after a brief consultation, showed him into a drawing room. 'Please to wait,' she said. 'Frau Professor Einstein is come.'

Mileva still used her ex-husband's name and title, though they'd

been divorced for thirteen years. Was it out of lingering affection? Or was she laying claim to a share of her ex-husband's fame? If so, the ploy had been a failure. Outside Switzerland her very existence, like that of her sons, was all but unknown. As far as the newspapers were concerned, Elsa was the only wife Albert Einstein had ever had. Even worse, they usually assumed that Elsa's daughters (in fact the issue of her first marriage), were Albert's daughters too. It was perhaps proof of Einstein's indifference to popular opinion that he had failed to set the record straight. It was possible Mileva had never truly accepted the divorce. If she'd been religiously minded or merely old-fashioned, she might have regarded her marriage bonds as dissoluble only by death. Retaining her husband's name might have been a matter of entitlement for her, a matter of honour.

The room was airy, with high ceilings and white walls. The furniture was of dark, polished wood. A baby grand piano stood in one corner, a large table in the middle, neatly stacked with books and papers. An eclectic mix of etchings and watercolours hung around the walls. On a sideboard, above a radiator, stood a row of small cactus plants in earthenware pots. French windows led out onto a balcony. Outside was an expanse of grass and fruit trees and, beyond that, the snow-covered roofs of the city.

Mileva's family photographs were displayed on a side table. Women in high collars were gathered around bearded patriarchs in carefully posed groups. Chubby-faced toddlers in sailor suits stared stupidly into the lens. In one picture – the oldest, judging from the blotchy condition – three generations were lined up in rows, all facing front. The men wore no jackets, only waistcoats, and the women had scarves tied round their heads. Like their dress, their weather-beaten faces suggested lives of rural toil. The sharper, newer pictures were less formal: a baby in a Christening robe being bounced on a woman's knee; two young boys in hiking gear smiling on a woodland path; a handsome young man in a sunlit garden, women either side of him. Kirsch searched for an image of Albert Einstein, but could find none.

Something about the young man was familiar: the broad forehead, the delicate mouth, the wary expression. He reminded Kirsch

of an American movie star, one Alma said was the new Valentino. Then it came to him: he hadn't seen the face on the movie screen. He had seen it in Mariya's sketch-book.

He's a writer.

He picked up the photograph and turned it over. Nothing had been written on the back. Was it the same man? On closer inspection, he wasn't sure.

Out in the hall, a grandfather clock struck the half-hour. Church bells joined in across the city. Kirsch had never been to a place where the passage of time was marked so assiduously. There was no need to own a watch.

'I see you've found Eduard.'

A woman in a black dress was standing in the doorway. She was small and wore a double string of pearls at her neck. Her fine dark hair was streaked with silver and loosely secured at the back of her neck. Her pupils were like black glass. It struck him that they might once have made her beautiful, but her prominent mouth and strong jaw gave her face an almost simian quality.

Mileva Marić, Einstein's wife for sixteen years. Mariya's mother, perhaps. Kirsch searched for a resemblance, thought he could detect some similarity in the cheekbones and the eyes and the angled arch of the eyebrows. He put the photograph down, stammered a greeting, but she seemed in no hurry to commence the formalities.

'That picture was taken three years ago.' She closed the door behind her. Her accent was the same as Mariya's, if less pronounced. 'Just before we had to send him away. He's put on a little weight since then. The food they give him at the Burghölzli, it's all potatoes and dumplings.'

The Burghölzli was a psychiatric hospital, the most famous in Switzerland. Karl Jung had worked there for many years.

'This is your son?'

Mileva gestured towards a sofa, seating herself in an armchair. It was as if she'd been expecting him. 'They say he has a schizo-affective disorder. Is that a particular field of yours, Dr Kirsch: schizophrenia?'

It occurred to him that Professor von Laue had anticipated his coming, and tipped Mileva off. What else could explain her getting down to business so quickly? Unless this was just the way she was: intelligent, eccentric, with a pressing interest in psychiatry, but none whatsoever in small talk.

'It's a subject I've looked into,' he said. 'Although, to tell the truth, I'm sceptical that such labels are really useful. I'm not satisfied their basis is scientific.'

'I see. And does this scepticism extend to Dr Freud and his ideas?'

'I believe we have to remain sceptical about everything until we know it to be true. And when it comes to mental illness . . .'

An arch smile formed briefly on Mileva's lips. 'A sceptical psychiatrist? I can see why my husband would call on *you*.'

Kirsch wished he knew what she was talking about.

'Albert has no time for the modern psychiatric theories. He believes madness is in the blood, something that runs in the family, like . . .' She paused, the smile returning. '. . . like a dislocated hip. And there's nothing that can be done about it, except to stop breeding.'

'Frau Einstein —'

'Eduard, now *he's* a great disciple. In fact, he knows more about Freud than the people who treat him. They told me psychoanalysis is useless where he's concerned: he outwits them every time.' Mileva glanced at the photograph of the two boys hiking through the woods. Kirsch recognised Eduard as the younger of the two. 'He's always had a remarkable imagination. At school his teachers said he should write professionally. His compositions were always outstanding. His principal said it was he who'd inherited the Einstein spark of genius.'

In Kirsch's scrapbook was an interview Albert Einstein had given to a magazine three years earlier. *Imagination is more important than knowledge,* he had said. *Knowledge is limited. Imagination encircles the world.*

'And you should hear him play the piano.' Mileva was looking at him. 'But I expect his father's already told you all this.'

At last he understood: Eduard Einstein had been in a psychiatric

hospital for the past three years. For some reason, his father had been dissatisfied with the treatment he was receiving, and had insisted on sending a psychiatrist of his own choosing from Berlin. Mileva had simply assumed that he, Martin Kirsch, was the psychiatrist in question. It was the only explanation.

'I'm afraid there's been a misunderstanding,' he said. 'I've not had the honour of meeting Professor Einstein.'

Mileva stared at him. 'He didn't send you?'

'I'm afraid not.'

She was still for a moment. 'You've just joined the Burghölzli, I suppose. And Eduard is your patient.'

Kirsch shook his head. 'My patient, the patient I'm concerned with, is in Berlin, at the Charité Psychiatric Clinic. Her name is Mariya Draganović.'

He let the name hang in the air, wanting to study its effect, hoping for some evidence of affection or concern. Just before his departure for Zürich, he had looked up the facts of the first Einstein marriage, which had been recorded in detail at the Berlin Town Hall at the time of the divorce. Einstein and Mileva Marić had married at a civil ceremony in Berne, Switzerland on 6 January 1903. That was five months after Mariya Draganović was born, according to the papers she had presented to the Alien Registration Office.

He saw a flicker behind Mileva's eyes. But her face betrayed no emotion.

'A student of mathematics,' he added. 'She is known to you?'

Mileva did not answer. Without explanation she got up and went to the door. Kirsch noticed for the first time that she walked with a limp, that one of her shoes had a built-up sole. *Runs in the family, like a dislocated hip.*

It seemed the interview was at an end.

'Frau Einstein, I can assure you I have no wish to pry into your private affairs. But I believe –'

'Biljana!' Mileva was calling down the corridor, demanding something in a language Kirsch could not understand. She glanced back

208

at him. 'You will take coffee, Dr Kirsch?' she said, and before he could answer, she gave a nod and disappeared down the corridor.

When she returned a few minutes later her demeanour had changed. It was as if she were trying to make up for her previous indiscretion. Kirsch sensed a brittleness about her that didn't augur well. As for his enquiry about Mariya, it was as if he had never made it.

While the maid poured the coffee, he explained the facts of the case, leaving out only two significant details: the level of press interest and the letter found among Mariya's possessions. Mileva listened without interruption.

'She's clearly of Serbian origin,' he said, accepting a cup with both hands. 'And the fact that she studied mathematics here in Zürich, I thought it possible you'd come across her.'

'Thank you, Biljana,' Mileva said. The maid left them. 'Do you take sugar, Dr Kirsch? Some cream?'

'No, thank you. I showed some of her work to Professor von Laue, at the Prussian Academy. He was very impressed. In fact, he was curious to know who had taught her.'

Mileva's expression softened. 'Von Laue is a good man. He has honour. More than can be said for the rest of them.'

'Was I mistaken, Frau Einstein? You've never heard of Mariya Draganović?'

Her dark eyes fixed on his. He saw for a moment a younger woman: intense, clever, but awkward – an awkwardness born of isolation, perhaps. A child prodigy who couldn't dance.

'You weren't mistaken, Dr Kirsch,' she said. 'Miss Draganović was my pupil. I taught her for a month or two last autumn. On a private basis.' She nodded towards the table in the middle of the room. It was here the lessons had been conducted, pupil and teacher seated side by side opposite the window. 'I'm sorry to hear she's been unwell. I hope it's nothing too serious.'

'It may be serious. She's suffering from an acute form of amnesia. The cause, I believe, is psychological. Unless I can discover more about her history – and quickly – I fear it may become permanent.'

Kirsch was sure this revelation would be enough to break down any reticence on Mileva's part. No natural mother could stand by and let her child suffer harm, however great the distance between them.

Mileva was silent for a moment. Then she said: 'I had no idea she was in Berlin. I assumed she'd gone home.' She turned her cup round on its saucer. 'I believe that was somewhere near Novi Sad. She never gave me an address. But I think she came from around there.'

'Novi Sad?'

'That's in Yugoslavia. In the province of Vojvodina. It was part of the empire before the war, the Austrian empire. But all that's gone now.'

'Isn't that where you come from?'

Mileva studied him. It was not the sort of information a stranger would possess unless he had gone to some trouble. 'No. I was born in Titel. Quite some miles away.'

'But still in Vojvodina?'

'Yes.'

Mileva was perfectly calm. Kirsch detected no hint of distress in her face or her voice. It was disappointing.

'You must have had a great deal to talk about,' he said, because he couldn't think of anything else.

Mileva shook her head. 'Miss Draganović came here to study, not to chat. Our talk was of physics.'

'Quantum physics?'

'She was anxious to secure a place at university. She'd come into some money, you see. Her father had recently passed away.'

I remembered finding his grave. The snow and the fresh earth.

'Did she come to Switzerland alone?'

I remember the feeling very clearly.

'Oh yes, quite alone.'

I felt free.

Kirsch reached for his handkerchief and dabbed at his forehead. The walk up the hill had drained him. The possibility that he had

been mistaken, that Mileva had nothing of value to tell him, drained him more.

'Are you all right, Dr Kirsch?'

'Yes, yes, thank you. When did you last see Mariya?'

'A few months ago. September or October.'

'Where did she stay?'

Mileva sucked her teeth. 'She lodged in town. I forget the address. It was somewhere near Baschigplatz.'

Kirsch reached inside his jacket and took out an envelope containing the photograph of Mariya from *Die Berliner Woche*. It was still the only picture he had.

'This is her?'

Mileva studied the picture. 'She looks thin.'

The paper trembled slightly in her hand.

'It's important I make contact with her family. Could you help me with that? In the strictest confidence, of course.'

Mileva continued to look at the photograph. 'I've told you all I know.'

'You can't remember anything else?'

She handed the picture back. 'I'm afraid not.'

Kirsch put the cutting back in the envelope. Years spent studying the human mind, and yet he couldn't tell if he was being lied to or not. 'Frau Professor Einstein, did Mariya say anything . . . ? Was there ever any mention of a child?'

'A child? What are you talking about?'

'It's just a possibility.'

'Mariya was unmarried. Why would you say that?'

The indignation seemed genuine. Kirsch was pleased to have elicited some reaction, some small indication of hurt. But how to exploit it?

'It wasn't clear to us if she'd been married,' he said. 'She's quite old enough to have been widowed or divorced. And therefore to have had children.'

'Well,' Mileva visibly relaxed, 'I *can* help you with that. She told me quite distinctly that she had never been married.'

'I'm still not clear how she came to be your student.'

'Most of my students are young women from that part of the world, from the Balkans.'

'So you were recommended.'

'I've never needed to advertise my services. I suppose I'm known in certain academic circles.'

Kirsch tucked the envelope away in his jacket. Mileva didn't trust him. Why should she? She had no way of divining his motives, of judging his integrity. Perhaps she would trust him in time. But then, time was the one thing he did not have.

'Did Mariya talk to you about Berlin?'

'Not that I recall.'

'Why did she go there?'

'So many questions, Dr Kirsch.'

'She must have said something.'

'Not to me.'

'Is it possible she went to see Professor Einstein? Might that have been the plan?'

Mileva picked up her coffee again and stirred it deliberately. 'It's a long way to go for a public lecture, Dr Kirsch, even assuming you can get a ticket.'

'Perhaps she hoped to meet him face to face.'

The stirring stopped. 'That would have been most presumptuous of her. Professor Einstein's time is precious. More precious than you can imagine.'

'Perhaps she felt they had something in common.'

Mileva was very still, perched on the edge of her seat as if afraid a single movement might see her fall. Kirsch wished she *would* fall.

'Presumptuous again,' she said. 'For your information, Mariya never struck me as the presumptuous type.'

'How *did* she strike you?'

'She was a good student. Gifted. Such people are often . . . different. What the Lord gives with one hand, he takes away with the other.'

Kirsch edged forward. '*How* was she different?'

Mileva sighed and looked out of the window. The snow had stopped falling, but the wind was gathering strength. It nudged against the frames, rattling the glass.

'Mariya is suggestible, Dr Kirsch. A dreamer. One might say a fantasist. Plant the seed of an idea in her mind and . . .' She raised a fist and flipped open the fingers as if releasing a small bird. 'In her studies she understands the importance of rigorous proofs; not so in other matters.'

Kirsch shifted in his seat.

'What did she fantasise about exactly?'

'Oh, finding happiness in various unlikely ways, beginning a new life. Love, I dare say. She was lonely. Yes, lonely. People like that grow up to rely on their imaginations for company, more than is good for them. Their lives may be quiet, but their dreams run wild. You must have observed such things in your work.' Mileva glanced at the clock ticking on the mantelpiece. 'I'm afraid I have a pupil. Is there anything else you'd like to know?'

He could have shown her the letter. There was nothing fantastic about that. It was there in his jacket pocket. He could have asked her what it meant and how she accounted for it being among Mariya's possessions. He could have asked her about Lieserl. But what was the use? By now she would have had her answers and evasions ready.

'There is one other thing. Your son, Eduard, did he become acquainted with Mariya as well?'

Mileva's eyes fixed on him again. 'Is that what she told you?'

It was hard to hold her gaze. 'She remembers him quite clearly. Clearly enough to draw pictures of him.'

Mileva shook her head impatiently. 'My son is unwell. You must understand that. He's not capable of normal relationships with the opposite sex. It was just such an entanglement that led to his first relapse.'

'And Mariya . . . ?'

'I told her to keep away from him, but she didn't listen. She saw him behind my back.'

'At the Burghölzli?'

'He was staying here at the time. We'd hoped he was on the mend. There had been no trouble for some time. But then, he became worse than ever.' She brought a hand to her throat. 'It's quite possible Mariya was to blame. I don't know. I'd stopped teaching her by that time.'

'Are you saying they had an affair?'

The question came out more bluntly than he had intended.

'No, Dr Kirsch, I am *not* saying that. I only know that Eduard took a shine to her in his way. And she . . .'

'She . . . ?'

'She did nothing to discourage him. Even after I'd explained about his state of mind.' Mileva shook her head regretfully. 'She meant no harm, I'm sure. Perhaps she'd grown fond of him. But it did him no good, coming on top of everything else. No good at all.'

'Everything else?'

Mileva made no attempt to elucidate. 'So you see why I was — why I *remain* anxious to see that their acquaintance is not renewed. My son's health is paramount.'

'I understand.'

'I hope you do, Dr Kirsch. I hope you would not seek to treat one patient at the expense of another.'

In the hallway, the clock struck four. Mileva put down her cup and rose to her feet. Her pupil would be arriving any moment. She escorted him to the door.

'Will you be returning to Berlin at once? Or have you other business here?'

He would probably go first thing in the morning, he said. It was clearly what she wanted to hear.

'I do hope your treatment is successful,' she said as they shook hands. 'And that Miss Draganović will be able to return home.'

'Shall I send her your best wishes, at the appropriate time?'

Mileva hesitated. 'All things considered, Dr Kirsch, it would be best if she did not dwell any further on her time here. I think that would be best all round.'

* * *

214

There was no sign of a pupil, not on the stairs, not in the entrance hall, not in the street outside. Mileva had heard all she wanted to hear and said all she wanted to say. Kirsch felt sure there was more she could have told him. But she had come to regard Mariya's presence in Zürich as an intrusion, perhaps a threat, and already she saw him in the same way. Was it really her son's peace of mind that she was so anxious to protect? Or her own family honour? Or neither of those things? Was it Albert Einstein who had to be protected, his reputation, his unimpeachable name?

Kirsch could have called on Mileva again, of course, try to catch her in a more cooperative mood. But he felt sure that when he returned, whatever the day, whatever the hour, he would find she was regrettably unavailable.

Crossing the road, he looked back at the apartment. It took him a moment to realise that she was standing at one of the windows, a small dark figure, partially obscured by the reflected sky. He gave her a nod, but she simply stood there, framed like a painting, watching him walk away.

He ate supper at the Hotel St Gotthard and killed the evening at a crumbling picture palace a block away from the railway station. He sat in the smoky darkness, thinking about Mariya as the images danced on the patched and yellowed screen, and about Mileva.

How had she and Einstein ever made a couple? She was conventional where he was free-thinking, suspicious where he was open, remote where he was warm and sociable. Above all, she was secretive, whereas he had given his life to unravelling secrets. Max von Laue said Mileva understood Einstein's work, had shared in it once. Mariya's notebook suggested she was following it still, as best she could.

After the short feature came the newsreels. Kirsch sat up as General Schleicher's image flashed up on the screen. He was seen hurrying into the back of a motor car with a hard frown on his face. The commentary said he had failed to secure a majority in the Reichstag and had resigned from the government. Adolf Hitler had been

appointed Chancellor in his place. Kirsch recognised the Kaiserhof Hotel, small figures in long coats making their way through a thronging crowd, arms outstretched on every side. The picture cut to a victory parade of Brown-shirts and army veterans, thousands marching out of the Tiergarten and along the Charlottenburger Chausee towards the Brandenburg Gate. Kirsch hardly recognised the place. It was as if, in his absence, his city had been taken over by an alien horde. Bands formed up playing Prussian marches. Outside the French embassy they stopped and sang the old war song, 'Siegreich wollen wir Frankreich schlagen', their voices swelling like a drunken ocean. Then they marched on with their flaming torches – bank clerks and bus boys, eager as ever for the thrill of battle and the restitution of German honour. In the meantime, the Brown-shirts would have the freedom of the streets, to deal with their enemies as they saw fit, and no one would stand in their way.

And it occurred to Kirsch that if Mariya really was an Einstein, he would have to keep that knowledge to himself. Nobody could be allowed to know the truth, perhaps not even Mariya herself. There could be no publications in the medical press, no reports in the news-papers, however advantageous. It would have to be a secret, perhaps for ever.

He still wanted it to be true, though, in spite of the dangers. He wanted it to be true more than ever.

Twenty-nine

The Burghölzli Psychiatric Clinic lay in the southern suburbs of the city, with the Zürichsee on one side and the Zürichberg on the other. It was a grander building than the Charité, with a lofty stone-clad exterior reminiscent of an English stately home. The grounds were larger than anything on offer in Berlin, and the views from the upper floors were impressive, marred only by the busy railway which ran along the shore of the lake.

There were other differences. The Burghölzli boasted a special first-class section, like a passenger liner where, for an additional fee, patients could be accommodated in a suite, with fully furnished sitting and dining rooms. First-class patients were also excused work in the grounds or the workshops, which other patients were given as part of their general rehabilitation. The arrangements were discreet. Most of the second- and third-class patients were said to be completely unaware that they existed. Presumably, Kirsch reflected as he stepped out of the taxi, knowledge of their inferior status was thought likely to interfere with their treatment.

Albert Einstein's younger son was one of those who resided in the first-class section. Kirsch presented his card to a nurse at the front desk and was escorted down a series of corridors towards the south side of the building. The air seemed to improve as he went, the stench of boiled food and disinfectant being slowly replaced by subtler, more agreeable aromas: drapery, wood polish, flowers. This was more like the exclusively private clinics and sanatoriums that he had heard about. Found all over the Swiss Alps, they had once catered to wealthy consumptives, promising clean air, rest and gentle exercise in a conducive setting. Many had since moved into psychiatric care, offering water treatments and the latest cures, along with

copious amounts of peace and quiet – for a price. In Switzerland, madness, like the wars of its neighbours, had become a considerable source of profit.

They went through a locked door. On the far side a second nurse took the place of the first. She was tall and red-haired, with pale, lightly freckled skin. They climbed a flight of stairs and then she too disappeared, leaving him to wait on a landing. There he spent several minutes looking out of the window at the snow-covered grounds. He had no idea if Eduard Einstein would see him, but in his experience people confined to institutions rarely passed up an opportunity to escape the monotonous routine of their daily lives. The alternative was to go through his doctors, but they were sure to consult Mileva, an eventuality he wanted to avoid at all costs. Eduard was his last chance, the one person remaining who had known Mariya in Zürich and who might know the truth about her origins.

In a nearby room, a piano struck up: a rapid scale, ascending, descending. Then chords, heavy and dramatic. Kirsch strained to listen, but then the music abruptly stopped. He heard three or four bars of a waltz, then it too stopped on a single note, a note that repeated and repeated, as if the pianist was unhappy with the tuning.

The tall red-haired nurse returned. 'If you'll follow me,' she said.

Eduard Einstein sat at the piano with his back to the door. He was dressed in a white shirt and a pair of baggy checked trousers, secured by braces and a sturdy belt. His hair was dark and slicked back. The piano was an upright, the tuning dubious in the upper registers, but he played well, everything delicately phrased and note perfect.

The room was decently furnished, but untidy. A waste-paper basket was crammed full to overflowing. Piles of newspapers, a number from Berlin, were scattered across a kneehole desk, along with magazines and journals. An ashtray was overflowing with cigarette butts. A silk dressing gown had been slung over the back of an armchair. Kirsch found it uncomfortably warm, a large iron radiator trickling away beneath the double-glazed window, across which

a pair of iron bars had been fitted. The pervading smell was one of stale tobacco, mixed with an expensive variety of cologne.

When the piece was over, Eduard got to his feet. He took a deep breath, his shoulders slowly rising and falling, before finally turning towards his visitor. His mother was right: he had put on weight since the photograph in the garden. His cheeks and jowls were fuller. A prominence in his upper lip suggested a moustache where there was none. But he was still handsome: tall, dark like his mother, with the same strong mouth and lustrous eyes.

'Bravo,' Kirsch said.

The young man smiled but didn't look him in the eye. 'The Partita in D minor.' His voice was soft, hesitant. 'Not everyone likes Bach. They find him dry.'

'He can be a little mechanical in the wrong hands.'

Eduard lowered his gaze towards the patterned rug on the floor. 'My father likes Bach. He plays the violin. Not all that well. Not as well as he thinks he does, though nobody tells him that. They want to be able to say "I played with the great Professor Einstein". They don't care how rough it is. All they can think about is how they'll tell their friends.'

He encircled the fingers of his right had with his left, squeezing so that the knuckles cracked. Then abruptly he sat down on the edge of a nearby sofa.

Kirsch removed his coat and sat down opposite. People connected to Albert Einstein always seemed to mention him at the earliest opportunity. Even with Max von Laue it had only been a matter of minutes. But there was more to it than name-dropping – name-dropping was hardly necessary in Eduard's case, or in von Laue's. It was as if the man was constantly in their thoughts, a lens through which all things were seen.

'He'll play Mozart too, on occasion,' Eduard said. 'We always play Mozart together. But anything later he won't touch. It upsets him. Beethoven or Brahms – especially Brahms.'

'It's too difficult?'

'No. It has too much emotion. Too much feeling. He doesn't care for that.'

Kirsch watched the young man closely: he was evidently talented, but also conscious of his psychiatric condition, of his difference from other people. The two elements mingled to produce a shyness mixed with bursts of loquacity that was quite distinctive. He had seen it before among the most gifted patients; and he had often wondered if the gift owed something to the abnormality, or if the abnormality owed something to the gift.

'He won't go to the pictures for the same reason,' Eduard said. 'The sad scenes upset him. He's like a child in that way.'

'A child?'

Eduard nodded. The way he kept looking at the floor reminded Kirsch of a blind man.

'It makes no difference to him that the story isn't real. That's what I mean. He feels it no less than he would if it *were* real. No less and no more. That's why he stays away. He prefers tranquillity. He thinks he needs it to see.' Eduard placed his hands between his knees. 'Are you here for a second opinion, Dr Kirsch?'

'In a way.'

Eduard didn't wait for further explanation. 'I've been diagnosed with a schizo-affective disorder. But that's just because the psychiatrists here cannot agree about me. At first Dr Zimmermann diagnosed me with schizophrenia because my thoughts were disordered. My mental associations had loosened, making me incoherent.' He glanced up at Kirsch for a moment, as if appealing against this judgement. 'Also, he was of the opinion that I demonstrated conflicting emotion and attitudes towards other people. He had in mind my mother, I expect.'

'Your mother?'

'I attacked her. Didn't they tell you? I only meant to frighten her. I was angry. My father's the same. He has no control over his anger. Like a child, as I say. Mother thought I was going to throw her off the balcony. She's kept the French windows locked ever since.'

'I see.'

'A loosening of associations and emotional ambivalence are two of the criteria for diagnosing schizophrenia, according to Dr Bleuler.'

A twitchy smile formed on Eduard's lips. For the first time, Kirsch noticed that his teeth were slightly crooked and stained with nicotine.

'Dr Zimmermann is a follower of Dr Bleuler,' Eduard said. 'But Dr Schuler isn't. In his opinion, I lack the clear evidence of hallucinations, which he regards as necessary for a diagnosis of schizophrenia. He says I suffer from a mood disorder, a depressive mania possibly with an hereditary component. There may be something in that. My mother's frequently depressed. She's been that way since I was a boy.' He sniffed loudly. 'Have you met my mother?'

'Yes.'

'Some people say she was different once. Before my father went to Berlin. She was actually happy.'

He sat staring for a moment, then looked up suddenly, frowning. 'Yes, yes, they could not agree. But then they heard about this new disorder from America: the schizo-affective disorder. And that seemed like a good compromise, being schizophrenia with manic interludes.'

'They explained all this to you?'

Eduard talked so quickly Kirsch found it a struggle to follow him.

'Oh no. The other way around. I explained it to them.'

'I'm sorry, I don't –'

'It was me who suggested the diagnosis.' Eduard's hands slid out from between his knees and settled on top. 'I have more time for the psychiatric journals than they do.' He nodded towards his over-crowded desk. 'I have nothing to do but read. I read all day.'

Eduard showed every sign of being starved of conversation. It came as no surprise. Psychiatric nurses, while often compassionate, were not inclined to sit around and chat, certainly not on the more erudite topics that Eduard was drawn to. If it was true that he had inherited his father's genius, it was a genius without the same clear goals, a restless undirected force that put him at a distance from the world around him, but brought no benefits to compensate. If there was a goal, it was only that he should gain his illustrious father's attention and hold it for as long as possible.

'I'm not here to make another diagnosis, Herr Einstein.'

'Your card says psychiatrist.'

'That's right.'

'Then you can give a second opinion – or a third.'

'But who would I give it to?'

Eduard looked puzzled. 'To me. One can't have too many opinions. The more you have, the better your chance of finding one to your liking.'

'I'm not sure my opinion would be of any value. Besides –'

Eduard put his head on one side. 'What is the general view of Dr Jung in Berlin? Dr Jung says what we call mental illness is usually a creation of the unconscious – a crisis that forces us to recognise obstacles to our development as individuals. He says we should embrace it.'

'So I've read.'

'What people call mental illness is just a new way of seeing things. A way they don't like. It's a comforting idea, don't you think, that there's some point to being mad? A reason for unreason.'

Eduard smiled again, tentatively. It seemed to Kirsch that everything he did was tentative, except for his piano playing. He spoke rapidly, hurrying on from one idea to the next, as if anxious that none should be examined too closely. Kirsch realised he was sweating. The heating in the room was up way too high.

He took out a handkerchief. 'I'm not aware of a consensus in Berlin,' he said, 'regarding Dr Jung's ideas.'

Eduard smiled. 'I expect Freud is in the ascendant, being established there. I find his writings most persuasive, especially his analysis of the family. Have you read *Totem and Taboo*?' He ground the heels of his hands together, as if squeezing the words out from under his skin. 'Freud says every son instinctively wants to kill his father, to supplant him, while feeling guilty about it, of course. The father's role is to tame the son's instinct, to guide him so that he is capable of looking outward, beyond the family – beyond the clutches of the mother, in particular. To have the confidence to strike out into the world. But then, if there is no father . . .'

Kirsch dabbed at his forehead. It wasn't just the temperature in the room: he was running a fever. He could feel it in the tightness of his scalp, and the dull aching of his joints. And the way Eduard

talked, the ideas and opinions coming one after the other, that was feverish too.

'Herr Einstein,' he said, 'the reason I'm here ... I came to ask you about Mariya Draganović.'

Suddenly Eduard was very still. Either he was feigning surprise or he was surprised. Then he smiled. 'Mariya? I haven't heard from her in months.'

'Can you be more precise?'

'She sent me a postcard from Berlin. It was October. Just a postcard, then nothing.' Eduard frowned. 'How do you know her, may I ask?'

'She's a patient.'

'A patient?' The joints in his fingers clicked.

'She's suffered a kind of breakdown. I'm trying to uncover the circumstances surrounding it.'

Eduard stood up and went to the window. Two small cactus plants, like the ones in Frau Einstein's sitting room, were resting on the window sill. They were dome-shaped, the flesh beneath the needles a ghostly shade of green. Was that why the heating was up so high: because that was how the cactuses liked it?

'What are the symptoms?' he asked.

'Memory loss, primarily. At first she had no idea of her own identity. She's made some improvement, but the causes of her condition remain unresolved. It's possible she was attacked, but the police aren't sure.'

Eduard squatted down beside the big iron radiator. 'Attacked where?'

'In woods, outside Berlin.'

'Where exactly?'

'Somewhere near Potsdam. Why?'

Instead of answering, Eduard slowly turned the valve. 'But she remembers me?'

'From what I can gather, you were close.'

Eduard smiled again. 'She's very bright, you know. Like my mother when she was young. Mama didn't want to teach her at first. She was quite angry with Aunt Helene for sending her, but when she saw her

work she couldn't resist. A brain like that can't go to waste, she said. We have a responsibility.'

'A responsibility? Were those her exact words?'

Eduard nodded. 'I heard her talking on the telephone.'

Kirsch remembered the letter. *I urge you to be cautious in this matter and observe the agreements that have been entered into.*

'This Aunt Helene wouldn't be Helene Savić, by any chance?'

'She's not really my aunt. Just an old friend from my mother's student days. She's Austrian, but she married a Serb – the opposite to Mama: a Serb who married a German. A kind woman and clever. All Mama's friends are clever. She lives in Belgrade. Have you ever been to Belgrade, Doctor?'

Kirsch shook his head.

'Its name means "white city". That's rather beautiful, don't you think?'

'Your mother says she gave Mariya lessons for a couple of months, but then the lessons stopped. Why was that?'

Eduard brushed some dirt from his palms. 'Because Mama had nothing left to teach her. If you knew the kind of work she was doing . . .'

But Kirsch did know. Professor von Laue had told him.

'I believe she was working on the unified field theory,' he said. 'Specifically a five-dimensional geometry recently proposed by your father.'

Eduard blushed. 'My mother's idea.' He stood up abruptly and went over to the piano. 'She still follows everything my father does. Uncritically, of course. Have you ever delved into quantum physics, Dr Kirsch?'

Kirsch was anxious to avoid another of Eduard's academic digressions, but then he recalled that it was quantum physics that had filled Mariya's notebook, calculations of a type and complexity that even Max von Laue had been intrigued.

'I've read the odd thing,' he said.

'My father brought it into the world. He gave it life, but now he wants to disown it. He wishes it had never been born. He says if

224

quantum mechanics is real then the world is mad.' Eduard looked up at a faint brown stain on the ceiling. 'And nothing horrifies him more than madness.'

'He's not alone in that,' Kirsch said.

'Do you know why my father finds quantum theory so threatening?' Eduard said. 'The real reason?'

'The issues are beyond me, I'm sure.'

'Oh, they're as much visceral as intellectual, I assure you. Bohr and the others, they've created a world he can't stand to be in.' Eduard extended a finger and played a single note high up on the keyboard. 'Quantum theory says all observation is interaction. The physicist can't step outside reality and observe it objectively, any more than he can step outside the universe with a stop-watch and a measuring stick. In the quantum world, to see things is to shape them, and until they *are* seen, their nature remains in flux: potential but not actual. Bohr says physics is not about defining reality; it's about ordering the human *experience* of reality, which is quite a different thing – some would say, a lesser thing.' He played the first few notes of a melody, then stopped. 'So you see, quantum physics strips the scientist of his detachment. There's no escape from his own humanity. He's part of what he dissects, whether he likes it or not.'

'It sounds like you want your father to fail,' Kirsch said.

Eduard still had his back to him. 'Of course. But then I have a vested interest.'

'I don't understand.'

'If the world is mad, then I'm at no particular disadvantage. It's the rest of you who don't fit in.'

For a moment there was silence. Eduard seemed to be waiting for something. Either that or he had forgotten that he was not alone. At times, Kirsch felt the young man's intelligence like a pressure, bearing down. Perhaps it was the same for Eduard himself: not an advantage, a means to success or happiness, but the cause of his loneliness, a burden he could never set down.

'So is that why Mariya went to Berlin?' Kirsch said, finally. 'To continue her studies?'

'Perhaps.'

'Or was she hoping to find her father?'

Eduard remained very still. 'I thought her father was dead.'

'That would depend on who her father is, or was.'

Eduard sighed. 'You know, you can't help her like this. You're wasting your time.'

'Why do you say that?'

'Because Mariya isn't mad.'

'I never said she was. In any case, *mad* isn't a recognised psychiatric term, as I'm sure you know.'

'Ill then. *Defective*. Mariya is changing. It's a process, you see, a preparation. Aunt Helene understood. She understands everything.'

'A preparation for what?'

Eduard answered with a shrug, as if he could say more, but saw no reason why he should.

'Why did Mariya go to Berlin?' Kirsch asked again.

'The first I knew of it was when I got the postcard.'

'She didn't confide in you?'

Eduard played a single note, quite loud, then let his fingers run along the keys, revealing another fragment of melody. 'It isn't sensible to confide in mental patients. They can't be relied on to keep the secret.'

'What secret is that?'

'Any secret. I was stating an issue of principle and prudence.' The melody became a waltz, the same waltz Kirsch had heard while waiting on the landing. 'I hope you don't mind, Doctor. I have to practise for my father. Though it's more than he does. I'm expecting him any day now.'

Kirsch stood up. According to Professor von Laue, Einstein was in America and was not due back for more than a month.

'Thank you for your time, Herr Einstein,' he said, but Eduard went on playing, nodding in farewell – or was it simply in time to the music?

Outside in the corridor, the red-haired nurse sat waiting. As they descended the stairs together, the waltz abruptly stopped.

Thirty

I had forgotten about Aunt Helene's friend by the time I was old enough to attend the university at Zagreb. All I knew was that the money had been found for my fees and for a small living allowance, and that in some way Aunt Helene had played a part in obtaining it. Nor did I ask to be enlightened on the matter, for fear that my fortune would be snatched away from me. For though my father continued to take credit for my success and to boast of it whenever an opportunity arose, I did not feel in the least able to count on his support. For one thing, he had begun to drink a great deal, not just at night, but on and off throughout the day. His intervals of sobriety became increasingly fleeting and his mood subject to sudden and violent change. Even when he praised me to my face, which he did now and then, especially when in the early stages of intoxication, I did not feel reassured. He would invite me to join him in a glass of wine, making a big show of treating me behind my mother's back. Then he would tell me I was becoming quite a pretty little thing and that I should have to watch myself or some young devil would lead me astray. I was uncomfortable with such talk and would escape his presence on whatever pretext I could think of.

Late at night, when he was no longer sober enough for such pleasantries, I would hear him coming up the stairs. When his step was heavy I would stay in my bed. But sometimes I could hear him trying to make as little sound as possible so as not to be heard. And then I would leap out of bed and lock myself in the water closet or hide up in the attic. For I knew that when he was quiet, he had it in mind to say goodnight to me in my room, the idea of which made me uneasy. I lived in those years much like a cat, or so it must have appeared to him. For, like a cat, I would disappear rather than be alone in his company without some visible means of escape. All this I did while trying never to displease

him. For I felt sure that should he remove me from my studies, I would be condemned to a life of imprisonment beneath his roof. For you must remember that I was entirely without means of my own.

I suppose most girls in my position would have looked for a new life in marriage. But the truth is, it would have been a far from simple matter for me to find myself a husband in Orlovat. Our father did not entertain a great deal, considering himself too good for most of our neighbours and we, in turn, were not often entertained, except occasionally by relatives. Nor had I many friends from my schooling, except for a handful of girls who lived in Bečkerek. Besides, the idea of marriage did not much appeal to me. The men roundabouts were mostly of the rude country kind, with no learning and even less regard for it — like the boys who once threw pebbles at me, only grown larger and more sure of themselves. For them, any young woman who went to the city alone was a kurva, or would become one before very long, and the very last thing I wanted was for such a notion to reach my father's ears. For I knew that there could be no greater disgrace to a family than to have a kurva in it, as I was taught from a very young age, even before I knew what a kurva was. (When I asked my grandmother, she would say only that it was a Jezebel, which shed no great light on the matter, Jezebel being, to my mind, a princess in the Bible who worshipped Baal and was thrown out of a window.)

But go to Zagreb I did, to be enrolled in the Faculty of Science. I was one of just three women in my year, and the only one taking mathematics.

I could have rejoiced more at my departure, had it not been for my sister. I felt regret at leaving her, and some guilt as well. Senka now lived like a servant in our house, making herself scarce whenever there was company and having, besides me, no society at all but that of the animals, and sometimes the women who came to work in the orchards. I was afraid she would be lonely without me. I had less fear that our father would mistreat her as he had done in the past. Her presence no longer seemed to anger him. He provided for her better than he had during the war. She ate at the table as often as not, and had sometimes new dresses and boots and stockings in the winter. I imagined my mother had reminded him of his obligations and he had gone along with her wishes so as to appease her. Only Senka took these meagre things as

evidence of paternal love, which I could all too plainly see in the hundred little things she did to try to please him, from saving him the very largest, freshest eggs, to cleaning his pipe and fluffing up the cushions on his chair. I should perhaps have guessed that there were other reasons for the change in his behaviour, but Senka said nothing to me. We had begun to spend less time together, what with all the studying I had to do. I suppose I didn't want to see what was under my nose. Had I seen it, or imagined it, then I would have been forced to speak out – and in the process all my hopes would certainly have been dashed.

I had been at Zagreb about a year and a half when I had word from my mother that Senka had gone down with a fever. She did not ask me to return home, but I could tell from her letter that she was fearful, for she said she had moved into the same room as my sister so as to watch her all night, and be there to calm her when she was in her delirium. So I set off the next day with a small suitcase and a trunk full of books – for there were mathematics examinations six weeks away and I had no idea how long I should be away. To be truthful, I was very much afraid of performing badly, for all manner of reasons. Not the least of these was the certainty that if I did, people would say it was proof that I had taken my female intellect as far as it could go in such a rigorous sphere – for, to be sure, they were saying it already, without any cause whatsoever.

When I arrived home, things were not as I had expected. Senka was all but recovered, but now it was my mother who was sick. The doctor, whom our father had only now sent for, said she was suffering from pneumonia. Our father wanted her removed to a hospital, but the doctor, who came every day all the way from Novi Sad, said that the journey would only make her worse (for it was very cold, being February). In any case, the hospital could do no more for her than was being done already. And he said it had been most unwise of my mother to stay in such proximity with Senka, for the best thing to do with infections was to keep a distance as much as possible. At the same time, several of our animals died for no clear reason, and the doctor remarked, somewhat severely I thought, that this was very likely where the trouble had begun. I wondered at his being so free with his speculation and wished he had kept his opinions to himself. It was not wise or fair, it seemed to me,

to dish out blame in such circumstances, especially when there was no way of knowing how or where it might rebound.

On the third day I was taking a bowl of broth to my mother when she took hold of my sleeve and bade me sit down by her bed. She was pale and thin in the face, and for the first time I could clearly see the impression of her skull through her shrunken flesh, the round eye sockets and the rows of teeth that her thin lips barely covered. I sat down with the bowl of soup and the tray on my lap and thought this is how Death comes, not with a knock at the door, but from within. He is there inside us, waiting to come out. After that, I did not want to look at my mother any more, for fear that I would only see Death there, and not my mother at all.

She took my hand and told me that something had been troubling her, and asked if I would set her mind at rest, to which I said I would with all my heart. She said she was much afraid about the future and in particular for Senka. She asked me to promise that I would take care of her and see that she was always provided for, as much as it was in my power. 'You will be all right with a husband,' she said. 'But poor Senka will be all alone one day, but for you.'

Her concern seemed to me somewhat one-sided. For, as I have said, I saw no great prospect of a husband in my future. I was almost as much alone in the world as my sister, and certainly as dependent on our father's good will. But I held my tongue and promised that I would do as she said. As if by way of consolation, my mother then patted my hand and said she had no worries where I was concerned, for she had always known I had some bright stars in my destiny and that they would take care of me. And at once I thought of how fortunate I had been with my education and the money that had been found to pay for it, and wondered if there was not more to the matter than destiny alone.

The next day my mother seemed somewhat improved. She had some colour in her face, had regained some appetite and was more animated generally; so that we had cause to think the worst had passed. But two nights later the fever returned more strong than ever. She was delirious and woke us all with her crying out. Then she was suddenly quiet again and fell asleep, and by morning she was dead.

I never thought there was any great love between her and our father,

especially on his part, for he was always complaining at her. I had never been able to picture them as a courting couple, solicitous with each other and ardent in their feelings. But when my mother died, it was as if our father had lost everything that mattered to him, as if the greatest love imaginable had been brought to a tragic end. He wept and moaned and carried on such that I could not bear to be near him, but instead took my grief outside the house and shared it with poor Senka, who I was afraid would not understand what had happened or why. We huddled in a corner of the stable and clung to each other and wept, as our old horse looked on, shifting his weight from hoof to hoof. When it was at last time to go back into the house, the geese gathered all around us, following close behind like an escort of mourners. Not one of them hissed at me that time or showed any sign of hostility, which I appreciated even in my distracted state.

There is no need to describe further those days, except to say that it fell to me to make the funeral arrangements and that I was glad of the occupation. I also found that in being mindful of my sister's sorrow and doing my best to comfort her, I found no small comfort for myself. There is no better way to make light a burden than to take up another's, as I am sure you have observed.

I was concerned that without a woman to cook and clean, my father would let everything fall into chaos. So I made arrangements for a woman in the village, a respectable widow by the name of Maja Lukić, to keep house. She had worked for my mother once before, as a nursemaid and help around the house, and had always given a good account of herself. Father slowly regained his composure and, after a period of a week or so after my mother had been laid to rest in the churchyard, went as far as to ask if I did not have studies to attend to in Zagreb.

A short while later I bade farewell to Senka and made my way back to that city, grateful for the chance to devote myself to my work, but with a sense of foreboding that I could not fully account for. Father was quiet, quieter now than he had ever been, and Senka was fully recovered from her illness. Yet I sensed something brittle in this tranquil state of affairs, like a thin layer of ice over a skating pond, just waiting to crack.

Thirty-one

Robert Eisner forced open the drawer using a screwdriver and the heel of his shoe. The filing cabinet wasn't usually locked. He had delved into it before without recourse to such drastic measures. Sometimes he was curious to know how Kirsch was handling his cases (Kirsch was so much better at keeping up with the latest thinking). More usually he was on a hunt for items of stationary or official forms, Kirsch's office being a lot closer to his own than the store cupboard two floors below. On this occasion his motives were financial, although the very fact that Kirsch had locked the cabinet on his departure for Switzerland was curious – not to say provocative. After all the favours Eisner had done him, Kirsch was not entitled to secrets.

The top drawer came loose with a jolt. It slipped from its mountings and crashed onto the drawer below. Eisner froze, listening. It would be embarrassing to be caught in Kirsch's office with a screwdriver and a ruptured filing cabinet, but it was half past six and most of the patients and staff were having supper. He turned off the overhead light. Working by the desk light alone, he hauled the drawer back into place and got on with rifling through the files.

The first thing that caught his eye was the letter from Dr Eugen Fischer of the Kaiser Wilhelm Institute. It seemed Kirsch had won himself a lucrative commission. *I consider this work to be of the highest importance, and I feel sure it will result in a significant publication.* Eisner sniffed. So that was it: a fat cheque *and* a significant publication. He wondered what Kirsch had done to deserve such preferment. Alma's father must have put in a good word. What other explanation could there be? Unless Fischer had seen Kirsch's name in the newspapers: *the eminent psychiatrist assigned to the case.*

What a joke that was. *The eminent Dr Kirsch*. What an outrageous piece of luck.

There were voices on the other side of the door. Nurses. Eisner eased the drawer shut and picked up a book, preparing to look nonchalant. The nurses laughed, the clack of their shoes growing louder before retreating down the corridor.

Eisner went back to the cabinet. At first, de Vries had been content with verbal information about the case – impressions, observations, gossip – for which he paid surprisingly well. Eisner had told him as much as he could, which was not a great deal, Kirsch being lately so secretive and untrusting. But lately the reporter had grown more demanding. He wanted facts, case notes, details.

'You want me to steal them?' Eisner had protested.

'Of course not,' de Vries had replied. 'I want you to borrow them, for a fee.'

Patient E's file was the fattest in the drawer. Eisner spread out the contents on the desk: newspapers, postcards of Berlin, sketches in pencil and charcoal. Faces loomed up out of the dark shading, like ghosts from the grave: a kindly old man with white hair, a matinée idol type, frowning thoughtfully. Here was Heinrich Mehring's shiny dome; Nurse Auerbach with her glossy painted lips, lips he planned on kissing, if nothing better came along. And here was Kirsch himself. His portrait was bigger than the others, his features rendered in bolder lines. He looked sad. But what did he have to be sad about? A luckier man had never been born.

But something was missing. Where were the notes? The reports of interviews, diagnoses, formal and informal? Where were the reports of medication and treatment? Patient E's was not a medical file. It was a collection of keepsakes. As if Patient E were not really a patient at all.

But if she were not a patient, then what was she?

The telephone rang. Eisner jumped to his feet. Someone must have spotted him sitting at Kirsch's desk – perhaps Kirsch himself. Eisner looked over his shoulder at the narrow window. It was too dirty for anyone to see in. Or was it?

The telephone went on ringing then abruptly stopped. Eisner eased himself back into the chair, a hand over his pulsating heart.

Near the bottom of the file was some kind of receipt. It was for advance payment of a month's worth of rent, dated a week before Christmas. But the name at the bottom was not that of Kirsch's usual landlady, Frau Schirmann. This landlord was called Mettler and his premises were on Wörtherstrasse.

Kirsch kept a city street map in the top drawer of his desk. Eisner ran his finger down the index. Wörtherstrasse. He had heard the name before. The grid reference told him it was somewhere north of Alexanderplatz – very near Kirsch's place, in fact. Why would Kirsch be renting two apartments, juts a few streets apart?

That was when he remembered.

Kirsch had called it a ladies' rooming house. It was where the Einstein girl had been staying before she lost her memory. But why was Kirsch paying her rent? And how long had he been doing it? A week? A month? A year?

The bulb in the desk light was emitting a high-pitched buzz. It burned suddenly brighter then went out with a loud pop. Eisner sat in the dark, thinking about Kirsch and Mariya Draganović, trying to work out what was going on; trying to see what he had missed.

There had always been aspects of the affair that were distasteful, not to mention odd: the way Kirsch had cornered the case, thrusting himself into the limelight at the first hint of press interest, launching himself at photographers like an aspiring actress at an opening night. Eisner had assumed that this was simply a matter of self-interest. A famous psychiatrist was a valuable psychiatrist. Private clinics would pay good money to put a recognised name on their staff. Was there more to it than that? Was there another story, besides doctor and patient, that he knew nothing about?

If so, how much would de Vries pay for that?

The door of the rooming house was open no more than three inches, a chain across the gap thick enough to strangle an ox. It was a raw

night, frost already glistening on the cobbles, making them treacherous underfoot.

'I'm a reporter with the *Berliner Morgenpost*,' Eisner said, because that was the best lie he could think of. 'I was hoping for some background on your old tenant, Fräulein Draganović.'

Herr Mettler, dressed in a greasy chef's apron, squinted at him through steamed-up lenses. An unappetising smell of boiled flesh drifted out into the night.

'I've nothing to say,' he said, putting his shoulder to the door.

'I'd pay.' Eisner reached into his pocket and produced three five-Reichsmark notes, holding them up where Mettler could see them. 'For your time and trouble. I realise it's late.'

The door remained ajar. The chain rattled against the wood.

'Herr Mettler?'

'What do you want to know?'

'Just what you told the doctors at the Charité. About your tenant.'

'Why don't you ask them?'

'You mean Dr Kirsch?' Mettler did not reply. 'He's left the country, unfortunately. No one knows when he'll be back. Besides, you know how doctors are.' With a twist of thumb and finger, he fanned the banknotes out. 'Ten minutes of your time. And I promise not to quote you. No one will know I was here.'

A truck was approaching, yellow headlamps flickering among the avenues of trees, long shadows reaching across the road like claws. Over the roar of the engine, Eisner heard shouting.

Herr Mettler took off the chain and held open the door. As soon as Eisner was inside, he shut it again, bolting it top and bottom. The uncomfortable thought occurred to Eisner that he was now a prisoner. He hunched his shoulders and glanced around the hallway, took in the faded green wallpaper with its floral pattern, the row of empty pigeon-holes, the grandfather clock in the corner with one hand missing. The smell from the kitchen was awful – not a cooking smell at all, but the smell of bones being boiled up for stock. And he thought suddenly of Carl Grossmann and Georg Haarmann and the other

famous murderers who had cooked up their victims' bodies to make potted meat.

Herr Mettler closed the kitchen door and held out his hand for payment. 'I don't keep tabs on my tenants,' he said. 'As long as they pay up, then as far as I'm concerned, they can do as they please.'

Eisner handed over the notes and waited to be shown into another room, but it seemed the interview was to be conducted in the hallway. Herr Mettler squinted at the money then squirrelled it away in the folds of his apron.

'That was one thing I wanted to ask about. *Has* she been paying up?'

'The room's still hers for the time being.'

'Thanks to Dr Kirsch. He's been paying for her?'

'He's made arrangements on her behalf.'

'Very kind of him. Most unusual for a doctor, wouldn't you say?' Mettler said nothing. 'How long are these arrangements going to continue?'

'You'd have to ask him.'

Herr Mettler squinted at Eisner, his tongue working around his grey incisors, as if in anticipation of a meal. There *was* something furtive about him, a demeanour of concealment. Perhaps it had something to do with his tenants. Maybe they weren't all studious young ladies, come to Berlin to improve their minds.

'I'd like to see her room, if I may.'

If Kirsch and the girl were already lovers, there would be some proof of the fact up in that room. There would be a love letter, a photograph – a book, knowing Kirsch. A book that might be revealingly inscribed.

'What for?' Herr Mettler said.

'Background. What's the number?'

'Three.'

'Does it have a double bed or a single?'

'Single. All my rooms have singles. This is an establishment for ladies.'

Eisner glanced up the stairs, saw no sign of light. 'Which floor?'

'A let room is a private room. This isn't a fairground.'

'Of course not. Fifty Reichsmarks for a quick look around.' From the kitchen came a hissing sound. Eisner eased the last of his banknotes into view. 'The girl's lost her mind, for God's sake. Why should she care?'

Herr Mettler sniffed and pushed his spectacles back up his nose. 'Sixty. And everything stays put.'

'Agreed.'

Herr Mettler eyed the money. 'I'll get the key.'

He went back inside the kitchen. Another belch of fetid carcass wafted into the hall. Eisner brought a handkerchief to his nose and turned away, his gaze coming to rest on a letter lying propped up in one of the pigeon-holes, beneath the number 3.

The letter was addressed to Mariya Draganović. It bore a foreign stamp and a postmark that clearly read: ZÜRICH. Was it Kirsch's handwriting? It was hard to tell.

There was no time to think it over. He took the letter, slipped it inside his wallet and tucked the wallet back inside his coat.

Herr Mettler reappeared with a key in his hand.

'You know what?' Eisner said, moving back to the door. 'Maybe I'll come back another day. I've already taken up enough of your time.'

Back on the train, Eisner tore open the envelope. There was a letter inside, though the motion of the train made it impossible to read more than a few words at a time. The handwriting was cramped and untidy, obscured by frequent crossings-out, occasionally switching into schoolroom clarity, with neat, upright letters, before collapsing back into a scrawl.

The writing was not the only strange thing: the envelope was addressed to Mariya, but the letter inside began *Dear Elisabeth*. Was that a mistake? Eisner wondered. If not, which was the correct name?

He got off at Friedrichstrasse. They had installed new electric lights above the platform. Round and white, they were lodged in the whitewashed ceiling like a row of sightless eyes. He pulled out the letter again and read from the beginning:

Zürich, 1 February

Dear Elisabeth,

I thought you hadn't answered my letter, or if you had, that they hadn't let me see your reply. I didn't want to write again, because what could I say if I was being spied on? I usually give my letters to a nurse here who is friendly. She posts them outside with the money I give her, but it is possible she gives them to Dr Zimmermann first. I don't know if I can trust her. So this time I am posting the letter myself on one of our trips out. There is a confectionary shop with a post box outside. We are always led inside to look at the sweets, as if we are all children, and we are allowed to buy something if we have some pocket money. It's a pathetic exercise, but I play along.

I've been waiting for you to come back from Berlin and hoping fervently for the success of your mission. I never believed you had forgotten me, but I did fear that you had given up all hope of success and returned to Vojvodina. I had many bad thoughts about it, but I never guessed that you might have fallen ill, or rather that they would say you are ill so as to watch you and make sure you keep quiet. I feared there would be dangers for you in that troubled city, but perhaps I didn't realise how great those dangers would be. The world is changing. Ignorance is safer than knowledge; lies a lighter burden than the truth. Still, I hope you don't blame me for telling you what I know. I could see how very great was your need, if only because of the child.

Earlier today, while I was practising the piano, a doctor arrived from Berlin, a psychiatrist called Kirsch. He said you had suffered a breakdown, but he also said you had been attacked in the woods, which made me suspicious. He said you had amnesia, but that you remembered me, which was the one thing I felt I could believe. It made me happy for a while, because – I admit it – for a long time I thought you had forgotten me. I even feared that you might have decided to go to America, alone. If only I could see you again, I could make everything clear. I fear that without my guidance, you have been overcome with doubt.

The doctor from Berlin asked all kinds of questions. Mostly he wanted to know why you went there, which is just what I would expect

238

from a private detective, if a private detective had been hired. He would want to know what you know and how you know it, if you could prove your claims and what the dangers are that there will be a scandal. When I see my father I am resolved to tell him about you, though it will not be easy. These are things I am still not supposed to speak about. Besides, his mind is all on the quantum question, those seeds of madness he has unleashed on the world and now wishes to lock away again, as Mr Rochester locked away his poor, mad wife. But I will find a way to do it for your sake; so that you may be free, at least, from the fears that haunt you.

I wonder if this Dr Kirsch is really treating you, as he says. Is he really a psychiatrist? He has the look of a haunted man and his hands shake, although he tries to hide it. It cannot be that he is afraid of me, but he is afraid of something. He is desperate to know the truth about you, as if his own life depended on it. I have never before seen a doctor so devoted to his case, so anxious to learn rather than to pronounce and prescribe. For a doctor he knew a certain amount about physics, which is not the usual way of things.

For all my doubts, I did enjoy talking with him. I didn't feel so much like the 'bad seed' in his presence – perhaps he is a 'bad seed', too. I sensed something of the kind. For sure, he is not like the doctors here. When he asks a question it is because he wants to know your opinion and not merely so that he may judge you – I mean, the state of your mind and the degree or character of your derangement. He seemed content to argue with me as an equal, which made it difficult for me to guard my answers. It was tempting to tell him everything, but of course I did not do that. I have a feeling I will see him again. He knows there is more to learn about you and me.

I think of you often, Lieserl. When I open my eyes first thing in the morning, it is your face I have before me. So I know I have been dreaming of you even if the dream itself has slipped away. I imagine you travelling through the great city, your face lit by shop windows and the passing glare of street lamps. I imagine you reading by a window, reading the manuscript I gave you perhaps – no doubt frowning at the untidy prose and the strangeness of the story, which to those

locked up in the prison of commonplace perceptions will probably make very little sense. I imagine you liking it, of course, or at least feeling the need to finish it. Because if you do not finish, you will never fully understand what it is you have read. And remember, I am still counting on you for a title.

I long for your return to Zürich, though I wonder now if it will ever come about. If not, I urge you to burn what I gave you, rather than let it fall into the hands of those who would silence me once and for all.

I must go now or I may be discovered.

Yours always,

Eduard

Thirty-two

Einstein's family and friends had taken a vow, so it seemed to Kirsch. Enquiries about the physicist's private life, like his whereabouts, were greeted with silence or evasion. Those who knew the most said the least. Those who knew next to nothing – newspapers, politicians, clerics – felt free to pronounce on the innermost working of his mind and the content of his soul. Eduard Einstein still offered the best hope of establishing the facts. Illness and isolation might have weakened his resolve and his loyalty. He might reveal what he knew he shouldn't. But could his account be trusted? His grasp of the world was unconventional and unsettling, coloured with thoughts of persecution and paranoia, concealed beneath a veneer of scholarly objectivity. He might say anything it suited him to say.

Kirsch went through the proper channels, disguising the real nature of his interest. He wrote letters to the director of the Burghölzli, Hans-Wolfgang Maier, and to Dr Jakob Schuler, asking for their help with his study of diagnostics. He didn't mention Eduard Einstein. He was afraid they might not agree to discuss his case, given that he was a first-class patient and the son of such a famous man.

After two days, he changed rooms to one overlooking the street. He read the newspaper and watched the procession of pedestrians and motor cars, the regular circuits of the trams, the punctual opening and closing of shops marked at the hour and the half-hour by the chorus of bells. He imagined the young Einstein looking down from the Polytechnic, observing these conventions of time and imagining different ones: a universe perhaps in which time was not strictly linear, but moved like a pendulum, accelerating, decelerating, then reversing altogether, running backwards to the point where it began,

the laws of physics running backwards with it. Or a universe in which the pace of time corresponded to the beat of the human heart, the seconds compressing during excitement or exertion and stretching during rest – finally stretching to infinity with the last heartbeat of all.

Or a universe in which the rotation and orbit of individual planets was irregular, like the motion of sub-atomic particles. The length of each day and night would have been unpredictable; likewise the procession of tides and seasons. Sundials would have been useless. Clocks would never have been invented, because it would have been impossible to synchronise them. Instead of watches, people would have carried astrolabes or sextants, so as to be able to measure the elevation of the sun and stars. The rhythm and structure of life would have been tied not to the abstract and the notional, but to what was tangible and real.

And when we're back again, we can argue about the non-existence of time.

That was what Max had said that last day on the lake, anticipating an argument with his unenlightened brother. It was almost the last thing Kirsch could remember him saying. For years it had bothered him the way this fragment of chat – trivial and impersonal – stuck in his mind. What if it *was* true, that time had no real existence? What if it *were* only a useful convention mistakenly elevated to the status of absolute? The world was full of tenuous abstractions, dressed up as absolutes. Civilisation was not built on relativity, let alone quantum mechanics. It was built on faith. A man had to believe in something, wasn't that what everyone always said? You had to nail your colours to one mast or another. If not, where was loyalty, duty, sacrifice? Where was morality? Where was love?

Looking at Zürich through his hotel window, Kirsch rehearsed this notional argument for the hundredth time. Along with Einstein's book, it had been Max's parting gift. And, like the book, when he immersed himself in it, it brought Max back: a living, animated presence only just out of sight.

* * *

By night his dreams were stark and lucid. He dreamed he was back at the front, guns rumbling in the distance, wounded coming in on stretchers. He dreamed he had no instruments to operate with. He'd mislaid them, an offence meriting court martial, like a private soldier losing his rifle. He dreamed that Karl Bonhoeffer had died, leaving Dr Mehring in charge at the Charité; and that Mehring wanted his patients for a new experimental treatment involving electricity applied to the brain. More often he dreamed of Mariya. He saw her at the Tanguero, dancing with a tall, handsome man, who he only realised on waking was Eduard Einstein. She was wearing the blue dress and stockings from Karstadt's. Everything was back the way it was. But when he asked her what had happened, he couldn't hear her answer over the noise of the band. Then they were running for a train to Potsdam, where she made him jealous taking a boat out alone with Max, drifting into the mist so that all Kirsch could hear was the faint echo of their laughter. And he wondered at himself for having made such a naïve mistake, it being obvious that Max was a far better match for Mariya than he was. But when the boat came back to the shore, he saw that Mariya was no longer on board, and instead of Max there was just an old man with a face so badly disfigured, he could hardly bear to look at him.

It was possible such visions would soon invade his waking hours, the way they had during the war. The important thing was to be prepared. He could still function with an overactive imagination. For the present at least, there was no reason why anyone else had to know.

One morning on his way down to breakfast, the bellboy handed him a telegram. It was from Dr Bonhoeffer's secretary, Frau Rosenberg.

VACANCY POSITION DEPUTY DIRECTOR STOP
RETURN BERLIN SOONEST STOP

Kirsch sat at a table by the window and counted the words. Perhaps the telegraph office charged in blocks of ten these days, or five.

Either way, the wordage was inadequate: two sentences juxtaposed, the connection between them left open to any number of inter-pretations. Dr Mehring's position had apparently fallen vacant; and he was expected to cut short his stay in Switzerland and return to Berlin. Was it to cover for the deputy director until a replacement could be found? Was the vacancy permanent, or had Dr Mehring merely taken a temporary leave of absence? If so, six words would have been enough:

MEHRING ILL STOP RETURN BERLIN STOP

Outside, it was snowing again, light flurries descending from a misty sky. He brought his coffee cup to his mouth, the lip rattling gently against his teeth. Perhaps Frau Rosenberg thought it improper to broadcast Dr Mehring's condition across the telegraph network. Perhaps she considered it a medium unsuitable for private infor-mation, whether personal or professional.

MEHRING PILES STOP RETURN BERLIN STOP

He let out a nervous laugh. Better than illness, a resignation squared with Mehring's volte-face over the Nurse Ritter incident. If he had been lining up a new position for himself at another clinic, he might have wanted to tie up loose ends at the Charité, rather than leave the whole messy business unresolved. Of one thing Kirsch was certain: he wasn't being invited to step into the deputy director's shoes. Among the staff were other clinicians with more experience and more seniority than him.

He didn't want to leave Zürich yet. There was still too much to learn, information that might secure Mariya's future. But what choice did he have? As things stood, he was the one who made the deci-sions concerning Mariya and her treatment. But if the staff changed, that might change too. Heinrich Mehring was not the only psych-iatrist eager to try out new treatments aimed at pacifying the insane.

* * *

Immediately after breakfast he telephoned the Burghölzli and asked for Dr Schuler.

'I'd hoped to call on you before my return to Berlin.'

Schuler was apologetic. If he had received the letter, the contents had slipped his mind. He seemed flustered by the possibility that he had shown professional discourtesy, and invited Kirsch up to the hospital that same afternoon. 'I'm sure we'll be able to assist you,' he said. 'I'm a great admirer of your Dr Bonhoeffer. He's done so much for the profession over the years.'

Kirsch set off on foot. He took a small hipflask of brandy to keep out the cold, and struck out along the eastern shore of the Zürichsee. The journey took him longer than expected, and the light was fading by the time he reached the outer suburbs, the sun's last rays falling on snow-capped mountains far to the south. On an empty, wooded road he stopped to catch his breath. Down below, the lake had turned a mineral blue.

He took a swig of brandy and stood listening to the silence, a silence broken only by the sound of his own breathing. He listened intently for some other sign of life, but there was none. He felt suddenly hot. The hair on the nape of his neck was damp.

He reached for a handkerchief. The effort of searching his pockets left him breathless. His sight clouded over, swirling red-black masses masking the road and the sky. He had to steady himself against a telegraph pole. The thought occurred to him that he was dreaming again, still lying in his bed at the hotel. The city below him was a dream city, occupied only by ghosts and memories. He had dreamed his way into the hinterland of Professor Einstein's life, to a place where his presence still echoed among the narrow cobbled streets, where those he had touched now lived as if trapped in the amber of those precious days.

He took a deep breath. Darts of light swam in a river of blood. He wasn't dreaming. Exertion and alcohol were responsible. Perhaps a touch of fever. He straightened up, his vision clearing. The sweat at the nape of his neck had turned cold.

A locomotive's whistle echoed across the valley. He was in danger

of being late. He carried on up the road, picking up the pace. He had just gone around a bend when he became aware of movement to his right: a man, also walking, keeping pace with him at a distance of perhaps fifty yards. Kirsch could make out his slender form quite distinctly out of the corner of his eye: a young man silhouetted against the distant patches of light. But when he turned to look, he saw nothing but trees.

A flock of birds swooped by, their wings scything the air. He hunched his shoulders and walked on. The man was still there. He moved silently from shadow to shadow, disturbing nothing, like a hunter stalking prey. He wasn't trying to hide, though. He wanted Kirsch to know he was there.

Thirty-three

Dr Jakob Schuler was a slight, dapper man with gold rings on his fingers, a salt-and-pepper moustache and tidy, thinning hair. A pair of close-fitting spectacles lent him an appearance of owl-like wisdom, which must have impressed his patients greatly. He was senior enough – just shy of sixty – not only to have worked alongside the previous director, the renowned Eugen Bleuler, but to have openly disagreed with him as well.

'He wasted too much time on Freud.' He spoke rapidly, his voice clipped but loud. 'Always trying to appease the fellow, telling him how important he was: the Copernicus of the mind and that sort of nonsense.'

They were walking down a long corridor, Schuler levering himself along with the aid of a stick, his white coat unbuttoned.

'Bleuler was fundamentally insecure, an incorrigible fence-sitter. He was afraid of being cast into the outer darkness, among the *unbelievers*. You know how it is with Freud.'

'You mean, you're with him or against him?'

'Correct.'

This part of the building was brightly lit and noisy with the constant coming and going of staff. The second- and third-class patients were having supper in the refectory, providing an opportunity for the wards and other areas to be cleaned and searched – the regime being strict about the prohibition of alcohol, tobacco and other stimulants, except by permission of the doctors. Despite the antiseptic appearance of the place, there was a faecal taint to the air, not completely covered by a more powerful aroma of bleach.

'That particular brand of *belief* is all very well,' Schuler said, 'when your clients are paying fifty francs an hour, but in a place

like this it's nothing but trouble. People don't take kindly to enquiries about their sexual impulses, especially when their mothers are brought into it.' We stepped around an orderly who was on his knees, sponging a dark spattered stain from the wall. 'I have no objection to the basic approach. The emphasis on childhood is quite persuasive. But his sexualised model of family relations is doctrinaire.'

Karl Bonhoeffer had a similar view of Freud's theories. Perhaps this had predisposed Schuler to cooperate with Kirsch's researches, once it had been established that the identity of his patients would be properly concealed.

'The degree of subjectivity in these diagnoses is a constant source of friction,' he said. 'And by looking at family histories you may also shed some light on the hereditary question. I'm always reading that mental instability is passed from generation to generation, but it would be good to see some data.'

'My aim is to focus only upon diagnostic criteria,' Kirsch said. 'I want to establish if they're consistent; and if the current classification of mental illness is scientific.'

Schuler frowned, the rubber tip of his stick making sharp contrapuntal squeaks as he limped along. 'And what happens if you find it *isn't* scientific? Are we supposed to give up psychiatric medicine altogether?'

'Why should we?'

Schuler look surprised. 'Well, Dr Kirsch, it seems to me our claim to be doctors, to be working in a branch of medicine, rests upon our ability to identify discrete illnesses. If we can't say what people are suffering from, what else are we good for?'

Kirsch remembered what Dr Fischer had said when they first met: *Status. It's the Achilles heel of the whole profession.*

Schuler fished out a key from his pocket. 'Until we started calling insanity an illness, and as such susceptible to medical treatment – at least potentially – most sufferers were simply locked away like guilty secrets. Bad seed, and all that. Illness carries less in the way of stigma. Medicine, however rudimentary, at least offers hope.'

'A little more consistency in diagnostic methods is all I'm looking for. To arrive at an objective frame of reference.'

'I see,' Schuler said. 'An objective frame of reference. Well, we could all do with one of those.'

The Burghölzli's older records were kept in a musty basement, along with stacks of disused institutional furniture: benches, a blackboard and several iron desks of the kind Kirsch hadn't seen since his school-days. After a brief tour and an explanation of the indexing system, they adjourned to Schuler's office, a capacious room with scores of potted plants lined up around the walls. Schuler explained that the hospital not only enjoyed extensive gardens, but boasted a conservatory where tropical plants were cultivated. Unfortunately, several panes had been broken by one of the patients throwing things out of an upstairs window, and in order to preserve the more delicate botanical specimens it had been necessary to house them indoors until the repairs were complete.

'We've found horticulture to be excellent therapy for many types of patient,' he said, lifting a weeping fig from the seat of a chair and indicating that Kirsch should sit down, 'so long as they can see the fruits of their labours. But a late frost causes untold distress.'

'You don't by any chance grow cactuses?' Kirsch asked, looking around at the masses of yellowing foliage.

'Cactuses? Oh dear, no. The conditions are quite wrong, even in the conservatory.' Schuler found a place for the weeping fig on his desk, where it only partially obscured his face. 'Although there's a patient here with a couple of very fine specimens. His father brought them back from America. Why do you ask?'

'I think I saw them. If you're talking about Eduard Einstein.'

'I am indeed. How did you . . . ?'

'I came to visit him last week. In a semi-private capacity.'

In the broadest terms, Kirsch explained his professional interest in the Draganović case, without mentioning Mariya by name. 'Since I was here already, I thought I might as well find out what Herr Einstein recalled of her, since they were acquainted. I should have

contacted Dr Maier first, but I didn't want to burden him with anything so trivial.'

Schuler sniffed, the one indication that he was discomforted by Kirsch's professional corner-cutting. 'And did you find Herr Einstein cooperative?'

'Up to point. Some of his remarks were puzzling, though. I'm still not sure what to believe.'

Schuler sighed. 'Well. Dr Zimmermann is overseeing that case for the time being. I suppose you should talk to him.'

Schuler picked up the telephone and made several calls around the building. A few minutes later, Dr Zimmermann walked into the room clutching a cardboard folder. He was twenty years younger than Schuler, small in stature, clean shaven and gaunt, with spectacles and a heavy thatch of dark hair set in waves across his head. His left earlobe was bandaged.

He shook Kirsch's hand eagerly. 'I hear you've just come from Berlin,' he said, imparting significance to the remark by raising his eyebrows.

'A few days ago, yes.'

Zimmermann nodded gravely. 'How is it?'

No doubt he had seen the same newsreels and newspaper reports as Kirsch had: Hindenburg appointing Adolf Hitler as Chancellor, the crowds and the torchlight parades, events that Kirsch himself had missed. The lack of an accent suggested Zimmermann was German by birth.

'Dr Kirsch hasn't come here to talk politics,' Schuler said. 'He wants to know about our resident Einstein.'

'Herr Einstein, well . . .' Zimmermann looked around in vain for an unoccupied chair. 'He's certainly an interesting case. Clear psychiatric disturbance combined with remarkable intelligence and knowledge. His writing was highly accomplished, according to his academic reports. And he's the best pianist we've had for years.'

In the ensuing discussion it became apparent that Dr Schuler and Dr Zimmermann disagreed as to the precise nature of Eduard's condition, just as Eduard had implied. But if this was a source of

animosity between them, they kept that animosity in check, at least for his benefit.

'Eduard studied at medical school for several years,' Zimmermann said. By now he was perching on the end of a table between a rubber plant and a dwarf acacia. 'It makes diagnosis much more difficult. He knows all the various symptoms and can present them at will.'

'He does it to amuse himself,' Schuler said. 'There's a manipulative side to his personality: passive but effective. Not unlike a woman's.'

'He has an ambivalent attitude to the whole idea of psychiatry, as with so many things,' Zimmermann said. 'He's clearly very interested in the subject, but at the same time he likes to adopt a sceptical attitude, as if the entire field is unsound.'

Kirsch nodded. 'I sensed exactly that when I saw him.'

'It's an attitude he gets from his father,' Zimmermann went on, 'which I suspect is the heart of the matter. Whatever his father won't accept, he can't bring himself to accept either, not completely. Unfortunately for Eduard, his talents and inclinations lie in areas his father has no time for, music being the one exception. You can see how this presents him with a dilemma.'

At first, Kirsch did not see. The presence of Eduard in Mariya's life was increasingly a source of confusion. Einstein's son had knowledge, but also imagination; and, he sensed, a mischievous side, perhaps even a malicious one.

'A dilemma,' he repeated. 'What do you mean?'

Zimmermann pushed his spectacles up his nose. 'Eduard either sets himself up in opposition to his father – which is a hopeless cause, his father being an intellectual colossus without parallel – or he submits to the dismissal of almost everything that might establish his own place in the world – one might even say his own identity.' He opened up the folder and produced a sheaf of papers, loosely bound with a length of blue ribbon. 'Here's something Eduard wrote: philosophical aphorisms, he calls them. He sends them out in letters periodically, but fortunately he's vain enough to keep copies.'

He handed Kirsch the papers. They were covered in neat hand-writing, like something laboriously copied out. One sentence had been underlined: *Nothing is worse for a man than to encounter someone beside whom his existence and all his efforts are worthless.* Kirsch turned over a page and found another sentence given the same treatment: *The worst destiny is to have no destiny, and also to be the destiny of no one else.*

'Touching or maudlin,' Schuler said, 'depending on your taste.'

Zimmermann put the papers back in their folder. 'There's a book too. Several hundred pages long.'

Schuler frowned, as if Zimmermann had said something he wasn't supposed to say.

'What kind of book?' Kirsch asked.

'A work of fiction, apparently. We heard him say he was working on it a couple of times, but we never believed it actually existed. Then one of the nurses found him wrapping up a manuscript. Unfortunately, by the time we went to see for ourselves, it had vanished. We think he must have given it to someone. It's most frustrating.'

Kirsch could hardly believe his ears. Several hundred pages of imaginative outpouring, however disorganised, might have offered a level of insight that years of analysis couldn't match. The book had been right under their noses, but they hadn't seen it, simply because they didn't *believe* it was there.

'Have you any idea what it was about?'

'It's set in a psychiatric hospital,' Schuler said. 'And the hero's a psychiatrist. That's all we know.'

Given Eduard's interest in psychiatry, the choice was not surprising. Perhaps in fiction he could make choices he didn't dare make in life.

'Are you saying Eduard's relationship with his father is actually the root cause of his condition?' Kirsch asked.

Zimmermann nodded.

'And Professor Einstein is aware of this?'

Schuler shrugged. 'We send reports to Eduard's mother. We *assume* they're passed on, but . . .'

Zimmermann and Schuler looked at each other. Zimmermann touched at the bandage on his ear. 'We've seen no evidence of . . . interest. Of course, the professor is a busy man.'

'There's no doubt Eduard feels abandoned,' Schuler said. 'Judged unfit and cast aside. That's why he detests his father. Just as he worships him. Such a conflict of feelings isn't healthy, especially not for a sensitive young man.'

'It's destroying his mind,' Zimmermann added. 'The worst part is, I think he knows it.'

The analysis made sense, with or without recourse to the strict tenets of Freudian psychoanalysis. It was an observable fact that children frequently blamed themselves for a parent's absence or neglect, however irrational that might be. Add to the mix a father who cast a shadow longer than any man living, an irreproachable being beloved by millions, and it was easy to see how feelings of guilt or inadequacy might become deeply rooted. But as far as treatment was concerned, the only approach with a hope of success was to change the nature of the relationship. A bond had to be recreated between father and son that was nurturing instead of destructive, before the damage became irreparable. It was an approach that demanded devotion and time.

'The sense we get is that Professor Einstein doesn't agree with any of our assessments,' Schuler went on. 'He believes his son's mental illness has nothing to do with him. It's inherited, like congenital syphilis, only less susceptible to treatment. According to Eduard's mother, the professor has a great fear of inherited insanity – an irrational fear, one might say. When his other son, Hans Albert, got engaged to an older woman a few years ago, he had her investigated by a private detective. And when it turned out she'd undergone a brief spell of psychiatric treatment, he opposed the marriage tooth and nail.'

'I'm sure he had his reasons,' Kirsch said.

'Apparently he believes the Marić family have insanity in their blood too. So marrying into a family with the same curse –'

'Couldn't he be right?'

Schuler shrugged. 'Eduard's mother *is* prone to fits of depression – at least, Eduard says so. And his aunt, Zorka Marić, she spent two years here at the Burghölzli during the war. Alcoholism and a breakdown of some kind, although quite likely trauma-related, according to the case notes.'

'Inherited or not,' Zimmermann said, 'it would be easier to address the patient's difficulties if the sense of rejection could be reduced. Eduard's behaviour became markedly more disturbed when he learned his father might be leaving Europe for good.'

Kirsch thought of Eduard, alone in his room, practising the piano every day in anticipation of his father's visit – a visit that, so far, had not come.

'*Is* he leaving for good?'

'Very possibly,' Zimmermann said. 'Frau Einstein told us he's been offered some highly lucrative positions in America. Apparently Eduard found out, though he wasn't supposed to.'

'He intercepted a letter from his father,' Schuler said. 'It turned out he'd been doing it for some time, going through his mother's papers and such. She thinks some were stolen.'

Kirsch sat up. 'Letters?'

'We assume so. This was a few months ago. In any case, as far as Eduard is concerned, just the thought of his father abandoning Europe is profoundly disturbing. It seems to have affected relations with his mother at the same time.'

Out in the corridor an electric bell sounded. Schuler pulled a watch from his top pocket and got to his feet, explaining that he had a meeting to attend and would have to be excused.

'Just let me know when you want to make a start on the archives and I'll make sure you have access and a quiet place to work. In the meantime, do give Dr Bonhoeffer my warmest regards.'

Dr Zimmermann escorted Kirsch back through the building. The evening meal was at an end, the patients silently shuffling back to their quarters, some eyeing the stranger warily as he went by, most staring into space with a familiar mixture of hopelessness and

bewilderment. At least the general mood was more sedate than at the Charité, but perhaps that was simply because the patients were more liberally sedated.

'I hope we've been of some use,' Zimmermann said. 'You wanted to know if Herr Einstein is a reliable source of information, and I'm afraid the answer is probably not. There's simply too much going on in his head.'

'You're obviously worried about him.'

Zimmermann nodded. 'I worry this may end in self-destruction. It's possible he already craves some form of martyrdom at the hands of his father.'

'Perhaps that's what he had in mind for his fictional psychiatrist,' Kirsch suggested.

Zimmermann shrugged. 'I fear we'll never know.'

Again Kirsch pictured Eduard at the piano. He played so well, with such acuity, it was hard to believe he was other than completely sane. It was evidence of the degree to which the human mind was compartmentalised; one part performing at the highest level, another entirely dysfunctional. In which part lay his writing? Had the vanished manuscript been authored by Einstein the genius or Einstein the madman?

'I do have one last question,' he said. 'If Eduard can present symptoms at will, how can you be sure his behaviour hasn't been a charade from the start? Is it possible this is just an appeal for help? A way of getting his father's attention.'

'Anything's possible, but it would be unique in my experience. You've only got to look at the deterioration in his handwriting to see that something's amiss. Besides, some of his behaviour has been quite extreme.'

'Such as?'

'Rages, slamming doors, banging the piano with his fists for ten minutes at a time. And then he attacked his mother when she tried to restrain him. Tried to push her off the balcony.'

'He told me he was just trying to scare her.'

'That isn't all. His mother tutors young women – maths and music

and such. Eduard took to walking in on the lessons stark naked. His bedroom walls were covered in pornographic images. His mother didn't dare let anyone in there, not even the maid.'

They had reached the main entrance. The bare space echoed with the sound of closing doors.

'My patient in Berlin, she was one of Mileva Einstein's pupils. But I'm still not clear how Eduard got to know her.'

Zimmermann frowned. 'What's your patient's name?'

'Mariya Draganović.' Kirsch nodded towards the folder still tucked under Zimmermann's arm. 'Didn't Eduard ever mention her?'

Zimmermann pondered the question. 'You know, I don't think he did, as a matter of fact, although of course —'

'She's a Serb, from the same region as his mother.'

'Yes, I know. I remember her quite clearly.'

Kirsch wasn't sure if he had understood. 'I'm sorry? You don't mean you've actually met her?'

'Well, yes, of course. She was a patient here for a while. In the first-class section. You didn't know?'

'No. I didn't.'

'Eduard was here at the time,' Zimmermann said. 'So I expect this is where they met.'

Thirty-four

Mariya had been a psychiatric patient before she ever set foot in Berlin. The proof was right there in her file. She had been at the Burghölzli for two weeks. And who was to say she hadn't been a patient before that, elsewhere? It seemed Inspector Hagen had been right all along: it was pointless trying to unravel Mariya's purpose in Germany, or the events leading up to her discovery. It was pointless trying to reconstruct cause and effect as you would in the investigation of a crime. There had been no crime, no rationale, no purpose. Only delusion.

Kirsch read the file in Dr Zimmermann's office, while Zimmermann himself shuffled about, trying to look busy. It was a slender dossier, but complete. The facts of the case – dates, times, observations, procedures – were all faithfully recorded and signed. Hard information. Data. Objective fact. Exactly what he had come for: insight into Mariya's state of mind, solid foundations for a new beginning. But it was not the new beginning he had been banking on.

She had presented herself at the hospital in September. In the notes there was no mention of a referral or of anyone accompanying her. She had arrived, it seemed, entirely under her own steam. She had claimed to be suffering from insomnia, sleepwalking, bouts of panic and intervals of memory loss that left her disorientated for several minutes at a time. A Dr Vogt had conducted a preliminary examination. Since there was no evidence of head trauma, his first concern had been that she might be suffering from a brain tumour, but memory loss aside, the normal symptoms associated with that diagnosis were absent: Mariya suffered no headaches, no drowsiness, no sickness – a fact about which she was emphatic. He noted that the patient seemed agitated, *although outwardly determined to*

appear calm. The next hypothesis was that she had suffered a nervous attack, brought on by emotional stress, the best treatment for which was complete rest in a tranquil environment. At Dr Vogt's suggestion, she had booked herself into the first-class section a few days later.

Memory loss. It was there in black and white. Had the problem continued? Had the intervals become longer, culminating in the continuous state of amnesia Kirsch had observed in Berlin?

He read on. Mariya's stay at the hospital had been uneventful. Besides rest and various forms of sedate recreation, she had begun a course of hydrotherapy, a fashionable new treatment for which the Burghölzli had recently been equipped. As Kirsch understood it, patients were wrapped tightly in wet sheets before being immersed in water at different temperatures. Zimmermann said the process had been found to lessen anxiety and delusions in paranoid and schizophrenic patients and to induce periods of tranquillity without the use of drugs. Kirsch could believe in the relaxing properties of prolonged immersion in water. The experience of partial weightlessness was certainly beneficial. But he found it hard to accept that it amounted to a lasting treatment. In any case, Mariya's course had been cut short after the first session. The notes didn't say much about why. They stated only that she had become 'uncooperative' and 'vocal', and had shown signs of distress.

The last note, written by Dr Vogt, said only: *After improvement, the patient once again exhibits disquiet and a lessening in powers of concentration. Recommend a thorough psychiatric evaluation commencing early next week.* But by that time, Mariya had paid her bill in cash and discharged herself from the hospital. She left no forwarding address.

Vogt had never challenged Mariya's claim that she was ill. But neither had he observed any concrete symptoms for himself. The evidence of a disorder was patchy and second-hand.

It was not unusual for people to check themselves into a psychiatric establishment for a period of discreet recuperation. Rest cures were common in moneyed circles, although the Burghölzli wouldn't

have been a fashionable choice, there being too many genuine lunatics on the premises. It could have been coincidental that Mariya had followed Eduard into the hospital a couple of weeks after his return. But if it was not a coincidence, what was it? The pursuit of some strange fascination? Or something more calculating? Perhaps Mariya had sensed the same exploitable weakness that Kirsch had: a back door to the truth.

The possibilities crowded in, unwelcome but intractable. Even after all this time, none could be dismissed. Eugen Fischer thought Mariya was party to an elaborate fraud. Even that theory was still tenable.

Kirsch pulled off his spectacles and rubbed his eyes. Why had Mariya gone to Berlin? Where had the idea come from? Perhaps the Einstein connection was all in his mind. Had he elaborated scenarios that had no basis in fact?

He closed the file, realised that Zimmermann had been staring at him from behind his desk.

He smiled nervously. 'Found what you were looking for?'

It was still surprisingly bright outside, though it was late in the afternoon. The snow gave off a phosphorescent light, making it easy to see the way, even as the sky darkened. A solitary pair of tyre tracks made parallel lines on the winding surface of the road.

Kirsch had forgotten about the man he'd glimpsed earlier among the trees, but as he went around the bend below the hospital he saw him again, leaning against the trunk of a pine, smoking a cigarette.

'You took your time,' he said.

Kirsch didn't have time to be surprised. He had a vague recollection of having made an arrangement with this man. 'I'm sorry,' he said.

Max threw the cigarette away and stepped up onto the road. His old overcoat was draped across his shoulders. He had been hiding here all these years, in neutral Switzerland, gravitating inevitably towards Albert Einstein's old stamping ground in Zürich. It had been their secret, just the two of them, a secret Kirsch had kept so well that he'd almost forgotten there was any to keep.

'Why are you still here?' Max said.

Kirsch hunched his shoulders and walked on. 'I'm here for my patient. There are some things I need to understand.'

'Mariya's the one with the answers. You won't find them here.'

'I might find out who she is.'

'Don't you mean who she was?'

'I don't see the difference. What's the difference?'

'Who do you want her to be?'

It was just like Max to ask the awkward questions.

'Lieserl. I want her to be Elisabeth Einstein.'

'Why?'

'How can you ask me that? You of all people.'

'You think it'll make her well again?'

'Yes.'

'Like Eduard Einstein. He's *very* well.'

'That's different.'

Max shrugged. He was sceptical about psychiatry generally, like his hero. As far as he was concerned, it wasn't a proper medical science. 'It's very noble of you to go to so much trouble. If it turns out you're right, she'll be in your debt for ever. So will her father.'

They were just above the lake now, where the grey mass of water met the featureless sky. It was like standing before a huge unfinished mural. Only the woods and the town were complete.

'That's not why I'm here,' Kirsch said. 'I need the facts. I'm tired of conjecture. I need a solid hypothesis.'

Max pulled the coat closer about him. Kirsch felt guilty for having taken it from the house without asking him.

'I suppose gratitude is something,' Max said. 'She'll remember you, at least, won't she? After you're gone.'

'It's not like that.'

Max lit another cigarette. He never used to smoke. But he was older now. 'What *is* it like?'

Kirsch walked on without answering. After a few seconds he realised that his brother was no longer keeping up with him.

He looked over his shoulder. Max was standing in the road, his hands at his sides.

'You haven't much time,' he said.

Kirsch awoke in his hotel room. Blue dawn light bled through a gap in the curtains. It was freezing cold. For an instant he thought he saw Max standing in the corner, watching him. But it was just his raincoat hanging on the side of the wardrobe. He let his head sink back onto the pillow and pulled the covers up to his chin. It had definitely been a dream. He was sure he had taken a taxi back from the Burghölzli. He clearly remembered Dr Zimmermann telephoning for one.

He tried to recapture the sound of Max's voice, the detail of his face. But in the dream it had been too dark to see clearly. He could recall only a dark figure, stark against the snow. And the voice, had that really been Max's? Kirsch was no longer sure he would recognise it if he heard it.

He took the raincoat off the wardrobe and slung it over the back of a chair.

Thirty-five

Later that morning, Kirsch sat down at the desk in his hotel room and wrote a letter to Alma. It was not the ideal form of communication, given what he had to say. But he was not at all sure, given her father's illness, when he would see her again; and it seemed wrong to summon her specially to Berlin just to break off their engagement. In a letter, at least, he could give her a clear explanation. He could set out the argument without fear of interruption; so that she could see for herself that a break was in her best interests. It was a cowardly choice, but no other was left to him. He had already waited far too long. And why? Because, for all that time, voices in his head had told him that his feelings for Mariya were not real. They were a passing fad, a fantasy constructed in the convenient void of her amnesia. But as a truer picture of Mariya began to take form, he had come to see that it was his love of Alma that lacked substance. He had yearned for the idea of her: clean, wholesome and undaunted, like the sun in a cloudless sky.

He addressed the envelope first: the easy part. Then he began to draft, making three false starts before half a page was written. With each new attempt, his explanations, rather than becoming more solid and coherent, seemed to disconnect and disintegrate. *I have an illness,* he wrote, *from which it is more than possible that I shall not recover.* He did not say what the illness was. *It is doubtful that we would be able to have children.* He was not, in any case, the man to make her happy, he said. She would see that very clearly in time. He did not talk about love. Love, he knew, would only confuse the matter. All the same, without it, everything he wrote sounded hollow and false, as if it had been dictated by someone else.

He looked at his watch. It was time to go. He placed the letter

unfinished in the envelope, and left the envelope on the desk. He would finish it later or, more likely, start again from scratch. By the time he had reached the lobby he had decided not to write a letter at all. He would make a special journey to Oranienburg on his return, and explain himself face to face. It was the least Alma could expect.

Unfortunately, while Kirsch was away, the chambermaid took the letter and gave it to the concierge who affixed a stamp and sent it out with the rest of the mail, making the appropriate addition to Kirsch's bill. Kirsch did not discover what had happened until his return.

By the time he arrived at the Burghölzli, the sun had begun to break through the clouds, making rafts of white light on the surface of the lake. But inside the conservatory it was gloomy, the glass roof being covered by a blanket of snow. On one side, several panes had been smashed, shards of glass framing the sky like broken fangs. Only there did the sunlight shine through.

Eduard was tending a row of shrubs in earthenware pots, tying lengths of rag around the ends of the branches. He wore an unbuttoned overcoat over a red dressing gown and a pair of pyjamas. His hair flopped untidily over his forehead.

'Camellias. See, they've already started to open.' He showed Kirsch a sliver of pink petal, peeping through the folds of a waxy green bud. 'One hard frost and they'll be ruined.'

His breath made clouds in the air.

'We should go inside,' Kirsch said. 'You'll catch a chill out here.'

Eduard began to wrap up the bud. 'I didn't think you were that kind of doctor. Are you qualified for general practice?'

'I was a surgeon before I was a psychiatrist.'

'Really? Why did you stop?'

Kirsch hunched his shoulders. Eduard's mood was combative. It had caught him off balance. 'Does there have to be a reason?'

'Now *that's* an interesting question. Does the human mind belong to the world of classical physics or quantum physics? Is there an

unambiguous reason for every thought and desire? Or can they arise spontaneously?'

'Let's say I needed a change.'

'You don't have to tell me, if it's a secret.' Eduard carried on wrapping up the bud, splitting the end of the rag and securing it with a knot. '*I* stopped because I didn't like the cadavers. After a few dissections I started dreaming about them. And that terrible smell. Even formaldehyde can't hide it. I expect you know what I mean.'

'Yes.'

'I could never get rid of it. It was as if it had seeped into my brain, into my mind. I could smell it on my pillow when I went to bed. And on other people, living people. That's why I began to stay away from them. I didn't want that smell on me.'

At the front they used to store the dead in the nearest available cellar until they were ready for removal. But during the big offensives against the Russians the cellars would always fill up – though they laid the bodies on top of each other, three deep – and they would have to make do with tents. The orderlies wrapped up the corpses if there were spare sheets available. Otherwise they simply dressed them again and placed sacks over their heads. Either way, the sickly smell always found its way back to the field hospital within a day or two. In no time the whole placed smelled of death, and no amount of chlorine or phenol would cover it. As more wounded men were brought in, they could see the crows and the ravens lined up along the roof. Eduard was right: once you had lived with that smell, you never forgot it. The olfactory imprint was permanent, and any reminder of the time or place would bring it back with sudden repulsive force.

'When it comes to the mind, I veer towards the quantum view myself,' Eduard was saying. 'Isn't thought composed of electricity? And aren't electrons *quanta*? At any rate, I don't believe the operations of the brain are purely mechanical. Cause and effect. Tick tock. There's more to it than that.'

'You mean, there's the soul.'

Eduard tut-tutted. 'Turning to the supernatural won't get us anywhere. One simply swaps one set of unanswered questions for another.'

'Then what did you mean?'

Eduard fingered a camellia leaf. The tip had turned yellow. Soon it would fall. 'The difficulty is one of language. In the quantum world there are things for which we have no words: objects that crystallise in time and space only when observed; position and form that exist potentially but not actually. Human language doesn't recognise such spectral states of being. An object can't be in more than one place at a time. It exists or it doesn't exist. But that's not the quantum world – which is what all the others are made of. Niels Bohr said when it comes to atoms, the only language that's any use is the language of poetry.'

By now Kirsch was shivering. 'I have some questions, Herr Einstein. I hope you don't mind.'

Eduard reached into his pocket for another piece of rag. He tried to tear off a strip, but the material twisted in his hands. 'Have you got a penknife on you? Or scissors?'

Kirsch kept a penknife in his top pocket, mainly for sharpening pencils. It had an ivory handle, yellowed with age. He hesitated, then took it out, folding out the blade before handing it over.

'It doesn't matter. I can guess why you stopped being a surgeon.' Eduard weighed the penknife in his hand. 'There's something about cutting into the dead. The desecration. At the anatomy classes people used to laugh and give them nicknames – the cadavers, I mean. Good morning, Kasper; good evening, Molly. Only so much meat, they used to say, like a butcher's shop, only not so fresh. We used to keep them in a cold store, but it wasn't cold enough in the summer. I used to dream they came back, all blackened and mangled from the class.' He tested the blade against the palm of his hand. 'I expect it's different with living specimens. I suppose they can't come back to haunt you if they're still alive.'

'I shouldn't think so.'

'Unless they die right there on the table.' Eduard folded the rag

tight over the blade, and pulled down on it until it tore. 'It must be a terrible thing, to have someone's life in your hands. Suppose you make a mistake?' He reached for another camellia bud, rubbing his thumb over the surface. 'Why don't you sit down, Doctor? You look pale.'

There were several canvas deckchairs stacked up against the back wall. Kirsch considered fetching one, but then it came home to him how peculiar it would look, him sitting while Eduard was on his feet. As Dr Bonhoeffer would have said, such things undermined the bedrock of the patient–doctor relationship.

'I knew you'd come back,' Eduard said. 'You want to talk about Mariya again, don't you?'

'If that's all right.'

'Oh yes. I like talking about Mariya. It helps me remember her. She's pretty, don't you think?'

'Yes, I do.'

'And so clever too, though it isn't obvious when you first meet her. When you meet her, she seems merely innocent. Like a visitor from a better world. You feel embarrassed that your own world isn't like that, because it should be.'

'Your mother said Mariya was suggestible and easily led.'

Eduard sniffed. 'My mother's ashamed.'

'Of what?'

Eduard turned his back and walked on to the next plant, stooping to smell a bloom, though it had not yet opened.

'Eduard?'

He shrugged. 'It's like I said: the world isn't how it should be. That's all I meant.'

Kirsch reached for a cigarette and lit it. He needed the facts. The cause and effect. Stick to that.

'When we talked before, you didn't tell me that Mariya had been a patient here. Why was that?'

'I thought you knew.' Eduard went back to work. 'I put her in a story, you know. You might say she was my muse.'

Kirsch watched Eduard cut into another length of rag. He was

glad he hadn't sharpened the blade in a while. 'Dr Zimmermann told me about your book.'

Outside, two workmen dressed in overalls came around the side of the building, carrying a ladder between them. They stopped outside the conservatory. The man in front peered through the glass.

'It's set in a psychiatric hospital,' Eduard said.

'So I understand.'

'It's about a psychiatrist who falls in love with a patient.'

With a loud bang the workmen leant their ladder against the side of the conservatory.

'That's an interesting premise,' Kirsch said. 'Why does he do that?'

'Why does anyone fall in love? Because they find someone who can give them what they want, or what they need. Someone who can set them free.'

'I see. And how does it end?'

'Not happily, I'm afraid. Endings have to be credible or the reader feels cheated. There's nothing like an unlikely ending to spoil a good story. I hope you don't mind.'

'Why should I mind?'

Eduard began wrapping another bud. 'Perhaps it's a quantum story, Doctor. Prose instead of poetry. Have you thought of that?'

Kirsch tapped the ash from his cigarette into an empty flower pot. Eduard was playing with him, trying to keep him off-balance. No doubt he had played the same games with Mariya. It was his way of having fun, an outlet for his warped and restless brilliance.

'What about you, Eduard? Is that the real reason you came here, to research a book?'

'Research *is* important. For the setting. The setting has to be convincing too. Readers expect it nowadays. The willing suspension of disbelief – that's what they call it. You need it to make your readers believe.'

'And what about Mariya? Why did she come here?'

Eduard didn't answer. Once again he seemed too absorbed in protecting his precious camellias. The buds were wrapped up now like small bandaged fists, waving pugnaciously in the air.

One of the workmen outside was holding the ladder. The other had climbed it. All that could be seen of him were his feet and ankles.

'That's Hermann,' Eduard said, without looking up. 'Manic depressive disorder. Sometimes they let him come and listen to me play the piano. Inordinately fond of Schubert. Likes Mozart too, but I have to be careful or he starts dancing around.'

A small cascade of snow fell from the roof. A column of sunlight parted the gloom. Hermann's face appeared above them, a mask of concentration, his tongue sticking out between his lips. Kirsch took in the stubble, the slack jaw, the village-idiot haircut.

'They're afraid the glass roof will cave in,' Eduard explained, 'especially now it's been damaged. It happened once before, a few years ago, when the snow got too thick.'

For the first time Kirsch noticed that the frame of the conservatory was creaking. 'Tell me more about your writing,' he said. 'Do you show it to people?'

'Not usually.'

'What about some of the other students your mother taught?'

Eduard shook his head.

'But I heard you got on very well with them. Fräulein Anka Streim, for one, and Maja Schucan. You definitely played for them. And you went out dancing.'

It had all been in Eduard's file: how Eduard would come in at the end of the lessons and give short recitals. Mileva had encouraged him. She was proud of her younger son and anxious that he should not sink into introspection and depression as he had at university. Generally, her pupils found Eduard charming. He accompanied them on outings and evenings out. But then his behaviour had begun to deteriorate. Instances of jealousy and 'inappropriate conduct' put an end to any prospect of romance.

Eduard shrugged.

'Those relationships didn't last, did they?' Kirsch went on. 'So I suppose when Mariya came along, you must have worried the same thing would happen.' He stepped closer, speaking as gently as he

268

could. 'Is that why you gave her the letter, Eduard? I mean, the letter you took from your mother's room, the one about Lieserl.'

He watched for some reaction, some sign of confusion or denial, but there was none.

'I was wondering how Mariya came to have it. I can't believe she took it herself. When would she have had the chance? I'm quite sure now that your mother didn't give it to her. So that only leaves you.'

Hermann eased himself further up the ladder, placing one foot on the roof as he pushed his broom through the snow. The man on the ground yawned.

'If she was your sister,' Kirsch said, 'then things would be different. Is that what you thought? She'd stay with you. She'd be a part of your life for ever, no matter what. And you wouldn't have to worry about romancing her. You could sidestep all that.'

Eduard did not respond. He worked on, winding a strip of rag round and round, a frown of intense concentration on his face. It was tempting to ask him if had really believed Mariya was his sister – if he still believed it. But it had come to Kirsch on his drive up the hill that even Eduard's opinion shed little useful light on the matter. Only his mother could know the truth for certain, and she was clearly not going to share it. Still, it might be something to know what Mariya herself had believed.

Kirsch had been lying awake in his hotel room when it came to him: it was Eduard who had been pulling the strings. That Mariya was an Einstein like him was an idea he could have planted in her mind. Superficially she was a strong candidate for Lieserl, the long-lost daughter: she was roughly the right age; she had been brought up in the right part of the world; she had a natural aptitude for mathematics. And with both her parents dead, there was conveniently nobody around to refute the idea once it had taken hold.

It would have been a perfectly credible story. The child known as Lieserl had been conceived and born out of wedlock. At the time, Albert Einstein had been struggling to find work. His application for Swiss citizenship had not yet been approved. Both he and his

future wife had been foreigners, liable to have their visas revoked on the whim of the authorities. A scandal might have proved disastrous. Albert was still technically liable for military service in Germany. So Mileva had gone home to Serbia to have the child in secret. There, her friend Helene Savić had arranged for a discreet adoption. It might have been intended as a temporary arrangement. The Einsteins might have planned to bring their daughter back to Switzerland once they were married and established there. Or perhaps that was what only one of them wanted. The issue was the kind that might easily contribute to the breakdown of a marriage. Whatever the truth, family honour had been protected. Lieserl had remained in Serbia with her adopted family, as Helene Savić had put it, *for the good of all*.

Standing by her father's grave, Mariya said she had felt liberated. She was psychologically predisposed to believe she had been adopted. And hadn't Eduard's mother made it plain that Mariya was a fantasist? *What the Lord gives with one hand, he takes away with the other.*

'Did she believe you, Eduard?' Kirsch asked.

'Believe what?' Eduard was searching for more buds to tie up, but they were all done.

'That she was Lieserl, your sister.'

Eduard shook his head. 'I don't have a sister.'

'Then why did you give Mariya the letter? What was it for?'

Eduard looked down at his hands and at the penknife. He began folding and unfolding the blade. Now that there was more light, Kirsch could see that his eyes were bloodshot and there were circles under them. He wondered what kind of treatment they were giving him for his schizo-affective disorder. He had been so focused on Mariya, he hadn't thought to ask.

'Eduard –'

'My father *did* send you, didn't he?'

'It's just as I told you, Eduard: Mariya is my patient. I want your help.'

Eduard turned, the knife open in his hand. 'What does it matter what *I* say? What does it matter what *I* think?'

'You and Mariya were close.'

'She's gone. She's . . . *no one.* You're too late.'

He took a step closer and for a moment Kirsch thought he was going to stab him with the knife. But instead, Eduard lifted his head and placed the point of the blade against his own throat, against his carotid artery, pressing hard so that the flesh went white. Dr Zimmermann's words sounded in Kirsch's head: *I worry this may end in self-destruction.* And with a knife Kirsch had given him.

There came a bestial shriek from above. Instinctively, both men looked up. Hermann must have been watching them. He was lying flat against the roof, his face pressed against the glass, hammering with the flat of his hands so that the whole conservatory shook. Kirsch sprang forward, reaching for Eduard's wrist, but Eduard was too quick for him: he smartly stepped aside, pivoting on one foot like a matador. Kirsch lurched past, tripping over a stack of flower pots and crashing to the ground.

Eduard looked down at the knife that was still in his hand. He blinked, as if unsure what it was doing there. Then he carefully folded away the blade and handed it back.

'Thank you, Doctor,' he said. 'I have to go and practise the piano now. My father gets upset if I don't practise. Good day.'

Thirty-six

It was a compound of sodium and sulphur: ten grams of yellowish powder at the bottom of a small unlabelled bottle. The porter at the main hospital assured him it was the real thing. All Eisner had to do was make a two and a half per cent solution with sterilised water and inject it into a vein. The pentobarbital powder was stable and could be stored indefinitely, but in solution it had to be used within forty-eight hours. After that it started to corrode the glass.

'Two hundred and fifty milligrams,' the porter said. 'That's your maximum dose. Of course it depends on the body weight.'

'Of course.'

'Careful you don't go over. Too much too quick and they go into shock.'

'How long does it last?'

'Depends. About fifteen minutes.'

Eisner was disappointed. Fifteen minutes wasn't very long for the interrogation he had planned. He wondered how many doses of pentobarbital it was safe to give, and at what intervals, but he didn't want the porter getting too curious. He handed over the money and went back to the clinic. He would proceed by trial and error. He had already helped himself to needles and syringes from the store room. He had also acquired a second-hand set of apothecary's scales and a measuring cylinder. But where was he going to get sterilised water?

That afternoon he went to the kitchens and boiled a kettle, pouring the water into a clean coffee pot. The fact that there was no coffee inside went unnoticed. He carried the pot up to his office and locked the door. Sitting at his desk, he made up enough solution for three hypodermics, which he filled there and then. He was impatient to

make a start, but it was safer to wait until after supper. He did not want to be interrupted, or to attract unnecessary attention.

The prospect of making his own minor medical breakthrough excited him. Kirsch was not going to like him doing experiments in his absence, but what could he do about it? A man with so many secrets had to be careful how he threw his weight around. How would he like explaining to his fiancée why he was paying the rent at Herr Mettler's, for example?

Eisner held up a syringe to the light. The fluid was clear and colourless, as seemingly harmless as water. It was some time since he had administered an injection. The trick was to find a vein, taking care not to go in one side and out the other. When you had leakage into the surrounding tissue there could be all kinds of complications. It was probably a good idea to strap the subject down. He didn't want her jogging his hand.

Eisner squeezed the syringe until a single tear of fluid welled up at the tip of the needle. It was important to avoid injecting air. A bubble could cause blood vessels to rupture. If it travelled up into the brain, it could cause a stroke. The whole procedure would have been safer if Martin had agreed to participate. It would be his fault if something went wrong.

The problem with Kirsch, Eisner decided, apart from his tendency to become sanctimonious where his patients were concerned, was his refusal to share. He grabbed the interesting cases and then treated them like his own private projects. He rarely discussed his thinking. He would not allow colleagues any input, the Einstein girl being a case in point. It was selfish, not to mention ungrateful. Robert had introduced him to Alma. Robert had ushered him into the Siegel fold. On those grounds alone, he deserved a little more respect.

The barbiturate might turn out to be useless. It might not unlock the subconscious, or override the ability to dissemble as people were saying. But no truly dispassionate observer could blame him for putting it to the test. It was only through such experiments, successful or unsuccessful, that human knowledge could be advanced.

Kirsch had been dead against the experiment. Over his dead body,

he had said. But that was not going to be a problem, because neither he nor his body, dead or alive, was anywhere to be seen.

Mariya was asleep on the bed when the orderly came into her room.

'Dr Eisner wants to see you downstairs.'

Male staff were not normally seen in the women's wing after dark. Mariya thought this must be a rule for all but the doctors. The way the orderly stood in the doorway, eyeing the pictures pinned up around the walls, told her she was right.

She turned her back to him, though her eyes remained open. 'I'm tired,' she said. 'I want to sleep now.'

The orderly's name was Jochmann. He was a stocky, bull-necked man with a surly manner. She had noticed how the male patients avoided him.

'It's important,' he said. 'Come along now.'

She lay still, refusing to move or answer. Eisner was not her doctor. She did not trust anything the orderly said.

She heard the door close. She thought he had gone. But then she heard his heavy footsteps crossing the room. It came to her that she should call for help, but as soon as she opened her mouth she felt a hand on the back of her neck, thrusting her face into the pillow. Jochmann twisted her arm behind her back and held her down. She struggled for a few seconds, but his strength and weight were too much for her. She managed to twist her head to one side, just enough to breathe.

She forced herself to relax. He could not rape her without letting go with at least one hand. As soon as he went to unbutton himself, that would be her chance. But he did not let go. He held her tightly until all resistance had ceased; then he hauled her to her feet.

'There's no sense being difficult,' he said. 'It's for your own good.'

He marched her out into the corridor. She had the sense that all this was familiar to him, routine. Was this why the orderlies all looked so strong?

'My doctor is Dr Kirsch,' she said as he marched her out into the corridor. 'He's my doctor.'

'Well, now you've got two,' Jochmann said. 'Aren't you lucky. Twice as many doctors; you'll be cured in half the time.'

He led her down some back stairs that she had never used before. After a few flights he let go of her arm. They went down and down until they came to a warm, dimly lit basement where pipes ran along the walls and there was a strong smell of fuel oil. Cement dust and soot clung to the soles of her feet. She could run, but how far would she get? She could scream, but would anyone hear?

'Nearly there,' Jochmann said.

He pushed open a heavy swing door, holding it open for her. On the other side was a bare half-tiled room with sinks along one wall. In the middle of the room was an iron bed with straps attached to the frame. Dr Eisner was sitting near the end of the bed, his hands between his knees and his legs dangling, like a schoolboy killing time. He jumped to his feet when he saw Mariya come in.

'Where's Dr Kirsch?' she said.

Eisner looked slightly hurt. 'Right at this moment, I couldn't say. He's taking some kind of sabbatical.'

'When will he be back?'

'You've every right to feel a little neglected. But that's all going to change now.' Eisner stepped away from the bed. 'Now I want you to come and lie down.'

fugue

Thirty-seven

I never finished my studies at Zagreb. It was not through idleness or disappointment that I left, or even that I grew lonely for my home, although I was very often alone. It was because of what happened in Orlovat in the spring of my final year, which, even now, is hard for me to think about, and harder still to relate, though I must if you are to understand why I am here and what it is that I must know from you.

It was a very wet season that year. Returning on the train for Easter I saw mile upon mile of flooded land. In places it was hard to see where the fields ended and the sky began – which was a pretty sight, even if, as I knew, it meant hunger and hardship for those whose crops were rotting in the ground. I had sent word ahead of my arrival, but there was nobody there to meet me at the station, though it was raining again and starting to get dark. So I walked through the village alone, jumping over the puddles from one sliver of muddy ground to the next until I stood outside the courtyard of the Draganović house.

The front door was not locked. A lamp was burning in the kitchen, but I could find no one at home. I put down my suitcase and wandered through to the back, thinking that at least Senka would be about, tending the animals. I found the horse gone. The geese and chickens were scattered about the yard and the orchard, some beyond the fence, others huddled around the trees at the edge of the field. That was when I became afraid. Senka would never have left her flock to wander about. She would have gathered them into their huts for warmth and safety. But the huts were all empty, except for one solitary bird, which looked scrawny and thin. I tried to gather up her precious geese, but they hissed at me or ran away, and on no account would take any direction from me no matter how I cajoled and pleaded with them.

Then I remembered the housekeeper, Maja Lukić, and set off for her

house. I had not gone twenty yards when she appeared, hurrying along the road, her clothes as wet and muddy as my own. We went back inside and she told me how Senka had gone missing the day before. Maja and some of the villagers had been searching roundabout for some sign of her, but as yet they had found not a trace. I could tell that there was more to this story, and that Senka would not run away without cause. I asked where my father was, and if he had played any part in the matter.

At this time I did not know Maja Lukić well. When Senka and I were children, she would bake biscuits for us, and hide them wrapped in muslin among the branches of the trees. This I remembered. But she had stopped working for us when I went to school and I had seen little of her since. Now her position as housekeeper brought her money that she needed and had, no doubt, grown accustomed to. So it is no wonder that she feared to speak badly of her employer, for fear that he would replace her. Nevertheless, I found her evasions intolerable and asked her bluntly if my father had sought to punish poor Senka for some alleged offence and, if so, with what results.

Maja Lukić reassured me that nothing of the kind had occurred, as far as she was aware. On the other hand, she admitted that when he was alone and had been drinking, my father would sometimes rail about Senka on account of our mother's death. In that inebriated state he took this to be her fault – all because of what the doctor had said about the disease being first among the animals and then carried into the house by Senka. Maja Lukić was circumspect in her description of these outbursts, but I could all too easily imagine their violence. Where his own worth and station were concerned, Senka's very existence was to Zoltán Draganović like an open wound: for she was his flesh and blood, and there was nothing he could do about it. For some reason which I did not yet perceive, the credit I brought him through my scholarly efforts never fully made up for Senka's deficiencies, and never would. Now, of course, I know why.

As to Senka's disappearance, I was still not satisfied with Maja Lukić's explanation, and told her so. After some hesitation, she led me into the drawing room where she said she had been cleaning the previous morning. It had not been much in use since our mother died, though a fire was

always lit in the grate to keep out the smell of damp. Maja took our family photograph album from its place on the writing desk and showed it to me. She had found it open on the floor, she said, and feared Senka had come across it. I did not understand what she could mean, but then I opened the album and saw what our father had done. He had removed every picture of Senka, even the ones of her wearing her Christening robes. Where she had appeared in the photographs, such as the family groups we had taken at the studio in Novi Sad, he had carefully cut out her image with a blade. In some pictures, all that remained of her was a shoe or an arm or a few locks of hair falling over an inch or two of shoulder. In one picture, our mother held Senka upon her knee, with her arm around her waist. Clearly, it had not been possible to remove Senka without taking our mother's arm with her. The solution to this problem had been to cut off Senka's head instead. Now our mother appeared to have nothing but a headless dummy on her lap, and to be smiling at the fact, as if it were a joke.

When I saw this new cruelty, I was filled with a hatred such as I had never felt before. It is not in my nature to be violent – no more, at least, than any human being. Still, at that moment, only blood could have answered the rage I felt on my sister's behalf. It was, I know, a selfish impulse: vengeance offered to assuage the guilt of my own absence and neglect. Fortunately, my father was nowhere to be found. He had left the village that morning on some pretext, which even Maja Lukić could not disguise as anything more profitable than his usual quest for intoxication.

There was no hope of finding Senka in the darkness, but as soon as it was light we went looking for her again. It was a Sunday, and while many in the village went piously to church to pray for the health of their crops and their pocket books, no more than six or seven of them came out to help us, though the rain had stopped. No doubt the rest thought poor Senka was prone to wandering off, not being right in the head, and was just as likely to wander back again. But I knew better, and with much trepidation set off towards the river with two companions. It was there I felt that the greatest danger lay, for the water was flowing fast. The old stone bridge resembled a weir, with the water foaming as it

coursed beneath the arches. I was afraid of what might happen to Senka were she to have fallen in, for neither of us had learned properly to swim as children, there being little occasion for swimming in that part of the world.

We followed the river downstream. I took one side and my companions – a cousin of Maja Lukić's and his wife – took the other. A short way from the village the river meanders for a half-mile or so. It is a place the fishermen like to go with their rods and lines because there is shade, and the shallow waters bring their quarry within easier reach. But here the banks had burst, flooding the meadows and the birch woods on either side. I waded up to my knees through muddy, tangled waters, fearing that I would be sucked under, so clinging and treacherous was the ground beneath my feet. I soon lost sight of the others on the far side of the river, but I could hear them calling Senka's name, which I did also. Our voices did not carry far. Already the water was draining from the land, and it seemed to carry the sound away with it. I saw the cloying blackness of what it left behind and panic almost overcame me. I cried out for Senka until my voice was all used up, and nothing came from my mouth but sobs. Already in my heart I knew she would never answer.

Then Maja's cousin was shouting. He had seen something. I ran through the trees towards the sound, tripping and falling. I must have looked like a madwoman, soaked from head to foot and plastered in mud, but for a few brief moments I was filled with hope.

Maja's cousin was still on the far side of the river. He was pointing towards a clump of willows on his side. As I made for them, a handful of crows started from the trees and flew away. A moment later I saw what looked like an old tangled sheet caught up in the lowermost branches. It was only when I saw her dark hair trailing in the water that I knew it was my sister. She was dead: drowned and carried downstream on the flood. She lay on her back, one shoulder slightly raised, and an arm resting across her eyes, like one of those grieving figures carved in marble that guard the tombs of great men. I do not know how long she had been there: a day or so, I think, for the crows had already begun to feed on her poor, upturned face and mouth, the sight of which I have struggled these ten years to forget.

The hours that followed are unclear to me: the order of things and what I myself did and said. For some minutes or hours, I was not in my right mind. I know that Maja Lukić found us and that she and her cousins took poor Senka down and covered up her face. Others came to help carry her away, then more people and the village priest too, all anxious to offer what help they could or simply to witness the horrible spectacle for themselves. They laid Senka out on the kitchen table, but then the priest said she must be taken somewhere cooler because in her state she would already have begun to rot and would rot faster being wet. And an argument broke out as to where such a place might be found and whose property was most suitable. The church was the coolest place that anyone knew of, but the priest would not allow Senka to be taken there until, he said, the circumstances of her death had been ascertained. So they wrapped her in a bed sheet and carried her away to some other part of the village, and I never looked on her again.

The one person absent during these deliberations was our father. Maja Lukić fretted that, as the head of the household, it was his right to make the decisions regarding his daughter, but no one seemed anxious to go and find him. I think they enjoyed taking charge of affairs in the big house from which they had mostly been barred. So, in the end, it was Maja Lukić herself who commandeered a horse and trap and set off for the next village, leaving me alone in the house. She has often told me since how bitterly she regrets that mistake and wishes she had stayed with me. For years afterwards she blamed herself for what happened. But I do not blame her. She was in my father's employ, not mine. She was only acting to protect the rights and honour of the family and the Draganović name, which in a place like Orlovat is what matters more than anything, more even than life.

I sat for a long time in the kitchen — how long exactly, I cannot say. It must have been an hour or more, because by the time I stirred, the sun was low enough in the sky to peep beneath the canopy of the clouds. I lit a lantern above the table. Then I got up and went into the scullery and took off my filthy dress. I stood in my chemise before the mirror wiping the black mud from my face and arms and rinsing my hair under the tap. Why I did this, I do not know. I had a strong need to be clean,

to scrub away all trace of the day. Even more, I wanted occupation, to keep from thinking any more. I scrubbed and scrubbed until my skin was raw.

I was there in the scullery when I saw my father walk through the gateway into the courtyard, pulling his horse behind him. It was apparent to me that he was still oblivious of what had taken place, for he was humming as he came and even chuckling to himself, as if recalling some reprehensible joke.

I have said before how I had learned instinctively to avoid being alone in that man's company. But the cold anger I felt at that moment, the urgent need for revenge, eclipsed the habit of self-preservation. What I should have done, I suppose, was to leave by the back door. How different everything might have been if I had. For sure, I would not be here, now, writing this account for you. More than likely, our paths would never have crossed at all.

But, as you will surmise, I did not leave. Instead, I calmly put down the scrubbing brush, went through into the kitchen and picked up the biggest knife I could find.

Thirty-eight

Berlin, 3 February

Dear Professor E,
Since my last communication I have learned the following regarding the matter of interest to you.

The case in question is presently assigned to Dr Martin Kirsch (b. 1890, Wittenberg, Sachsen Anhalt). Kirsch served as a military surgeon during the Great War, attached to the 9th Army on the Eastern front. He received several commendations before being discharged in September 1918 as psychologically unfit for duty. According to hearsay, Dr Kirsch was on one occasion spared court martial (grounds unclear) by the personal intervention of his CO, Col. Gustav Schad.

Dr Kirsch is considered by colleagues to be intellectually arrogant and politically apathetic. On occasion he has proven both disloyal and insubordinate. Such conduct would be more reckless, it is said, had he not successfully cultivated connections in wealthy and influential circles. In particular, he is engaged to be married to the daughter of the industrialist Otto Siegel. He has proven accommodating when offered professional or financial advantage.

Dr Kirsch has taken an unusual interest in the Draganović case, reportedly at the expense of other duties. The fact that the case has been in the public eye (ref. newspaper cuttings, see enclosed) may account for this. Kirsch appears ambitious and, left to his own devices, is likely to exploit the case in any way he considers personally beneficial.

Dr Kirsch recently took a leave of absence in Zürich, ostensibly to undertake research for an academic paper. There he visited the Burghölzli Psychiatric Hospital, where records show Fräulein Draganović was a patient for several weeks in September last year.

To date, I have not been able to ascertain his exact reasons for doing so. However, given his persistence and his determination to uncover his patient's history, it cannot be ruled out that Dr Kirsch believes a connection exists between yourself and her, which, if proven, could be exploited to his advantage.

I fully appreciate the importance of anticipating such a development and am prepared to take all necessary measures to ensure that your interests are not compromised in this regard.

Your servant,

H. de Vries

Thirty-nine

Nobody spoke to him on his way through the building; so Kirsch was not prepared for what greeted him when he opened the door to his office. The room was empty. The filing cabinet had gone. His desk was bare: no typewriter, no papers, no files. The shelves, normally bowed beneath the weight of books and journals, held nothing. He pulled open the drawers of the desk: all that remained was an old bookshop receipt from Speyer & Peters and the stub of a broken pencil. Even his white coat, which he always kept on a hook behind the door, had disappeared. He picked up the telephone to call Frau Rosenberg, but the line was dead. He ran the flex through his hands and found himself looking at two tufts of bare wire.

Kirsch's briefcase now held the only evidence that he had ever been a psychiatrist at all. Had Bonhoeffer changed his mind again? Had there been another complaint? To be dismissed *in absentia* was unheard of, but then, Kirsch had been all but dismissed once already. He would have been gone by now – his desk cleared, his shelves empty (but what had they done with his books?) – had it not been for Dr Mehring's unexpected change of heart.

Outside, the rain was coming down steadily. He clutched his brief-case against his chest. His hands felt clammy. Was it possible he had imagined Mehring's retraction? Or dreamed it? His dreams were so vivid, so bound up with his waking concerns, that it was hard to tell in retrospect if they were dreams at all. He fumbled for the telegram he had received in Zürich. Perhaps he had dreamed that too. He rummaged through the briefcase, then emptied his pockets one after the other. The Swiss francs were still there in his wallet, but there was no sign of the telegram.

VACANCY POSITION DEPUTY DIRECTOR STOP
RETURN BERLIN SOONEST STOP

He had wanted desperately to see the back of Heinrich Mehring and his quackish experiments; to handle things his way without interference. And that was exactly what had happened. He had never stopped to question whether it could all be real. Rainwater dripped from his chin, making his collar wet. The barrier between perception and imagination was fragile, but crucial. He knew too well what happened when it began to break down.

Max's voice whispered in his ear: *You haven't much time.*

He made his way up to Bonhoeffer's office. At the bottom of the stairs two nurses were talking. Before he could say good morning, they split up and walked away. Passing by the wards, he caught glances from other members of staff, but no smiles of recognition, let alone a greeting. A male patient was having his chest examined by a visiting physician. The physician was busy with his stethoscope, but the patient stared at him, as if at a ghost, his grip visibly tightening on the edge of his iron bed.

How long had he been away? He'd planned on a week or so, but had it been longer? It felt as if an interval of time had gone missing. Was that why his things had been removed: because he had been away too long? Or perhaps he had never actually told anyone he was going. Perhaps that too had been part of the dream. As far as Bonhoeffer and his staff were concerned, he had simply disappeared. Outside the deputy director's office he paused. If Heinrich Mehring was there, Kirsch would know, one way or the other.

He knocked gently, then louder, but there was no answer. It was nine o'clock by his watch. Mehring could have been on his rounds, or down in the basement conducting his insulin experiments, making his patients less 'complicated' – but which patients?

Kirsch pushed open the door. It was months since he had been on the other side. He remembered a smell of Turkish tobacco, a chaise longue with yellow tasselled cushions, tinted etchings on the wall of Vienna and Budapest, a coyly erotic slave market scene in

the corner, partially obscured by a rubber plant. His heart sank: everything but the cushions was still in place.

He left the door ajar and stepped inside. It was cold. Instead of tobacco smoke, there was a smell of disinfectant. He looked along the glass-fronted bookshelves and was surprised to see that Mehring owned many of the same books as he did. He even kept them in the same order. Here was Eugen Bleuler's book on schizophrenia; here was Karl Jasper's philosophical autobiography, here was a copy of Alexander Moszkowski's *Dialogues with Einstein*. Kirsch took the Moszkowski from the shelf and flipped through it, finding annotations in pencil. He found more annotations in Emil Kraepelin's *Manic Depressive Insanity & Paranoia*: the same annotations *he* had made.

He knew then what had happened to his books, at least: Mehring had taken them. He must have thought his insubordinate junior had no further use for them. And what of his papers, his notes? Kirsch went to the filing cabinet and opened the drawers. Sure enough, the papers inside were his papers. He went to the desk. His letters – letters plainly addressed to Dr M. Kirsch – were there in Mehring's in-tray.

He picked up the telephone. The operator put him through to Frau Rosenberg's extension.

'This is Dr Kirsch.'

'Good morning, Doctor.'

'My office, it's . . .'

But what was it?

'Is it to your satisfaction?'

He sat down behind the desk. 'My things. They've all been taken to the deputy director's office.'

'Yes.'

She didn't seem to think any explanation was necessary.

'Well, I . . .' There was a pause on the line. 'My filing cabinet has been opened. I left it locked.'

'Are you sure?'

He wasn't sure of anything. He was expecting any moment to wake up. But where, and when?

Perhaps it's a quantum story.

'Yes, I'm sure.'

'Is anything missing?'

'Not that I know of, but . . .' He noticed that a white coat was hanging behind the door. 'Where is Dr Mehring?'

Frau Rosenberg hesitated. 'Dr Mehring is no longer with us.'

'Where is he?'

'He resigned.'

Kirsch looked at the pictures and the chaise longue and wondered why Mehring hadn't taken them with him. 'I didn't know.'

There was another pause.

'Is there anything else you need?'

'Why did he resign?'

'You'd have to ask the director. He isn't here at the moment.'

There was an unfamiliar hesitancy in Frau Rosenberg's voice, a distance. In the past she had always been friendly, like an indulgent aunt.

'Is there anything else?' she said again.

Kirsch's gaze fell on a large envelope at the top of his in-tray. The words *University of Berlin* were printed on the front.

'No thank you,' he said, and hung up.

He opened the envelope. It contained a short paper published by the Institute of Psychiatry together with a typed letter. But the letter was not from Professor von Laue, as he had expected.

Dear Dr Kirsch,

I trust your researches are proceeding well and that you will soon be in a position to start gathering data. Recent events on the political front have greatly improved the prospects of reforming the psychiatric profession both in Germany and elsewhere. Your work is now more valuable than ever in helping to change outmoded and self-serving attitudes.

I enclose an article — one might call it a manifesto — just published by my friend and colleague Dr Ernst Rudin. Copies are being circulated to senior staff at all psychiatric establishments, with the approval of the authorities. As Dr Rudin points out, the interventionist approach

to psychiatric medicine has failed. It is a science built largely on untested suppositions, and dubious classification. As such, it offers only false hope (cures, etc.). In the long run, the only way we can hope decisively to reduce mental disease and degeneracy in the population is through the introduction of mental and social hygiene programmes. These alone will empty our asylums and protect future generations. I believe Germany now has a government that is prepared to assume this responsibility, assisted, of course, by the relevant centres of learning.

You will be pleased to see that Dr Rudin has quoted extensively from your preliminary study, published in the Annals of Psychiatric Medicine, as providing evidence of the unscientific nature of current approaches to schizophrenia. I hope this will convince you of its importance.

Yours cordially,

Dr Eugen Fischer

The coat was his, but there was something unfamiliar about it. It was tighter than before and a more brilliant shade of white. It gave off a detergent smell. In his absence, Kirsch realised, it had been laundered and starched.

He put the coat on and made his way to the women's wing. In the recreation room a sewing class was in progress, the patients in their grey smocks sitting in a circle, heads bowed over their work. Mariya Draganović was not among them. He went up to her room. A new patient, a woman with wild hair, lay on the spare bed, but on what had been Mariya's bed there were neither sheets nor blankets. The mattress had been rolled up. He opened the wardrobe: her clothes were missing.

'Where is she?'

The woman propped herself up on her elbows. Her hair was long and grey like a fairytale witch.

Kirsch pointed at the naked bedstead. 'Mariya. Do you know where she is?'

'On no,' the woman said, sitting up, slinging her legs over the side of the bed. 'It's my turn now, Doctor. I've been waiting.'

* * *

He found Nurse Auerbach smoking a cigarette outside the laundry room, blowing the smoke through a tiny window that overlooked the kitchens. Seeing him, she threw the cigarette away and gathered up a pile of sheets.

'I'm looking for Fräulein Draganović,' he said. The nurse looked blank. 'Patient E?'

'I know who you mean, Doctor. She's not here.'

'Not here?'

'They took her away. A couple of days ago.' Nurse Auerbach put her head on one side, adopting an attitude of concern that was no more convincing than it was genuine. 'Didn't you know?'

Forty

The storm troopers now called themselves 'auxiliary police'. Three of them stood outside the entrance to Triage, pacing up and down with their thumbs in their gun belts. When an ambulance pulled up, they gathered round, as if on the look-out for contraband. The crew climbed out of the back, carrying a man on a stretcher. One of the storm troopers pulled the blanket off him; another poked at him with a rifle. They wanted to know if he had any bruises or broken bones. Kirsch heard someone say 'appendicitis' and the stretcher was allowed to pass.

Inside, the hospital was quieter than usual. The staff appeared preoccupied and determinedly silent. They went about their business briskly, speaking, when they had to speak, in low voices. As a doctor of psychiatry, Kirsch enjoyed no special privileges when it came to visiting hours. But nobody challenged him, even when he asked for directions.

According to Nurse Auerbach, Mariya had been taken ill three days earlier. She had run a high fever and become delirious. When she started bleeding from the nose, a doctor was sent for. Fearing she had succumbed to an infectious disease, he had recommended that she be moved out of the clinic and into the main hospital. There the diagnosis changed. Mariya was said to have suffered an allergic reaction, although to what the nurse did not know.

Kirsch found Mariya in one of the women's recuperation wards. Eight identical beds with white iron frames stood either side of the aisle, with identical white tables in between. All but two of the beds were occupied. Mariya lay asleep on her side. She wore a nightshirt, the sleeves rolled up, one arm resting outside the covers.

He stood watching her. He wanted to sit down beside her and to

take her hand, but there were no chairs. One of the patients at the far end of the room had a dry, insistent cough. The sound echoed off the bare walls and the shiny wooden floor.

Months had gone by since he had first found her at the hospital, and yet here they were again, the interval between the two events compressed into a sliver. Mariya's hair was longer now and there were no bruises on her face, but in every other way she was the same. Everything was the same. All his enquiries and strategies had made no difference. Certain material facts had come to light, but in themselves they explained very little and promised even less. Mariya's mind, like her predicament, remained obscure. He had enough information for theories and conjectures, but not enough to understand, let alone to heal. All the while, time had been running out – for her and for him. Because the longer she was without her memories, the harder it would be to recover them. Memories, like dreams, disintegrated when unrehearsed.

He sat down on the edge of the bed. Mariya's sketch-book lay on the table. He picked it up and flicked through the pages. His portrait was on every one, his and nobody else's. Even the old man and the matinée idol had been forgotten. Was this progress: a sign that the delusion Eduard Einstein had encouraged was finally losing its grip? Or was it evidence of further decline?

She had captured him in a variety of attitudes and moods: sitting, standing, smiling, frowning, animated, pensive. But as Kirsch turned the pages, the images became gradually rougher, less precise, less identifiably him. By the time he reached the last sketch, the image was just a few lines suspended in space. His collar and spectacles were drawn in more detail than his face. After that, the pages were blank.

Mariya stirred. Her skin was pale and waxy, her hair wild. But seeing her again – seeing life in the dark eyes, the brow, the soft contours of her mouth – quickened his heart.

'Good morning,' he said. She squinted at him, but her face expressed nothing. 'I'm back.' He became aware of the other women watching him over the tops of their blankets. 'I was away too long. I'm sorry.'

She brought a hand to her mouth, tracing her lips with the tips of her fingers. 'Was it long?'

'A few weeks. Longer than I'd planned. If I'd known . . .'

She held her hands out in front of her, flexing the fingers, digging the nails into her palms. 'Am I awake?' she said.

He pulled the screen across and sat down again. 'Of course you're awake. Mariya?'

She did not answer. She kept on clenching and unclenching her fists, as if her fingers were something new to her.

'I shouldn't be here,' she said. 'I told them: there's somewhere I have to be. Someone's waiting.'

'Who's waiting? Eduard?'

She slung her legs over the side of the bed. 'I must go back.'

He had never seen her this confused. It had to be the effect of some analgesic. He supposed they had given her something to take away the pain.

'Mariya? You know who I am, don't you?'

He held up the sketch-book, showed her his picture on the first page. 'It's me, Dr Kirsch. *Martin* Kirsch.'

She peered at the sketch, then at him. 'Martin,' she said. He thought he saw the flicker of a smile. 'The writer.'

There were footsteps on the other side of the screen.

'Who put *this* here?'

With a clatter, the screen was folded back against the wall.

'Dr Kirsch.' It was Dr Brenner with the ward sister. 'What are you doing here? Visiting hours are two till four.'

Kirsch stepped back as the ward sister bustled over.

'Come along now,' she said, lifting the covers.

Obediently Mariya lay down again and closed her eyes. She had confused Kirsch with Eduard. That had never happened before.

'Will she be all right, Doctor?' Kirsch asked.

'I'm hopeful of a full recovery, though it was touch and go for a while. She's improving daily.'

'What was wrong with her?' Kirsch asked.

Brenner regarded him steadily. 'As a matter of fact, I was hoping you could shed some light on that.'

'They told me an allergic reaction.'

Brenner glanced over his shoulder. It was obvious he didn't appreciate having an audience. 'That was *one* idea. The swelling, the rash. Of course, without all the pertinent facts, it's largely guesswork.'

He had never known Brenner's tone to be less than brisk, but now it was almost accusatory.

'What pertinent facts?'

'A history of her medication, for one thing,' Brenner said. 'That *might* have been useful. I sent a request to your office, but no one bothered to respond.'

'I'm sorry. I've been away. In any case, she's not been given any medication. None at all.'

Brenner pushed stubby fingers through his lank grey hair. 'Thank you, Sister,' he said.

The ward sister stopped tucking Mariya in and marched away.

Brenner stepped closer. 'The treatment of your patients is your affair, Dr Kirsch. I wouldn't dream of interfering in your experiments. But please do not insult my intelligence.'

'What are you talking about?'

Brenner took hold of Mariya's wrist, turning it over to reveal the underside of her arm. The flesh around the elbow was swollen and there were clear signs of haemorrhaging beneath the skin. Then Kirsch understood: two blobs of dried blood revealed where the cephalic vein had been punctured.

'Well, it's the first I've heard of it. Is he absolutely sure?'

They were outside the back of the clinic. Eisner, in his shirtsleeves, was busy trying to repair his bicycle. The vehicle stood upside down between them, the rear wheel jammed between the railings.

'I've seen it for myself,' Kirsch said. 'Two injections at least.'

'Recent injections?'

'*Very* recent. How did they get there?'

Eisner was struggling with the chain, trying to force it over the

sprocket. 'Have you any idea how short-staffed we are, Martin? I've been fully occupied just keeping the lid on things. What have *you* been doing?'

'So you've no idea what happened?'

'I've ideas. Just no information.'

'What ideas?'

'Maybe someone wanted to put her to sleep. So they could take advantage of her.' Eisner looked up through the spokes of his front wheel. 'Wouldn't be the first time, Martin. Or maybe they sold her something. You know how it is. Stuff goes missing from the stores: sedatives, opiates. The orderlies had a proper racket going the last place I worked.'

'I don't think so. Mariya couldn't pay. She's got no money.'

'Maybe it wasn't money they were after.'

Eisner let go of the chain and looked at his hands. They were covered in soot and grease. He sniffed in disgust. It was only recently that he had started cycling to work. Before that, he had enjoyed the use of a stylish but decrepit automobile, a pre-war Adler. But the engine had finally died on him and the cost of resuscitation was beyond his means.

'You said something once about barbituric acid,' Kirsch said. 'This truth serum. You wanted to conduct an experiment.'

'That's right. And you were dead against it. Don't tell me you've changed your mind.' Eisner frowned at the bicycle. 'I'm going to have to take this whole damned thing apart again. I can't believe it.'

'I haven't changed my mind. I'm thinking you went ahead anyway. Did you?'

'Of course not. I'm surprised you have to ask.' Eisner wiped his hands on a rag. 'Look, maybe it was Mehring.'

'Mehring? What are you talking about?'

'Come on, Martin. He's always had it in for you, hasn't he? And Patient E, well . . .' He picked up a screwdriver and examined the business end. 'Everyone knew her case was important to you. The *eminent* Dr Kirsch? Maybe he thought he'd throw a spanner in the works, as a parting gift.'

Kirsch planted a hand on the railings. He didn't want to think about Heinrich Mehring. 'I don't believe it. I don't believe a word you're saying.'

Eisner looked up at him. His pale eyes were very still. 'Suit yourself.'

He went back to struggling with the bicycle chain, using the screwdriver to lever it over the sprocket.

Kirsch took a step closer. A bead of sweat broke from his temple and darted down his cheek. 'If I find out you're responsible, your time here will be over.'

Eisner sighed and stood up. He was about to say something, but Kirsch couldn't bear to hear it. He put a hand against his chest and pushed. Eisner was caught off balance. He took a step backwards, knocking over his bicycle and falling awkwardly on top of it. Kirsch left him sprawling.

'Congratulations on the promotion, by the way,' Eisner called after him. 'Best man for the job by far.'

Forty-one

Robert Eisner picked himself up and carried on working on his bicycle, confident that even if Kirsch looked back, he would not see the flushed cheeks or the shaking hands. He even tried to whistle, but his lips were too dry and all that came out was a hiss. Only when Kirsch was well and truly out of sight did he get up, march back to his office, and pick up the telephone.

He had been undecided about what to do with the file; likewise the mysterious letter from Zürich. Handing them to the press might lead to a scandal, but it was naïve to assume that Kirsch's downfall would necessarily work to his colleagues' advantage. Events unravelled under scrutiny. What if Eisner's own role in the story came to light? It might mean the end of his career, or worse. Besides, Kirsch was his friend, or so he'd always thought. Friends in the ascendant were more useful than friends on their way down, even if they did rather less for one's self-esteem.

But Kirsch was not his friend any more, apparently. Prudence demanded that he strike, while he was still in a position to do so. Look what had happened to Heinrich Mehring. He had fled the country after threats to his life. But no one was in any doubt who had arranged them.

The operator connected him. At the other end of the line the phone rang. Eisner had a sense that he was about to do something momentous, reckless. But Kirsch had given him no choice.

'De Vries.'

'Eisner.'

Furniture creaked: de Vries sitting up or sitting back.

'Well, what can I do for you, Doctor?'

Eisner covered the mouthpiece with his hand. At the tips of his fingers the grain of his skin was etched in black. They stank of grease and soot. 'It's more a case of what I can do for you.'

Forty-two

The entire village of Reinsdorf had turned out for the Service of Dedication. Kirsch could not find a seat in the pews and had to squeeze onto the end of a bench, one of several jammed in between the porch and the old font. After the service the congregation filed out into the sunshine, heading for the crossroads where the war memorial was to be unveiled. It was not until they were out of the churchyard that Kirsch was able to catch up with his family. He was surprised to see his mother in a brand-new double-breasted coat. It was long and black, with wide cuffs, a belt and big buttons at the waist and the shoulder. She wore a matching black hat and a fawn-coloured fur around her neck. He had never seen her looking so fashionable. Arm in arm with her husband, she strode along, head held high, as if off for a pleasant evening at the opera.

Kirsch's sister Emilie followed a few paces behind. She had put on lipstick and was accompanied by a gaunt-looking stranger of about thirty, with a stiff bearing and a gold watch-chain hanging from his waistcoat pocket. He hovered at the edge of the party, keeping such a respectable distance between himself and Emilie that for a while Kirsch wondered if he was actually with her at all.

'This is Reinhard,' Emilie said finally. 'My brother, Martin.'

The stranger stopped, held out his hand and bowed formally. 'Reinhard Poppel. Honoured to meet you, sir.'

They shook hands and carried on walking, the memorial in sight now, hidden beneath an expanse of dark red velvet. The villagers hung on to their hats as a sharp wind veered across the open space.

'I understand, sir, that you also served.'

It took a moment for Kirsch to realise that Reinhard Poppel was addressing him.

'Served? Yes, I did, after a fashion.'

Poppel stared at the site of the memorial.

'Alas, I was just too young.'

Emilie blanched. It was a struggle for Kirsch to keep from laughing. 'Alas indeed,' he said.

In a flash, Emilie's expression changed from embarrassment to anger, her eyes narrowing, as if to say: *Do you want me to die an old maid?*

Kirsch put his hands behind his back and set about asking polite questions. It turned out Herr Poppel was an educational inspector and had met Emilie on one of his school inspections.

'I was struck immediately by how attentive her classes were, and how eager the children were to learn,' he said. 'Even in mathematics the girls showed real enthusiasm.'

'You sound surprised.'

'Well, it's rare – understandably, perhaps, given how unlikely they are to need it.'

'You're forgetting the household accounts,' Kirsch said, looking into the distance.

'Oh, indeed. But this was a class in geometry, not arithmetic. I fear Euclid is not much help in the larder.'

'Curdles the milk.'

Herr Poppel laughed obligingly, delighted to be getting on so famously with his sweetheart's eminent brother. 'Emilie is lucky,' he added. 'There's no doubt she has found her true vocation.'

Privately Kirsch doubted it. It was his impression that what Emilie had always wanted was to be a musician, to have attended one of the great schools in Berlin or Dresden, and to have travelled the world giving concerts – and perhaps she would have done it, had it not been for the war.

The villagers had formed a wide semicircle around the memorial, parents carrying their children or holding them firmly by the shoulders, as if afraid of what might happen if they got too close. Herr Poppel was no longer with them. Kirsch searched the faces of the onlookers, hoping for his sister's sake that he had not been too

unfriendly. He finally spotted him talking to a man in a brown uniform. Beyond them, more storm troopers were jumping down from a truck.

'What are *they* doing here?'

'They're the band,' Emilie said. 'The only ones who would play for free.'

A retired lieutenant-general in full uniform appeared beside the monument, shaking hands with local dignitaries and members of the steering committee. As the church bells struck twelve, the slab of granite was unveiled to a smattering of applause. Naked, rough-hewn and massive, it looked utterly out of place among the tidy houses and rustic outbuildings. A single large wreath was propped up against the stone. The lieutenant-general made a short speech about the duty of remembrance, his voice small in the gusting wind. The erection of memorials such as this, many of which were shame-fully overdue, he said, played a vital part in the restoration of national dignity now in train across Germany. At that the Brown-shirts clapped, followed by a section of the crowd. Then the lieutenant-general read out a list of the fourteen fallen heroes of Reinsdorf, together with their ranks and regiments. Some people in the crowd took out handkerchiefs. A small child cried in its mother's arms because it had spotted a duck waddling across the road and wanted to touch it. Then the brass band struck up with '*Ich hatt' einen Kameraden*' while photographs were taken for the local press.

'I didn't think we'd raised enough money for this,' Kirsch said, as they stood waiting for the formalities to finish. 'I thought we were short.'

'We were,' Emilie said, 'before Alma pitched in.'

'What are you talking about?'

Emilie frowned at him, pressing a finger to her lips, obliging Kirsch to edge closer.

'Her father made up the difference,' Emilie said. 'Just last week.'

Kirsch felt unsteady on his feet. He had resolved to tell no one about the end of their engagement until he had spoken to Alma in person. He had telephoned the house at Oranienburg twice, leaving messages, but they had not been returned. She was hurt, he supposed,

even insulted. Perhaps she didn't believe that he was ill at all. It had sounded unconvincing to him even as he had written it. He still planned to visit her, to tell her everything: that his breaking off the engagement was a lucky escape for her. But it was hard to see her agreeing to a meeting designed solely to salve his conscience, and which could only bring her further humiliation. He would just have to go up to Oranienburg and present himself at the door, and risk whatever came next.

'Are you sure, Emilie? Are you sure it was Alma's father?'

Emilie nodded. 'Five hundred Reichsmarks. Where else do you think it came from?'

'She never told me.'

'Of course not, Martin. Why would she tell you, when she knew perfectly well you'd find out?'

So that was Alma's response: charity, pity, condescension. There was no reason why his family should suffer, just because he was a black sheep. But that seemed too complicated for Alma, too calculating. Kirsch stood staring at the memorial and it came to him that Alma simply did not accept what he had written. She considered it an aberration, caused by overwork and an unhealthy proximity to the insane. She was sitting at home, awaiting another letter from him, retracting what he had said in the first. In the meantime, everything would be business as usual.

Emilie was shaking her head. 'You know, Martin, sometimes I think you don't know your fiancée very well.'

The steering committee had organised a lunch party in the old school house, with sandwiches and potato salad on offer, beer for the gentlemen and punch for the ladies. The band stood outside playing marching songs. The lieutenant-general shook some more hands and left after ten minutes, but the mood of satisfaction lingered. If nothing else, the fourteen fallen heroes of Reinsdorf had put their village on the map, and the modern style of the memorial was generally considered superior to the limestone obelisks and crosses that had gone up in neighbouring districts. Kirsch helped

himself to a beer and wandered about the room, nodding to old childhood acquaintances, accepting occasional congratulations on his upcoming marriage. His mother was one of the main centres of attention, it being well-known that it was she who had saved the day. She stood surrounded by the more eminent members of the community, the conversation punctuated with further requests to smile for the camera. At one point, she took her husband by the hand and led him into the shot so that they could pose arm in arm. It was a long time since Kirsch had seen them so calm and happy in each other's company, his mother so serene. The memorial had brought people together. The village was a family, it reminded them. They had suffered as one and remembered as one. And now, with their names carved in stone, it was as if the fourteen heroes had actually died there too, giving their blood for its very walls, homes and soil – victoriously, because the walls, the homes and the soil were all still there.

After a while the band stopped playing and made their way inside. Kirsch passed them at the door, ignoring the way they stepped back to let him through, smiling like dogs eager for a congratulatory pat. He checked his watch: another hour and he would have to set off for the station again. He had just lit a cigarette when he realised his mother had followed him out.

She put a hand on his arm. 'I know you had a part in getting us the money.'

'No, I didn't –'

'It can't have been easy asking Alma to intercede. I know how proud you are, and no one likes asking for charity.'

'You're quite wrong. I didn't even know about it.'

But she was not listening.

'To tell the truth, I wasn't sure you really approved. I know how you feel about the war . . .' Her gaze drifted towards the memorial. From a distance of a hundred yards it looked to Kirsch like an asteroid that had just fallen from the sky and buried itself in the ground.

'Of course I approve,' he said.

'We'll talk over supper.' His mother squeezed his arm and turned

back to the school house. 'I had such a nice letter from Alma. You are staying, aren't you?'

That evening after the meal, Kirsch stole up to the top of the house. He felt sure Max would be waiting for him, ready to vent his disgust at the day's proceedings: the mendacious waste of good stone, the fantastical cant about national honour. Kirsch wanted to assure him that he was in complete agreement. But when he got to Max's room, he found that it too had changed. The bed had been moved to the opposite side of the room, the old counterpane replaced with a quilt made up of pastel blues, greens and pinks. Instead of the old faded satin curtains, there were now new ones made of brightly printed cotton in a zigzag pattern. A new rug lay on the floor and the large chest of drawers, in which so many of Max's old things had been stored, had been moved into the corner and was now littered with hairbrushes, clips, combs, nail scissors and a powder puff in a silver case. Max's faded photograph was still there, but everything else had disappeared.

This was where Emilie slept now. After thirteen years she had finally moved out of the box room. These were her things on the chest of drawers, her clothes hanging behind the door. She had taken possession, putting everything to her use, according to her taste.

A small bookshelf had been put up above the head of the bed. The books were mainly novels and collections of poetry. Sylvan patterns embossed in gold ran up and down the spines: Goethe and Schiller, Shakespeare, Balzac, and some other writers Kirsch had not heard of.

What had they done with Max's books, his clothes, his boyhood toys? Had they been consigned to the attic? Or had they been sold in aid of the memorial fund? Most likely the latter, he thought, it being deemed appropriate. He doubted if they had made much money. The clothes were old, the toys mostly broken, the books of a kind that did not enjoy wide appeal. Mostly people would have bought them out of sympathy. In a short time they would probably throw them out again, since they held no sentimental value. They would be left out for the dust cart, or tossed into an incinerator. And no one would ever miss them.

Forty-three

Kirsch's new position was confirmed by letter. Heinrich Mehring's caseload became his. He unpacked the files, which had been boxed up in the corner of the office, and went through them one by one. The records of the insulin coma therapy treatments he found in a special folder with its own lock — a lock he forced, there being no evidence of a key. Mehring had been thorough. Every step of every treatment had been meticulously recorded: dosages, times, responses, all according to a prearranged schedule. The patients were examined in the same way, the questions and stimuli being standardised for ease of comparison. By Mehring's own measure, it was clear that his patients' responses had become more appropriate over the course of their treatment. Paranoid and delusional claims had become less pronounced. In some cases, patients denied that they had ever made them. Almost all became more cooperative when asked to carry out tasks, both intellectual and physical, and expressed a willingness to rejoin society. *On the renewed desire to please rests the best hope of the patient's returning to a productive existence in the future,* Mehring wrote after one especially satisfactory session.

Kirsch found the record of Sergeant Stoehr's treatment. Of the incident on 30 October, in which Nurse Ritter had been injured, Mehring had written: *Session terminated before completion. See addendum.* But Kirsch could find no addendum.

He put the whole file in the incinerator. It was not something he had ever thought he would do, data being data, but once the job was begun he found it surprisingly satisfying. The following day he had all the equipment stripped out of Mehring's laboratories: the beds, the drips, the stores of glucose water. The insulin itself he sent over

to the main hospital, with a note saying it should be checked for contamination.

The patients, on the other hand, remained. Incurable schizophrenics, especially those deemed dangerous or suicidal, were usually removed to asylums, where they were kept under permanent sedation. To keep them at the clinic, it was usually necessary to carry on some form of treatment with a view to improvement. But Mehring's notes were focused entirely on aberrant symptoms, collected for the purposes of identifying a pre-defined disease. He had cared little for his patients' histories. The possibility that experience might have driven them to extreme or troubling behaviour had been ignored. Kirsch did not know where to begin.

The rest of the staff were not helpful. Perhaps because of Kirsch's rank, they kept their distance, carrying out instructions promptly, but volunteering nothing. It was as if he were back in the army, a chain of command both above and below him. He toured the wards, the workshops and recreations rooms, trying to make time for each and every patient, to listen and record; but there were too many of them, too many stories. Though troubled with vivid dreams and bouts of fever, he worked longer hours than ever, without tangible progress. He began to wish the clinic was in Switzerland, in some picture-postcard valley, so that he could at least prescribe peace and clean air and exercise, like one of those private institutions he had once considered a sham. As it stood, the clinic provided only shelter and security – and less and less of that.

He discharged patients wherever possible, encountering no opposition from colleagues. His attempts at thinning out the ranks was assumed to be a cost-cutting measure. It was widely known that the institution, like others of its kind, was under pressure to reduce its expenses. Cuts in staff had already begun at the main hospital.

Some families were pleased to hear that they were not in any danger from their afflicted relatives, and that the best treatment for them was consideration and care. Most were not pleased at all. Often they refused point blank to take their relatives back. Some of the patients had no family in any case, at least none remotely close

enough to provide a home. Where they were concerned, there seemed even less hope of care than there was of recovery. It struck Kirsch as never before that where the mentally ill were concerned, there was simply not enough compassion to go around.

Kirsch went to see Mariya every day, though visiting hours were strict and limited, and the setting far from conducive to private conversation. After a week, she was discharged by Dr Brenner. Her physical symptoms, he confirmed, had finally disappeared, and her mental state appeared stable. Only the amnesia remained. At Kirsch's insistence, she was readmitted to the clinic.

The same day, Kirsch received another communication from Dr Fischer, congratulating him on his promotion, and asking for information:

> You will be pleased to learn that the Commissioner for Health and Medical Services at the Reich Ministry of the Interior has accepted the recommendations of the Kaiser Wilhelm Institute regarding the redefinition of priorities within psychiatric medicine. All psychiatric establishments will soon be instructed to prepare comprehensive lists of patients past and present, who exhibit or have exhibited symptoms of incurable mental or neurological disease. In accordance with the precautionary principle alone, these must henceforth be regarded as congenital and therefore likely to have an hereditary component. Patients listed should include those suffering from any form of:
> — schizophrenia
> — manic depression
> — epilepsy
> — hereditary blindness and deafness
> — grave bodily malformation
> — hereditary alcoholism
> — congenital feeblemindedness.
> Such information will enable the state to protect the population as a whole, and future generations, from the ravages and misery of inherited disease.

*As a practitioner at one of Germany's most respected establishments,
it would be to your advantage to begin work on this immediately. A
willingness to show leadership in support of this crucial initiative will
ensure the continued trust and support of those in positions of authority.*

* * *

Frau Rosenberg told him the director was on the telephone. Kirsch
said he would wait. For ten minutes he sat in silence in the outer office,
while Frau Rosenberg tapped tentatively on the keys of her typewriter,
determined, it seemed, to avoid his eye. When he was finally admitted
into Bonhoeffer's presence, he found the old man on his feet in front
of the window, fiddling irritably with the latch. A cigarette burned
unattended in an ashtray. Something in his appearance was unusual,
although at first Kirsch could not identify what it was.

'Damned draft,' Bonhoeffer mumbled. 'Take a seat, Dr Kirsch.'

Kirsch remained standing. He handed Bonhoeffer the letter. The
director looked at it dubiously, then reached into his top pocket for
his spectacles. It was then that Kirsch realised what had bothered
him: Bonhoeffer was not wearing his white coat. He glanced around
the room, trying to locate it. But the only white coat he could see
was his.

Bonhoeffer handed the letter back. 'I'm aware of the commissioner's demands. Though I appreciate you keeping me up to date.'

'They want lists. Patients past and present.'

'Apparently.'

'What for? What's it all for?'

Bonhoeffer looked at Kirsch over the top of his spectacles. 'Why
don't you ask your Dr Fischer?'

'Dr Fischer? I hardly know the man.'

The lines deepened in Bonhoeffer's brow. 'How strange. He seems
to know you rather well. And not just by reputation.'

He slid the letter back across the desk. Reluctantly Kirsch picked
it up. His connection with Fischer was too complicated to explain.

'What's it for?' he asked again.

The director regarded him steadily. 'The names on the list will be removed to special facilities. When, I don't know.'

'What kind of facilities?'

'Surgical facilities, I should imagine. Certainly psychiatry as we understand it will not be in evidence.' Bonhoeffer sat down at his desk and began shuffling papers. 'Of course, compulsory sterilisation will require a change in the law, likewise euthanasia, although I'm sure it won't be long in coming. They'll have to find the surgeons, of course.' He reached for the cigarette, examined the end, then screwed it into the bottom of the ashtray. 'But I doubt if that will prove an obstacle. Our colleagues in the mainstream profession have never believed in the value of psychiatry.'

'You don't intend to cooperate?' Kirsch placed his hands on the desk. Bonhoeffer stared at them, as if afraid they were merely pausing en route to his throat. 'You're not going to give them those lists?'

'Naturally I shall do what the law requires.'

'Hang the law.'

Bonhoeffer laughed. 'Be careful. Or the law may hang you.'

Kirsch could have sworn that the building was swaying beneath his feet.

'Are you all right?' Bonhoeffer said. 'You look pale. And tired.'

'I won't cooperate.'

'Are you sure you won't sit down?'

'It'd be better to shut the clinic. Better to empty the place, if this is what our patients can expect.'

'Empty the place?' Bonhoeffer put his head on one side. 'Haven't you made a start on that already? Hasn't that been your aim all along?'

'My aim? My aim is . . . has always been . . .'

Kirsch did not want to sit down, but his legs would not support him. He felt a burning around his chest, as if his skin were shrinking onto his ribs, stretching and tearing. Bonhoeffer offered him water, but he refused it.

'Herr Director, you can't surrender those records. It's unthinkable.'

'On the contrary: I think you'll find it's been thought about a

great deal. The hereditary health of the European race? Your reading has been too selective, I think.'

'They can't force us to comply.'

'Not legally, not yet. But I expect it's only a matter of time.'

'Then it's time we must use.'

Bonhoeffer leaned back in his chair. Kirsch was a difficult man to read. In the beginning he had been dedicated and inquisitive. But slowly his ideas had hardened into a disregard for authority and accepted practice – that, at least, was Bonhoeffer's perception. It had been the start of a general moral disintegration. Kirsch's arrogance had fed his ambition and his ruthlessness. Heinrich Mehring had fled the country after threats to his life and that of his wife. It was widely rumoured that Kirsch's powerful friends were responsible.

Now Kirsch wanted to do the honourable thing, regardless of the consequences. Was it a change of heart, Bonhoeffer wondered, or had he misjudged the man completely?

'I'm not sure I know what you mean,' he said. 'Use the time how?'

Forty-four

No one at the clinic was surprised when the new the deputy director assumed responsibility for compiling the list. When the psychiatric staff received Kirsch's memorandum, instructing them to go through their records, many assumed that this eagerness to comply with the ministry's request was the real reason for his promotion. The tone of the memorandum was brisk. All files relating to patients, past or present, who met the health commissioner's criteria were to be surrendered without delay. Where the diagnosis was uncertain – in particular, where schizophrenia or manic depression were suspected – the relevant file was also to be handed over. Even the files of the dead were not to be left out. There might be relatives still living – brothers, sisters, children and grandchildren – all with the potential to scatter the seeds of feeblemindedness and insanity, endangering future generations.

Kirsch was vaguer about the fate of the patients themselves. He emphasised only the gathering and sharing of data; data which the Commissioner for Health and Medical Services would use to shape future policy. Even so, he knew there would be objections. Mental illness was a curse families had always been anxious to conceal. The stigma of congenital insanity was deep and enduring. It had taken the psychiatric profession years to change attitudes, to be trusted with family secrets the way physicians were. Surrendering sensitive information to the authorities – names, addresses and medical histories – would surely destroy that trust for ever.

As soon as the memorandum had been sent, Kirsch set to work at the top of the building, a damp-smelling attic where the oldest records were stored in mouldy cardboard boxes and bundles tied up with ribbon. Many were almost a hundred years old and pre-dated

Emil Kraepelin's first classification of mental illness. Kirsch sifted through the remainder, pulling out anything that might, in the ministry's view, indicate congenital disease. The task proved difficult. Instances of mania, dementia or alcoholism occurred in most of the case histories; instances of possible epilepsy in hundreds more. The only way he could be sure no cases of hereditary illness had been missed was to take them all.

Within twenty-four hours the first files arrived from Kirsch's colleagues. Some were delivered in person; others were stuffed into his pigeon-hole outside the common room, with notes attached. *These are the cases from the past three years. I shall go into the remaining cases directly.* By the end of the second day they made a pile two feet high. In the event, none of his colleagues protested. None of them asked for a more complete explanation, or even when they could expect their files back. The data flowed unquestioned and unconstrained. Kirsch found further notes inside the files, clipped or pinned to the reports, volunteering additional information: *On several occasions the nursing staff have found Herr Göschel with alcohol. Furthermore, I can report that his father has the complexion of a man who drinks.* Others were even more conscientious: *This patient's intellect is technically superior to that of an idiot. However, I have it on good authority that at least one of the siblings is mongoloid.*

By the end of the week, Kirsch had all the files he needed to compile a comprehensive list. He doubted if anything like it had existed before. Matched to the public records of births and marriages, it might be possible not only to follow the progress of past mental illness, but to predict where mental illness would occur in the future. It would be tempting to intervene. Prevention, after all, was better than cure, especially since cures were not available. If psychiatric institutions across the country were as thorough, congenital insanity might one day be eradicated altogether, like the dodo or the bears that had once roamed the great German forests.

That evening after supper Kirsch sat alone in his office, waiting for the clinic to quieten down. The weather did not help. A strong

gusting wind rattled the windows and shrieked over the roofs. Rain fell in short, intense bursts. Storms always unsettled the patients. Many found them terrifying and had to be sedated. With others the wildness of the elements unleashed something wild inside them. They shrieked and babbled and danced. The storm was a champion, a transient deity at whose feet they worshipped. Occasionally bad weather provoked violence or self-mutilation. Kirsch was called to several disturbances on the men's wing and ordered that the lights be kept on for an extra hour.

Around midnight the dormitories at last fell silent. Making as little noise as possible, Kirsch went down to the kitchens and fetched a trolley. He loaded it with files and dragged it down the back stairs into the basement. By the dim electric light he set about stoking the boiler, piling coal into the furnace with a rusty shovel. It was dirty work. For a long time the coal seemed reluctant to burn, producing only black smoke that billowed in his face and left sooty smudges on his spectacles. It took another nine journeys to the top of the building to collect the old files. He could not take too many at once. The trolley would become heavy and difficult to manoeuvre, its iron wheels thumping down on the stairs. The noise echoed through the building like artillery. It was another exhausting hour before he was ready to start.

His own files went first. In the move from his old office they had become disordered. He had found some of Mariya's sketches mixed up with correspondence from Eugen Fischer. Other case notes had been split up and scattered. But it didn't matter. He was going to burn them all. To have been a patient at the Charité, regardless of the diagnosis, or how brief the stay, was now something to be hidden; and this was the best way to hide it. His research went too, including the records he had gathered and analysed for his paper in the *Annals of Psychiatric Medicine*.

'I expect you don't approve,' he said aloud to the shadow flickering on the wall behind him. But the shadow did not answer, although from the way it moved across the sooty brickwork, he had the impression it was shaking its head.

315

When the evidence of his work in psychiatry had been reduced to a heap of embers, Kirsch threw on the other records, file by file, bundle by bundle. The old papers, in particular, were slow to burn. They hissed and popped like cooking flesh. The furnace choked on the ashes so that Kirsch had continually to rake them over to keep it from going out. He worked on into the night, until the sweat ran in streaks down his face. The last thing to go into the flames was his white coat. He would not be needing it any more. He had already written the letter of resignation. It was lying in Dr Bonhoeffer's pigeon-hole, waiting for his arrival in the morning.

He cleaned up in the washroom as best he could and then made his way into the women's wing. One of the duty nurses could be heard snoring at the end of the corridor. The other was nowhere to be seen. Kirsch went to Mariya's room, knocked gently and let himself in.

Mariya was sitting at the end of her bed with the lights off, staring out at the night. She had her boots on and Max's old overcoat draped across her shoulders. Her sketch-book sat in her lap.

'Are you ready?' he said.

They went out through the kitchens. It was nearly five o'clock, dawn a hint of blue in the furrows of distant clouds. A taxi was waiting. They rode east in silence through the empty rain-washed streets. Kirsch felt hollow and strangely elated, the two feelings separate yet proportionate, like object and reflection. For the first time in years, he was no longer a psychiatrist, no longer a man of medicine; and Mariya was no longer his patient.

She sat beside him, her face silhouetted against the pulse of passing street lights. Again it struck him how little he knew about her. Every answer prompted more questions; and no matter how many questions he answered, the core of her, the essence, remained beyond his reach. In that elusiveness there was a kind of power. He saw now how he had been seduced by it, drawn to explore the limits of his understanding, to behold the infinity of what he could never know. If there had been no Einstein girl, what would have become

of him? It was a question he had asked himself often. But still he had no answer.

They let themselves into Herr Mettler's and went up the stairs without turning on the lights. Above them, water was coming in through a hole in the roof, the drips landing in a metal bucket on the second-floor landing. The room smelled of damp. It had been unoccupied and unheated for too long. Kirsch got down on his knees and tried to light the fire. Scraps of old newspaper lay under the coals, but, like the old Charité files, they did not catch easily.

'We'll soon get the place warmed up,' he said, striking a third match.

Mariya sat down on the bed, looking around the room at the drab furnishings and the possessions – the doll with its china face, the hairbrush and hand mirror, the shoes behind the door – that were supposedly hers. In a moment her gaze would come to rest on the spot where she and Kirsch had held each other and kissed, the spot by the window where the floor was bare and the boards creaked. It took an effort of will for Kirsch to keep his back to it, not to refresh the memory of that moment with a few incidental details: the pattern of the curtains, the height of the ceiling, the fittings on the window. For a few minutes it had felt like a starting point, a second chance against all the odds. Now the shared memory of that moment weighed down on them, rebuking them for their unrealistic dreams.

In the fireplace a tongue of flame drifted over the surface of the coal. A minute ago Kirsch was cold; now his skin was burning.

Mariya tucked her hands under her thighs. 'Am I done with the clinic now? Am I ever going back?'

'No. You mustn't go back there, not ever. It might seem like home to you now, but it isn't safe any more. This country isn't safe.'

In a few days' time she would have a new passport and an address. Kirsch had already explained the situation to the Yugoslav embassy. They had agreed to look up Mariya's records in Belgrade and inform him of the essentials by return. He would give her enough money

to go home, wherever home was. There she would find neighbours, colleagues, friends. They would tell her what she needed to know.

'The important thing is that you leave,' Kirsch said. 'The sooner the better.'

'What about you?'

'I've resigned.' Kirsch stood up. 'I wasn't doing any good there.'

'But what will you do?'

Kirsch had to brace himself against the mantelpiece. The dizzy attacks didn't usually come on until the middle of the day. He had learned to anticipate them, to avoid being where his debilitation might be observed. But this time he had been caught off guard. 'I may set up in private practice somewhere.' He forced a smile. 'It's what old army doctors do.'

'Somewhere? Not here?'

'I'm finished with Berlin too.'

He wished he could explain: about the ministry's list, about the paper he had written in the *Annals of Psychiatric Medicine*, about his brother Max and the war memorial; most importantly, about Dr Schad and the test for neurosyphilis that had proven positive. He was tempted to share it all, if only so that she would understand why he could not go with her. Why, in whatever life awaited her, there could be no place for him. But another part of him was wary of burdening Mariya with too much understanding. Her feelings for him had surely faded by now. With luck she would come to think of him as a cold, clinical man so fixated on the functions and operations of the mind that he had lost the capacity to feel. It was better that way, simpler, cleaner.

'It's about time I had a change of scene,' Kirsch said. 'Twelve years is too long in one place.' He patted his jacket and fished inside it for his wallet. His head was starting to swim. It was all the smoke and the night without sleep. 'Here's some money to tide you over. The shops open in a couple of hours. Try Grenadierstrasse. You'll find everything you need there. Herr Mettler can direct you.'

He held out the notes. It felt awkward, as if there were something sordid about it. 'I'd better go.' He put the money on the chest of drawers. 'I'll be back as soon as your passport arrives.'

318

It was a struggle to walk normally, to keep his head upright. By the time he reached the door, his vision was so cloudy he could not find the handle. He heard Mariya's voice behind him, but for once he could not grasp the meaning of her words.

He just had to find the handle and he would be out in the hall. Out of sight, out of mind. He didn't want her to see him staggering like a drunk.

'Get some rest,' he said. His jaw and his tongue were heavy too. 'For the journey. It'll be a long journey.'

He was in darkness now, a churning granular mist of tiny squares and triangles, like schoolbook doodles. He would be able to keep his feet if the mist cleared just for a moment, if someone brought some light. But then he was falling. Instinctively, he raised his arms to protect himself, but his hands smacked against iron bars. A bedstead. He hung on to it but the bedstead was falling too. He looked down and saw water flowing beneath him: a wide black river, tiny points of light moving on the glassy surface. He wasn't sure if he screamed out loud or only in his mind.

Someone took him by the wrists and pulled him up onto the jetty. It was Eduard Einstein. *Perhaps it's a quantum story.* That was when Kirsch knew he was in a dream.

As he lay on the ground, breathing hard, Heinrich Mehring took out a pocket handkerchief and carefully dusted his hands. The handkerchief came away blackened with ash.

'Your case, Dr Einstein,' he said and turned away. In the distance a woman was crying.

Kirsch learned afterwards that the fever lasted three days. It came and went, changing in intensity and effect. His waking hours were fragmentary and confused, his dreams often lucid. Memories became unreliable, subject to constant revision. People he thought were dead appeared at his bedside, calmly explaining the reason for his mistake. The living he saw laid to rest and buried beneath wooden crosses or granite headstones that bore a host of names. Through sweats and chills and searing headaches, he fought to

maintain an idea of place and time, an order of concrete things that he could believe in, a catalogue of the indisputably real. He clung to his sense of the external world and his place in it, gripped with the fear that to let go would meaning losing them for ever.

Mariya cared for him. If nothing else, he was sure of that. Almost always when he woke she was there, sitting by the bed, bringing him food on a tray or lying asleep on the floor with a blanket over her. More than once he opened his eyes to find himself back at Frau Schirmann's with his books and papers around him, but he learned to distrust those visions, not least because of the people who were often in the room with him, although seemingly oblivious to his presence. One of them was Eduard Einstein. He rummaged through Kirsch's papers, frantically searching for the letter he had stolen from his mother. Members of Kirsch's family also appeared, even his elder sister Frieda, whom he had never before seen in Berlin. They sat in the shadowy corners of the room, his father behind a newspaper, like mourners at a graveside vigil.

In a dream he asked his brother Max to fetch Colonel Schad. They were back at the clinic, down in the basement with Mehring's equipment all around them. But some time later Colonel Schad actually appeared. He told Mariya to open the window, because the room was too hot, his voice reverberating, as if in a brick bunker. Kirsch wanted to tell him that there were no windows. They were in the basement. Then he felt the room grow cooler and found he was back at Herr Mettler's again.

'No more than twenty-three degrees. And not too many blankets.' It was definitely Schad's voice: brisk but mellow. 'Plenty of fluids – clear broth is excellent – and aspirin twice a day to thin the blood. I shall return in two days. Oh, and take this for his mouth. One application every few hours.'

An instant later Schad was gone – another dream, Kirsch assumed. Or a hallucination. It was hard to tell the difference. But then Mariya was beside him, gently dabbing his cracked lips with petroleum jelly. Her fingertips were cool – her touch, he recalled, was always cool – and he could feel her breath on his cheek. He was sure both

sensations were real, but he was afraid to turn and look at her, in case she too disappeared.

Max appeared in a dream, sitting on the end of his bed, leafing through his copy of the Einstein book. Mariya had brought it with her from the clinic.

'I don't think she read it,' Kirsch said.

Max did not look up. 'Don't be stupid,' he said. 'She doesn't need to. What were you thinking?'

Kirsch wanted to ask what he meant, but Max was already gone, taking the book with him.

The last time he saw Mariya was at least a day later. She was standing by the window. Moisture clouded the glass and brought a sharp chill to the air. The old travelling trunk had been dragged into the middle of the room. The lid was open.

'Mariya?'

His voice came out as a croak. Mariya did not look up. She was peeping round the curtains at the street below.

He cleared his throat. 'What's the matter?'

She came over to the bed. A bowl of soup lay cooling on the table. 'Nothing. You must eat.'

'What were you looking at?'

She picked up the bowl and a spoon. 'Herr Mettler says it's just another newspaperman.'

'A newspaperman? What did he look like?'

'It's nothing.'

She refused to discuss it further until he had finished the bowl. After that he needed to empty his bladder; and after that he needed to sleep again.

'I'm going out for a while,' Mariya said, as she pulled the covers over him. 'To get some things. I won't be long.'

As far as Kirsch could tell, she never came back.

Forty-five

Colonel Schad returned to Wörtherstrasse just as he had promised. By that time Mariya had been gone for hours. He couldn't shed any light on her whereabouts.

'Perhaps she went in search of new lodgings. Got tired of sleeping on the floor, I expect.'

He was listening to Kirsch's lungs with a stethoscope. He seemed satisfied that he was over the worst, at least for the time being.

'She would have told me,' Kirsch said. He swung his legs off the bed. 'I must find her.'

Schad put a restraining hand on his shoulder. 'You're not going anywhere, Dr Kirsch. In your weakened state a chill could be fatal.'

'Something's happened. She may have got lost or . . .'

Kirsch tried to get up. He felt clear-headed but hollow, like a papier-mâché doll. Where were his clothes, his shoes?

'Martin.' Schad was looking at him, a look of forbearance on his face. 'She knows what you have. The disease. I don't know how. I didn't tell her. Perhaps she guessed. But you can't be surprised if she feels a little distance would be . . .' He sighed. 'I did warn you. Even loved ones assume the worst.'

Kirsch caught his reflection in the wardrobe door. With his shirt open, the marks on his body were plainly visible. They had spread across his chest, joining up into long curved lines like the claws of a giant crab.

'I think I told her,' he said. 'I hadn't meant to.'

Schad grunted and reapplied the stethoscope. 'Well, that's very commendable.'

It was obvious to Kirsch what Schad thought: that Mariya had

been his mistress. But being wrong about that didn't make him wrong about everything.

'These fevers may come and go,' he was saying. 'It's to be expected. Your system is fighting the infection. This time it won, I'd say.'

Kirsch thanked him and asked for a bill, but Schad wouldn't hear of taking payment. He was happy to oblige for old times' sake.

'Besides, it's the young lady you should thank,' he said. 'She's quite the little nurse. You were in very good hands there. No doubt about it.'

As soon as Kirsch could stand, he went looking for her. He went from rooming house to rooming house, all through the eastern districts. There was no sign of her. In the days that followed he tried the hospitals, the clinics, the asylums. Many people had heard of the Einstein girl; nobody had seen her. He made enquiries at police headquarters, even looked at snapshots of unidentified females found dead around the city. He trailed from dive to dive around Alexanderplatz and along the Kurfürstendamm, armed with his photograph from *Die Berliner Woche*. As a last resort, he tried to recruit the Berlin press. They had once been fascinated by the story. Here at last was a new twist. But the editors he talked to were not interested in reporting Mariya's disappearance, or disappearances in general. 'These days we have more important matters to focus on,' one told him. 'We are privileged to live in historic times.'

He went back to Wörtherstrasse every day, hoping that Mariya might have returned or left word for him. He continued to pay the rent for her room. But she did not return; and there was no word. Towards the end of March he arrived just as a truck loaded down with furniture was pulling away from the kerb. He was almost run over trying to flag down the driver. It turned out the furniture was on its way to be auctioned. Herr Mettler had sold the property and left. The new owners appeared in no hurry to move in. The following week the windows had been boarded up.

* * *

A few days later he took the train out to Potsdam. It was still too early in the year for the steamer service; so Kirsch rented a bicycle outside the station and cycled south up the winding paths of the Telegraphenberg. The Einstein Tower stood on the far side, a few hundred yards beyond the summit. Smooth and white, it rose up out of the wooded hillside like the conning tower of a giant submarine. The windows were swept back, curved and organic in form, as if streamlined by evolutionary forces for speed of movement. Only the silver dome on top, beneath which stood the great vertical telescope, betrayed an element of pure function.

It was said Einstein didn't care for the building created in his honour. He wasn't attuned to the architect's Expressionist sensibilities. He had visited only occasionally, despite being chairman of the foundation that ran it. But Mariya would have gone there, Kirsch felt sure. The tower was the only place in Berlin that bore Einstein's name. She would have wrapped up warm and come to mingle with the day-trippers for whom the Telegraphenberg was also a favoured spot, if only for the views and the clean air and the ornamental gardens laid out around the summit. Perhaps she had gone there the day before she was found by the boys on their bicycles. Perhaps, Kirsch thought, she would go again, without necessarily knowing why: hers a mind cut adrift from the comforting certainties of linear time. Everything instead repeating. A cycle of crisis, amnesia, recovery, crisis, with no end but death.

The day-trippers were absent that day, though the rain had eased and the sun was breaking through the clouds. The doors of the tower were locked and secured with a chain. Scaffolding clung to one corner of the structure. A loose tarpaulin flapped in the wind, heavy ropes lashing the ground.

Kirsch headed down the slopes on the far side. The paths were steep and slippery. He was soon gathering pace, his wheels skidding on the bends. The brakes on his bicycle were dangerously stiff. Every time he squeezed them he was almost pitched over the handlebars. He was forced to use his feet. For several minutes he fought to keep his balance, before finally the path levelled out.

He freewheeled to a halt. He was deep in the woods by this time, somewhere south of the Telegraphenberg. The trees all around were tall and sparse. Rainwater dripped from their branches, making a stealthy pitter-patter on the leafy earth. Kirsch listened, turning his head this way and that. It was hard to shake off the sensation of being watched. A memory came to him of the young pastor at Reinsdorf, something he had said about fallen leaves and the fallen of the war. It had always struck him as a poor metaphor, misleading and weak.

A gunshot ruptured the stillness. It was some way off: a hundred yards, at least. People hunted in the woods around Berlin, with or without a permit. A dog barked. Kirsch heard a man shouting. Then nothing. A bird was sitting hunched on the limb of a tree no more than ten feet above him: a crow or a rook. Its black feathers were bedraggled, especially around its neck. Kirsch clapped his hands, but the bird didn't fly away. Sick or stunned, it continued to watch him, unconcerned.

The gravel path had become a track. Kirsch cycled on, his wheels sinking deeper into the mud. Black water welled up out of the ground, filling the ruts, spattering his face and his clothes until he could taste it on his lips. He rose from his seat, putting all his weight into the peddling to keep up his momentum. Black pools appeared ahead of him, as big as shell holes. The woods were drowning in them.

After a mile it became impossible to pedal. He dismounted and pushed the bicycle, skirting round the pools, plunging through undergrowth and ferns, often losing the path altogether, only to find it again a few hundred yards further on. Burs and bindweed clung to his trousers and his sleeves. Roads were supposed to intersect the forest. Sooner or later he was bound to come across one. His watch told him he had been cycling for an hour, but when he looked more closely, wiping the mud away from the face, he found that the hands were no longer moving.

At last he could make out smudges of gold in the sky. They told him he was heading south-west. He couldn't have been far from the lake. He left the path and turned due west, wanting to reach the open

water as quickly as possible. The ground beneath him began to rise, then fall again. In this part of the forest the trees were choked with ivy. Only the pines and willows were still alive.

He didn't see the house until he had stumbled into a corner of the garden. It stood in a small, landscaped clearing, a red-brown clapboard building with white shutters. A broad roof terrace, reached by an external staircase, and a peculiar port-hole window on the ground floor lent the premises the look of a seaside villa. Kirsch had seen the house before in newspapers and architectural magazines. Except for its foundations, it was built entirely of Oregon pine and Galician fir, an example of the Bauhaus style. Although the exact location was never disclosed, he knew where he was. He had reached the outskirts of Caputh. He was standing in the garden of Albert Einstein's summer house.

The cuttings were still there in his scrapbook. He had other photographs of Einstein standing in front of the French windows with various distinguished visitors, or staring from the roof terrace towards the lake, pipe in hand. In his mind the house had been bigger and more beautiful – not palatial, but elegant and homely. It had reflected the warmth and wisdom of its owner. The reality seemed shrunken, cramped, as if Einstein's absence had sucked the spirit out of it.

Clover and weeds choked the lawns. Moss had invaded the paths. The plants in the window boxes – flowering in the photographs – were dead. Kirsch laid his bicycle down and walked onto the cement veranda, aware as he approached of a faint sound, a muffled impact, like the lazy pounding of a machine.

The outside staircase was slimy underfoot. On the landing halfway up, one of the railings was broken. Leaves had gathered in wet heaps around the roof terrace. A rolled-up parasol lay on its side. A short distance away, the lake was a strip of grey water, obscured by trees. Kirsch shivered. His clothes were cold and wet against his skin.

The noise began again. It was coming from inside the house. A door led off the roof terrace, but it was locked. Kirsch went around to the north side of the building, peering through the shutters as he went. Everything inside was dark.

A dirty green Mercedes with the top down stood in the driveway. It seemed someone was home after all. But it couldn't be the Einsteins. Albert Einstein was in hiding abroad. The regime had seized his bank accounts and what remained of his property. A pro-Nazi newspaper had put a bounty of $50,000 on his head, dead or alive.

Kirsch went to the front door. He was about to knock when he noticed that the wood was splintered around the lock. Beneath the handle was a large muddy footprint. The door had been forced. A nudge of the shoulder was all it took to get in.

A dark, narrow hallway with a chequerboard floor. A damp, musty smell. The walls and ceilings were of wood. A narrow staircase led up to the first floor. A door, ajar, led down into a cellar. Kirsch moved towards the back of the house, where bands of light peeped through the shutters.

There was little of interest to thieves. The furniture was sparse and plain. There were no display cabinets showing off the family silver. He stepped into the kitchen. Next to a pepper grinder, a bag of flour lay ruptured. Thousands of tiny ants swarmed over the counter and the sink.

He felt a gentle draft on the back of his neck. The noise was coming from the other side of the interior wall: a nonchalant knocking, an ironic summons. Knives lay on the kitchen table, but none was sharp enough to serve as a weapon. He moved out into the passage. Papers rustled. Someone was in there, in the next room. He eased back the door.

The sunlight hurt his eyes. The windows were broken. The shutters hung from a single hinge. They swung back and forth, knocking against iron railings on the outside. The room – a small study – had been ransacked. Books and papers were strewn across the floor. Behind a plain pinewood table a man was on all fours, hastily gathering them up. It took Kirsch a moment to recognise him.

'Professor von Laue?'

The professor looked up, startled. 'Who are you? What do you want?'

'Martin Kirsch. From the Charité. Don't you remember me?'

The professor continued to stare. His collar had become detached from his shirt, revealing a sliver of flesh at the base of his neck. 'The door, it was —'

'What do you want?' von Laue said again.

'I'm looking for someone.'

'Who?'

'A patient. Ex-patient. The one you were curious about.'

'The student?'

'She's missing.'

Von Laue frowned, then shook his head, his alarm visibly subsiding. 'Well, you won't find her here. No one lives here any more.'

'So I see.'

The professor deposited a stack of files on top of the desk. It came to Kirsch that he had given the man quite a shock.

'Well,' von Laue said. 'Well. Never mind. You can help me get these papers together. Make yourself useful. It's only a matter of time before they come back.'

'Who? Before who comes back?'

'Who do you think? We need to get all these to the car. They'll have to stay at his apartment until I can think of a safer place. Find some boxes or something.' Von Laue looked at him. 'Well, what are you waiting for?'

Kirsch did as he was asked. He found some old luggage under the stairs and some vegetable crates in the larder. Back in the study they got busy, filling them with papers.

'The books too?' Kirsch asked.

'Anything annotated. Otherwise no.'

They worked on in silence for a few minutes. Kirsch sensed that von Laue was embarrassed by the hostility he'd shown. He could feel the older man groping for some way to make amends.

'What made you think your patient would be here?' he said finally.

Kirsch paused to mop his brow. His only thought had been to seek out the place where she had been found by those two small boys on their bicycles. It was a way of getting closer to her, the only way he could think of.

'She was originally found less than a mile from here,' he said. 'I think it's possible she was on her way to meet her father.'

Von Laue sighed and began sifting through the bookshelves. 'You're a good man, Dr Kirsch. You mean well, I can see that. But your energies would be better directed elsewhere.' He picked up a volume, examined the spine and replaced it. 'Trust me: nothing can come of that line of enquiry.'

'How can you be sure?'

Loose papers fell on Kirsch's feet, adding to the mass already carpeting the floorboards. Bending down to pick them up, he felt breathless.

Von Laue was flicking through a book. 'People think Albert Einstein's work is all about distant stars and galaxies. They don't think it has anything to do with *them*. What they forget is that we're all part of the universe. We're as much an expression of its physical laws as anything else, whether we like it or not. Therefore to change your understanding of the cosmos is to change your understanding of Man. And that is a very significant thing.'

Kirsch was packing books. In his hand was a copy of the work Max had given him: *On the Special and General Theory of Relativity, Generally Comprehensible*. Max must have shared von Laue's opinion, to some degree. Why else would he have chosen such a gift for his brother, the military surgeon?

'Are you saying Professor Einstein would have no time for his own daughter?'

Von Laue smiled. 'Time *is* an issue, but not in the way you mean.'

'Then in what way?'

Outside, clouds moved across the sun. The room grew suddenly darker. Von Laue glanced out of the window into the woods. For a moment, Kirsch thought he saw someone standing there, watching from the shadows.

'What do you suppose lies behind these great leaps of understanding?' Von Laue said. 'You've studied the human mind, Doctor. How is it Albert Einstein can see what's invisible to everyone else? How can he conceive of what to others is inconceivable?'

'I suppose he's more intelligent.'

Von Laue shook his head. 'More intelligent than Poincaré? More intelligent than Max Planck? I doubt it. I doubt *he* would say so. The difference, the critical difference, lies in the independence of his thought. His scepticism, if you like. Somehow he has developed the ability to step back from any assumption, any abstraction, however deeply sunk into the bedrock of the human mind, and establish exactly what's real and tangible, and what's not. Linear space and absolute time were more than sacrosanct, Dr Kirsch. They were the foundation stones of rational thought. No one even *considered* questioning them. Einstein didn't just demonstrate that they were illusory. He saw that they were.'

Kirsch's brow felt warm, the fever gently pulsing at his temples. 'I'm not denying his uniqueness. But I don't see –'

'But you *do* deny it. You imagine these extraordinary perspectives can be reached without sacrifice, without change. But that's how the truth is discovered. To perceive the world, one must step *outside* the world. In the gospels it says the truth shall set you free. What it should say is: the truth will set you *apart*.'

What had Eduard Einstein said at their first meeting. *Mariya is changing.*

'This is all science,' Kirsch said. 'Surely it has nothing to do with . . . with a man's family.'

Von Laue shook his head. 'You don't want to understand me. But I think you do.' He pulled a pair of volumes from the shelf, holding one in each hand. 'If instinctive notions of space and time are invalid, then the conventions of human society are hardly likely to be infallible. Honour, community, country, God. What are these concepts built on? Solid and tangible foundations? Something absolute, like the speed of light? Or assumptions so dubious and inconsistent the rational mind hardly knows where to begin?' He packed the books away, then opened a drawer in the table. More papers lay inside. 'In a sceptical world truth and certainty would go together. But look around you. Is that what you see?'

Kirsch brought a hand to his face. He was sweating. He closed

his eyes and saw the monument at Reinsdorf, the shiny black granite and the big bold lie: FOR GOD AND THE FATHERLAND.

'It doesn't have to be like that,' he said. 'People could learn.'

Von Laue laughed. 'What makes you think they *want* to learn? My dear fellow. For the mass of humanity, it's only delusions that make life bearable. That's the tragedy of the human condition, if you ask me. Men need to pretend there's meaning where reason says there isn't. Without it what would they have in common? Human ties would dissolve. Society would disintegrate, and they'd be left to face the indifference of the universe alone. That, more than anything, is what they want to avoid; and for that, even war is a price they're willing to pay.'

Wind gusted against the side of the house. The shutter slammed against the frame. Von Laue picked up one of the boxes. 'We'd better get this done. I don't want to be here after dark.'

He went out to the car. Kirsch went back to work, sweeping the papers by the armful into a small leather suitcase. He tried not to think of Mariya making her way to the house in her new dress and her new shoes, hopeful of finding the Albert Einstein of the newsreels: the compassionate prophet, the benevolent father. He tried not to think at all.

He was almost finished when he came across a bundle of mail, all unopened: bills, several invitations in embossed envelopes, what felt like periodicals, to judge from the heft. At the bottom was a thick white envelope with Einstein's name and address written in a tidy feminine hand. According to the post mark, the package had been sent on 26 October from Berlin postal district C, close to where Kirsch lodged. He knew then where he had seen it before.

Inside there was a stack of lined pages covered in the same tidy writing. They made up the complete folio of a notebook. Tucked into the final page was a sketch a few inches square: Albert Einstein, standing in front of a lectern, a kindly smile on his face.

The first page began: *How do I come to be here after all this time?*

light

Forty-six

I was a fool to think I could overcome a man of Zoltán's size, even in his intoxicated state; and more of a fool to imagine that I had it in me to bury a knife in his heart. I wanted his death. He had driven my sister to hers just as surely as if he had drowned her himself. But some instinct checked my hunger for revenge and kept me from flying at him as soon as he opened the door, which would have been the wisest and most effective form of attack. It was not pity that stopped me, still less fear. It was a sense — unfamiliar yet hard, like a tumour in the flesh — that to take a human life was alien to me; that once I took that lethal step I would be changed for ever. My old self would fade away and I would begin a new existence, one where history and the ties of blood had to be forgotten, where the mind might be lively, perhaps, but where the heart would always be silent.

I stood in the kitchen with the knife in my hand, hesitating on the threshold of that bleak new existence. That was how things were when Zoltán Draganović walked in from the yard.

He stood looking at me, at first shocked, then affronted, then amused, all three emotions jostling for pre-eminence in his stupefied brain.

'What's all this?' he spluttered finally. Then his eyes narrowed and I could see he was trying to explain to himself what might lie behind this unexpected hostility. 'Have you been talking to your sister? What's she been telling you?'

What might she have told me, if she had still been alive? Or if I had been unselfish enough to ask her? I could imagine well enough, now that it was too late. But I could not bring myself to speak of it, even then. Some small part of me still hoped I was wrong.

Zoltán stepped closer. I jabbed the knife towards him, pointing at his throat. One good thrust, I told myself, and he would bleed to death like

a slaughtered lamb. I fought to find that last ounce of willpower. But the thought of my own guilt, of my silent complicity in Senka's fate, left me weak.

Zoltán sensed that the moment of danger was past. He laughed as I waved the knife in front of him.

'This is my house,' he said, holding his arms wide. 'If you want it, you'll have to take it.' He swaggered towards me, offering his chest as a target, daring me to attack.

I told him I did not want his house. But I could not say out loud what I did want: to change the past and stay at my sister's side so that no harm could come to her; to hear her laughing as she climbed up into the branches of an apple tree, or sit with her in the orchard and share again the whispered confidences of our childhood; above all, to know that her trust in me had not been misplaced. But all these things were now beyond me and even Zoltán's death would not bring them within reach.

'Then what do you want, young lady?' he said. 'What's got you all in a stew?' He put his head on one side, as if I were an interesting puzzle to which he was beginning at last to perceive a solution. 'Maybe your sister's got you a little jealous.'

Before I could reply, he snatched at the knife, which I pulled away just fast enough to cut him along the palm of his hand. He screamed and struck me in the face so hard I fell against the table. My head swam and I could taste the blood in my mouth. He pushed me back and down, then with one arm lifted my legs clean off the floor so that I fell back onto the table, the same kitchen table where my sister's body had been stretched out only hours before. Then his weight was on top of me, such weight that I thought would crush the life out of me. The lantern above the table was swinging back and forth so that the whole room seemed to sway. Zoltán spoke all the while, saying he would not have troubled with my sister if he'd known I was game for it; and more things besides that I would not hear. For even as I struggled, I found myself withdrawing from that place and time, retreating into an oblivion where nothing could touch me, where there were no consequences and no dreadful realisations, because there was no knowledge. From this insensible place I could watch the man and the woman wrestling with each other on a table beneath the

light of a swaying lantern – and see only that. The man had no name, nor the woman either. And the table was just a table; and the lantern threw shadows over them so that it was hard to tell if their embraces were the embraces of lovers or of mortal enemies locked in a fight to the death. It was only afterwards, when I awoke and found myself alone, that the bitter truth became clear to me and I realised what my weakness and guilt had cost me.

I was scarce on my feet when Maja Lukić returned. She must have guessed what had happened. She wrapped me up in a coat, picked up my suitcase and took me straight away to her house, going the back way. I was in no state to question her choice, but of course she was afraid we should be seen on the main street even though it was almost nightfall. Later the injustice of this made me angry. But Maja Lukić was not an ignorant woman. She knew well the little place in which she lived, and that a woman's honour once lost, however unjustly, could never be regained. Such are the primitive cruelties of the place where I grew up, where men profess their devotion to modernity and the blessings of enlightenment (who will not travel by steam train, or avail themselves of the best medicine, or electrify their homes when they can?) but leave their hearts in the past, among the shadows of superstition. How well do I understand your impatience with that foolish, rotten old world and your need to be free of it!

I doubt if Maja Lukić shared these opinions, but her concern for me was real. She determined that it would be best if I made my escape from the village as soon as possible. She told me she had thought for some time that Zoltán was not in his right mind, and that she had come close to quitting her position as housekeeper more than once. She feared Zoltán might rather kill me than have me level accusations against him. She gave me all the money she had in the house and sent me to Belgrade the next day, armed with a hastily written letter of introduction to a relative by marriage. I did not argue with her. I did not know where else to go. I could not remain in Orlovat; and without Zoltán's money I could not continue my studies in Zagreb. I also had it in my mind that he would seek me out there. In short, my state of mind was such that rational decisions were best left to others. Even my memory became unreliable;

so that on more than one occasion I awoke not knowing where I was, thinking Senka — and even my mother — were still alive and that the family I once belonged to still existed.

Svetlana Lukić was the sister of Maja's dead husband. She owned a small dress shop close to Saint Sava's cathedral and was at heart a kind woman, although somewhat prim and set in her ways. Her principal fondness was for cats, which was unfortunate, for she could not afford to keep any in the house in case they left their fur on the dresses or clawed the fabric. Instead, she would feed the strays that lived in the grounds of the cathedral.

I did my best to help around the shop. I had no skill with a needle, but was able to assist in the ordering of her accounts, which were in such a shambles that any tax inspector would have had her at his mercy. Then, after a month or so, I set about looking for a teaching position which I found with ease, there being a great shortage of female teachers in the fields of mathematics. In the years that followed I tried as best I could to continue my own education. Thanks to the intervention of a tutor at Zagreb, I was granted access to several of the most important academic libraries, and was even able to attend certain lectures at the university of Belgrade, which fed my appetite for physics and the many startling discoveries in that field. I do not suppose my efforts at self-tuition were any substitute for a proper degree, but the rigours involved in following this science and the contemplation of its mysteries did much to bring me peace in those times, even if that peace was incomplete.

But I am letting my account run ahead of itself. There is more I must tell you of that torrential spring when my sister died, though it is hard. Besides myself I believe only Maja Lukić knows everything. Soon you shall know too. You must, or my long journey here will have been for nothing. You see, I offer you my long-guarded secrets in hope of receiving one from you in return. This is what I ask of you and only this.

I was still staying with Svetlana when I began to receive letters from Maja Lukić. I opened them always with a heavy heart, knowing that they would contain tidings of people and things I wanted only to forget, saving of course my poor sister. Maja informed me that Senka's body had been removed to Novi Sad, the provincial capital, and buried in the

Draganović family plot. To this day I wonder why Zoltán went to the trouble. I can only suppose he was concerned to keep up appearances. Now that his daughter was dead, he could afford her all the honours in the world and receive the world's sympathy into the bargain. I wished I could have been there for that final farewell, but what I wished even more was that she had been laid to rest elsewhere and in better company.

It became clear to me that, just as I had felt some responsibility for Senka's fate, so Maja Lukić felt some responsibility for mine. From her letters, awkward but sincere, I could see that she was tormented with guilt. Perhaps my scant replies deepened those feelings, for she became ever more desperate to set my mind at ease. In this vein she began to hint, then suggest, then assert as if it were a matter of record that Zoltán Draganović was not my father. She repeated something I had once heard from my grandmother about my mother having had a baby before me who had fallen sick with scarlet fever. I had all but forgotten this story, assuming it to be some fancy of my childhood. As far as the world was concerned, I was the first-born. I had gone down with the fever at six months old, but recovered. That was the end of the matter. But Maja Lukić told a different tale.

She had been working in our house at the time and saw the first-born child close to death. My mother, she said, was in a dreadful state and inconsolable. Then Maja had been sent away for a fortnight or more. No one was given admittance to the house, not even the priest, which was unusual; for when a child was thought likely to die it was the common practice to bring forward the Christening so as to make safe its soul. When Maja was eventually permitted to take up her duties again, she found the child as right as rain – except that it was not the same child. 'This baby was older by two months at least,' she wrote. 'She had a rounder face and darker eyes.' In her opinion, there was only one explanation: I had been adopted in secret, either to compensate my mother in her grief, or because Zoltán was afraid he might otherwise have no children at all. On the other hand, she had no idea where I might have come from, or whose child I truly was.

Maja Lukić was afraid that I might be upset or insulted by this revelation, even after what had happened. It was one thing not to be my

father's child; quite another not to be my mother's also. But when I read that letter, it was as if a puzzle I had been grappling with all my life had suddenly been solved. For years I had felt like an outsider in the Draganović family. Here at last was the reason. It came as a shock to have my feelings so suddenly and decisively confirmed. But it was also a comfort, more than even Maja Lukić could know.

I could, I suppose, have demanded that Zoltán tell me the truth. But nothing would induce me to contact him, let alone reveal to him my whereabouts. Finally, some nine years later, I received word from Orlovat that he was dead of a stroke. His lawyer came from Novi Sad to settle his affairs, but could find no will, except for the one that he had drawn up before my mother's death. There being no other surviving kin, I was informed that the residue of the estate, once certain creditors had been satisfied, would fall to me. The value was more than I had expected, for, although Zoltán regularly drank the proceeds of his meagre pension and the rents that came in from his land, the land itself had remained in his possession. In addition, he had left certain family effects, as well as the house.

I returned to Orlovat to take possession of the estate. I made certain sales of land for a fair price and then turned my attention to the house. I had put off the task of going through Zoltán's papers, but was advised that the job was a necessary one, and so finally sat down to do it. Everything was in a chaotic state, and I was tempted to put the whole lot on the fire. But then I came across a number of notes from his bank in Novi Sad, going back more than ten years. In each case the bank informed my father that funds had been received from a bank in Zürich. Three times a year moneys had been sent from a Frau Einstein-Marić – enough to pay for a university education. Furthermore, the payments had ceased around the time I had abandoned my studies and gone to live in Belgrade.

You may imagine how curious this made me. I remembered Aunt Helene's taciturn companion, and the effect her presence in the house always had on my mother and father. More particularly, I remembered what I had learned subsequently of her achievements and her fame. It was at that moment, sitting alone in the very room where Frau Einstein had once sat as our visitor, that I dared to believe Maja Lukić's story.

A few weeks later, I sought out Aunt Helene in Belgrade. I had not seen her for many years, but she remembered me and offered me her condolences on the death of my father. I told her that due to my changed circumstances, I now intended to continue my studies abroad. I asked her where I should go and if she could suggest where I might gain the necessary tuition in mathematics and physics such that I might re-enter the academic world. She greeted my enquiry thoughtfully and, I thought, with some pleasure. In due course, as I knew she would, she suggested I go to Zürich, and seek out a teacher known to her there. I need hardly tell you who that teacher was.

I did not tell Aunt Helene the truth, or at least not the whole truth. I should have liked nothing better than to study again. I have dreamed of grappling with those strange and beautiful riddles once again, of striving for the final and absolute enlightenment which I know now occupies you. To win that prize, if it can be won, will surely prove the crowning achievement of mankind. Nothing could be more important or worthwhile. But my purpose in travelling to Zürich, my purpose in coming to Berlin, is simpler: to discover my parentage and learn, once and for all, if Maja Lukić's story is true. I believe only you can help me. Those others that could speak, I am certain, will not do so while you remain silent. Such is the hold you have over them. It seems you are twice blessed: not only with the power to command men's minds but also their loyalty and love — a consequence that flows, I have no doubt, not only from your very great wisdom, but from goodness and kindness too. So it is with confidence that I place myself in your hands, safe in the knowledge that to you, of all men, the perpetuation of a lie is an intolerable thing, however convenient its continuation may be to men of narrower vision and lesser principle.

Forty-seven

Le Coq sur Mer, Belgium, April 1933
The sun beats down through a film of haze, making the shadows
pale. The sea is a dead, unnatural calm, the horizon melted into a
white sky. From the veranda of the Villa Savoyarde Albert Einstein
watches one of the detectives pace the water's edge. His name is
Gilbert and he spends most of his time patrolling the beach and the
tall dunes that surround the villa. An assassin might attempt to land
by boat, he explained to Elsa one morning. Besides that, he has said
very little. Mainly he smokes cigarettes and stares at the trawlers as
they chug up and down, fishing for grey shrimp. Beyond them, in
the far distance, the ferries can just be seen slipping out of Ostend
harbour on their way to England.

Another detective is always in the house. His name is Flemish
and therefore unpronounceable. He sits in the hall, accepting cups
of coffee and watching the driveway. Whenever visitors appear,
he leaps to his feet, challenging anyone he does not recognise.
The locals in Le Coq have been asked to feign ignorance when questioned about Einstein's whereabouts, but this has had little effect.
Every day more and more people come wandering along the beach,
some affecting nonchalance, others blatantly rubbernecking or snap-
ping photographs. Both Gilbert and his colleague have become
noticeably edgier. They frequently check their revolvers and make
hushed phone calls to their superiors about the lack of a viable
perimeter. There have been altercations in the dunes with reporters
and a newsreel camera crew, not to mention several delegations of
academics. Less than three weeks *in situ* and the sense of siege is
palpable. Elsa spends hours upstairs, locked in her bedroom. There
can be no question that this refuge, provided gratis by the King of

Belgium, will be purely temporary. Nazi Germany is too near, its reach too long. Working here has become impossible.

Einstein's private secretary, Fräulein Dukas, a plain, thin woman with raven hair, looks up from her shorthand notebook. Einstein has paused mid-dictation: a letter to Lord Rutherford concerning the upcoming visit to Britain. Memorial lectures at Oxford and Glasgow. Rutherford needs to confirm the dates.

Without having to be asked, Fräulein Dukas reads back the last line: 'I hope to arrive in Dover no later than May twenty-sixth . . .'

Normally the diary is her affair. She knows her employer's commitments and obligations by heart, and those of his wife. But there are some commitments she cannot schedule for him, some obligations only he can evaluate.

A trip to Zürich is long overdue. He promised to visit in May. But for how long should he stay? Three days? Four? Elsa wants him to stay at a hotel, but that would be churlish and needlessly proper. Mileva has a perfectly adequate guest room in her Huttenstrasse apartment. On the other hand, there is a danger that she will bring Eduard back from the Burghölzli so as to maximise their time together. Father and son will play musical duets, which will be painless, and converse on the subjects of psychiatry and literature, which will not be. He will avoid talk of final farewells. He has been careful never to say anything to the press about settling in America permanently. His public comments about the Land of the Free have been disparaging. All the same, he longs to bid farewell to the complications of the old world once and for all, to set down the burden of caring about it, publicly or privately. The old world, like his old life, is a distraction, an itch he cannot quite reach. The thought of putting an ocean between it and him is more attractive every day.

Three days and three nights. More than that and Mileva's good humour wears thin. Resentments surface. Her pleasure and pride at seeing him is gradually superseded by her innate sense of grievance. Mileva the martyr. No encounter is complete without some allusion to broken promises or neglect. In that sense their younger son is the perfect weapon, a living reproof. Two years ago she turned

up unannounced in Berlin at the wedding of Elsa's daughter, bearing bad tidings about Eduard's mental state. But the madness doesn't come from his side of the family. Just look at her sister, Zorka. She's been in and out of psychiatric hospitals most of her adult life. Now she lives alone in Novi Sad in a house with forty cats.

Three days and *two* nights. That should be enough.

Einstein turns to Fräulein Dukas. 'I hope to arrive in Dover no later than . . .'

On the table lies a stack of unopened mail. The range of national postage stamps is even more impressive than usual, but one large brown envelope catches Einstein's eye. It has no stamps at all. Nor does it bear his name; just the words *Villa Savoyarde*.

'Where did this come from?'

Fräulein Dukas looks up from her notepad, waving away an importunate sand fly. 'It was delivered by motor-cycle messenger. He wanted to give it to you in person, but Detective Dejaeck . . .'

She nods towards the hall. The envelope is sealed with wax and marked *Confidential*. Fräulein Dukas does not open mail marked *Confidential*.

Einstein tears open the envelope. He knows who it is from. Only de Vries sends his mail by private courier.

'I'll just be a moment,' Einstein says and carries the papers inside.

In the sitting room he stops and listens. A rustling sound from the hallway reveals that Detective Dejaeck is reading a newspaper. Elsa is upstairs. The carriage clock on the mantel ticks lightly twice a second. Even before he reads, Einstein feels the clinging fingers of the past. They reach out to claim him. Will an ocean away be far enough? Will he reach his chosen haven at Princeton only to find his old sins hidden in his luggage, waiting to be unpacked?

De Vries's latest report is reassuring on the main points. He has uncovered no hint of a conspiracy in the Draganović affair, no suggestion that fraud or blackmail was ever contemplated. If Mariya Draganović had a conspirator, it was her psychiatrist, an ambitious but apparently unstable character whose devotion to her case has given rise to comment. There are suggestions of a liaison between

the two of them, rumours of a more than professional attachment, but nothing more troubling. That still leaves the possibility that the girl's claims were the product of a deluded mind, that somewhere, probably in Zürich, she heard the story of Lieserl Einstein and made it her own. Such fantasies are often concocted by damaged minds, perhaps as a means of repairing a chronic sense of insignificance or isolation. Even so, the psychiatrist in Berlin noted no such tendency in Mariya Draganović, no sign of advanced psychosis. Nor was it Einstein's impression that she was insane. If the woman had been obviously insane, he would have let the matter rest.

Whatever the truth, the girl is no longer being treated at the Charité. De Vries considers it unlikely that she will ever surface in any significant way again. All Einstein's fears, it seems, were unfounded.

He lowers himself onto the sofa, letting one hand come to rest on the edge of the seat. He finds he craves detail. There is still too much he does not know, uncertainties that may one day coalesce into something threatening, like the remnants of a tumour imperfectly excised.

If the girl was not lying and if she was not mad, then she must simply have been mistaken. Lieserl has been dead for years. At least, that was what they told him. He tries to recall the moment when Mileva gave him the news, the exact circumstances. But he can't.

A small photograph is glued to the bottom of the final page, the kind used in passports and passport offices, which is probably where de Vries acquired it. This face is more like the one he remembers. Mariya was there in the crowd at the Philharmonic Hall. He had hardly begun to speak when he noticed her. There are usually pretty women at his public lectures, but something in her face held his attention. He found himself looking at her again and again. 'Have we met?' he asked her afterwards, as she came through the crowd towards him. It was not a conversational gambit, an opening line. It was the only explanation he could come up with: that they had met before, the memory hovering just out of reach, tantalising and sweet.

What does it matter? There's no threat here any longer, no potential scandal to prevent his settling in America. The girl is gone and

will never return. Only the photograph remains troubling – the very sense of recognition that he once found so compelling. Was it his own flesh and blood he recognised? Was that it?

He pushes his fingers through his long white hair. Why would Mileva lie? To hurt him? But he wasn't hurt, not a bit. The news of Lieserl's death, true or false, had no practical consequences whatsoever. Or did that very fact make the deception possible – in fact, easy?

Enclosed with the report is a letter, addressed to the girl. De Vries has attached a note. *This item of correspondence appears to have been sent by a resident patient at the Burghölzli Psychiatric Clinic. He calls himself Eduard, but I have not yet been able to ascertain his full identity.* Einstein already knows it. The handwriting is unmistakably his son's.

He begins to read. With the stiffening sea breeze the house is getting cold. He needs his pipe and his jacket. The clock ticks on the mantel. Eduard. He never thought of Eduard, assumed he was far away in a world of his own, incapable of scheming. Or did someone put him up to it? Did someone arm him with information he was never supposed to have? In his absence, old grievances have festered, becoming cankerous.

When he has finished reading, he tears up the letter and de Vries's report and tosses the pieces into the fireplace. Then he goes out again onto the veranda.

Fräulein Dukas picks up her pad and pencil. 'I hope to arrive in Dover no later than May twenty-sixth,' she says, reading back his dictation.

Einstein sits down, shielding his eyes from the sun. Soon the past will loosen its grip. Soon. His life will be lighter, clearer. He will do great things in Princeton. He will tame the Young Turks of quantum mechanics and rescue the sanity of science, once and for all. Once he is free.

He picks up his pipe from the ashtray. The fire in the bowl has gone out. He sucks on cold, tarry air. 'No later than June first. I shall need to be away a little longer than I thought.'

Forty-eight

Orlovat, 28 April

Dear Dr Kirsch,
*Please forgive me if the curiosity that drives me to write this letter is
unwelcome to you. It is a month since I left Berlin. In that time I have
tried my best to do as you told me: to forget the city and everything
that happened there. But I find there are things I have to know and
equally things I need to tell you. For though I am no longer your patient
or your responsibility in any other way, I fear my sudden departure
might have caused you anxiety, or that it might have left you with the
wrong impression of my feelings or my state of mind. I think often of
the time you spent on me, the protection and care, and the possibility
troubles me that I have in return caused you only disquiet.*

*The first reassurance I seek is that you are well and recovered from
the fever. Your friend Dr Schad assured me that you were on the way
to recovery and I had reason to believe he was right. Your temperature
had fallen; you were at last eating, and you had begun to sleep peace-
fully without those violent dreams that so frightened me during those
first two days. I wish now that I had stayed longer, if only to satisfy
my own anxiety, but when you know the truth I hope you will not judge
me too harshly.*

*One of the last things you told me was that you thought you had
done no good at the Charité. I had the impression that you thought
you had failed me, that your efforts had been for nothing. I want to
inform you that you were wrong. If you had recovered a little sooner
or if I had left Berlin a little later, you would have seen this for
yourself. Today as I write, my memory is all but restored. There are
some moments, some episodes from my recent past, that I still cannot*

347

recall clearly, but they are few and getting fewer all the time. I have recovered a solid sense of who I am without recourse to invention or second-hand memories. I have needed mental strength to do this, to face what an instinct deep within me was determined to bury in the deepest, darkest place. But that strength, I now know, I found thanks to you. From a distance it is clearer to me than ever: without you I would have continued to exist only as a ghost of myself, learning in time perhaps to play the part, but never to live it.

I was tending you at Herr Mettler's when the knowledge I had lost began to resurface. It reappeared little by little, in no clear order. At first I hardly noticed that it was there at all. While you were sleeping that first night I explored the room where once I had stayed, and examined the possessions that were presumably mine. I found the travelling trunk and went through the contents: the books on science, at once so formidable and familiar, the many postcards I had bought but never sent; the photograph album with its empty frames – a clue that sadness lay in my history and would be there for me should I insist on rediscovering it. Gradually the memories of what these things were and what they meant to me drew closer, like something on the tip of the tongue that cannot quite be grasped.

I did not struggle too much to reach them. These were idle moments I passed between sleeping and caring for myself and my patient, for which occupation I was very grateful. Did you know that Frau Mettler let me use her kitchen, and even helped me prepare the food once she learned how ill you were? I found my way around the district quite well, and to Dr Schad's as you requested. I even took a short cut back from Grenadierstrasse one morning without thinking about it. That should have told me that my memories were returning, but it was another, more concrete clue, that brought the realisation home.

I took seriously what you told me, about Germany not being safe for me any more, but I had no clear idea what form the danger might take. All Herr Mettler would tell me was that people were in the habit of disappearing, and that I should keep off the streets at night. I followed his advice and even when I ventured out during the day – when, I admit, everything seemed quite as normal – I tried to keep my

wits about me. I supposed that if I was to disappear, I would first have to be seized and overcome. So I mostly avoided the emptiest streets and alleys, while checking over my shoulder regularly in case anyone was following me. Sometimes I got myself into quite a state, imagining that I had seen this or that stranger before. When I saw someone watching me, it was often all I could do not to turn and run away. Then I did see someone, not following me, but watching the house. I had seen him that morning as I went out to buy bread and milk, hanging around the gates of the Jewish cemetery: a rough-looking man with a florid complexion and a hard, steady gaze. He was there when I returned, not in plain view, but this time inside the cemetery, moving aimlessly from stone to stone, his hands in his raincoat pockets. Herr Mettler thought he was most likely a reporter. Reporters had turned up at his rooming house before, he said, asking impertinent questions. But the man outside did not strike me as having anything to ask. He struck me as a hunter, waiting patiently for his prey to break cover.

Back in the room, I went to the window. I could see no sign of the man, but that did not mean he had gone. Part of me was afraid, part of me said the fear was irrational. The man might simply have been a mourner come to pay his respects to a loved one. But in the back of my mind I must already have been thinking of flight, for as I was weighing the possibilities, I went to a drawer in the chest of drawers where I had a stack of clean petticoats and chemises. Without thinking about it, I reached into the middle of the stack and took out a passport and a handful of banknotes. This was where I had hidden them months before. It was only when I held them in my hand that I realised what I had done: I had remembered.

Dr Schad visited later that day. You were right to put your trust in him, for he was very solicitous and clear in his prescriptions. I asked him about your underlying condition and if what you had told me in your feverish state was true. Perhaps mindful of your privacy he said little. All the same, I had the impression he thought the news must have come as a great shock to me, enough to change whatever feelings I might have had for you. Then he said that I was lucky, being young enough to fix my sights on someone new. He seemed to be under the

impression that I was more to you than a patient. I did not correct his assumptions, though at times I wish I had. You see, it was not on account of your illness that I left you so suddenly.

It was the postcards that were responsible, the postcards I must have purchased but never sent. It was the morning of the fourth day. I had left the house as usual to buy food, going out the back way via Herr Mettler's kitchen. As usual I went to the little bakery at the far end of Tresckowstrasse, but they had run out of bread so I walked a little down the Prenzlauer Allee, looking for another. I had not gone far when I passed a little shop selling newspapers and tobacco. On a display outside the door were postcards of Berlin just like the ones in the room: the exact same views of the exact same places, and others besides. It was the shop where I had bought them.

I had no conscious purpose in stopping, but I did stop. I began to sift through the pictures, especially the newer, coloured ones. It was something I had been in the habit of doing ever since I left my home country. Besides the streets and monuments, some of the cards had pictures of animals: dogs, horses and cats with long fur and bows around their necks. I chose a postcard of some cats and went to pay for it. That was when I remembered who the postcards were for, who they had all been for. I stood in the shop motionless as the memories toppled into my consciousness one after the other, question following answer following question with such speed it made my head spin.

I dropped the postcard and ran out into the street. By now it was busy with people going off to work. They were crowded onto the trams and streaming along the pavements towards Alexanderplatz station. I had my passport and my money in my coat. There was nothing to stop me getting on a train there and then. I felt safe in that crowd, shielded and hidden by its numbers. If I went back to Wörtherstrasse, I was afraid I might never get away again. The watchers would come for me and your warnings would have been for nothing. So when I reached Alexanderplatz I bought an underground ticket to the Potsdam station and from there took a tram to the Anhalt station. There was a train to Munich leaving seven minutes later. This stroke of luck seemed like a confirmation that I was doing the right thing. I bought a ticket and hurried aboard.

I hope you will understand the need I felt to be gone when I tell you that the postcards had all been intended for a child. It is she I remembered in that little shop, she who had heard nothing from me for five long months. She is my daughter. Her name is Anna and she is nine years old. A few days after I left Berlin we were reunited. I am determined now that we shall not be separated again.

It is troubling to me that anything so precious could have been driven from my conscious mind. Often I feel guilty that my love for Anna was not strong enough to hold fast, even against the darkness that enveloped me. What kind of mother is capable of forgetting her child? I have to remind myself that children are all too often forgotten in this world, and that it is not always by choice that the innocent are abandoned. The good opinion of society is an imperative few men have the strength or the courage to resist.

For most of her life Anna has been forced by the circumstances of her birth to live apart from me. It is difficult for a woman with a child out of wedlock to find work as a schoolteacher, even in these modern times. Be that as it may, Anna now lives with me. We have moved back to the country, to the village where I was born. Here the disapproval of the school authorities may be outweighed by their need for staff, or so I have been led to believe. In any event, Anna and I will never be parted again.

You asked me often why I had come to Berlin. I can tell you now that it was on her account. I hoped to dispel a shadow that has hung over Anna's life since birth, though she has always been unaware of it and always will be if I have my way. Please forgive me if I do not set down in writing the exact nature of it. If I have the good fortune to see you again, I will conceal nothing from you. But for the time being, suffice it to say I failed in my task. The questions remain unanswered, though they trouble me now less than they did. I wonder sometimes if this, like so much else, is thanks to you. In any event, I see more clearly now that this shadow is mine and mine alone. It will die with me and vanish. Neither Anna nor those that go after her will see it, even in their dreams. Light is not truly light until it is observed, so the great minds tell us. In the same way, there can be no disgrace in a story that is never known.

It is my selfish dream that one day you will come to us here. Anna is a bright and beautiful child, full of curiosity and kindness. There is so much she would delight to learn from you. Even if the time given to us is brief, I would gladly take every hour of it, no matter what care you might need from me. You told me you were done with Berlin. Perhaps this unlikely haven will provide you with the tranquillity you crave and so richly deserve.

If not, please know that you have for ever my gratitude and love.
Your friend,
Mariya

Forty-nine

The train rumbled into Belgrade over a massive iron bridge. His first sight of the white city was of crowded waterfronts and wooded slopes crowned with churches: a southern city of squat houses and red roofs. It wasn't until he was in a taxi that he found the obligatory grandeur of statehood: wide boulevards and palatial buildings with cupolas and wedding-cake façades. On the streets the horse-drawn carts and carriages outnumbered the trucks and motor cars. The dress of both men and women was funereally sombre and devoid of contemporary style. In the afternoon heat, the city had a lethargic, provincial air: puffed up and vaguely menacing, the kind of place where gentlemen carried knives, the better to avenge any slight to their honour.

In the lobby of the Hotel Moskva, Kirsch consulted the city telephone directory. It was a slender booklet containing just a few thousand names, although the concierge made a point of flipping through the pages, as if to emphasise its heft.

'Exchange *automatski*,' he said, pointing to a telephone cabin at the far end of the lobby. 'Absolute private.'

Kirsch found the name and number he was looking for, and wrote it down on a scrap of paper, along with the corresponding address.

'Do you know where this is?' he asked.

The concierge squinted at the paper. 'Yes, yes.' He gestured over his right shoulder. 'Kataníceva Street.'

'Can you give me directions?'

The concierge looked doubtful, as if surrendering such precise intelligence to a German-speaking foreigner was potentially treasonable. 'Wait,' he said, and summoned the bellboy.

The bellboy produced a grubby street map from his back pocket

and led Kirsch out into the square. Kataníceva Street was a little way south of the city centre, behind what the map seemed to indicate was a large public building set in a park. Kirsch bought the map and jumped on a southbound tram. The other passengers stared at him as he fumbled for the fare, proffering dinar notes that the conductor merely shook his head at. The women averted their gaze as they moved off. The men continued to stare without a hint of apology. More than anything, a fatty, butcher's shop smell told him he was a long way from home.

The large public building turned out to be a church: vast, white and domed in the Orthodox style. The walls had been recently repainted; so that as the sun came out, Kirsch had to shield his eyes. There were swifts in the sky above, their piercing shrieks small in the open space. An old woman sat by the gates, a case of souvenirs and lucky charms open beside her. Kirsch stopped to buy a postcard.

The houses on Kataníceva Street were several storeys high, with shutters, red roofs and stucco façades, some plain, some decorated with bas-relief cherubs and classical urns; houses, once imposing, now shrunk unwillingly into quaintness by the scale and power of the industrial age. Number 10 was one of the larger properties, its exterior hidden beneath a dead vine. Its fibrous limbs were wrapped like skeletal fingers round every ledge and prominence. The upstairs shutters were open, but otherwise the house had a crumbling, unoccupied look.

Kirsch rang the bell. Feet shuffled hesitantly across a stone floor. The door opened.

'*Dobro jutro.*' Kirsch removed his hat. 'Frau Helene Savić?'

He could see nothing of the woman opposite him but the pale oval of her face and a stout silver crucifix swinging from her neck. She blinked at him, whether from surprise or the strength of the light, he could not tell.

'My name is Kirsch, Dr Martin Kirsch.'

He held out his card. The door opened a few inches further. The woman was dressed all in black with a black scarf wrapped around her head. She was middle-aged, roughly the right age for Aunt

Helene, he supposed, although he hadn't expected to find her dressed like a nun.

Aunt Helene was reportedly Austrian by birth, a native German-speaker, as her letter to Mileva Einstein-Marić had confirmed; but this woman betrayed no sign of understanding him. Kirsch looked down, saw the huge felt slippers and the cloth with which she had evidently been polishing the floor.

'Frau Helene Savić,' he said again. 'Is she here?'

The woman took the card. 'Moment,' she said, and beckoned him inside.

The hallway had the same look of neglected elegance. The fine striped wallpaper was dull and peeling; black mould had broken out in patches on the ceiling; a large gilt-framed mirror was cloudy with oxidation. The woman – a housekeeper, Kirsch assumed – disappeared upstairs. He heard voices: a man's, gruff and irritable, the woman's insistent. He listened for a third voice, the voice of another woman, but there was none. Thirty years had gone by since Helene Savić had written her letter to Mileva Marić. Perhaps she and Milivoj had separated since then. If so, Kirsch hoped they were still in touch.

It was through Aunt Helene that Mariya had become reacquainted with Mileva. Eduard Einstein had told him that. He had also revealed that his mother was angry with Helene on that account. Kirsch could understand why: Helene was meddling in family business, picking recklessly at an old and shameful wound, bringing an unwelcome ghost back to life. Mileva had other children to think of now, besides her own peace of mind. And there was the famous Einstein name, to which she had clung even after her divorce.

I urge you to be cautious in this matter and observe the agreements that have been entered into. That was what Helene had written to Mileva thirty years earlier. Something must have brought about the change of heart. A sudden attack of conscience, perhaps? A religious awakening? Or were there material motives? In 1903 Albert Einstein had been a patent clerk; now he was the most famous scientist in the world. Looking around the shabby hallway, breathing in the smell of mildew and stale liquor, Kirsch could imagine how

thoughts of profit might take hold. If the Einsteins accepted Mariya, she might find ways to express her gratitude. And if they didn't, if Mileva refused to acknowledge the truth, then there might be a price for silence too.

Kirsch had decided that the truth would be his gift to Mariya: the knowledge that Zoltán Draganović had not been her father, that she was an Einstein, and her daughter too. He assumed Helene Savić would be an ally in that cause. Aunt Helene was kind and clever, Eduard had told him. She understood everything.

Upstairs, a door opened. A man appeared at the top of the stairs: six feet tall, heavy-jowled and obese. He was tying the belt on a quilted dressing gown that was too short for him. He looked down the stairs and frowned, as if faced with an unpalatable challenge.

'Good morning, Dr . . .' He squinted at Kirsch's card, apparently focusing with difficulty.

'Kirsch. Martin Kirsch.'

'Who are you? One of *his* people, I suppose.'

Milivoj Savić spoke German with a heavy Slavic accent.

'I'm here on my own account, sir.'

The man was unsteady on his feet, though he struggled to conceal the fact. The housekeeper brushed past him and came down the stairs, muttering.

'Is it a medical matter?'

'I'm here about Mariya Draganović. I'd like to speak with Frau Savić, if possible.'

Herr Savić sniffed, arching his back, as if that made him appear less drunk. 'My wife is not here at present.'

'May I ask when you expect her back?'

'Two or three days. She's in Novi Sad, visiting . . .' Savić planted a steadying hand on the banisters. '. . . friends.'

This seemed to be all the conversation he could muster. He turned unsteadily and walked back to his room. 'I shall tell her you called,' he said, and closed the door.

Fifty

Helene Savić, fifty-three years old, petite and grey-haired, sat by a window in the Queen Elisabeth Café with a cold glass of tea in front of her, waiting.

When she was a child in Austria, tuberculosis germs had attacked Helene's joints, and in particular her left knee, affecting the growth of her leg. Like her friend Mileva Marić, who suffered from a congenital hip displacement, she had worn an orthopaedic shoe all her life. It was an ugly thing, heavy and black, and impossible to disguise. The best she could do was conceal it beneath full-length skirts, which was one reason why she had continued to wear them long after they had gone out of fashion. She knew they made her look older than she was, even a little ridiculous during the summer months, but Belgrade was not Vienna, let alone Paris. And since Milivoj had lost his job at the ministry, fashionable clothes had been beyond her means in any case. Only now, when it was too late, did she wish she could wear something prettier, a tailored outfit perhaps, with matching jacket and a calf-length skirt, like the ones she occasionally glimpsed in fashion magazines. Just for this one day, she wished she could look young again.

She stared out across the square beside the theatre, squinting into the light. Thin cloud moved silently across the face of the sun. Her grip tightened on the scuffed leather satchel that lay in her lap.

The satchel belonged to her eldest daughter, Julka. The meeting with Albert had been arranged a fortnight ago – that, at least, was when she had received the telegram – but not until that morning had she thought about what to put the letters in, letters that, until then, she had kept locked away in her desk. Julka was grown up and married now, with two children and a volunteer job at the

General State Hospital. She had no use for the satchel, but still Helene worried that she might miss it, that it might hold some sentimental value. She blushed at the thought of having to explain that she had given it away.

A wagon went by outside, horseshoes clattering over the old Turkish cobbles. The clock behind the bar read half past one.

It had been a mistake to choose a table by the window. Albert wouldn't want to sit where he could be seen from the street. But it was too late. Helene could not ask to move without drawing more attention to herself, and hence to Albert. The waiters were quite attentive enough already, fussing around her with menus, cake trolleys and suggestions of the day. She wondered briefly if they would recognise him. It was twenty-five years since he had been a regular visitor. But then, of course they would: Albert's was a face the whole world knew. What was less certain was whether he would recognise her.

There was a knife on the table. She edged forward, trying to catch her reflection in the blade. How changed she would seem to him now, how old and worn out – by time, by childrearing, most of all by the inexorable erosion of hope. Sometimes she wished she had never left Austria or, like Mileva, had found herself a husband in Switzerland, where life was easier.

Albert had never approved of Milivoj Savić. He considered the man too stupid for her, too limited. He had all but said so to her face. She had not been put out. If anything she had been flattered that Albert should have such a high regard for her intelligence. As for his liaison with Mileva Marić, that had made Helene equally uneasy, though for very different reasons. Albert had never understood Mileva. He had never understood the depths of unhappiness of which she was capable, or her need for love.

Mileva had all but resigned herself to spinsterhood before Albert came along. She was pretty enough in her way, but fate had given her a limp and a shy, melancholy nature. She could not dance or flatter her way into a man's affections. The only man she had even tried to please was her father, Milos Marić, and there, at least, she

had succeeded. Mileva had been his favourite, his greatest source of pride – until, of course, she had dishonoured him.

What had Albert seen in Mileva? Surely not her command of differential calculus, her ability to understand his experiments and theories – although that was certainly a great novelty where females were concerned. Perhaps it was simply the way she took care of him, the cosiness and companionship that came with complete, unquestioning devotion. Then there was Albert's mother. She detested the little Serbian cripple, as she had once called her. She slandered and ridiculed her so viciously that word of it regularly brought Mileva to tears. But it only made her more appealing in Albert's eyes. Looking back, Helene saw it clearly: the way he had cultivated detachment. Even in the face of his own instincts and desires, he had forced it on himself. Defying his mother, the most important woman in his life, was hard, no doubt. But that was why he had felt compelled to do it. It was a test he could not allow himself to fail.

What he had not seen – or had not cared to see – was how love changed Mileva's life: how everything became centred on him and dependent on him. There was no greater proof of that than the conception of Lieserl. In Vojvodina, such transgressions against family honour were paid for in blood. Even a fiancé who anticipated his wedding night could easily end up with his throat cut. For his impregnated lover, exile and disgrace were the least she could expect. Perhaps Mileva had not cared because she was in exile already. The great Einsteinian cosmos had become her country, her world.

Albert's telegram had been more of a summons than an invitation. There had never been any suggestion that he might come to Belgrade. Presumably he did not want to meet Milivoj, or feared that he might be uncooperative. Unemployment had hit Helene's husband hard. Perhaps Mileva had told Albert about his drinking and his ranting; the way he would not leave the house for days at a time. If so, Helene regretted having told her. Such things were between them. Milivoj, for all his faults, had always been an honest man.

The waiter came and took away Helene's glass. She was too

preoccupied to stop him. He came back with the bill. She was taking money from her purse when a stranger walked into the café. He had wrinkled, freckly skin, like a peasant's, but his shirt was crisp and his suit fashionably double-breasted. He took off his hat and looked around the room, his gaze going methodically from table to table. Then he was staring at her with a pair of pale, penetrating eyes.

The purse slipped from her grasp and fell to the floor. She bent down to retrieve it, almost losing the satchel from her lap. When she looked up again, the stranger had gone.

A dusty blue motor car had pulled up outside. A group of young women went by, talking in whispers. They stopped right outside the window and looked back at the vehicle. Then they turned and hurried away, giggling and clutching each other by the arm. Albert had arrived. The girls must have seen him draw up: an old man who bore an extraordinary resemblance to Professor Einstein. It would not have occurred to them that he actually *was* Professor Einstein, not here in this small Serbian town, where there were neither tele-scopes nor a university to elicit his attention. Besides, Albert was too famous, too much a legend, to be truly incarnate in any one place and time. It struck Helene that he had become, like the divini-ties of monotheistic religion, universal. Everywhere and nowhere. She wondered if that had been his aim all along, the secret longing that fuelled his insatiable curiosity.

He wore an unfamiliar black hat, with a wide brim and a tall crown and a crease in the top like a cowboy's. A pipe was clenched between his teeth. His striped tie was secured with a small, untidy knot. He came towards her, acknowledging her with a wave of his pipe. He pulled off his hat as he sat down. His hair was longer and wilder than it used to be, streaked with grey and white, the original colour only visible above his ears. Apparently the second Frau Einstein did not take as much care of him as the first.

'So,' he said, 'here I am.'

Immediately the waiter reappeared and handed him a menu.

'Coffee, black,' he said, handing it back again. 'Two cups.'

It was as if he had been away for an hour or two, instead of

twenty years. He fished in his pocket for a box of matches. The smell of tobacco was heavy on his clothes. As a young man he had struck Helene as quite dapper, despite his modest means, but now there was a slovenliness about him. Appearances, she supposed, were no longer of any use to him.

It came to Helene that she was staring. 'Albert,' she said. 'Dear Albert.'

Dear Albert? What was she saying? She blushed – blushed like a schoolgirl at her first dance. 'It's good to see you.'

Albert gave her an indulgent smile, his dark eyes glistening. He struck the match and applied it to the bowl of his pipe. The smoke gave off a surprisingly fruity smell. Helene found it much more agreeable than the dry, chemical stink of her husband's cigarettes.

Einstein seemed to read her mind. 'An American blend,' he said, tossing the match into an ashtray. 'They call it *Revelation*. With a name like that . . .' He tucked his thumbs into his waistcoat pocket and took in his surroundings. 'This place feels different.'

'It's the same. A little shabbier.' Helene glanced at the scuffed furniture, the white cotton curtains, now yellowed with age, the chipped and smeary wainscoting that had been badly re-varnished so that its flaws were more obvious than ever. 'It hasn't been done up for years. There isn't any money.'

'It's the only place I could remember,' Albert said brightly. 'Always excellent coffee.'

Helene felt sure the coffee would be a let-down as much as the café itself. The standard of provisions had declined, along with the affluence of the local bourgeoisie. Before the war, Novi Sad had enjoyed a certain strategic importance as a border town. Its bridge over the Danube was a crucial point of entry into the Austro–Hungarian empire. In the customs service and the military there were government jobs aplenty, and commercial opportunities too. These days, Novi Sad found itself marooned in the middle of Yugoslavia, a market town with more than its share of grand buildings; the last stop before Belgrade.

'I shall miss that,' Albert added. 'The Americans know tobacco. But the art of making coffee is completely lost on them.'

Helene had heard that he was going back to America. Could it really be for ever?

'Where are you staying?' she asked. 'On Kisacka Street?' Albert looked puzzled, as if the name meant nothing to him. 'The Marić house.'

'Oh.' Albert frowned. 'No. Zorka lives there now.'

He tapped the pipe against his teeth, as if spelling out the implications of this statement in Morse code. Albert had never shown much consideration for Mileva's younger sister; and she, in turn, had always been terrified of him. She had been psychologically scarred by what had happened to her in the war (Helene still shuddered to think of it). Probably no man, certainly no Serbian man, would have been eager to marry a woman who had been raped by a gang of soldiers, even assuming she had been willing. But that was no reason to avoid her. She had never hurt a soul in her life.

'If she's alone then there's surely more room for a guest,' Helene said.

Albert sucked thoughtfully on his pipe. 'The house is full of cats, apparently. She picks up strays from the street. It drives the servants mad, and her mother's too old to stop her.'

'I'm sure you'd still be welcome there.'

'The hotel's quite adequate. We're leaving tomorrow in any case.'

'We? You aren't here alone?'

Albert glanced out of the window. The taxi was still there, waiting. 'I'm obliged to travel with a companion. Elsa insists, and so do my American paymasters. These days I can't take a walk on the beach without detectives falling in behind me.'

'He's a detective?' Helene said, craning her neck.

'When paid to detect, yes. On this occasion he has other duties. Elsa imagines Nazi agents round every corner.'

'A bodyguard.' The idea struck Helene as fantastical and perverse. How could anyone think of killing Albert Einstein? 'Does he have a gun?'

'I don't think so.' Albert briefly examined the bowl of his pipe. 'He has no conversation whatsoever, but at least he carries my luggage. My back is grateful for the lack of employment, but my tongue is quite dismayed.'

The coffee arrived, along with a small jug of milk. In Zürich, when they were all students together, it had seemed to Helene that Albert lived on coffee – coffee, tobacco and sausages, and those not always of the best quality. Mileva used to worry that he would end up with rickets and started cooking for him as the only way of ensuring his survival. It had all backfired horribly when Albert told his mother to send her food parcels to Mileva's address. The suggestion that they were already sharing rooms outraged Frau Einstein's sense of decency. The two women had been on bad terms from that moment.

'Have you brought the letters?' Albert said, pouring the coffee.

Helene blushed. So that was it for small talk. It had been brief; civil, but without warmth. She and Albert had not been in touch since his divorce, but she had expected him to take some pleasure in the rekindling of old memories.

'They're all here. Some got lost, of course.' Albert watched her in silence. 'I'm still not clear why you want them. They're Mileva's letters, after all.'

'Mileva wants them too.'

'You're taking them back to her?'

Albert slid a cup of coffee towards her. It was a foolish question. The letters were going to be destroyed: too much information on an unhappy marriage; too much information about an illegitimate child Albert had never seen. With the fame and the money had come paranoia. There was no other explanation.

Helene picked up her cup and then put it down again. 'You've really nothing to fear, you know. I *can* be trusted.'

Albert took a mouthful of coffee and frowned, either because he was troubled by her words or because the coffee was as disappointing as she had expected. 'I'm sure you can. But what if something happened to you? Who would have the letters then? What if you were robbed?'

'I can destroy them as easily as you can, if that's what you both want.'

Albert reached into his jacket pocket and took out a white envelope. 'I couldn't ask you to do that. They'd be valuable one day. It wouldn't be fair.'

He propped the envelope up against the salt cellar, as if it were a birthday card. Helene looked at it, found herself mentally checking the thickness.

'Why now?'

'You have to ask?' he said. 'The business with Mariya Draganović. That little bit of mischief.'

A look of annoyance crossed Albert's face. Helene remembered how quick his temper could be, the sudden explosive rages that so terrified Mileva – though she would only speak of them in whispers. He was not a strong man, but from an early age he had been adept at harnessing the power of gravity. Anyone who upset him was in danger of being thrown down the stairs: children, servants, even his wife. Mileva said it was as if a different Albert took over, a man who had no control over his emotions, a man prey to all the passion and violence that, at all other times, he so feared and despised.

'I wasn't making mischief, Albert. I gave sound advice to a very bright girl. She was looking for a teacher and Mileva was the obvious person. That's all there is to it.'

Albert shook his head slowly. 'You can stop pretending, Helene. Mileva told me everything. I know who Mariya Draganović is.'

Helene felt the blood drain from her face. It had not been her idea to lie. It had been Mileva who had insisted. *I shall tell him Lieserl is dead*, she wrote to Helene in a letter. It was the year Albert went to Palestine, the year he delivered his Nobel lecture in Sweden. Ten years ago. *It is best if he never thinks of his daughter again: best for him and for her.* She wanted Helene to keep the secret.

'I'm sorry, Albert. I only did as Mileva asked. She wanted me to keep quiet and I did.' Albert sucked on his pipe. 'Besides, it's not as if you ever asked me about Lieserl. It's not as if you ever took the slightest interest.'

She found it hard to hurt Albert, even though he deserved to be hurt. He had always been like a child in that way. Guilt always rebounded on those who tried to scold him.

'She came to Berlin,' he said. 'She had it in her mind to find her father.'

'Mileva must have told her. I didn't say a word, Albert. I promise.'

Albert shook his head. 'I know, I know. It was Eduard. He came across some old letters in Mileva's apartment. About Lieserl. I don't know when exactly. Perhaps years ago.' He sniffed. 'So. Now you understand why I'm here.'

Helene hugged the satchel to her. 'What happened?'

'Happened?'

'In Berlin.'

'Nothing.'

'Nothing?'

Albert shrugged. 'She came out to the summer house.' He pushed the coffee cup away from him, his tongue smacking disgustedly against his hard palate. 'I shan't come here again. It's not like it was. A pity.'

'Then what?'

Albert picked up his pipe again, but it had gone out. He regarded the bowl with an expression of indifference, as if it no longer mattered to him if it produced smoke or not.

'There was a misunderstanding. She approached me at a public lecture. Women often do. I'd no idea who she was. She *said* her name was Elisabeth. She taught mathematics. So I invited her to visit. I have a lot of visitors these days. More than I'd like.'

Stories had reached Mileva about Albert's life in Berlin, and some of those stories had reached Helene. His second marriage – to his cousin, Elsa – was as stormy as his first, apparently, and considerably less intimate. Albert would not be ruled by his wife in anything. She was not permitted to interfere in his life. He came and went as he pleased, ate when and where he pleased, entertained whomsoever he pleased. In Caputh it was even reported that Elsa was required to vacate the house entirely so that Albert could carry on with his

female admirers without fear of embarrassment or interruption. These reports were whispered in Mileva's ear by well-meaning allies. She was better off without him, they meant to say. But the reports only made Mileva angry. They were disloyal, she thought. Albert deserved better friends. In all the years since their divorce, Helene had never once heard Mileva speak ill of him.

'So she went out there. I suppose you were alone.'

'I was working. I wanted to get back to work. You have no idea how much is asked of me nowadays, Helene. It isn't at all like it used to be, in Zürich. I was a free man then.'

Helene began to feel uncomfortable. There had always been a suggestion of waywardness in Albert's behaviour, even when they first met, a touch of the Lothario. In those days, Helene had seen it more as a pose than reality. But now, armed with the aphrodisiac of fame, freer than ever from the constraints that applied to ordinary mortals, he would have had ample opportunity to live the part for real.

Mariya was to be another conquest, a brief amusement. Had he become that perfunctory with his 'visitors'? Was there a routine? A favourite place in the house – an upstairs sitting room perhaps, with a commodious sofa?

'She explained herself? You found out who she was before . . . ?'

'She said she was Lieserl. Can you imagine? Out of the blue. I thought I was being blackmailed. What else was I to think? Thanks to you.'

Helene could picture it: Mariya hopeful, elated, tongue-tied, her heart in her mouth; he interpreting all this as the swooning devotion of a pretty young fan. How flattering. How arousing. And then to be baulked, ambushed by an outrageous claim that could not possibly be true.

'You were angry.'

'I threw her out.'

'Down the stairs?'

'What?'

'She hurt herself. That's what Mileva said.'

366

'She fell. It was raining. The steps were wet.'

'Steps . . .'

'I went after her, but she ran away. She probably thought . . .'

She thought her father was going to rape her. Helene felt faint. She did not want to hear any more, but Albert kept talking, anxious now to justify himself.

'She stole my rowing boat. Jumped in and pushed off. I knew it would take in water, but she wasn't listening.' He tapped out his pipe in the ashtray. Unburned tobacco spilled out, along with the ash. 'She was mad. I thought she'd pass out the rate she was breathing. I let her get on with it.'

'You still didn't know who she was?'

'How could I? Nothing she said made sense. I only saw some sense in it when I learned her psychiatrist had turned up in Zürich.'

Across the room, a local eminence and his wife were watching them. The man wore an indignant expression on his face, as if the presence of a genius in the café was an unmerited assault on his own importance.

'All very unsettling,' Albert said. 'I was out of sorts for days. I'm determined nothing like it will *ever* happen again.'

Helene gathered herself. 'I'm sorry she disturbed you. I hope no harm was done.'

Albert sighed. His breath smelled rank and sickly. 'Not so far.' He took out a tobacco pouch and began to refill his pipe. 'But you can see why I'm inclined to be cautious, Helene, with so many people anxious to cast a stone at a stone.' He chuckled at the pun on his name. 'These days I'm a great graven image. Some people feel compelled to worship; others just want to cast me down.'

The waiter returned to remove the cups. Before she could stop herself, Helene had snatched up the envelope, to keep it from his reach. When she looked up again, Albert was smiling.

Once the waiter had gone she put the envelope back.

'They used to have music here,' Albert said. 'What happened to the musicians?'

'Viennese waltzes aren't the fashion any more. Things have changed here, Albert.'

'It was nice to just sit here and listen,' he said. 'Without the constant need to chatter.' He looked at his watch. 'I must be going.'

Helene placed the satchel of letters in front of him. 'They're all here.'

'Ah yes,' Albert said, as if the letters had slipped his mind. 'Thank you.'

He put the satchel over his shoulder and rose to go. It looked faintly comical on him, the strap being far too short for an adult, but he did not seem in the least bothered.

'Albert.' Helene reached across the table and put a hand on his arm. 'Don't be angry with me. About Mariya. I didn't feel I had the right to stand in her way. I never meant to cause a problem.'

He patted her hand with his. 'Problems are there to be solved. How dull life would be without them.'

Helene smiled, although she did not feel like smiling. She felt she was losing something precious, this time for ever.

'Don't get up,' Albert said. 'Best I slip out unnoticed. A shame I can't stay, but I have one more assignation here before I take my leave.'

He put on his strange black hat again, and clenched his pipe between his teeth.

'May I ask with whom?'

'Just someone.' Albert pulled some change from his trouser pocket and dropped it on the table, smiling. 'Someone who shall be nameless.'

Fifty-one

Kirsch blinks awake. An old woman is shaking him gently by the knee, talking to him, though he can't understand her. He has fallen asleep on the train. He sits up smartly, straightening his spectacles, aware of other people watching him. He's short of breath and sweating, his shirt wet.

The old woman nods and sits back, offering some explanation to the other passengers: the young man has been having a nightmare, probably something he ate. The other passengers laugh.

The compartment is hot and airless. He finds it hard to breathe. The old woman makes another remark as he makes his way unsteadily into the corridor, tugging at his collar. She points to one of the luggage racks above the seat. She is telling him not to forget his suitcase. Doesn't she know he has already lost it in the flood? He is halfway down the corridor before he realises that the flood was just a dream.

After his visit to Kataníceva Street, he left Belgrade on the first train. There was no point in waiting for Helene Savić. She might not return for weeks, if she returned at all. She might not talk to him even if she did. But the journey from Berlin had exhausted him and it would have been better if he had rested for a while.

At Novi Sad the stationmaster tells him there is a branch line running north-east via Titel. According to a large map on the wall, it will take him within a few miles of Orlovat. But the last train has already gone. He will have to stay the night.

'I recommend the Hotel Queen Maria.' The stationmaster says. His German is unusually good. 'Oldest establishment in the province and still the best. Used to be the Queen Elisabeth before the war, but *she* was Bavarian, so . . .'

He shrugs apologetically. Not an enthusiast for the Yugoslav federation, clearly. Kirsch frowns. The story is familiar. Then he remembers: like the hotel, Mariya was Elisabeth once. She was Lieserl. Does the stationmaster know that? Is he making a joke?

'I don't understand.'

The stationmaster's face falls. 'No offence, sir.' He points towards the street. 'The taxi will take you.'

Across the town, heavy, clanking bells strike two o'clock.

Mariya Draganović hears them from the lobby of the Hotel Queen Maria. The sound echoes around the square outside, putting a flock of pigeons to flight. She folds her hands in her lap and waits. She has been waiting for half an hour already, nervousness churning her stomach.

Ten days ago she received a letter from Mileva Einstein-Marić in Zürich. After enquiring after her health, it stated that her ex-husband was intent on a visit to Novi Sad and wanted to meet her. He was anxious to reassure himself about the state of her health and to clear up any misunderstandings that may have arisen in Berlin. The letter was followed a few days later by a telegram. It asked her to respond by return. The meeting is to take place at two o'clock today.

She feels warm in her plain grey dress and her heavy travelling boots. The front door of the hotel has been propped open, to encourage a draught. Across the road a small child crouches on the cobbles, playing with a spinning top. She saw him before with his brothers and sisters, but they moved on some minutes ago with their mother. It appears the little boy has been forgotten. But he doesn't seem to mind. All his attention is on the spinning top, which he examines on all fours, his cheek almost touching the ground, prostrate, as if the top is some tiny wooden deity, deceptive in the extent of its power.

Mariya's memories of Caputh are still incomplete, the fragments sharp and wounding: shards of a broken mirror. She took a steamer. It was the very end of the season: rows of empty seats, sunlight veiled and shimmering on the grey water. She took a path through

the woods, surprised at the close, resinous air. She remembers fanning herself with the map she had bought herself. The flier for Einstein's lecture kept falling out from between the folds. Finally she picked it up and tucked it into her chemise. Caputh was further away than it had seemed. Her dress grew heavy, tugging and flapping around her legs. Near the house, a car pulled out onto the road. A woman with untidy grey hair gave her a disdainful stare from the passenger seat.

The whole house creaked like a ship. By the door was a space to leave your shoes. She felt breathless and unsteady as she stood in the hallway, tugging at her boots. The sitting room was upstairs. From a roof terrace steps went down into the garden, the white railings bright against the darkening sky. A tartan rug lay draped across a sunlounger.

'Elsa has gone to Berlin for the afternoon. The shops and such.'

They were alone. Mariya was pleased. She and Einstein had a lot to discuss, secrets to share. It would not do to be overheard.

He had not received her letter, though she had posted it first class three days before. The postal service was not reliable, he said. Strikes were frequent. Besides, he had too much mail from members of the public. He only read what his private secretary told him to read. When she pressed him to check, he became irritable.

'What could you have to tell me that you can't tell me now?'

But there was a lot she could not tell him. That was why she had written it down: to put the whole story before him so that he might understand her, know her as she wished to be known. She was hot from the walk. The room was stifling and the heavy wood smell faintly nauseating.

'Can we get some air?'

She got up and went to the French windows. The handle was stuck. Einstein watched her from the sofa, looking amused as she struggled to make it turn.

'Take off your jacket,' he said. 'I want to have a look at you.'

She remembers telling herself that this was natural enough. Why shouldn't a father want to look at a long-lost child?

She said she was thirsty. She needed time to gather her thoughts. Einstein disappeared and came back with something dark and sweet in a cut-glass tumbler. He had on baggy trousers and a tennis shirt. His skin looked tanned against the white fabric.

She did not know how to begin. The shame was too much. She felt faint. She took off her jacket. The heavy cotton blouse clung to her skin. Then they were both on the sofa. Einstein asked her about the lecture. Had she been able to follow it? Had he spent too much time on the field equations? Was the differential geometry comprehensible? It was as if he had no real idea who she was or why she had come. Yet at the Philharmonic Hall he had seemed to recognise her at once. She only had to say her name for him to draw her aside. 'We must talk,' he said. 'The sooner the better. I've been hoping you would seek me out.'

She gulped down the drink. It burned in her throat. Einstein patted her on the knee. 'Now, what did you want to tell me?'

At some point she fainted. When she came around she thought she was dreaming. She was in Orlovat. Everywhere flooded land, the river dark and swollen, the crows picking at her sister's lips as she lay in the branches of a willow. The kitchen table with the lantern above it, swinging back and forth above her. A voice in her head that said: *This is not me. I am not here.*

'There's no need to swoon on my account.' Einstein's face was close to hers. His breath smelled of tar. 'I assure you, I think no less of a lady who prefers to be fully conscious when making love.'

The glasses went over, smashing on the floor. Elisabeth Einstein. I am Elisabeth Einstein. I am Lieserl. Your daughter. She remembers screaming the words in her mind. But out loud?

Blackness then. She has searched for the moment, but nothing comes back to her. She remembers only a taste of blood in her mouth. No idea how it got there.

'Cunning little slut.'

He had a spray of blood on his white tennis shirt, just above his heart.

They were outside on the roof terrace. She saw the rowing boat

bobbing up and down by the shore. Einstein's hand was around her arm. His grip was strong: a sailor's grip. Like a claw.

'Who put you up to this?'

She broke away, reached the top of the steps, but she could feel him at her back. Then she was falling, arms reaching out into the yawning void. She must have somersaulted most of the way down. Pain lanced through the panic. She remembers asking: *have I broken my arm?* Her hands were peeled and bleeding.

The staircase shook beneath her. He was coming down, heavy footfalls pounding on the wood.

Then in the rowing boat, her heart beating so fast she could hardly catch a breath, looking back at the house: no sign of Einstein, no sign of anyone. Where had he gone? Then the chill water welling up around her feet. Sinking. She would drown in those heavy clothes. They would drag her down like a leaden shroud. But what if he saw her swimming for it? What if he had been following her along the shore? She had to make more distance. She had to get out of sight.

The sun was long gone. The water was the colour of slate, the surface turning choppy in the stiffening breeze. She tore at her clothes, retching up water as the boat fell away beneath her. The last thing she remembers was the shock of cold as her head ducked beneath the surface, a fleeting dread as she felt herself falling from the light.

A telephone rings. Mariya looks up. The old man who works behind the front desk comes towards her. Nearly all the staff at the Queen Maria seem too old for their positions.

'Miss Draganović?'

She nods.

'There's a car for you outside.'

She peers out at the street. The boy with the spinning top has gone. Instead there is a motor car, black and shiny. Someone is waiting in the back, smoking a pipe.

The houses in Novi Sad are like the houses in Belgrade, only older. Time and gravity have pulled them out of shape, robbing them of

perpendicularity and, in the process, their dignity. The streets are broad, treeless and empty. The inhabitants of Novi Sad are mostly indoors, Kirsch supposes, taking refuge from the heat. As he rides towards the middle of town, he imagines them watching him from behind their flaking shutters.

A horse-drawn wagon, loaded high with beer barrels, is partially blocking the road. His driver moves to overtake, slowing to a crawl. Coming the other way, another motor car does the same. Both vehicles slow to a crawl. As they pass, Kirsch sees Mariya seated in the back beside an elderly gentleman in a black broad-brimmed hat.

At first he isn't surprised. These days, when he thinks of Mariya, it often happens that she appears before him, at least for a few seconds. The same thing happened during the last year of the war, with the spectres of dead men. He has seen Mariya jump onto a moving tram; he has seen her hurrying along a crowded platform. He has seen her reflection many times in shop windows. Then, with a jolt to the heart, it comes to him what he is seeing. The sights and sounds of the present rush in. And she has vanished.

But this time she does not vanish. She turns her head, looks directly at him. He smiles at her. She does not smile back. The look on her face is one of shock, as if this time she is the living one, the one of flesh and blood, and he is the lifeless apparition.

As they move off, the elderly gentleman leans forward, curious to share whatever it is that's so interesting to his companion. Kirsch sees his face.

He insisted she call him Albert. So far, though, she has not called him anything, because she doesn't know what to say. It doesn't seem to matter. Professor Einstein seems content with the occasional nod of her head, a 'yes' or a 'no'. After the first incoherent moments she has even detected a hint of euphoria in his demeanour: in his voice and the way he puffs appreciatively on his pipe, as if a burden has been lifted. He is apparently unsure of her reaction at meeting him again, and is relieved to find her cooperative. There was a misunderstanding in Berlin, he says, for which he intends to make

reparations before his departure for America. He does not refer to her amnesia, either because he has not been told about it or because he does not believe it to be genuine. He thanks her courteously for taking the time to travel from Orlovat. He knows it's a tiresome journey, he says, the Serbian roads being what they are. It's as if they're old friends.

A stranger in a double-breasted suit is driving. His close-set eyes watch her in the mirror – eyes, she feels sure, that have watched her before.

'Who is he?' Mariya asks, quietly so as not to be overheard.

'That's de Vries. Don't worry about him. His purpose is mainly counter-gravitational.'

'Counter-gravitational?'

'He carries my luggage.'

Up ahead, a wagon rolls out into the road. The driver brakes. They are on the corner of Kisacka Street, halfway to the railway station. Another taxi is coming the other way. There is barely room for the two of them to pass.

Kirsch tells the driver to stop, but the driver doesn't understand. He thinks Kirsch is complaining about the route. 'They dig here,' he says, jabbing his thumb over his shoulder, then makes circling gestures with his hand. 'Go round.'

Out of the back window Kirsch sees Mariya's taxi pick up speed again, throwing up eddies of dust.

'That way.'

He points after it, but the driver shakes his head. That's not the way to the Hotel Queen Maria. He points his chin at the road ahead, sounding his horn, as if that will get them there quicker.

Kirsch hesitates. What good will it do to follow her? Mariya no longer needs his help. She has found her father; or he has found her. They will not be separated again. She and her daughter will go with him to America, where there will be no need for secrets. And it will be a painless emigration, because they have no ties left to sever.

375

Kirsch plants a hand on the driver's shoulder. The driver jams on the brakes.

'That way,' he says. 'Follow.'

The driver curses and does a U-turn. Mariya's taxi turns right into a side street. A woman carrying a basket watches it go by.

'There. That way!'

But the driver has had enough. He pulls over, orders Kirsch out. The lunatic foreigner can walk, as far as he is concerned. Kirsch grabs his suitcase. There are no other taxis in sight, no traffic at all. He has no choice but to continue on foot.

A rusty iron sign on the corner reads *Almaska*. The street is narrow, the house fronts dilapidated and sooty. Not a street that leads anywhere. Maybe this is as far as they're going. Maybe this is Mariya's final destination.

A hundred and fifty yards away, he can see a church surrounded by trees, a tall baroque affair with a sloping red roof and a white bell tower. He runs on, looking for a hotel sign, a school, anything that makes sense, but there are only houses, a bakery with its shutters down, rusting iron balconies and peeling paint – and the church.

Births, marriages and deaths. What can they want in a church? Then it comes to him: churches have records. The church is where they give you your name. Is this where Mariya was given hers?

But what does it matter now? Some old ritual, ancient and useless. What would Albert Einstein care about that? Maybe Mariya needs a visa to go to America. Maybe the Americans want proof of who she really is.

Kirsch leans against a doorway. The running has left him breathless and giddy. Barking erupts from within. Canine paws scamper across the flagstones. The door jolts, iron bolts rattling.

Almaska Street opens out into a tiny square. The church stands in a graveyard with iron railings surrounding it. A breeze stirs the trees. At the far corner of the square, a man in an apron is winding down an awning. The screw makes a squeaking sound. Kirsch has never been here in his life, but something about it feels familiar.

It occurs to him, just for an instant, that he is dreaming again, that none of this is real. That's when he sees them through the gates of the churchyard, walking among the headstones: Albert Einstein and his first-born child.

He stops. This time Mariya does not look up. Her father is speaking and she is listening intently. What is he saying? What is he explaining? Kirsch wishes he could hear. He wants her to know that he came, if only to bid her a final farewell.

Then he spots the other car. It's parked on the other side of the road, the engine running. A short, thickset man stands a few yards away, lighting a cigarette. He looks up and down the street. His demeanour, his way of standing, his face – everything is strangely familiar, but at first Kirsch can't place it.

The reporter. The one he saw with Robert Eisner. The one he saw hanging around outside the clinic. What's *he* doing here?

Kirsch checks his pace. The reporter must be here for Einstein. What else would bring him all this way? But how has he found his man? How did he know where to look?

Then I did see someone watching the house . . . a rough-looking man with a florid complexion and a hard, steady gaze. He was there when I returned, inside the cemetery, moving aimlessly from stone to stone.

Mariya has been followed and the trail has led to Albert Einstein. Was that blind good luck? Or was it envisaged, anticipated, planned for?

Who would make such a plan? Who had the patience, the data, the means? Not a humble reporter. Not a man who worked for a newspaper. But perhaps a man who worked for the state. A secret policeman, a spy.

They could have stopped Mariya from leaving Germany, but they had let her go. Kirsch comes to a halt. Suddenly it's clear. Mariya was no use to them in Germany. Einstein would never return to the Reich. But in Vojvodina, a place he once knew, he might think himself safe. He might drop his guard. The Einstein girl is bait, and hook.

And now he is here too. Just in time to witness the assassination of Albert Einstein.

The stranger's gaze fixes on him. His eyes narrow in puzzlement, or is it disgust? In that moment the last doubts evaporate. Propelled by Destiny, Kirsch starts to run, not away from the assassin, but towards him.

Hans de Vries recognises Martin Kirsch a few seconds after Kirsch recognises him, and after an instant of rushed reflection, reaches the same conclusion. Kirsch is ambitious and mentally unstable – a man, as they say, on a short fuse. His jealous and obsessive focus on the Draganović case has been noted and suggests a degree of opportunism unusual in his profession. For an opportunist, the presence of Albert Einstein in Novi Sad might well be too good to ignore: it offers still further advancement, care of the new regime, not to mention fifty thousand Reichsmarks if the pro-Nazi newspapers pay up. All he has to do is kill Albert Einstein and escape across the border.

Any doubts de Vries has about this thesis are buried by the sight of Kirsch breaking into a run – running towards him, jaw clenched, as if bracing for impact. He is no more than thirty feet away when de Vries reaches inside his jacket. The Walther PPK is not there. It comes to him that he has left the pistol in the glove compartment. Three days of playing valet and chauffeur to Professor Einstein have dulled his sensitivity to danger. The scientist seems oblivious to the possibility of attack, exhibits such Olympian confidence it's hard to remain vigilant.

De Vries is standing on the driver's side of the car, the wrong side. Maybe if he makes a dive for it. He yanks open the door, knows at once it's a mistake. Kirsch slams against it, pinning him against the frame. De Vries can't get a purchase. He can't push back. Suddenly there are bells – heavy, clamorous bells – not in his head but above him. In the church the ringers are practising. Kirsch's spectacles have come off. They hang comically from one ear. He slams the door again, harder. De Vries feels a rib crack, and screams.

He staggers. Kirsch has let go of the door. He steps back and

aims a punch, connecting with the side of de Vries's head. It smacks off the roof of the car like a bony football.

Albert stops halfway to the south door and looks around, as if trying to get his bearings.

'It's been a long time,' he says. 'Mileva showed me once, but I'm not sure . . .'

He points his pipe first one way, then another, then grunts in apparent satisfaction and heads off around the bell tower, which shines a brilliant shade of white in the hazy sunshine. The church-yard is small but orderly, with yews and broad-leafed trees standing at intervals among the stones. Flowers, some weathered and brown, speak of quiet communions between the living and the dead.

They walk on for fifty yards.

'There it is,' Albert says. 'This is it.'

He leads her to a cluster of stones close to the church wall. The names on the stones read MARIĆ. He points to one of them. A clay vase of peonies stands at the head. Like the stone itself, they look freshly cut.

'This is Milos Marić,' Albert says. 'My father-in-law, as was. This is where Mileva would have ended up if she hadn't . . .'

He doesn't complete the sentence. He doesn't have to. Mileva had brought dishonour to the family by getting pregnant. In her father's eyes she turned out no better than a *kurva*. Then it comes to Mariya what Einstein is saying: *I don't make these rules. They have nothing to do with me.*

Albert turns and walks on a few paces, studying one stone after another. A few yards further on, partly obscured by a sprawling yew, is another family plot. The monuments here are less well main-tained: most of the stone is worn and weathered, the wrought-iron crosses pitched over at an angle by the importunate roots below. A simple wooden cross has a small brass plate nailed to the crosspiece. It reads: S.D. It is the only one of the Draganović graves with flowers at the base, though the flowers are withered and brown.

For Mariya, the Draganović family and the Marić family have

been separated by thirty years and a thousand miles. But here, in this graveyard, all that lies between them are a few metres of earth. Here they are neighbours, friends, dust of the same dust – only she was not allowed to know it.

Albert stares at the wooden cross. 'Do you know who this is?'

'Do you?'

Albert digs his hands into his pockets. 'I forget the first name. What was it?'

'Senka.'

'Ah yes. She drowned. Wasn't that it?'

'Yes.'

Finally Albert removes his hat. 'She told me it was you. My ex-wife, I mean. She said Lieserl was dead. Drowned. So when you claimed . . .'

'Why? Why would she do that?'

'Isn't it obvious?'

Family honour. That's what he wants to say. All this happened so as to protect the Marić family honour. But the lie would only have been necessary if Albert had threatened to upset matters, to seek out his daughter, to make her existence known to the world. And where is the evidence for that? Perhaps Mileva told her ex-husband that he no longer had a daughter because that was what he wanted to hear. It was one less potential encumbrance, one less earthly tie.

Albert reaches into his coat and produces an envelope. Mariya knows at once that it contains money. A parting gift. In return for her silence.

Mariya crouches down to pick up the dead flowers. She left them a few months before, on her way to Switzerland. 'You never came to see either of us, did you, the way Mileva did? You never made enquiries. Weren't you even a little curious?'

Albert shakes his head, puts his hat back on and turns away. For a moment Mariya thinks he's going to leave her there, but then he looks back. 'My dear, what on *earth* was there to be curious about?' He gestures at the sky, the sun, the light. 'Compared to this?'

A grandfather. Mariya has been waiting for the right moment to tell him. *This is why I came to find you. This is what I wanted you to know.* But now she sees, with diamond clarity, that the right moment will never come.

Albert is talking again, something about the circumstances and her right to an explanation, but Mariya can't make it out over the clamour of bells. They are ringing out across the little square, not a melodious peel of celebration, but a stiff, mechanical clanking that shakes the air. Albert holds out the envelope, then leans forward and drops it in her lap. It is then that she sees Martin Kirsch — there is no doubt this time — hurrying towards them through the churchyard.

It looks to Hans de Vries as if the gutter is swarming with black ants. There are millions of them, a seething mass that covers everything — except that, unlike the ants he has seen before, these have no collective direction, no discernible line of march. These are ants in chaos, purposeful and industrious, but devoid of a guiding purpose, their efforts doomed to counteract and conflict, so that the colony dies. He feels their legs on the back of his hands. He feels their tiny pincers on his arms.

He forces himself up onto his knees. The car beside him now stands on the slope of a steep hill. He wonders anxiously whether he remembered to put on the handbrake, and if the car will slide away from him before . . .

Before what? Then he remembers: before he can recover the pistol, *the pistol he needs to shoot Martin Kirsch.* He hauls himself to his feet, scrambles across the driver's seat, flips open the lid of the glove compartment.

The Walther feels solid and heavy. Simply holding it steadies him. As he climbs out, the car seems to right itself, like a boat coming slowly out of a capsize. He blinks, aware of something sticky in his eye, gumming up the lid. He rubs it. His fingers come away bloody.

He looks around the square. The church bells are ringing, but there is no one about. Where is Einstein now? How long has he

been gone? The idea jumps into his head that they are ringing the bells to mark Einstein's death. Or perhaps he is not too late, after all. Perhaps they are calling for help.

He hurries into the graveyard. His left eye is caking up with blood. He hears voices up ahead, shouting. Einstein is standing stock still. Kirsch is running towards him, one arm raised. Is there something in his hand? A knife? A gun?

De Vries sees Einstein look at him. He seems rooted to the spot. He points at Kirsch as if to say *do something*. De Vries raises the Walther, gripping it with both hands. He has only fired it once before, and that was more than a year ago, the day he bought it. He went out to the woods and shot at rotten apples, missing every single one of them. He needs practice, but the bullets are too expensive. What if he misses Kirsch and hits the professor? What will he do then?

Kirsch grabs Einstein by the arm. There is no more time. He must shoot. Now.

'God help me.'

De Vries's hands are shaking as he takes aim.

The unnatural way the body lurches, it's as if some web of invisible forces keeping him compact and upright has faltered. Coordination, form and direction disintegrate into shapeless disarray. For a moment Kirsch regains his balance, a questioning look on his face, before sinking to his knees.

Albert is running for the gate. De Vries is there with blood on his face, thrusting something into his coat pocket. It comes to Mariya that he must have fired the shot. It's all a mistake. It's all for nothing.

She runs to Kirsch, helps him onto his back. She can't see the wound. It must be under his coat somewhere. She tries to look but he grabs her by the arms, like a blind man.

'Is he safe?' His face is deathly white. 'Is he safe?'

It's all he wants to know. The bells have stopped ringing. From the square she hears the slam of car doors, the growl of an engine.

Kirsch gasps, begins to roll over. Mariya helps him down onto his side – it must be the side, she remembers that. On his side

there's less chance he'll drown in his own blood. She needs an ambulance, she needs to get Kirsch to a hospital. The churchyard is empty, but there must be people in the church. There must be people to ring the bells.

'I'm coming back,' she says. 'Lie still. Lie still now.'

His hands are still around her arm. Gently she prises them free and crosses them under his chin.

Fifty-two

The sun is bright in the sky. It shines in his face, almost blinding him. Has he been shot? He must have been. Better than a shell burst, at least. Better a bullet than shrapnel. Bullets are easier to extract, the wounds tidier. The hard part is stopping the bleeding.

Already he can see the surgeon cutting the clothes from his body, the nurses cleaning the wound with forceps and cotton. Soon they will give him the chloroform or morphine to take away the pain. If only his heart would stop pounding so hard. He doesn't want to pass out. He wants to know for certain that he wasn't too late.

He rolls onto his back. The sun is now two suns, yellow and hot. The nurses are dressed as nuns. With the masks and the habits, all he can see of them is their eyes: attentive yet void of expression. With a stab of regret it comes to him that the Draganović case is finally closed. There is nothing more he can do. He tries to console himself with the thought that one day, when the time is right and Mariya far away, he may write it up for a psychiatric journal. There may be lessons to learn, conclusions for men wiser than himself to draw.

A white curtain covers a window, billowing in the wind like a sail. One of the surgeons leans closer, the trace of a frown on his brow. Beneath his mask his lips move, but Kirsch can hear no sound.

He closes his eyes. Soon it seems that he is floating, not on the dark water of his nightmares, but on a glimmering, limpid sea. There are voices on the shore, some that he has not heard in a long time. They call to him. There was so much they want to know, so many stories he has to tell them. They have been waiting all this time.

Still he hopes he will not reach them too soon. He wants to stay with Mariya a little longer. He wants to know that everything is all right now. He wants to look into her face and see her smile – the

way she was smiling the first time he saw her. He wants a photograph or a sketch: something to remember her by. He tries calling to her, but his jaw is stiff and lifeless. His mouth will not form her name. What is her name anyway? Mariya or Elisabeth? What name will she chose, now that the choice is hers?

When he wakes again she is sitting beside him, holding his hand. His whole body feels heavy so that even turning his head requires effort. This time when he says her name it comes out loud and clear.

She leans closer. 'I'm here. Lie still now.'

Across the room a nurse is moving from bed to bed, distributing linen. She looks up for a moment, then continues with her work. The whitewashed ceiling is vaulted, as in a chapel or a medieval castle. An open window looks out onto trees. Then he remembers.

'Is he safe?' he says. 'Is *he* safe?'

'Quite safe.'

'You were followed. It was a trap.'

She nods, smiling, almost. 'It's as well you were there. Or he would be dead. You saved his life.'

The idea has not occurred to him before. He has saved Albert Einstein's life. No one could ask any more of him. Even Max would have been proud of him – Max more than anyone.

For a few moments he feels no pain at all. He feels light.

'He found you, at last. Your father.'

'Yes.'

She brings a glass of water to his lips. It comes to him that he is, in fact, thirsty. He drinks carefully, but still the water runs down his chin.

'Go to America with him. You and your daughter. It's safer there.'

Mariya takes the glass away and places it on the bedside table. When she looks at him again she is smiling properly.

'All right then. But you will have to come with us.'

'Me?'

She is holding his hands with both of hers.

'My father thought that was a fine idea. Will you come once you're better?'

He has often imagined America and what Mariya's life will be like there. He sees her now, sitting on the porch of a white clapboard house. She's hard at work, a pencil in her hand, a notebook in her lap, just like the one she had in Berlin. Through an open window he can see her father pacing up and down, puffing on his pipe as he awaits the fruits of her labours. In the yard a young girl is skipping on a rope, counting under her breath. Dry leaves tumble across the grass beneath her feet. He is walking up the path, wheeling a bicycle. Mariya looks up and smiles.

'Once I'm better,' he says and closes his eyes.

Mariya leaves the hospital half an hour later. The policeman dozing in the corridor does not stir. She has already given his superiors a statement to the effect that she was alone in the graveyard, visiting her sister's grave. Both the assailant and the victim are unknown to her, likewise the cause of the quarrel. So far no one has seen fit to challenge her testimony. Perhaps that will change now that there is a fatality to investigate, if the local investigators are diligent. But she doubts if that will be the case. The death of an unknown foreigner is curious, but little more than that. It poses no threat to the tranquillity of the town. Meanwhile, her father and his bodyguard are long gone.

Her daughter arrives with Maja Lukić just as Mariya is stepping out onto the street. In honour of the occasion, she wears her new blue dress and her dark hair has been tied back with a ribbon. Mariya crouches down and holds the girl close.

'She's been very good the whole way,' Maja says. 'She loves going on the train.'

'I wanted him to see her,' Mariya says. She doesn't want to cry in front of the child but it's hard to keep back the tears, hard to keep her voice calm and level.

'Him?' Maja Lukić's voice drops to a whisper. 'Do you mean the famous scientist?'

Mariya takes a deep breath. She stands up, brushes the dust from her skirt. 'No. His name was Martin Kirsch.' She takes her daughter's hand and leads her away. 'He was a doctor.'

Dear Elisabeth,

I am adding this final note to remind you of my request, and to ask that you do not judge too harshly this unruly flight of imagination, which will soon exist − if it exists at all − in your mind alone, to the exclusion of all others in the world. It is your story in more senses than one, since you are both inside it as a character and outside it as a reader. Knowing this, I hope you will not be offended by my presumption; for a reader, like a man of science, cannot help but shape what he observes according to his senses, experience and assumptions. So you and I, like parents, must share responsibility for the nature of this, our offspring, however unfair the circumstances of the conception.

I hope you found Dr Kirsch an agreeable companion over these many pages. In truth, I have yet to encounter a doctor of psychiatry quite like him. He is the kind of psychiatrist I should like to have been, had my temperament been stronger and my mind better ordered. I would even embrace the manner of his death, which is, in its way, happier than many states of life. Who would not rather die in a great cause, even an illusory one, than live without dreams?

I like to imagine that Niels Bohr and his allies would see the merit in my novel. But my father would be sure to hate it with every fibre of his being. That is why you would be well advised never to let him see it. He would deny his part in shaping its character, as he denies his part in shaping mine, and, for that matter, yours. He would have no hesitation in calling it the work of a madman, seeing as how its characters − in you and me and Dr Kirsch − exist in different places at once, like the quanta *he is so determined to pin down. But then, he calls many things mad that he does not care for. Perhaps that is easier than accepting them. Still, another part of me wishes he could see what*

I have written, however it disgusts him; so that he might know a little of the price that has been paid for his freedom.

I hope I have represented candidly my own character and conduct, and the nature of my disturbance. In retrospect, I find I can see my eccentricities quite clearly, as if they belonged to another man altogether. Nonetheless, it has been hard to recount the more extreme lapses of which I am, of course, ashamed – especially knowing that they will become more frequent and more intolerable with the passage of time. I am only glad that I have succeeded in completing this story before my treatment here begins in earnest. The effort demanded inspiration – inspiration which you gave me.

All that remains is to settle on a title. I have decided that the choice shall be yours. I will follow your suggestion, whatever it is. It is not much of a gift, but there is little else I have to give, having in this place no power and no possessions, only a few clothes, my music and my thoughts. At least you, Elisabeth, know what power may lie in the gift of a name, for better or for worse – you, of all people.

Whatever happens, remember me as I was.

Yours always,

Eduard

Historical Note

Following the proclamation of the Law for the Prevention of Progeny with Hereditary Diseases on 14 July 1933, around 400,000 people underwent involuntary sterilisation in Germany. The majority were patients in mental hospitals and other institutions. Between 1939 and 1945 a further 250,000 mentally and physically handicapped people were murdered as part of a covert operation known as T–4. The principal architects of the Nazi race hygiene programme, including Dr Eugen Fischer, were never prosecuted.

After his father's final departure for America in October 1933, Eduard Einstein's mental health deteriorated rapidly. He spent the remaining thirty-two years of his life as a patient of the Burghölzli psychiatric hospital in Zürich, where he underwent a variety of treatments, including insulin coma and electro-convulsive therapy. He never saw his father again.

After a clandestine arrival in New York, Albert Einstein took up a position at the Institute of Advanced Study in Princeton, New Jersey. There the quest for a Unified Field Theory continued to absorb his attention to the exclusion of almost all other problems. He was still making calculations in hospital in the hours before his death in April 1955. This labour of more than twenty-five years is today regarded by physicists as of little scientific value. The central tenets of quantum mechanics have yet to be successfully challenged.

In 1986 previously secret correspondence between Einstein and Mileva Marić was opened to public scrutiny. It revealed for the first time the existence of a daughter born to the couple a year before their marriage. The child was referred to as Lieserl (Elisabeth), and

was delivered on or around 27 January 1902, probably in Titel, a village in the then Austro–Hungarian province of Vojvodina. There is evidence to suggest she was mentally handicapped. Her fate remains unknown.

Acknowledgements

I should like to acknowledge the generous assistance in researching this book of Barbara Wolff of the Albert Einstein Archive at the Jewish National & University Library, Jerusalem and Osik Moses of the Einstein Papers Project at Caltech in Pasadena.

I should also like to thank Alice Meyer for her recollections of inter-war Germany; Claudia and Heiko Geithner, Jonathan Scherer and Clare Scherer for their helpful comments on the first draft; Christopher Zach for his many invaluable insights and suggestions; Peter Straus, Stephen Edwards and Laurence Laluyaux for their enthusiastic advocacy, and James Gurbutt for giving the book a chance.

Finally I should like to thank my parents, Peter and Dorothy Sington, for their unfailing encouragement and support through thick and thin.

www.vintage-books.co.uk

Contents